'Mum, I don't like this,' said Olive. It was true, of course, that her dad was hardly the liveliest bloke in the world. It was also true that now she and her sisters were all married, her mum was entitled to enjoy a bit more freedom. But leaving Dad, separating from him, well, that was hard to take. 'Look, stay and have some lunch with me and we'll talk about it some more.'

'I can't stay,' said Mrs Jones. 'Staying wouldn't change my mind in any case, especially as I've been invited to join the Stockwell Amateur Dramatic Society, which'll take up a lot of me evenings. I quite fancy meself on the stage, and I think I can hold my own with younger women when it comes to being costumed a bit glamorous. My, when I think of all the years I've spent living with a doorpost . . .'

www.booksattransworld.co.uk

THE PRICE
OF FREEDOM

Mary Jane Staples

CORGI BOOKS

TRANSWORLD PUBLISHERS
61–63 Uxbridge Road, London W5 5SA
a division of The Random House Group Ltd
www.booksattransworld.co.uk

THE PRICE OF FREEDOM
A CORGI BOOK: 9780552155571

First publication in Great Britain
Corgi edition published 2007

Addresses for Random House Group Ltd companies outside
the UK can be found at: www.randomhouse.co.uk
The Random House Group Ltd Reg. No. 954009

The Random House Group Ltd makes every effort to ensure that
the papers used in its books are made from trees that have been
legally sourced from well-managed and credibly certified forests.
Our paper procurement policy can be found at:
www.randomhouse.co.uk/paper.htm

Typeset in 11/13pt New Baskerville by
Kestrel Data, Exeter, Devon.
Printed in the UK by
CPI Cox & Wyman, Reading, RG1 8EX.

4 6 8 10 9 7 5

THE PRICE
OF FREEDOM

Chapter One

Crash!

Beer glasses smashed as they hit the sawdusted floor.

It wasn't that the pub on Brixton Hill was open, and that some drunken customers had dropped their glasses. No, it was just that a tray of them had slid off the counter, due to having been pushed.

'Here, what's the bleedin' game?' shouted the proprietor, who had been preparing for the morning opening time.

'Sorry about that, Stan,' said Muscles Boddy, as beefy Dan Boddy was known. He was five feet ten inches tall and five feet wide. 'Me hand slipped.'

'What for?' demanded the rageful proprietor. 'I've paid me monthly dues, haven't I?'

'And so you should, seeing your pub's kept nice and quiet for you and yer customers by me guv'nor's firm,' said Muscles. 'But according to a dicky bird that whispered in me lughole, you've been talking about complaining to the rozzers. Dear oh Lor'.' A sad sigh seemed to issue from his inappropriately jovial if knobbly countenance. Such a cheery expression was most incongruous on a man who dealt in bone-crushing violence. 'I don't want nosy bluebottles coming round to see me, do I? I ain't on friendly terms with any of 'em, and me guv'nor wouldn't like it no more than I would. He's worked himself near to death building up a business in Brixton. So I thought I'd come and let you know he's upset. What upsets me guv'nor upsets me as well, and ain't I said so before?'

'Would I complain, would I?' said the shaken proprietor.

Muscles Boddy reached over the counter and took hold of the man's collar, twisting and tightening it until he had his victim turning blue in his fight for breath.

'Well, here's hoping you won't, Stan,' he said, 'but suppose you had a rush of blood, eh?' He released the publican's collar in case the bloke had a fatal choking fit. 'Don't do it, or you might get taken to hospital with a leg off. Well, that's all, Stan, see you next month. No, wait a tick, if the flatties come and mention me monicker any time, let 'em know I'm your best friend, which I am, ain't I?'

'They'd believe that, wouldn't they?'

'Don't answer me back, Stan, it ain't what I

like,' said Muscles, and left, his boots crunching shattered glass.

A heavy East End gang had moved from Shoreditch into Brixton a year ago, in 1935, and established a lucrative protection racket. The people of Shoreditch would have been glad to see them go if it hadn't meant they'd been forced out by an even heavier mob.

In a house in Baytree Road, Brixton, Mrs Hilda Jones had just informed her youngest daughter that she intended to live a life of her own.

'Mum, what d'you mean?' asked the daughter, Mrs Olive Way.

'Just what I said, that I'm going to live me own life,' stated Mrs Hilda Jones.

'I wish I knew what you were talking about,' said Olive. 'How can you live your own life? There's Dad.'

'Well, he can live his own life too,' said Mrs Jones. 'He'll have to.'

'You can't mean you're going to leave him,' said Olive, shocked.

'That's exactly what I do mean,' said Mrs Jones.

'What?' Olive couldn't believe her ears. Twenty, she had been married six months, and she and her husband had set up home in this house in Baytree Road, off Brixton Hill. An attractive brunette, she was a likeable young woman who enjoyed helping her husband to apply new paint and new wallpapers to the rooms. There was nothing enjoyable, however, about the feeling that her mother had gone bonkers. 'Mum, you're not serious, you can't be.'

'Well, I am serious, and that's it,' said Mrs Jones. Forty-three, she was still comely in looks and figure. 'Now that I've seen all of my daughters married and settled, I feel I've done my duty as a mother, and I know I've done more than my duty as a wife. I've given your father the best years of me life. Twenty-five, I might point out, and now I'm going to enjoy the rest of my years by meself.'

'Mum, are you sure you know what you're saying?' asked Olive, incredulous.

'I've been thinking about it since your wedding day,' said Mrs Jones, 'and that's given me time to be as sure as I can be. I don't know how many socks I've washed or shirts I've ironed or meals I've cooked for your father. Thousands, I should think, and it's going to be a pleasure only doing things for meself.'

'I'll go dotty in a minute,' breathed Olive. 'I mean, are you talking about getting a divorce from Dad?'

'No, I don't want any messy divorce business,' said Mrs Jones. 'Well, I don't know, do I, if a woman can get a divorce on account of wanting to live her own life. The law's mostly on the side of men. Well, men make it, don't they? I'm just after a separation. I'm hardly likely to want to marry again and find meself washing some other man's socks. No, I want to be free to please meself how I spend my time, and to take up some lively interests.'

'I still can't believe you're serious,' said Olive. 'What's Dad going to say and what's he going to do?'

'He'll have to fend for himself for a change,' said Mrs Jones, 'and as for what he's going to say I don't suppose it'll be anything much. Well, he's never said anything much all his life.' Mrs Jones was a very talkative person herself, and forthright with it. If she wasn't as well spoken as Olive or her other daughters, that was because they'd had the benefit of a grammar-school education while she'd only had an elementary one, having been born of hard-up Camberwell parents. 'In fact, I don't know your dad's ever managed to hold a single decent conversation with me in all the years I've known him. I might as well come right out with it, Olive. Your dad is a boring old sod.'

'Why did you marry him, then?' asked Olive.

'I thought marriage would liven him up a bit, didn't I? It livens up other men, so I've heard.'

'But Dad's not a bad old stick, and he's sort of harmless as well,' said Olive, 'and you did marry him for better or worse.'

'Yes, but twenty-five years of being married to

someone that's about as lively as a doorpost, well, that's more than enough years for any woman,' said Mrs Jones.

'I know he's never been much of a talker,' said Olive, 'but he's never come home drunk or run after other women or been a rotten dad. And he did find money to make sure Madge, Winnie and I had a good education.' Madge and Winnie were her sisters. 'Mum, he's just the kind of man that's naturally quiet.'

'I've sometimes wondered if he's actu'lly alive,' said Mrs Jones. To Olive, her mother had seemed resigned to her father's quiet ways, apart from moments when irritation surfaced and she'd tell him he didn't even know how to listen, let alone know how to talk. Now she seemed a challenging woman, sprightly and active in her look and manner. 'Anyway, after all these years of having to put my fam'ly first, I'm going to start putting meself first.'

'But Dad's had to do the same,' protested Olive, 'he's had to put you and us first.'

'He's put the shop first,' said Mrs Jones. 'He should've married it instead of me. Olive, I've waited till you followed your sisters into wedlock, and now that you and Roger have settled in here, I'm going to get settled meself in a new home, a flat in Stockwell Road. That part-time job I've been doing is going to be full-time from next Monday, so what with the wage and what

12

savings I've made, I'll live quite comfortable. Mr Burnside, the manager, has been a lot more appreciative of what I'm worth than your father ever was. He's taken me for granted since the day I married him. Well, lots of women are beginning to feel their feet these days, and I'm one of them.'

'Mum, I don't like this,' said Olive. It was true, of course, that her dad was hardly the liveliest bloke in the world. It was also true that now she and her sisters were all married, her mum was entitled to enjoy a bit more freedom. But leaving Dad, separating from him, well, that was hard to take. 'Look, stay and have some lunch with me, and we'll talk about it some more.'

'I can't stay, I've got to be in the office by one o'clock for me afternoon's work, and I had a sandwich at home,' said Mrs Jones. Her part-time job, in the office of a Stockwell factory, filled her afternoons. It dovetailed with the morning work of another part-timer, who was leaving. 'Staying wouldn't change my mind, in any case, especially as I've been invited by Mr Burnside to join the Stockwell Amateur Dramatic Society, which he's president of and which'll take up a lot of me evenings. I quite fancy meself on the stage, and I think I can hold my own with younger women when it comes to being costumed a bit glamorous. In fact, if it turns out I've got a gift for the stage, I've been promised a part in the society's Christmas pantomime. My, when I think of all the years I've spent living with a doorpost, I know it's been wasted years except for the times I've enjoyed with you girls.'

'I don't see how you can say wasted years,' said Olive, 'and, anyway, Dad wouldn't stop you joining the society.'

'I don't suppose he would, or even notice that I'd joined,' said Mrs Jones. 'I don't suppose, after I've left him, that he'll even notice I've gone.'

'Of course he will,' said Olive. 'Mum, you're upsetting me something rotten.'

'You'll get over it,' said Mrs Jones, who felt a new and more exciting life was going to open up for her. It was May 1936, and she was looking forward to being free and independent for the first time since marrying Herbert in 1911.

She went on about her happy prospects until it was time for her to be on her way to her job. By then, Olive was almost glad to see her go. It was a relief to her ears. Her mother could get carried away sometimes by her gift for sounding off. That was when her father had most of his un-listening moments by going deaf.

The shop on the corner of the little Brixton street close to the borders of Streatham sold newspapers, periodicals, tobacco, cigarettes, confectionery and some simple grocery items such as tea, sugar, condensed milk and Camp coffee. It was a boon to local people, and was owned and run by Mr Herbert Jones. The freehold of the property had been left to Herbert by his father, who had run the shop before him. Above the shop was a flat that has been occupied for many years by an old lady, Mrs Goodliffe.

Oddly, the fourteen terraced houses extending from the shop in a solid row were all empty. The landlord, Walter Duffy, had sold the whole row to building contractors for development into attractive maisonettes, currently in favour with newly retired people who had a bit in the bank, and all tenants had been given notice to quit six months ago. The plan embraced the corner shop as well, but Herbert shocked the developers by refusing to sell, despite the original offer of a thousand pounds for the property and its prime site being upped to a thousand and five hundred. That, in the eyes of the developers, was a small fortune for any piddling corner-shop proprietor. Herbert said what good was one and a half thousand pounds to him when it would leave him without a business, without its turnover and without any property? Besides, he said, old Mrs Goodliffe had been his tenant for years, and his father's tenant previously. What was going to happen to her if he sold the place?

The developers said they'd find her a flat somewhere else, but Herbert didn't think much of that. They kept on at him, but he remained steadfast in his refusal to sell. Mind, he was forty-eight and beginning to think frequently about a new kind of life in which he wouldn't have to get up at six every morning, including Sundays, and work right through until six every evening, except Sundays, when he shut up shop at one o'clock. Nothing, however, would induce him to give old Mrs Goodliffe notice to quit. The flat was hers until she died. He had promised his father that. And he had let the developers firmly understand that the three-roomed abode was her own little world in her fast-declining years.

He'd lost some regular customers since the terraced houses had been vacated, but the shop still had a good turnover. He had money in the local branch of Barclays, and had always given Hilda, his wife, a generous housekeeping allowance to enable her to save a bit on her own account. Women needed something behind them in case they were left widowed. A widow's pension by itself didn't amount to much.

Hilda was a good wife. A bit of a gasbag at times, and always inclined to wear the trousers, but still reliable. And now that all the girls were married and settled, he'd made arrangements for her to enjoy a really posh holiday with him in the Isle of Wight come July. Two weeks and all, with Mrs Binns looking after the shop. Mrs Binns usually worked from seven thirty in the mornings until one in the afternoons, giving him needful assistance. From seven thirty until about eight, the paperboys and papergirls arrived to pick up their bundles of newspapers for delivery before they went to school.

It would come as a nice surprise to Hilda, two weeks holiday in the Isle of Wight at a posh Shanklin hotel.

At the moment, however, he was in a sorrowful state, a state that had come about two days ago, when old Mrs Goodliffe had gone at last, dying peacefully in her sleep. He'd known there was something wrong, because she hadn't come down for her pint of milk in the morning. He was the one who'd discovered her dead in her bed. A nice old lady, she deserved to slip away peacefully. If her going still saddened him, it was also giving him food for thought.

Mrs Nell Binns, a widow of forty-two and an invaluable help, interrupted his thoughts.

'It's half twelve, Herbert, time you had your sandwiches and your lunchtime cup of tea.'

'Be all right for a bit, will you, Nell?' said Herbert. He always said that. He was not a man of verbal versatility.

'Course I will,' said Mrs Binns. The shop being empty of customers for the first time that morning, she added, 'By the way, I've got to tell you I'm thinking of moving to Forest Hill, to keep house for an uncle of mine, a widower that's getting on a bit. It'll be board and lodging for me, and an allowance as well, and security for when I'm getting on a bit meself, so I'll probably say yes. It means I'll have to give you notice, Herbert, which I'll be sorry about.'

'I'll be sorry too, Nell,' said Herbert, 'but I can see you'd be wise to take up the offer.'

'I knew you'd be nice about it,' said Mrs Binns, 'and I'm sure you won't have any trouble getting someone to take my place, except now that old Mrs Goodliffe has passed on, will you be changing your mind and selling out to them builders?'

'I'll give it a bit of thought,' said Herbert, and went into the back room to put the kettle on for a cup of tea and to eat the sandwiches Hilda had prepared for him, as usual and as always. Someone came into the shop as he placed the kettle on the gas ring. A moment later, Mrs Binns called to him.

'Herbert, Mr Cawthorne wants to see you.'

Mr Lawrence Cawthorne, presumed Herbert. Joseph Cawthorne & Son (Building Contractors) Ltd was the firm that, having bought up the terraced houses, had been after his shop for ages. Their persistence and perseverance were still ongoing, and it was the son, Lawrence Cawthorne, who regularly came down from up on high to project his important self into the shop in repeated attempts to persuade Herbert to sell.

'Tell him to come in, Nell,' called Herbert.

Mr Lawrence Cawthorne entered the room, a little retreat from the shop. A brisk man with an engaging smile, he was in his element when negotiating for a contract on terms favourable to the firm, but he had found the quiet obstinacy of shopkeeper Herbert Jones difficult to break down.

'Here I am, Mr Jones, I've turned up again, but not like a bad penny, would you say?'

'Good morning to you,' said Herbert.

'Same to you,' said Mr Cawthorne. 'What's your present frame of mind?'

'I like to think it's tidy,' said Herbert.

It's still a hard job getting anything out of this character, thought Mr Cawthorne. Never speaks more than one sentence at a time, and never puts himself at a disadvantage.

'Mr Jones, is there no way we can overcome the one stumbling block, that of your tenant and the loyalty you owe her?'

Herbert could have said at once that his tenant was being prepared for burial at the undertakers, but paused to reflect on the matter before replying. Honesty winning out, he murmured, 'I'm sorry to say Mrs Goodliffe passed away two days ago.'

'She's dead?' said Mr Cawthorne not un-happily.

'I can't say it's surprising considering she was eighty-one,' said Herbert.

'That's a good run for anyone's money,' said Mr Cawthorne. 'Does that make you more willing to sell?'

'I wouldn't say I'm more willing,' said Herbert.

'But more open to a new offer?' suggested Mr Cawthorne. The firm was going to lose money unless work began on knocking the houses and the shop down within the next three weeks. The board had had to consider putting the houses back on the market unless the corner shop was acquired before the month was out. As it stood, the shop would be quite out of keeping with the superior quality and design of the maisonettes, whose proximity to the superior facades of Streatham would be emphasized. Further, the shop's site had always been necessary to the project.

'What d'you call a new offer?' asked Herbert.

'Well, look here,' said Mr Cawthorne, 'you've got us by the short and curlies, and you know it as much as we do. All right, then, what d'you say to us doubling the offer to three thousand? That'll look after you for the rest of your life. It's a more than generous amount as far as we're concerned, but it's on the table, ready to be picked up, providing you'll sign the contract inside a week from now.'

'Let's see, three thousand,' said Herbert, showing no signs of what the offer was doing to him. If he added his savings to it, he'd have three thousand eight hundred and fifty pounds in the bank. Invested in government stocks at four per cent, he'd collect interest of just over a hundred and fifty quid a year, a good three pounds a week. He and Hilda could sell their present house and buy one with a garden, and he could do what he'd always wanted to do, grow roses, sweet peas and vegetables.

'Come on, old chap,' said Mr Cawthorne.

'What with the shop, the flat, the wide frontage and the yard behind, I wouldn't say three thousand is overdoing it,' said Herbert. 'By itself it might be, but as part of what you've already bought, I'd say you'd still be getting a bargain.'

Mr Cawthorne blinked. All that was at least twice as much as this shopkeeper had ever come out with in one go, and what was more it meant he had a bit more up top than one gave him credit for.

'I'd say the bargain's more on your side than ours, Mr Jones, since frankly the yard's an eyesore.'

'You mean the people buying your maisonettes wouldn't like seeing it from their back windows,' said Herbert.

Mr Cawthorne blinked again. The shopkeeper

was proving that he wasn't simply an obstinate blighter.

'You've got a point, Mr Jones,' he admitted, 'but there's no chance of us offering a penny more. Three thousand is definitely the limit. In fact, old chap, that amount is going to make us feel skint.' Which statement was a bit of a porkie.

'Well, from where I am, the sale is going to make me feel I've lost my daily labours,' said Herbert, 'which could make me unsatisfied.'

'But a lot richer,' said Mr Cawthorne. 'Tell you what, we'll promise to pay all exes, such as solicitors' fees, yours as well as ours.'

'The kettle's boiling,' said Herbert, 'd'you want a cup of tea?'

'Not at this time of the day, thanks,' said Mr Cawthorne. 'All I'd like is an answer. In the affirmative.'

'Let me have the offer in writing,' said Herbert, 'and the day after I receive it I'll let my solicitors know I'll sign the contract. Can't say fairer, can I, Mr Cawthorne?'

Mr Cawthorne smiled. The man was almost loquacious today.

'I'll have the letter hand-delivered to you to-morrow, Mr Jones.'

'That'll do,' said Herbert, filling the teapot.

'Shall we shake hands on it?' asked Mr Cawthorne.

'Seems we ought to,' said Herbert. He put the teapot down and they shook hands on the deal, Mr Cawthorne thinking about a starting date for the demolition work, and Herbert thinking about delivering the good news to his wife.

Chapter Two

Herbert entered the kitchen when he arrived home. He and Hilda lived in their own house in Vining Street, Brixton. It seemed a bit of a hollow dwelling now that all their daughters were married and away. It wouldn't be a bad idea at all to move into a smaller house. There were some in the area east of Effra Road, two-storeyed terraced houses, three up, three down, with gardens – neat, compact and respectable-looking dwellings.

'Had a nice day, Hilda?' he said.

Hilda Jones looked at him. He had a sort of stolid, dignified appearance, with never a hair out of place, nor a tie ever creased, nor a button ever undone. And every evening of their married life he had said the same thing to her on his arrival home from the shop. Had a nice day, Hilda? Sometimes she didn't bother to answer, and he never pressed the question.

'Oh, in and out, up and down,' she said

now. She knew what he'd say to that. And he did.

'Oh, well, look on the bright side.'

It was a wonder she'd never thrown saucepans at him. She'd been a saint, really, in the way she'd put up with his dull and unimaginative character. She couldn't remember the last time he'd been an excitement to her in any way. In fact, she couldn't remember if he ever had been, even in bed, although she knew she'd always had a good body and still did. The marital act had probably been a sort of routine to him, and she wouldn't have been surprised if during his performances his thoughts had all been of his shop and his customers. He'd gone to work in that shop when his father owned it, since when he'd never been out of it, so to speak.

'Well, sit down, the supper's ready,' she said, and it occurred to her that that was how she'd responded to him every evening for many years. A born doorpost, that's what he was, and all she knew now was that if she didn't get away quick she'd turn into one herself. Mr and Mrs Doorpost, that's how they'd end up if she stayed.

Herbert sat down and she served rabbit stew.

'Well, this is tasty,' he said, which was more or less what he always said about any meal.

'There won't be many more,' she said.

'By the way, Hilda, I've got some news, I—'

'I said there won't be many more.'

'Many more what?' asked Herbert.

'Many more suppers cooked by me.'

'Pardon?' said Herbert, thinking supper was the right occasion for delivering good news, not for listening to remarks that didn't make sense.

'I'm moving to Stockwell next Monday, into a flat that's got its own bathroom,' said Hilda.

'Pardon?' said Herbert.

'Don't keep saying pardon, try and listen for once.'

'Did you say—'

'Yes, I did.' Hilda spoke positively. 'Now that all our girls are married and settled, I don't feel I'm obligated any more as a wife and mother. I've had twenty-five years fully obligated, so next Monday I'm moving out to live me own life. D'you understand me, Herbert Jones?'

'Well, no, I don't,' said Herbert, pretty sure he was either dreaming or not hearing her properly.

'I said I'm moving out on Monday. I want some fresh air and new faces in me life. We've come to a parting of the ways, you and me, Herbert. You take me for granted, you don't talk, you live for that blessed shop, you've got no real life in you, and you're about as exciting to a woman as a suet pudding. I'm leaving you before I go into a decline and lose me health and strength on account of aggravated depression.'

'Hilda, are you all right?' Herbert felt she was saying things that could only come from a woman who was suffering not depression but a serious attack of mental instability. 'I mean, d'you feel a bit ill or something?'

'No, I don't,' said Hilda, 'I happen to feel quite perky, like I've got a new life dawning, that's what. Look at you, always in the same suit, always saying the same things every day, and doing the same things every year. You wouldn't have noticed the difference if you'd married an empty flour sack or a bag of potatoes. Well, you can get hold of one to take my place. I'm packing me wherewithals on Sunday, and moving on Monday, like I said. The van will take part of the furniture, enough for what I'll need in the flat, and no more than I've worked and slaved for. I'll have me Savings Bank account, and I'll be working full-time instead of part-time, so you won't have any worries about having to keep me. I want to be independent, anyway.'

'Hilda, I don't understand, I've always been myself—'

'Don't I know it,' said Hilda. 'You've always been in need of having some fireworks tied to your coat tails, Herbert Jones. Still, just keep on being yourself and you won't miss me, you won't even notice I'm gone. And you'll always have the shop and your customers.'

Herbert, who had stopped eating during these last few minutes, looked down at his meal, then looked up at his wife, his brow furrowed beneath his handsome mane of iron-grey hair, his eyes dark with emotion new to him.

'I'm sorry, Hilda, about being, well, inadequate, I suppose, but I never thought—'

'I'm sorry too if I'm upsetting you a bit, but it's got to be said.' Hilda tried to look sorry for him. 'It's not your fault, I suppose, that you were born without any go. When we first got to know each other, I thought you were just a nice quiet type that I could help liven up, but after all these years I can't help thinking I ought to have seen my married life was going to be all work and no play, like. You ought to have sold the shop to the builders, treated me to some nice new outfits, put the rest of the money in the bank for both our benefits, then gone out into the world and got yourself a lively job that would've woken you up a bit, like with the Fire Brigade. Mr Murchison down the street is a fireman, and no-one could say he's not lively; he keeps Mrs Murchison in fits, so she says. Well, that's it, Herbert, I've said me piece, and now we're going to live separate lives. It won't hardly affect you, except you'll have to do your own washing and cooking, and I daresay you could soon learn what the gas cooker is for when—'

'Stop.' Herbert stood up. His placidity had taken one sharp arrow too many. 'I'm sorry for you, Hilda, I'm sorry for any woman who sees a husband like you see me. I never offered myself to you as anything but what I was at the time. After all you've said to me, I ought to throw you out here and now, and save you any more of your married suffering, but I can't do that, it's not in me nature. So I'm going out, I'm going to take a long walk and try to work out why you had to feed me salt and vinegar after all my years as a husband and father.'

'It wasn't easy,' said Hilda, 'but I had to speak my mind, and I'll tell you this much, Herbert, you've just said more to me than you've said in six months. That ought to make you think a bit.'

'It's doing that all right, Hilda, believe me.' Herbert was stiff with shock and flushed with humiliation. 'But if you don't mind, don't say any more, I've got the picture, thanks very much.'

The front door closed behind him a few minutes later, and it closed quietly, not with a slam.

Well, I've got that over with, thank goodness, said Hilda Jones to herself. I ought to have spoken to him years ago about the way he was turning me into a cabbage. If it hadn't been for the girls and the neighbours, I'd have felt buried alive. I did myself a really good turn when I went after that part-time job, it's been the making of a new life for me. All these years that I've put up with him and the same old suits, how did I manage to? Boring old sods shouldn't be allowed into women's lives.

*　　*　　*

During his long walk, Herbert made up his mind about what he wanted to do.

On his return, Hilda said, 'We don't have to act uncivilized to each other for the few days we've got left together.'

'No, we don't,' said Herbert.

'We can talk, if you want,' said Hilda.

'Better than that, I could let off a few fireworks,' said Herbert.

'That sounds a bit sarky,' said Hilda.

'Yes, I'm trying to put some sparks into me conversation,' said Herbert.

'You're too late,' said Hilda.

'Bloody shame, then,' said Herbert.

'Yes,' said Hilda.

'Sorry,' said Herbert.

'You'll be all right,' said Hilda, 'you don't really need anybody, not while you've got your shop.'

'Maybe,' said Herbert, keeping quiet about business events.

Hilda's other daughters got to know from Olive what was in the wind, and called on their parents the following evening. Their mother explained at length.

'Well, you can talk all night, but none of it makes sense to me,' said Madge, the eldest daughter. Twenty-three, she was buxom, healthy and assertive. She was also a lover of cats. She had three. She'd been married two years and her husband Brian Cooper kept wondering why his virility hadn't yet helped her to produce a child. Madge could have told him what the teachings of Marie Stopes had done for her, but didn't. She was happy with her cats. Cats weren't as messy or demanding as kids, and Brian would come to love them as she did. 'Does it make sense to you, Win?' she asked.

'No, it doesn't,' said Winnie, who was twenty-one, the mother of a year-old son by her husband Victor Chance, and a bit weird in her liking for standing at her open front door on a clear night and looking at the stars. She had a feeling that somewhere in the Milky Way was her own star. Victor, of course, often asked her how she was going to recognize it. She'd know, she said, as soon as she saw it. And then what? Victor asked. I'll come into a fortune, she always replied. And I'll come into a state of lumbago from all the draughts you're letting in, said Victor once, but that was as much as he did say in the way of a complaint. However barmy Winnie was about the Milky Way, she was a loving woman and couldn't be faulted in bed on Saturday nights. That was when she liked a kind of free-for-all beneath the sheets, on Saturday nights, give or take the occasional miss for one reason or another. 'Mum, you've had an over-forty brainstorm,' she declared now.

'Well, p'raps I have,' said Hilda, 'and if it surprises you, it doesn't surprise me. I wonder I haven't blown up ages ago.'

'Have you talked to her, Dad?' asked Madge.

'Not a great deal,' said Herbert.

'Talked to me?' Hilda laughed. 'He's never properly talked to me in twenty-five years. I could've been just an ornament. When he does open his mouth, it's only to say something he's said a hundred times before.'

'You don't have to be that unkind, especially not in front of Dad,' said Winnie.

'She can't help it,' said Herbert, 'it comes from her years of suffering.'

'Help, that's not like you, Dad, saying something like that,' said Winnie. 'You were born under a good-natured star, I've always said so.'

'Well, it must've just fell on me and knocked my brains about,' said Herbert.

'Being sarcastic won't help, Dad,' said Madge in her strong assertive voice, 'and you've got to face the fact that Mum's right about one thing. You hardly ever get sociable and talkative, and every woman ought to be able to rely on her husband to be good company to her.'

'D'you mind speaking a bit quiet?' said Herbert. 'Only I've got a slight headache in the region between me ears.'

His daughters stared at him, and his wife rolled her eyes.

'Dad, you're coming out with some unusual words,' said Winnie.

'He's had a shock,' said Hilda. 'Still, it's a change, a few unusual words from him.'

'Don't go on at him like that,' said Winnie. 'Being bitter won't help. But I must say, Dad, you could have taken Mum out and about a lot more than you have. I mean, how often have you taken her to the cinema or theatre?'

'Periodically, I have,' said Herbert.

'But how often is periodically?' asked Madge.

'Once a year,' said Hilda.

'A bit more than that, I'd have thought, but I've always wanted to save as much as possible for our old age,' said Herbert, looking apologetic. 'For when I retired from the shop and had time for us to be a bit more active together.'

'Not so we could live it up a bit, I bet,' said Hilda. 'As for that shop of his, he could've sold it months ago, and treated me to a trip to somewhere exciting like Paris without the expense hardly noticing. As it is, my mind's made up, I'm moving on Monday so's I can live a free and independent life. Your dad's accepted it, and you two girls and Olive have got to accept it as well.'

'I think the pair of you have got to act your age and have some sensible talk about it,' said Madge crossly. 'Winnie and myself, and Olive, don't agree with any separation, and we're not going to take sides, either.'

'I hope you all understand I've got justified reasons for wanting to live me own life,' said Hilda.

'The trouble is you and Dad don't have a lot in common,' said Madge. 'Now if you had a nice cat to look after, you could share the pleasure.'

'I don't like cats,' said Hilda, 'and are you sure your Brian does?'

'Brian has a natural liking for them, the same as I have,' said Madge.

'Well, your dad's natural liking is for his shop,' said Hilda.

An argument developed about shared interests, in which Herbert did not participate. He got up after a while and left his wife and daughters talking across each other.

They were so absorbed in making their points that they didn't notice he'd disappeared. Well, one could have said he'd always existed unnoticed in the background of their family life.

The argument didn't solve anything. Hilda remained adamant about having the right to be free after twenty-five years of slaving. Madge said she was out of her mind. Winnie said she'd come to regret it. Not me, said Hilda.

Chapter Three

The contract having been quickly prepared for signature, Herbert took time off on Friday to visit his solicitor in company with Mr Cawthorne, leaving the reliable Mrs Binns in charge of the shop for an hour or two. Mrs Binns was pleased for him. He was going to get a really handsome sum for his property, and the builders had allowed him two weeks to close the shop down. He was offering his customers a whole range of items at cost price, and every customer was being given a Roneo'd copy of a letter expressing his thanks and appreciation for their support over the years. Herbert Jones was a nice man, that was the firm opinion of Mrs Binns, even if he wasn't exactly electrifying. So it had shocked her all over to have him tell her his wife was leaving him. She'd had quite a conversation with him about it.

'But what for, Herbert? Is she having a fling, then?'

'A what?'

'You know, is she having it off with some man somewhere?'

'I'll have to ask you to choose your words a bit more careful, Nell.'

'Well, I wouldn't want to insult Hilda, no, nor you, Herbert, but I can't think why else she's leaving you.'

'It seems I'm not very exciting.'

'What?'

'It seems I'm a stodgy old bugger, Nell.'

'Hilda told you that?'

'That and more on the same lines,' said Herbert. 'She's right, of course, I'm no talker, and don't go in for playing a piano or doing a knees-up.'

'Well, you're a quiet man, Herbert, I won't say you're not, but that's better than being loud, rowdy and drunk, and there's plenty of that kind about when the pubs shut of a Saturday night. I don't want to say more than I should, like, but what's so exciting about Hilda that she thinks she's the cat's whiskers compared to you?'

'I won't talk about it, if you don't mind, Nell.'

'Well, let me just say I'm on your side, Herbert. Is she going to get half the money from the sale of the shop?'

'That's a private matter, Nell.'

'Oh, beg pardon, Herbert.'

'Still, after Hilda's left, I'll take you out for a

treat somewhere before you go and housekeep for your uncle. I couldn't have done without you in the shop these several years.'

'It's been a pleasure, Herbert, you've always treated me very friendly and fair, and as Hilda's leaving you and I'm a widow woman, why shouldn't you take me out before I go off to me uncle?'

'There's no strings, Nell.'

'Well, there wouldn't be, would there, Herbert, you're not that sort of man.' Nell mused on the matter for a moment or two. Then she said, 'Still, out of respect for the occasion, I think I'll wear me best hat and costume.'

Herbert and Hilda said their goodbyes to each other on Sunday night. Herbert had been sleeping in daughter Madge's old room since being advised by his wife that he wasn't much to write home about. And as he was always up very early, well before Hilda came down, he thought Sunday night the right time to say goodbye.

Hilda had done her packing. All her clothes and personal possessions were in a large trunk, and she had placed a slip of paper on each item of furniture she needed, which the removal men would collect. She had offered to discuss her furniture requirements with Herbert, but he said no need, she could take whatever she wanted. She said she felt she had earned ownership.

'Yes,' said Herbert, 'I appreciate you have.'

'Men don't always appreciate what their wives are entitled to,' said Hilda.

'No, apparently not,' said Herbert, 'especially us dull old buggers. Sorry I've been a bit negative.'

'Not as sorry as I've been,' said Hilda. 'Still,' she added, 'I don't want to go on at you any more, best if we say our goodbyes friendly like.'

The definitive goodbyes began at ten on Sunday night.

'Well, I'll say so long now, and then go up to bed,' said Herbert.

'All right, goodnight, then,' said Hilda. 'Oh, I suppose it's only fair to say not every day of our marriage has been dreary. More like a bit quiet, and I might remark there's even been them pleasant times, when the girls were young and you read bedtime stories to them. One thing I'll admit is that you weren't ever a neglectful father.'

'Just a bit of a stodgy one,' said Herbert.

'Well, even about that, no-one can help the way they're born, like I mentioned before,' said Hilda. 'If you're not born to set the world on fire, it's not your fault. I did try to buck you up a bit, but it didn't work.'

'There was no meat on the bone, I suppose,' said Herbert.

'What?' said Hilda.

'Not much for you to go to work on,' said Herbert.

'You're coming out with some surprising remarks lately,' said Hilda.

'No good me asking if you're likely to change your mind about going, I suppose?' said Herbert.

'No, I'm not going to change my mind, not now, thanks very much,' said Hilda. 'Anyway, I know you're not all that helpless, I know you'll be all right on your own. Well, it's not as if you've ever needed anyone to talk to, so I don't have to worry about you, which is a bit of a blessing under the circumstances.'

'Would you like me to come and see you once in a while?' asked Herbert.

'Yes, once in a while you could come,' said Hilda. 'Say for a cup of tea on a Sunday afternoon now and again. I'll drop you a line to invite you each time. Oh, I hope you won't forget to go and visit your daughters fairly frequent, Herbert.'

'I know I've got daughters, Hilda,' said Herbert.

'Yes, three of them, Madge, Winnie and Olive, and they're all married now, don't forget,' said Hilda.

Herbert nodded, looked at her with the eyes of a man who still didn't quite know what had hit him, and said, 'Well, I've got to thank you, Hilda, for being a good wife and mother all these years,

39

even if I don't understand how you could come to say all those things to me, or the way you said them. I suppose you had good reason, but it's fair knocked me sideways, I can tell you.'

'It was best for both of us, Herbert,' said Hilda, 'we'll both be better off living on our own, and I don't want you to feel sorry for yourself. It'll only make you brood. Why don't you take up darts at one of the local pubs? That's the sort of thing you need, a bit of activity, a lively atmosphere and some sociable company.'

'I'll go for some walks,' said Herbert. 'Well, goodbye, Hilda.'

'Goodbye, Herbert, and don't forget you've got to do shopping for yourself.'

'I won't forget,' said Herbert. 'By the way, I'll be gone, of course, before your removal van comes.'

'Yes, I know,' said Hilda, 'you'll be in the shop.' She rarely went there herself. That shop was something she'd been fed up with for years, mainly because she was sure he thought a lot more of it than he ever did of her.

'Goodbye, then, Hilda,' said Herbert.

'I'll tell you something,' said Hilda.

'What?' asked Herbert, halting on his way to the door.

'We've actu'lly just done some talking together,' said Hilda.

*　　　*　　　*

In the shop on Monday morning, Nell Binns kept giving Herbert inquisitive glances. She was sure he must be suffering a bit, seeing his wife had just left him. But he didn't seem fraught about it. At one point, when he was attending to two ladies who had dropped in to pick up their weekly magazines, he sounded very much like his normal self.

'Mr Carraway in the pink still, Mrs Carraway?'

He always asked that question of Mrs Carraway, a jolly woman with a jolly husband.

'I'll say he is, we went to a party Saturday evening where they gave us gin and tonics,' said Mrs Carraway. 'Gus had heard about gin and tonics, but never thought people outside of Noel Coward and his London toffs actu'lly drank them. Nor did I, but it seems they do in Streatham, which was where the party was. Well, the gin put Gus in the pink all right. There was a lot more of it than tonic. He's still got spots in front of his eyes, and I don't know how he's managing his greengrocer's shop this morning, or if I'm seeing any straighter meself than I was yesterday. You sure this is *Woman's Weekly*?'

'Quite sure, Mrs Carraway.'

'Well, I believe you, Mr Jones, you've always been a man to trust.'

'Yes,' said the other lady, Mrs Robbins, 'and I don't know what we're going to do now you've sold the shop, Mr Jones.'

'I hope none of my customers feel I've let them down,' said Herbert.

'Of course not – oops – ' Mrs Carraway let go an involuntary hiccup. 'Would you believe, that gin's still getting at me. I'll stick to port and lemon in future. No, we'll miss you and the shop, Mr Jones, but we don't feel you've let us down, especially if it means you and Mrs Jones can enjoy a nice retirement. Oh, and while I'm here, I think I'll have four packets of tea, three tins of evaporated milk and four pounds of sugar at the cost price you're offering.'

'I'll have the same,' said Mrs Robbins, 'and a jar of raspberry jam as well.'

'A pleasure, ladies,' said Herbert. He always expressed himself in that way over any purchases made by lady customers, and Nell Binns thought his wife just couldn't help seeing him as a middle-aged stick-in-the-mud. But what about his good points, his honesty and reliability? And he was still manly in his looks.

He caught her glance then and gave her a slight smile.

That's the stuff, Herbert, she thought, grin and bear it.

'Well?' she said later on, when the shop was empty at last.

'Well what?' said Herbert, his handsome mane of hair well brushed, his plain brown tie looking neat and tidy.

'Hilda's gone?' said Nell.

'As far as I know,' said Herbert.

'Hurting a bit, is it?' said Nell.

'I won't talk about it, if it's all the same to you,' said Herbert.

'I'm a friend, y'know,' said Nell.

'And a good woman,' said Herbert.

'Thanks,' said Nell. She was no beauty, but her features were pleasantly homely. 'Hope I'll be just as good as a housekeeper for me elderly uncle.'

'Bound to be,' said Herbert. 'I'd bet on it. Probably make the old lad sit up and take notice.'

'Complimented, I'm sure,' said Nell. 'And it's a nice change, hearing you say things like that.'

'Well, I suppose some of us can learn a few things, even if we're getting on a bit,' said Herbert.

Nell might have said he still looked in his prime, but a customer came in.

Muscles Boddy put in an appearance at the shop on the stroke of six, just as Herbert was closing. He always chose that time. It meant there were no nosy parkers about.

'Evening, 'Erbert old cock.'

'You're on time as usual,' said Herbert.

'Didn't want to miss you,' said Muscles Boddy. Strangely, he had a soft spot for Herbert. Well, he never gave any trouble, nor handed out any

43

lip. Muscles Boddy didn't like lip, not from people whose shops or pubs or other business premises were under the protection of the guv'nor. Herbert Jones, who ran a very profitable shop, according to the guv'nor, had seen the sense of being protected when it was put to him seven months ago. The opening conversation had been very agreeable to Muscles.

'Do I understand,' said Herbert, 'that protection means my shop won't catch fire or get smashed up or burgled?'

'Have yer been burgled, then?' asked Muscles.

'I've had three break-ins these last twelve months,' said Herbert. Old Mrs Goodliffe, a bit deaf, hadn't heard a thing, and if she had she'd have collapsed, poor old lady. Of course, he was insured against fire and burglary, which cost a bit, but it did cover shop and flat.

'Three break-ins? Dear oh Lor',' said Muscles, 'that's a cruel lot of dishonesty. Painful, I call it.'

'What did you say protection costs?' asked Herbert.

'Well, you ain't running a pub nor the Locarno ballroom, mate,' said Muscles, 'and me guv'nor's got a reputation for being fair. Ten bob a week suit yer, paid monthly?'

'Calendar months?' said Herbert.

'Eh?' said Muscles, his bulk taking up nearly half the cosy back room. 'Is that your lips moving?'

'It's January, February, March and so on,' said Herbert.

'Blind me, I think I've heard of them,' said Muscles, 'but two smackers a month means every four weeks on the dot.'

Twenty-six pounds a year is a lot, thought Herbert, but he could recognize what the alternative might mean. He knew all about the gang that had moved in, and he reckoned they'd had a good guess about the extent of his turnover.

'Sounds fair,' he said. He was a practical man, and his visitor was half the size of a mountain.

'Pleasure to do business with yer,' said Muscles.

'I'll be protected against break-ins?' said Herbert.

What a decent cove, thought Muscles, he's talking sweet. What a change from all the argufying he usually had to put up with from piddling shopkeepers. Break-ins? Well, they could be taken care of. It only needed for the word to be put around that the guv'nor required tuppenny-'a'penny operators to lay off this corner shop or else.

'You got my word, mate, that there won't be no smashed winders nor break-ins, providing you contract to me guv'nor. Mind, it won't be no written contract, just word of honour between gents. The guv'nor don't go in for a lot of writing, except to his loving ma on picture post-cards.'

45

'Good enough,' said Herbert.

'Let's see yer mitt,' said Muscles. Herbert put out his hand. Muscles smacked it. 'Done,' he said. 'Mind, payment in advance.'

'Of course,' said Herbert.

'Well, bugger me,' said Muscles, 'I like your style, 'Erbert.'

Herbert handed over two pound notes, then said, 'Like a nip?'

'Eh?' said Muscles.

'Scotch?' said Herbert.

If there was anything Muscles liked more than a pint of foaming wallop, it was a finger or so of Scotch.

'Sod me, I do like your style, 'Erbert,' he said, and Herbert took a bottle of whisky from a cupboard, together with two glasses. He poured two fingers into each glass. Muscles drank the health of his new client in two mouthfuls. Herbert drank his more slowly. Tomorrow he would give the insurance company notice to cancel coverage of burglary, break-ins and the like. He'd retain fire coverage, just in case. Allowing for the dues paid to this gorilla, he'd actually be in pocket.

Muscles considered the contract very agreeably settled. Corner shops generally couldn't come up with more than a measly quid a month, or even only fifteen bob. And some the guv'nor didn't even bother with. Clients like publicans or car dealers had to agree to ten quid at least.

Commission for Muscles was ten per cent of all collections.

He parted from Herbert on very friendly terms. Since then good old Herbert had paid up promptly and with never any lip. And there was always a nip or two of whisky offered. No wonder Muscles liked the bloke.

Today, however, the collector of dues looked sorrowful.

'Listen, 'Erbert, I heard this morning that you've sold the shop.'

'Yes, I have,' said Herbert.

Muscles took off his brown bowler and placed it over his heart.

'Well, I'm grieving, 'Erbert,' he said gloomily. 'I don't grieve much, having been brought up the hard way in a Borstal college, but I ain't above feeling sad sorrow for the end of our happy business relationship. Got a drop of reviver handy, have yer? It'll ease me sorrow a bit.'

'You've got a dubious way of earning a living, y'know,' said Herbert. 'I'm not sure you deserve a nip.'

'Here, come off it, 'Erbert,' protested Muscles, 'that ain't like you, giving me lip. Ain't it a bleedin' fact that since I've been keepin' me protective eye on your shop, it ain't ever caught fire, been burgled or had its winders broke?'

'It's a fact,' said Herbert.

'There y'ar, then,' said Muscles.

Herbert took the bottle of whisky from the cupboard, and poured a generous measure into one glass, and a modest amount into another. He paused, then added more.

'I think I'm in need myself,' he said.

'That's better,' said Muscles, 'that's more like it. What's friends for, eh, except to share a bottle when it comes to a sad parting?'

'Funny kind of friends,' said Herbert, handing the bruiser a glass. Muscles enjoyed a swig, then peered at Herbert.

'What's up, 'Erbert? You ain't your usual prime self.'

'My wife's left me,' said Herbert in a moment of bitterness, and took a mouthful of reviving Scotch.

'Eh?' said Muscles.

'After twenty-five years, she's walked out on me,' said Herbert. He owed this racketeer nothing except a kick in the crutch for crooked extortion, but there it was, an involuntary need to confide.

'She's done what?' said Muscles.

'Called me a boring old sod and left me,' said Herbert.

'Well, not having had the pleasure of meeting the lady, I ain't formed no opinion of her,' said Muscles, 'but calling you that and then walking out after all them years of you providing for her, well, she don't sound like my idea of an appreciative woman. I hope you ain't been soft enough to split the proceeds with her.'

'Proceeds?' said Herbert.

'Come to, 'Erbert,' said Muscles. 'What you sold the shop for. I heard it was a tidy sum, sort of mouth-watering.'

'Before I could tell her anything,' said Herbert, 'she came out with all her complaints about me imperfections, besides letting me know I was on a par with a sack of potatoes. So I didn't say a word to her.'

'Good on yer, 'Erbert mate,' said Muscles with an admiring grin. 'A tight north and south is a wise one, according to me guv'nor. But she's upset you, I can see that, plain as a sparrer on a lady's titfer. I ain't known you with a long face before. Below the bleedin' belt, that was, calling you names and walking out on you after twenty-five years. Listen, have you thought about pushing her under a bus accidental, like, and marrying again? There's always a welcoming widow woman somewhere about, ready and willing to get hitched to a steady bloke like you. I married one meself once. Pity she went and got drowned off Southend Pier one night, poor unhappy woman. Still, that needn't put you off marrying some other one that'll be more appreciative than yer present trouble and strife.'

'I'll be all right on me own,' said Herbert.

'No, that ain't for you, 'Erbert, you're a bloke

that needs his natural home comforts,' said Muscles, finishing his whisky. 'And you need a friend, don't you, matey? Well, you got me. Could you squeeze another tot out of that there bottle?'

'Don't know why I should,' said Herbert, 'not after what you've had out of me.' But he poured more whisky into the gangster's glass.

'Bless you, 'Erbert,' said Muscles. 'I ain't too fond of too many people, but I've always had a liking for you. You want a good turn done any time, you can rely on me, I promise yer.'

'You've got a good side, have you?' said Herbert.

'I ain't a cherub, I'll grant you that,' said Muscles, 'but I ain't been known to let a friend down. Cheer up, 'Erbert, you ain't lost nothing that counts. I suppose she ain't told you where she's gorn, has she?'

'She kindly left her address on a postcard on the kitchen mantelpiece,' said Herbert.

'That was kindly, was it?' said Muscles. 'Ruddy condescending, I call it. Gorblimey, 'Erbert mate, no wonder you ain't yourself.'

'I can go and see her now and again, if she invites me and if I feel like it,' said Herbert.

'I'm buggered if I'd feel like it meself,' said Muscles. 'Well, it's been sad, listening to you, matey, but there's always tomorrer, and you never know what tomorrer might bring, eh? A welcoming widow woman to start with. You got a notice in your winder, I see, advising customers your shop's closing down at the end of this here week. I ain't feeling too cheerful about that. Still, I'll collect your final donation while I'm here. Say a fiver.'

'It's two quid, the usual,' said Herbert. 'It's not even that, considering I'm closing down come Saturday.'

'Now, 'Erbert, we ain't going to conclude this pertic'ler relationship in an argufying way, are we?' said Muscles. 'You ain't even going to notice a fiver, not now the sale of your shop has earned you a sackful.'

'I think you're talking about bashing my head in,' said Herbert. Muscles grinned. Herbert, having emptied his till, took five one-pound notes out of his small canvas money bag, and handed them over. 'Meeting and relationship closed,' he said.

'Business relationship, eh?' said Muscles. 'We still got friendship, so I won't forget you, course I won't. Good luck to you, matey.'

Off he went, wide and big, and whistling.

Chapter Four

The following evening, Herbert kept his promise to give Mrs Nell Binns a treat. He took her to the Streatham Hill Theatre, and to a late supper after the show. It let her know how much he appreciated the job she had done for him in the shop. And Nell let him know she honoured his appreciation by putting on her glad rags, in which she looked very nice.

They had a very friendly chat over the meal, and it brought forth a lot more talk from Herbert than he was wont to produce. But an evening of mutual appreciation called for a fair amount of sociable exchanges.

That same evening, Brian Cooper took his wife Madge, Herbert's eldest daughter, to the Gaumont Cinema in Streatham. At the end of the programme they walked to a bus stop amid the night lights of Streatham. On the way, Brian emitted a low whistle.

'What's that for?' asked Madge.

'Cop what's on the other side of the road,' said Brian.

Madge looked. For the moment her view was blotted out by a moving tram. It passed on and she spotted a man and woman on the opposite pavement and level with her.

'Well I'm blessed,' she breathed.

'Your dad and friend?' said Brian.

'It's Dad all right, and she's Mrs Binns, who works in his shop,' said Madge, turning her head to follow their progress. Herbert and Nell were on their way to their late supper in a classy Streatham restaurant. 'I can hardly believe it.'

'He's found quick consolation,' said Brian. 'Didn't think the quiet old lad had it in him.'

'Wait till I get a chance to talk to him,' said Madge.

'Leave it alone, Madge,' said Brian, 'it's his own affair now your mum's left him.'

'It's not decent, neither is it right, not when the separation has only just happened,' said Madge.

'Point is, does the lady – Mrs Binns, you said? Yes, does she think like that? Your dad still looks a very healthy specimen, and the lady might fancy him in his nightshirt. Is she a widow, by chance?'

'Yes, she is,' said Madge. 'And look here, you clown. Dad doesn't wear a nightshirt, he wears striped pyjamas.'

'Well, she's free to fancy him in striped pyjamas, then,' said Brian, 'and he's free to oblige her, so good luck to him, even if he isn't any live wire.'

'Don't talk like that,' said Madge, 'it's not decent, especially when we're all hoping he and Mum can get together again. Which they will when they've come to their senses. All this nonsense at their age, it's ridiculous.'

'That's not much of a hope, their getting together again,' said Brian. 'I can't see your mother going back to someone she calls a doorpost, particularly now all you girls are off her hands. Listen, lovebird, isn't it time you and I started a family?'

'We've got a family,' said Madge firmly, 'you, me, Pinky, Floss and Fluffy.'

'Shoot Pinky, Floss and Fluffy,' said Brian.

'You don't mean that,' said Madge.

'Wait till I get you home in bed,' said Brian, 'I'll show you exactly what I do mean.'

'Well, I'll have to wish you luck, I suppose,' said Madge.

Herbert took some daily walks to keep himself occupied. One evening, after he had prepared and eaten a simple supper, he referred to the postcard propped against an ornament on the kitchen mantelpiece. There it was, Hilda's new address, written in her neat hand and plain

54

for all to see. He read it, not for the first time. The Flat, 25, Stockwell Road. He knew Stockwell Road. Some shops, some houses, some flats.

He didn't think he'd get invited too often. After all, he'd always be a boring old codger to her. His best bet was to turn up uninvited and give her a surprise. She wouldn't like that, she always preferred to have tidy arrangements. Still, it might be useful to get a picture of her new background. See if she'd bettered herself and if her plans for herself were working out. He had his own plans.

Olive popped in to see him later that evening. She wanted to know if he was all right and how he was getting on. Herbert said he wasn't all right, she couldn't expect him to be under the circs, but he wasn't going to put his head in the gas oven or anything like that. He'd soldier on, he said. Olive said she just couldn't get over the shock of him and her mum separating. It simply wasn't right, she said. One thing about Olive, she was pretty normal, he thought, not a cat-lover like Madge or a stargazer like Winnie.

'Dad, I can't help thinking it wouldn't have come to this if Mum had felt you cared a bit more for her than for the shop,' she said.

'What I cared for was making sure the shop takings gave the family enough to live decently,' said Herbert, 'to see you girls had the advantage of grammar-school educations, that you didn't go short of anything and always had nice clothes. Yes, and to see your mother was able to save for herself out of her housekeeping money.'

'Dad, wives and mothers need something more than their housekeeping allowance,' said Olive. 'They need to know they're appreciated and not taken for granted. I'd be very upset if I felt Roger didn't appreciate me.'

'What about husbands and fathers?' said Herbert.

'What d'you mean?' asked Olive.

'Well, don't some of us like to be appreciated, or is it something sort of exclusive to wives and mothers?' replied Herbert. 'I feel now that I was short of being appreciated meself. Your mother told me I'd taken her for granted for years, and it came to me only today that what I provided for all of you from me long hours in the shop, well, that was taken for granted too. I don't know that your mother or any of you girls ever said thanks.'

'That's not fair,' protested Olive.

'I paid out handsome for your schooling and for the weddings of all you girls, and I paid out with a good heart, like any decent dad should, but none of you gave me any special blessings. You took me paternal obligations for granted, just as your mother took all that generous housekeeping allowance for granted. But it didn't make me walk out on me family, it didn't even bother me a lot, because I don't believe in people having to go around thanking others for this, that and everything else. All I'm saying is that if I wasn't perfect as a husband, and I know I wasn't, it wouldn't do your mother any harm to take a look at herself in her mirror. Yes, that's all I'm saying.'

'You're saying quite a lot. Dad, considering you've never said very much before.' Olive put a hand on his arm. 'That was what got Mum really going in the end, that you hardly ever talked to her.'

'Well, that was a pity, and I'm sorry,' said Herbert, 'but I've never been much of a talking bloke. I admit your mother had a good reason there to pull me to pieces, except I always felt she liked the sound of her own voice much more than mine.'

'Dad, that's not fair, either,' said Olive. 'That's mean.'

'Yes, not very nice, I suppose,' said Herbert apologetically.

'Anyway, I don't think Mum meant everything she said to you, Dad, and I'm sure she's sorry about calling you boring.' Olive patted his arm consolingly, although she had agreed with her sisters that their father hadn't ever been an entertaining husband to their mother.

'Well, I never heard any woman complain

more than she did about me when she went for me,' said Herbert. 'I know I wasn't a talker, I've admitted that, but I could have said your ma was the other way about, a gasbag.'

'Dad, that's not a bit nice, talking about her like that,' said Olive. 'Look, I know what you mean, but don't mention it when you go to see her. Try your best to make it up with her.'

'I'm not going to make it up with her,' said Herbert.

'Yes you are,' said Olive.

'Not me,' said Herbert.

'Yes, you,' said Olive. 'You're both to blame, but you've got to be the one to make the first move. When you do see her, take her lots of flowers and make a kind of speech to let her know you can use plenty of words when you have to.'

'Turn myself into a talking husband, is that it?' said Herbert.

'Yes, that's it,' said Olive.

'I suppose you mean a gasbag,' said Herbert, and laughed.

'That's it, married gasbags making it up together,' said Olive, and she laughed too.

The door knocker sounded. Olive answered it and found Madge on the doorstep. In she came, and there was a brief family preamble before Madge enquired what her father had been up to just lately.

'Me?' said Herbert.

'Yes, you,' said Madge, 'you were out in Streatham a couple of nights ago with your shop assistant, Mrs Binns.'

'With Mrs Binns?' said Olive.

'Brian and I saw them together as large as life after we came out of the Gaumont,' said Madge.

'Did you?' said Herbert.

'Yes, we did,' said Madge in her meant-to-be-heard voice.

'Well I'm blessed,' said Olive, 'is that right, Dad?'

'It's right I was out with the lady that's been working several years in the shop,' said Herbert.

'Yes, you were on the other side of the road,' said Madge, 'and if I hadn't been so dumb-founded I'd have crossed over and spoken to you.'

'What about?' asked Herbert.

'About your being out with Mrs Binns,' said Madge. 'You're still married to Mum, you know.'

'I don't feel I am,' said Herbert.

'Don't be silly,' said Madge. 'How can you not feel married after twenty-five years?'

'It's a new feeling, I admit,' said Herbert, 'but it's risen up in me these last few days.'

'Something else has risen up in you,' said Madge.

'Has it?' said Herbert. 'What, might I ask?'

'Fretful talk,' said Madge.

'Can't be helped,' said Herbert.

'Yes it can,' said Olive, 'and then there's going out with Mrs Binns. Dad, you silly, you won't get Mum back if you start carrying on with other women.'

'Should I try to get your mother back?' asked Herbert.

'We insist you do,' said Madge.

'But what's the point?' asked Herbert.

'What d'you mean, what's the point?' asked Madge.

'Of getting your mother back,' said Herbert.

'Well, you don't really want her to live on her own, do you, Dad?' said Olive. 'You could go and see her, and promise to be more companionable to her, and a little more lively.'

'Stand on my head?' said Herbert.

'Do what?' said Madge irritably.

'Wear a funny hat?' said Herbert.

'I hope you're not going peculiar,' said Madge. Then, after a thoughtful moment, and an impatient jerk of her shoulders, she added, 'Well, even that might help to some extent.'

'It might,' said Herbert, 'but it's not me. I'm still the way I was born, I don't go in for funny hats or sawing a fiddle.'

'But you're going in for taking Mrs Binns out,' said Olive, 'which isn't your style, Dad. Heavens,

I hope it doesn't mean you're thinking of committing adultery.'

'Mrs Binns is a respectable widow,' said Herbert.

'It's not respectable being seen out with a married man,' said Olive.

'Especially as it looked to me as if she was wearing her best Sunday hat,' said Madge.

'Does wearing a Sunday hat on a weekday evening mean adultery's just round the corner?' asked Herbert.

'No, but wearing it for a man must mean she fancies him,' said Olive.

'I've just thought,' said Madge, 'have you been carrying on regularly with Mrs Binns, Dad, while she's been working in the shop?'

'I don't like that question,' said Herbert, 'it's a liberty.'

'That's not much of an answer,' said Madge.

'It occurs to me that as your mother's now calling herself a free woman, can I be called a free man?' asked Herbert.

'No, you can't,' said Madge, 'because all your daughters want you and Mum to get back together again. I think you'd better act your age and tell us if there's anything going on between you and Mrs Binns.'

'It so happens Mrs Binns has been invited by an old uncle of hers to be his housekeeper,' said Herbert. 'Which invite she's accepted. That shows she's sensible, not flighty.'

'She's leaving the shop?' said Olive.

'It's been a long time,' said Herbert.

'You can easily get someone else,' said Olive.

'The point is, I felt beholden to show my appreciation of her years in the shop by taking her to the theatre and then to supper,' said Herbert. 'I'm doing a bit of appreciating, which it seems I didn't do much of before.'

'I can't believe the way you're almost making speeches these days,' said Madge. 'Look, Olive and I won't quarrel with what you felt beholden to do for Mrs Binns, but you could have told us that five minutes ago.'

'I didn't feel I had to,' said Herbert. 'Still, you are my daughters, so I have told you. I'm sorry, mind, that I've been a dull old dad to you.'

'We've never called you that,' said Madge.

'No, but I know my faults,' said Herbert. 'And I realize now only too well that your mother would have liked a more entertaining husband. Someone like Max Miller, I suppose.'

'Dad, some of these things you're saying aren't like you at all,' said Olive.

'Must be because some heavy bricks dropped on my head,' said Herbert.

'Stop being silly,' said Madge. 'Come and have dinner with Brian and me on Sunday. Perhaps I could get Mum to come as well.'

'Very nice of you, Madge, but Mrs Binns has already invited me,' said Herbert. 'By the way, now that she's leaving and old Mrs Goodliffe has passed on, I'm giving up the shop.'

'You've sold it at last?' said Madge.

'Thought I might as well,' said Herbert.

'You'll be lost without it unless you get a job,' said Olive.

'Your mother suggested I might think about joining the Fire Brigade,' said Herbert.

'I'm not sure they'll take you at your age,' said Madge. 'Listen, are you giving Mum anything out of what you sold the shop for?'

'Well, she always made overnight sandwiches for me to take to the shop every morning,' said Herbert, 'so I'm thinking about a decent present for her.'

'How decent?' asked Madge.

'A set of new saucepans for her new abode,' said Herbert. 'Oh, and a bracelet for each of you girls.'

'Wait a minute, a set of saucepans for Mum?' said Olive.

'She'll throw them at you,' said Madge,

'I'll get the store to deliver,' said Herbert, 'and she can throw them at the carrier.'

'Well, I never,' said Madge in astonishment, 'I think you've just said something funny.'

'Not me, not my style,' said Herbert.

'Dad, a set of saucepans?' said Olive. 'You're not really serious, are you?'

'I'll buy the best quality,' said Herbert.

'You're joking,' said Madge.

'Never been a joker since the day I was born,' said Herbert, 'you all know that.'

'What I know now is that you're suddenly getting impossible,' said Madge.

'Sorry about that,' said Herbert.

'I can't stay arguing with you any more,' said Madge, 'I've got to get back to our cats.'

'You and your cats,' said Olive, but she departed in company with her sister. Both of them left feeling sorry for their father in his deplorable mood. It was shocking he wasn't going to do anything about getting their mother back, and very upsetting that he was only going to buy her some new saucepans out of what he got for the shop.

Things were quite different for Hilda that same evening. She was in very close company with a very close friend.

'Oh, you saucy devil, Rupert.'

'Can't help myself, can I, Hilda? And I can't tell a lie, either. You've still got a handsome body, my stars you have. You're an eyeful.'

'Oh, I can't hardly credit what you're up to, getting me all undone like this.'

'You should be like this, Hilda. I frankly admire you when you're all done up, but I admire you even more when you're not. It's all right to keep your proud bosom hidden when you're out shopping, but not when you're up here in private with me.'

'Lord, I didn't know you were going to take this kind of liberty.'

'Didn't you?'

'If I had known, I wouldn't have—'

'Yes, you would, you teasing woman. And it's not taking advantage, Hilda, it's doing what comes naturally, even if we're both past forty.'

'Rupert, stop that. Oh, I can't remember the last time I blushed, but I'm blushing all over now. Me at my age too.'

'You're no age, Hilda, not with your kind of body, and don't get worried. I mean, I'm not blushing myself, I can handle everything without getting embarrassed. You just relax.'

'Relax? I can't even get my breath – you're near to indecent.'

'Is that good or bad?'

'Oh, I've got to admit it's an exciting change.'

'From what old stodgy bones never did?'

'Don't let's talk about him, just mind what you're doing to my modesty.'

'Well, let's try your bed for an hour, you'll feel happier under the sheets. That's it, up you come. My word, you're a fulsome woman, Hilda, a warm weight in my arms, but it'll be what you might call a labour of love, carrying you to your bedroom. Off we go, then, in for a penny, in for a pound.'

'Oh, help, you don't care what you say, do you?'

'It's time we found out if we suit each other, Hilda, and we can't complain about the circumstances. The shop below is closed, and there's no-one above, except the Almighty.'

The bed sighed and sank a little as he laid her on it. She gasped a faint protest.

'Lord, I don't know I'm ready for this.'

But it happened, all the same, and afterwards he told her what a warm and exciting woman she was, then said, 'Is the old sod really coming to see you now and again?'

'Only when I invite him, and I suppose I'll have to, or my daughters will go on at me.'

'Will he take advantage of you, Hilda?'

'Him? Don't make me laugh.'

'Well past it, is he?'

'He was well past it ten years ago. But he's still got his shop to cuddle up to. Listen, you'd better go now, I don't want you staying all night, I don't want anybody talking.'

'Well, seeing we've found out we suit each other, I'm not going to complain about being sent on my way. After all, Hilda, there'll be other times.'

'Yes, I'm a free woman, but you mind you don't take me for granted.'

*   *   *

She went out the following evening to visit her eldest daughter in Streatham. Madge and her husband were pleased to see her, although suspecting she might already be regretting leaving the comfortable home she'd known for years. On the contrary, however, she was obviously enjoying her new-found freedom, and let them know how much she'd liked meeting all the members of the local amateur dramatic society and being enrolled.

Madge and Brian decided not to tell her that they'd seen Herbert out with Mrs Binns, but they did acquaint her with the news that he'd sold the shop.

'Go on, he hasn't, has he?' said Hilda.

'So he told Olive and me when we saw him last night,' said Madge.

'How much did he get for it?'

'He didn't say and we didn't ask,' said Madge.

'Didn't ask?' said Hilda. 'Well, you should have.'

'Must have got a few hundred at least,' said Brian, eyeing his wife's two potted plants on the window ledge. The leaves were a bright shining green. Madge being a healthy type, she liked everything around her to look healthy too. That included her cats. Her mother didn't spoil the picture. She looked blooming, and she had a remarkably good figure. So did Madge, a buxom and attractive young woman. 'Say five or six hundred.'

'Oh, I think the builders were offering a bit more than that,' said Hilda. 'Well, whatever he got, some of it's mine. My twenty-five years looking after him earned it for me. I'll speak to him about it when he visits. I might ask him to come Sunday week, say. Just for a pot of afternoon tea and a currant bun. I've got to say I wouldn't want him for longer. Well, it's always been painful trying to get him to make conversation. You'd think, wouldn't you, that he'd at least be able to talk about the Government, like most men can. Most men can talk their heads off about the Government. Or football. I don't care myself for talk about governments or football, but it would be something to hear Herbert talk about anything. I feel really sorry for him, not having any trouble myself in being entertaining. It's being entertaining that got me invited to join the amateur dramatics in Stockwell. I'm going to a reading evening soon, it's when I'll be asked to read from a play. I'm looking forward to it, I've got a nice feeling I'm gifted.'

Brian managed to get a word in at that point.

'How are you off for kitchen utensils and suchlike in your new flat?' he asked.

'Oh, I've got all I need,' said Hilda, 'I took what I wanted, and Herbert didn't complain.'

'What about saucepans?' asked Brian, and received a little kick from Madge. He'd roared with laughter when told that her father, in the money from the sale of his shop, was going to present her mother with a set of new saucepans. 'Got enough of them, have you?'

'Enough saucepans?' said Hilda. 'Yes, of course I have. What makes you ask?'

'Well, Madge and me like to think you're not short of anything in your new kitchen,' said Brian. 'D'you think you'll stay where you are, or d'you think you and Madge's dad might have second thoughts about any permanent separation?'

'He might, I shan't,' said Hilda, 'I like being free and independent, and I'm not giving that up. Were you thinking about making a pot of tea now, Madge?'

'I'll just give our cats their evening milk, then I'll put the kettle on,' said Madge.

'I've never heard of evening milk for cats,' said Hilda disapprovingly.

'In this house,' said Brian, 'there's morning, afternoon and evening milk for cats.'

'It's only what they need,' said Madge.

'They'll get fat,' said Hilda.

It was dark when she left, and a bus took her to Stockwell, and from the stop she walked down Stockwell Road. Halfway into her walk, she had a sudden feeling she was being followed. She looked back over her shoulder when she reached the light of a street lamp. But she detected no-one. Imagination, that's what it was, and having Herbert on her mind. He'd said some impertinent things to her and shown a bit of spite, and she thought now that he might be taking it on himself to come and watch her at times, and see if he could catch her out at something. No, but of course he wouldn't, he didn't have that kind of go in him. She wondered if he was even aware she was gone. She'd told him he wouldn't be.

Yes, that was it, she must have imagined there was someone a little way behind her. All the same, she hurried on, used her key to open a door at the side of a shop, closed it behind her and went up to her flat. It comfortingly embraced her and she murmured with pleasure that she didn't have to think about making overnight sandwiches for Herbert. She must have made a thousand in her time, always sandwiches, never anything else. It was a wonder he hadn't turned into something like a corned-beef sandwich himself. Well, perhaps he had because even if he didn't look like one, he had about as much up-and-go as one.

She laughed to herself.

Herbert was also late to bed that night.

Chapter Five

On Saturday, Herbert said a personal goodbye to every customer who came into his shop, and he also, by arrangement, had all his papergirls and paperboys call at ten thirty, when he delivered a few words to them.

'I've been very appreciative of your reliability, so here's a pound each for all of you.'

'Crikey, a pound? Ain't you a sport, Mr Jones?'

'We're ever so sorry you're closing down, Mr Jones.'

'I'm sorry too. Still, look on the bright side, that's what I always say.'

'Yes, you've told us that hundreds of times, Mr Jones.'

'Good luck, all of you, and if you want any sweets, Mrs Binns will weigh them for you at half-price.'

'Between you, you can have all that's left at half-price,' said Mrs Binns, and the boys and girls surged around the counters to make their choices from the depleted confectionery stocks.

At six that evening, Herbert helped a dealer load all that was left of his stock into a van, received the agreed price for it, then closed the shop for the last time and went home.

Nell Binns travelled to Forest Hill to see her elderly uncle, the one who wanted her to keep house for him. She needed to have a talk with him.

Hilda spent a thrilling evening with established members of the local amateur dramatic society. She was given excerpts from a play to read, and guidance from the director. She must have acquitted herself commendably, for listening members clapped her, bringing a flush of pleasure to her face, especially as she received handsome praise from Mr Burnside. Mr Burnside, the manager of the factory where she worked, was the society's president. He was also the director. A good-looking man of forty-seven, with a lot of self-assurance, his enthusiasm for amateur dramatics could bring out the best in a cast. Hilda felt he had already done wonders for her in the way he had made her approach her readings.

Having congratulated her on her first efforts, he addressed the company.

'I think we're all agreed that Mrs Jones has the makings of a good character actress.'

'Hear, hear,' said some.

'Well, I must say I've always had a feeling for going on the stage in a modest way,' said Hilda, 'and I do appreciate everyone's encouragement. It's kind of heart-warming.'

'Um, there's a subscription of five pounds a year,' said a young man, the society's treasurer. 'I should have pointed that out when you enrolled.'

'Never mind, and I can afford five pounds,' said Hilda. 'I can pay now, if you like.'

She paid and her membership was confirmed. She was delighted. What a lovely new life she was going to lead.

The evening ended at ten, when she had an escort to see her home to her flat. They conversed on the bus.

'If your husband divorced you, Hilda, you could marry again.'

'Not likely I couldn't. I'd end up washing socks and shirts again every Monday. When people talk about women's work never being done, they mean married women.'

'You'd escape that as far as I'm concerned, I'm not the marrying type.'

'Nor am I now.'

When they reached her door in Stockwell Road, a question arrived in her ear.

'Would you like me to come up with you, Hilda?'

'No, not this time of night, thanks. Someone will notice, and I don't want my new neighbours talking.'

'There's no-one about.'

'Might I ask what you want to come up with me for?'

'Well, together we could do what comes naturally again.'

She laughed.

'I never met anyone with more sauce than you,' she said.

'I like to feel I'm an exciting change from old stodgy boots.'

That made her laugh again, but she still didn't invite him up to her flat and her bed. A free woman could please herself what she did, she could have an intimate man friend even at her age. But it still wouldn't do to be careless about that in case her daughters found out. She felt she had a long way to go before the pleasures of independence made her indifferent to what her family thought of her. Just now, she especially didn't want details of her private friendship with Rupert to come to Herbert's ears. He might come round and act like a wronged husband. He really had been very impertinent and spiteful about being told his faults, and he might get extra spiteful about her having a fling. He was never going to understand that a woman was entitled to be free after twenty-five years as a slaving wife and mother. He simply didn't have any imagination.

Just before going to bed, Olive spoke to her husband Roger.

'I really don't know what's got into Dad.'

'So you keep saying,' said Roger, a personable young man of twenty-four. An engineering draughtsman, he wasn't advancing up the ladder as quickly as he'd have liked, but he was fairly happy-go-lucky about it, although he could have done with a salary increase. Olive had discovered that, with his easy-come easy-go nature, he had a tendency to let money slip through his fingers. During the last week of their fortnight's honeymoon in Devon, he'd asked if he could borrow some from her. They'd spent all that he'd brought with him, he said. Olive said she didn't think much of a bridegroom who had to borrow honeymoon money from his bride. Roger said he'd pay her back. She'd given him a pound, and he hadn't paid it back. She was having to watch his pockets for him, just in case they were empty when bills came in.

'Well, he was very upset about Mum leaving him, of course,' said Olive, 'but I didn't think it would make him go peculiar.'

'Peculiar?' said Roger.

'It's the things he says.'

'Are you surprised?' asked Roger. 'I'm not.'

'I can understand him being down in the dumps,' said Olive, 'especially now he's got a bee in his bonnet about not being appreciated himself.'

'He might have something there,' said Roger. 'Well, for a start, I'd like to know how much your mum's got in her savings account. That could tell us if your dad was generous or not in what he doled out to her. Generosity's worth some appreciation.'

'Well, yes,' said Olive, 'but saying he's going to make Mum a present of a set of new saucepans out of the money from the sale of his shop, and that she can chuck them at the carrier if she wants to, well, that's not like him at all.'

Roger grinned. He'd heard the story.

'I don't call that peculiar,' he said, 'I call that a bit of a laugh at your mum's expense.'

'Perhaps it is,' said Olive, 'but there's something about him that makes me feel uneasy.'

'D'you mean you feel he might be thinking about blowing his head off?' asked Roger.

'Roger, what a thing to say. That's awful. And no, I don't mean that, anyway, I mean I think he's got something up his sleeve that might come as a nasty shock to Mum.'

'Well, that'll make them even,' said Roger, 'he's had his own nasty shock.'

'Yes, I suppose he has,' said Olive. 'But I do feel that Madge, as the eldest, ought to keep her eye on him. That's if she can forget her cats for a while.'

'Brian might help.' Roger grinned again. 'He might drown them one day.'

'Roger, really,' protested Olive, although struggling to keep a straight face. 'I don't think you ought to be as unkind as that. Remember, what's said unkindly often comes to pass.'

'Someone had better warn the cats, then,' said Roger.

For the first time for years, Herbert enjoyed the experience of not having to open the shop on a Sunday. He'd planned a bus ride and a walk for the afternoon. Nell Binns had accepted an invitation to go with him after they'd had dinner together, he having discovered that with no shop to run, he actually fancied a bit of company.

Let's see, he thought, shall I take round a bottle of Guinness and share it with Nell over the meal? Does she like Guinness? I know a lot of working women enjoy a glass of same with their Sunday dinner, and no-one could say Nell isn't a working woman. She'd said she was going to do roast mutton with roast potatoes and garden peas. Not greens. A welcome change, garden peas would be. Hilda had put greens in front of him nearly every Sunday of their married lives.

The door knocker sounded. He answered it.

Muscles Boddy grinned at him from the door-step.

'Watcher, 'Erbert, how's yerself, matey?'

'To what do I owe the pleasure?' asked Herbert.

'To me good nature,' said Muscles, 'and me liking for sharing a couple of bottles of Sunday wallop with you.' He produced two pint bottles of Watney's stout from somewhere about his capacious person. 'Drink stout on a Sunday, do you, 'Erbert?'

'Not often,' said Herbert.

'Just occasional, like?' said Muscles. 'That'll do.' He stepped in. 'You lead the way, old cock.'

'All right, come in,' said Herbert, and took the affable crook through to the kitchen. The square room wasn't small, but Muscles Boddy's bulk made it look a bit undersized.

'Well, you keep a tidy place here, 'Erbert.'

'It's been kept that way by a tidy woman,' said Herbert.

'I take it you mean your ungrateful trouble-and-strife,' said Muscles, placing the bottles on the table.

'We won't talk about her,' said Herbert.

'Painful, eh?' said Muscles, and twisted free a rubber-washered stopper from one bottle. The black-looking stout sprang to life in reaction to the entrance of oxygen. It foamed, and the head spilled. 'Glasses, 'Erbert old cock?' Silently, Herbert brought two glasses from a dresser shelf, and Muscles filled them slowly, the foam rising to create a creamy froth. 'There y'ar, 'Erbert.' He handed Herbert a glass. 'Here's to your prosperity, matey.' He downed half his own stout in one swallow.

'Kind of you,' said Herbert, and took in a mouthful of the rich brew.

'I'll sit down, shall I?' said Muscles, and lowered himself into a chair, which emitted a sigh beneath his weight, followed by a creak of suffering wood. Herbert showed a small smile, then sat down himself on the opposite side of the kitchen table. He considered it wise to be able to look Muscles Boddy in the eye.

'All alone now, are you, 'Erbert?' enquired Muscles.

'Yes.'

'Gone, has she?'

'I'm bearing up,' said Herbert.

'Well, good on you, cully,' said Muscles, 'but as I mentioned previous, it ain't natural for a bloke like you not to have some home comforts. Looking around for a welcoming widow woman, are you?'

'Not so's you'd notice,' said Herbert.

'I know one or two meself that might take your fancy,' said Muscles.

'Well, you hang onto them,' said Herbert, 'I'm still a married man.'

'Got principles, have you?'

'Some,' said Herbert.

'Bleedin' crippling, that is, 'Erbert, having them kind of principles,' said Muscles, downing the rest of his stout. He refilled his glass from the second bottle, and topped up Herbert's. 'Me guv'nor's got principles.'

'Has he? What kind?' asked Herbert.

'The kind that stretch a bit,' said Muscles. 'Elasticated, like. More convenient, y'know, them kind. Still, you being a gent, they ain't your style. Strictly hon'rable, you are, matey, and gen'rous with your Scotch.' He rattled on in his gravelly voice about honourable blokes needing the help of friends, and Herbert said he was very appreciative of friendship as long as one half of it didn't relate to extortion. 'Here, that's a funny word,' said Muscles, 'I ain't heard of that one before. What's it mean?'

'That some friends need to be watched,' said Herbert.

Muscles grinned. It made his rough, craggy countenance look like that of a good-natured gargoyle.

'Well, I ain't one of that kind,' he said, and poured most of what was left in the second bottle of stout into his glass. He paused, then, as a good friend, he poured the meagre remains into Herbert's glass.

'Actu'lly,' said Herbert, 'I'm not one for making too many friends, I'm a bit of a loner.'

'I'm the same, y'know,' said Muscles, 'but you and me hit it off swell, 'Erbert, and I ain't the sort to let you down.' He made short work of the rest of his drink, then stood up. 'Got to see a bloke about a dog now, old cock. Nice to have talked to you. Just wanted to know how you was doing. I got the picture. Keep the bottles, there's tuppence back for the pair at the off-licence. See you again sometime.'

Herbert, relieved that the visit had been fairly brief, saw him out. Muscles shook his hand vigorously, and Herbert felt thankful he didn't end up with broken fingers. He hoped, quite naturally, that the bloke wasn't going to make a habit of calling on him.

On his way to Nell's flat, he bought a pint bottle of Guinness from the Jug and Bottle department of the local pub. Nell expressed pleasure and appreciation.

'Well, I do think a nice drop of Guinness with Sunday dinner's a treat, Herbert. How kind.'

They shared the pint along with the roast and the lush green garden peas. Nell talked, and Herbert said several words himself from time to time, which encouraged Nell to say she couldn't think why Hilda had complained that he wasn't much company. Herbert said he'd rather not talk about Hilda, and Nell said she could understand that.

After he had helped her with the washing-up,

he took her for the planned bus ride to the upper reaches of Streatham, and they enjoyed a long saunter all over Streatham Common. Herbert didn't have to say a lot, Nell being the kind of woman who didn't ask to be entertained. Like most chatty women, she was more in favour of a good listener, and Herbert was proving to be just that. She could tell he was, from his comments.

'Well, you don't say, Nell.'

'Go on, is that a fact, Nell?'

'Tell me more about getting caught with your skirts up in front of a young bloke at the Hampstead funfair.'

'Oh, I couldn't, Herbert, I'm already embarrassed, and I'm sure I don't know what made me say as much as I have. Seventeen's a very blushing age for a girl, and I could see that the young gent in question could hardly take his eyes off me frillies.'

'Girls of seventeen do go in for frillies,' said Herbert.

'Well, so they do,' said Nell, 'fancy you knowing that, Herbert. When we're that age, it's the pretty look of things that count most, even if you only get to show them accidental at a funfair.'

'Well, even showing them accidental, Nell, makes you a good sport,' said Herbert.

Nell laughed.

'I suppose it was a bit of a lark,' she said, 'and

the young gent, having near lost his eyesight, did help me to forget me blushes by treating me to a plate of cockles.'

'Worth all of that, I bet,' said Herbert.

'Beg pardon?' said Nell, dressed in her best costume and hat.

'Probably worth a plate of cockles and some fish and chips as well,' said Herbert.

'Herbert, you cheeky man,' said Nell. 'My, all the time that's gone by since then, with me pretties a thing of the past. Look at me now, I'll be near to being a middle-aged widow in a few more years.'

'Well, you don't look it yet, Nell.'

'Well, I hope I don't, not yet.'

They talked on and became very confiding and involved. It was really a very pleasant afternoon for Herbert.

It was also very pleasant for Hilda. Up to a point, that is. Her close private friend had taken her out into the country on a Green Line bus, and walked with her to a lovely quiet spot where there were only trees and chirping birds to observe them. Then everything became alarming.

'Rupert, oh, not here.'

'Here seems all right to me.'

'But supposing someone sees us— Oh, don't do that.'

'This, then?'

'Oh, that's worse.'

What was alarming became exciting, and of course she'd been starved of excitement for years. So she gave in to it, and considering she was in her early forties and he was in his late forties, no-one could have said either of them was short of health, strength and aptitude. The chirping birds, hopping from branch to branch, turned to twittering in their astonishment.

When it was over, and the surrounding country-side still looked empty of people, Hilda expressed faint words of indignation at having been treated like a tarty village girl.

'You didn't feel like one, Hilda, you felt a lot more like a wild woman.'

'Well, I was wild, I could hardly believe what was going on, all my respectability being dis-respected like that in public.'

'There's not much public around here, Hilda, just a handy collection of beech trees.'

'Now you know what I mean, Rupert.'

'I know what you're like, Hilda, you're a woman and a half.'

'And I know what you're like, you just can't be trusted.'

'Makes a change, though, does it, Hilda?'

'You can say that again,' said Hilda.

Chapter Six

Hilda was busy in the factory office on Monday morning. Her main job was to write out orders which arrived by letter or over the phone. She wrote them out on dockets, a docket for each order, with two carbon copies. The top docket was for the factory manager, who checked it and passed it to the foreman. The first carbon copy went to the invoice clerk, and Hilda was responsible for filing the second copy.

The factory made items for the hardware trade, like hammers, chisels, screwdrivers, drills, padlocks and so on, including many thousands of different-sized nails and screws.

The factory manager, Mr Burnside, popped into the office mid-morning. Hilda's desk was in a corner, well away from the typist and the clerk, both women.

'Morning, Mrs Jones.'

'Oh, good morning, Mr Burnside.'

He leaned over her, smiling. He had a winning

smile, as befitted a man who was both president and director of the Stockwell Amateur Dramatic Society.

'Write me out a docket for a dozen three-inch paintbrushes, two dozen four-inch, and two dozen hand drills, will you?' he murmured.

'Who for?' asked Hilda.

'Timms Hardware Stores of Mitcham.'

'My, they're real regular customers of yours, Mr Burnside,' said Hilda. The pad of dockets was in front of her. She put the carbons in place, and wrote the order out with a hard-leaded pencil. Mr Burnside was taking a lot of orders over the phone himself lately.

At the end of the day, when the factory was quiet, the workers on their way home, Hilda waited at the gates. Mr Burnside emerged from the door that led to the office.

'Hello, standing about for something, Hilda?' he said, informal now that they were out of the factory.

'I was waiting for you,' said Hilda, and he began to walk with her.

'People will start talking,' he smiled.

'They will if they get to know what I've just found out,' said Hilda. 'There's no copies on the file of all those orders I've wrote out for you, and I know I did file them. And there's no copies in Miss Taylor's invoice tray of today's order from Timms. I think someone's been making a habit of going into the office after work and taking the file copies and the copies I put in Miss Taylor's invoice tray. I'm talking about just the orders from Timms. It's upset me.'

Mr Burnside lost his smile.

'You bitch, you've been snooping,' he said.

'Here, watch your tongue, if you don't mind,' said Hilda, 'I didn't say I was going to tell the boss, did I? But you'll have to stop. I'm not going to write out any more dockets for Timms unless I know the carbon copies won't just disappear. In all me born years, I've never done anything dishonest, and I'm surprised to find I can't say the same about you.'

'Now look here, Hilda, you keep on doing as I tell you,' said Mr Burnside, far more nettled than discomfited.

'Not likely,' said Hilda, 'and don't come it over me, not now I know what I do know.'

'Just forget what you know.'

'You've been making money on the side,' said Hilda, 'and the firm could put the police on you.'

'Don't talk like that,' said Mr Burnside.

'If I went back to the office, I suppose I'd find the carbon copies of that docket for the Timms order today had gone missing,' said Hilda. 'Still, I'm not going to say anything.'

'Of course you're not,' said Mr Burnside.

'I was thinking,' said Hilda. 'The society's doing that play by Oscar Wilde in September.'

'Which one? Oh, *The Importance of Being Earnest,* you mean.'

'Yes, that's it,' said Hilda. 'I went up West once to see it with my eldest daughter. It was really good. I'd be ever so pleasured to play the part of Lady Bracknell.'

'Lady Bracknell?' Mr Burnside was sour. 'You couldn't play that part any more than my aunt's cat could. You can't even act yet. '

'You could coach me,' said Hilda.

'But the casting committee wouldn't give you the part.'

'You could use your influence,' said Hilda.

'Damn that, you monkey,' said Mr Burnside.

'You could think about it,' said Hilda.

'I get it, it's the part or else, is it?'

'No, of course not,' said Hilda, 'it's just that one good turn deserves another, like they say.'

'Well, sod me,' said Mr Burnside, 'there's more to you than meets the eye, Mrs Hilda Jones.'

They reached a bus stop, and there they parted, Mr Burnside to board a bus with the expression of a man trying to digest something that violently disagreed with him, and Hilda to walk on with a little smile on her face while thinking of the thrill of playing Lady Bracknell, and discounting any possibility that she'd be hopeless at it.

*　　*　　*

The following day. Muscles Boddy enjoyed an hour or so in a corner of a Brixton pub with a long-time crony from the East End. They shared a plate of cold beef sandwiches and each drank a couple of pints of the publican's best draught ale. They also exchanged a lot of chat without talking out loud. Well, most of Muscles' verbal exchanges with cronies were of the kind that shouldn't be overheard. It had been like that since he'd started his career of illegal activities with a crooked East End boxing promoter years ago. It hadn't taken him long to learn how to talk out of the corner of his mouth. His old-time crony had acquired a similar aptitude.

Eventually, taking a new tack, Muscles said, 'Well, I'll see you again tonight, then, in the Red Lion.'

'Look, we don't need to break the place up,' said his crony, nearly as big as Muscles himself, but not half as loud when at work.

'Well, course we don't,' said Muscles, 'we'll do it nice and quiet. The guv'nor says it's time we handed Alf some personal injuries.' Alf was the landlord, and Alf had been playing up lately.

'OK, I got you,' said his crony, 'soon as last orders is over, right?'

'Right, and you mind you keep a sharp look-out,' said Muscles. 'I don't want the rozzers interfering with the guv'nor's contracts.'

'You and me both,' said his crony.

'Them flatfeet have got a nosy way of turning up uninvited when the Red Lion's customers is leaving,' said Muscles.

'I dunno sometimes why coppers can't mind their own business,' said his crony.

'I tell you, they've been interfering with me all me ruddy life,' said Muscles.

'Me heart's bleeding for yer, Muscles.'

'Eh what?' said Muscles.

'Er, nothing.'

'That's better,' said Muscles, 'I thought for a tick you was giving me lip.' He came to his feet. 'Well, see you sometime tonight.' And off he went, larger than life.

'Roger, you're not short of money again, are you?' said Olive that evening.

'Me?' said Roger. 'No, of course not.'

'Why were you going through your wallet, then?' asked Olive.

'Just to see if I've got enough to stand my round after the meeting,' said Roger. He was a member of a cricket club and due to attend a meeting this evening. 'I'm covered.'

'Well, all right,' said Olive, 'I don't like thinking you're broke again. We don't want to end up as pawnshop customers.'

'Not a chance,' said Roger breezily.

'That's good,' said Olive. 'Don't be too late home, love.'

*   *   *

Later that same evening, Hilda arrived back at her flat after visiting her second daughter Winnie and Winnie's husband Victor Chance. She had enjoyed a glimpse of her little grandson before he went to bed.

After undressing for bed, she went to the bathroom. She found the bath full of water. It was right up to the waste pipe, and the tap was trickling a mixture of hot and cold. Well, that's funny, she thought, I don't remember running the bath before I left for Winnie's. I wasn't thinking of having one, anyway. Did I do it absent-minded or something?

She pulled up the right sleeve of her night-dress, bent over the bath and dipped her hand deep into the lukewarm water to release the plug.

At that moment, someone came up silently behind her.

It was an unfortunate evening for someone else. A little while after closing time the landlord of the Red Lion in Brixton lost some teeth, which happened when they made contact with Muscles Boddy's fist. The police weren't informed.

Chapter Seven

The factory boss entered the office at nine thirty the next morning.

'What's happening to the dockets?' he asked. 'Where's Mrs Jones?'

'She's not come in yet, sir,' said the typist, a Miss Simmonds.

'How's that?' asked the boss, Mr Richards. 'Do we know why?'

'No, she hasn't phoned or anything,' said the clerk, a Miss Taylor.

'Taken sick, I suppose,' said Mr Richards. 'Well, leave the invoicing, Miss Taylor, and take over the job of filling in the dockets. Mr Burnside and the shop floor are waiting for the first of them.'

'Yes, Mr Richards,' said Miss Taylor.

Mrs Hilda Jones remained absent all day.

During the evening, Olive and her husband Roger called on her mother by arrangement. But there was no answer to their several knocks on the door at the side of the shop.

'That's funny,' said Olive, 'she must have forgotten we were coming and gone out.'

'She's not a forgetful woman,' said Roger.

'No, she's not, especially about family arrangements,' said Olive.

'Perhaps she's just popped out to the corner shop.'

'It's not open this time of an evening,' said Olive. 'Perhaps she's already made friends with a neighbour and is having a chat. She'll remember in a minute about us. Let's go for a walk and then come back again.'

They did that and returned twenty minutes later. Roger knocked loudly. No answer.

'Wait a tick,' he said, 'perhaps she's been taken ill.'

'Or perhaps Dad's been round and they've gone out somewhere to make it up,' said Olive.

'Ruddy long shot, that one,' said Roger, 'and I'm not buying it. She wouldn't have gone out with anyone, not when she knew we were coming. Olive, I'm opting for trying to get in.'

'Oh, you can't break the door down, Roger,' said Olive.

'If she's been taken ill, we'd better do just that,' said Roger, 'we can't just walk away. Wait here a tick.'

Off he went to a neighbouring house, and

from the residents there he was able to borrow a crowbar. With it, he forced open the door at the side of the shop, and he and Olive went up to the flat.

A few moments later, Olive screamed and collapsed.

Roger stood staring. His mother-in-law was in the bath, fully immersed, a tablet of soap on the bottom of the bath and against her right hip. She was naked, and as dead as any woman could be.

Just after ten, Herbert, who was enjoying a quiet read while listening to some music on his wireless, heard a brisk rat-a-tat on his front door. He answered the summons. Two men were on his doorstep, one a good-looking bloke in a trilby hat and grey suit, the other a rugged type in a bowler and blue serge suit. They regarded him sombrely.

'Mr Jones? Mr Herbert Jones?' said the one in grey.

'That's me,' said Herbert.

'I'm Detective Sergeant Tomlinson of the Stockwell station, and this is Detective Constable Fry. Might we come in, sir?'

'What for?' asked Herbert.

'To talk to you, sir,' said Constable Fry.

'I can't think why, and it's a bit late, but all right,' said Herbert. They came in. He closed the door and led them into the living room. There wasn't much furniture. Half of what had been there now reposed in Hilda's flat. 'What's it about?' he asked.

'Your wife, sir,' said Sergeant Tomlinson.

'My wife? What about her?'

'I'm afraid it's bad news, Mr Jones.'

'Bad news about my wife?' said Herbert. 'Why, what's happened to her?'

'Something very unfortunate, sir.' Sergeant Tomlinson braced himself to deliver the news. 'I'm very much afraid I have to inform you she's dead.'

'What?' Herbert blinked. 'Dead? Hilda?'

'She was found dead in her bath earlier this evening by your daughter, Mrs Olive Way, and Mr Way.'

'I don't believe it,' breathed Herbert.

'D'you want to sit down for a bit, sir?' suggested Constable Fry.

'I want to disbelieve what you're telling me,' said Herbert.

'I'm sorry, sir, but it's true,' said Sergeant Tomlinson. 'Your daughter identified her. At the moment, all we know is that, according to the police surgeon, she died between about nine and ten thirty last night, and that your daughter and her husband discovered her at eight this evening after Mr Way had forced the front door.'

'Good God,' breathed Herbert, and he did sit down then, heavily. 'Hilda?'

'We understand, sir, that the two of you were separated, that she took up residence in the Stockwell Road flat last Monday week,' said Sergeant Tomlinson. 'D'you think that would have affected her to the point of committing suicide?'

'Never. Never, not Hilda.' Herbert sounded as if it was difficult to find words, any words. 'No, not Hilda. Is that – is that what she did, committed suicide in her bath?'

'We can't say, sir,' said Sergeant Tomlinson.

'But you said—'

'We don't know if it was suicide or not,' said Sergeant Tomlinson. 'We could say it looked like it. If it was, then a state of depression about the separation could have been the reason.'

'No. No.' Herbert kept swallowing. 'She wasn't depressed, she wanted the separation and couldn't have been happier about it, which hurt me, I can tell you. I can't believe she drowned herself in her bath.'

'We didn't say she'd drowned, Mr Jones,' said Sergeant Tomlinson, 'just that she'd been found dead. The cause of death hasn't been established yet, only the approximate time she died. We mentioned the possibility of suicide only because her separation from you might have badly affected her.'

Herbert looked as if he was trying to believe the unbelievable. It took him a little while to respond to the sergeant.

'My daughter Olive, the one you say found her, could have told you her mother wanted the separation far more than I did,' he said. 'I didn't want it at all. I don't believe in separations or divorce, only in trying to work things out. God, this is bloody awful. What did Olive say to you?'

'I'm afraid your daughter was too shocked to answer any questions,' said Constable Fry, 'but her husband did tell us your wife seemed all right in herself the last time he and Mrs Way saw her. But you'd have known her better, sir.'

'The day she left you, sir, was she upset or emotional?' asked Sergeant Tomlinson.

'I wasn't here when she actu'lly left,' said Herbert, 'I was at work in my shop.'

'She was here on her own when she went off, Mr Jones?' said Sergeant Tomlinson.

'Yes,' said Herbert, and wiped his forehead with the back of his hand.

The two CID men looked at each other.

'That would've upset her a bit, wouldn't it?' said Constable Fry. 'I mean, you not being here when she left. You'd had quite a few years together, hadn't you, sir?'

'I'd said goodbye to her on the Sunday night.' Herbert's face looked stiff now. 'She'd told me more than once she was looking forward to being on her own, and she told me again then. She was even excited about it, saying she'd be a free woman at last. Would you believe a wife could say that to a husband of twenty-five years?'

'I suppose she gave you her reasons,' said Sergeant Tomlinson. 'D'you mind telling us what they were?'

'Yes, I bloody well do mind,' said Herbert, 'but what's the point of keeping it to myself? Her main reason was that I was a boring old bugger.'

Constable Fry coughed.

'That upset you, Mr Jones?' said Sergeant Tomlinson.

'What do you think?' said Herbert, staring at the floor.

'Made you angry as well, I daresay,' said Sergeant Tomlinson.

'Shocked me to my core, I can tell you that,' said Herbert.

'Understandable, sir,' said Constable Fry.

'Shocked and angry, were you, sir?' suggested Sergeant Tomlinson.

'Well, of course I was annoyed when she kept on about my faults,' said Herbert, 'so I went out and walked it off.'

'That cooled you down, sir?' said Sergeant Tomlinson.

'Yes.'

'Could I put it to you, Mr Jones, that when you lost your temper you hit her, p'raps?' suggested Constable Fry.

Herbert raised his head, his expression one of disgust.

'Who said I lost my temper?' he asked. 'I didn't, and even if I had, I wouldn't have hit her, I wouldn't hit any woman for any reason. So don't make any more suggestions like that.'

'Didn't mean to upset you, sir, only trying to find out if your wife had cause to be in a bit of a state when she left you,' said Constable Fry.

'Give over,' said Herbert, 'I was the one in a bit of a state. Well, I ask you, after twenty-five years of working and providing for her and my daughters, what sort of a reward was it to be told I was about as useful as a doorpost?'

'It would have made some men furious,' said Sergeant Tomlinson.

'I daresay it would, but it only left me feeling like I was unconscious,' said Herbert. 'So stop trying to suggest I was in her flat last night, that I knocked her senseless and then drowned her in her bath. Last night I went out for a walk up to about eight thirty, when I called in on a friend of mine and got back here a little after eleven. You can check if you want.'

'We haven't said anything about your wife showing signs of having first been knocked senseless, sir,' said Sergeant Tomlinson.

'You've said enough to worry me,' said Herbert, wiping his forehead again.

'You're living here alone now, sir?' said Constable Fry.

'Yes. My three daughters are all married.'

Herbert bit his lip. 'Look, when d'you expect to know about the cause of my wife's death?'

'Tomorrow, sir,' said Sergeant Tomlinson. 'Well, that's all for the moment, thanks for putting up with us, and you can believe me when I say we didn't like having to bring you the bad news.'

'We'll see ourselves out, Mr Jones,' said Constable Fry.

Herbert didn't move from his chair or say anything as the CID men left.

'I'd be interested now to hear if his wife was asphyxiated, not drowned,' said Sergeant Tomlinson when he and Constable Fry entered their parked police car.

'Strangled before she was put into the bath?' said Constable Fry.

'What would you feel like doing to a wife who called you a boring old bugger and a useless doorpost before walking out on you after twenty-five years of marriage?'

'I'd feel like knocking her head off,' said Constable Fry.

'We should have asked him if he'd seen her since the day she left him.'

'And if he had a key to her flat,' said Constable Fry.

'Would she have given a spare key to someone she was glad to be shot of?' mused Sergeant Tomlinson.

'Well, that may be,' said Constable Fry, 'but in

my book, twenty-five years have got to mean something.'

'I tell you this much,' said Sergeant Tomlinson, 'if it wasn't suicide, then someone was with her in the flat last night. Someone who was well away from the place by the time Mr and Mrs Way arrived.'

'The husband, you remember, told us he was with a friend,' said Constable Fry. 'Should we check?'

'Now?' said Sergeant Tomlinson. 'It's too late for that, to get people out of bed, but once we've reported on our interview with Jones, we'll get orders to start checking tomorrow, you can bet on it.'

'Well, I know the form,' said Constable Fry.

'My guess is that what looks like suicide or accidental drowning is going to lead to an inquiry into suspicious circumstances,' said Sergeant Tomlinson. 'There was no sign of a break-in, so we're looking at how Jones felt about what his wife said to him. And did to him by walking out. I've got my doubts about suicide. It doesn't fit, not for a woman who sounds as if that was the last thing she had on her mind.'

'Could've been a sudden heart attack,' said Constable Fry.

'That's a thought, laddie, except it didn't occur to Jones, which it might have done if his wife was known to have had a weak heart.'

'Well, we'll get to know when the post-mortem's been done,' said Constable Fry.

The car carried them away then.

Herbert, watching from a window, went and poured himself a stiff whisky.

By now, having been told the terrible news, Madge and Winnie and their husbands were in the house of Olive and Roger. Olive was on her bed, still in a state of collapse, and Madge and Winnie were numb with shock. The three men were doing all the talking. Victor, Winnie's husband, wanted to know if his mother-in-law was lying flat in the bath when she was found. He pointed out that not many baths could take the full length of an adult.

'This one could,' said Roger.

'And did, apparently,' said Madge's husband, Brian.

'Listen.' Victor spoke quietly, not wanting Madge and Winnie to hear. The two women were seated on a settee, and Roger had found some brandy for them. 'Listen, do either of you think she simply got into the bath, laid herself flat under the water and then let herself drown?'

'I've asked myself that,' said Roger.

'So have I,' said Brian.

'In my opinion, the answer's no,' said Victor.

'Same here,' said Brian.

'There's got to be another answer, then,' said Victor.

'Too bloody right,' said Brian, 'considering Roger mentioned there was a cake of soap lying beside her. She wouldn't have bothered with any soap if she was going to drown herself.'

Madge spoke in a painful voice.

'What're you men saying?'

'We're just going round in circles, Madge,' said Victor.

'Haven't you thought Mum must have had a heart attack?' said Madge.

'It's on my mind,' said Brian.

'It's the only answer,' said Roger. 'The police will let us know tomorrow. If anyone would like some tea, put the kettle on, Brian, will you, while I just go up and see Olive again.'

Up he went, to find that Olive had recovered enough to come down. The atmosphere of the full gathering was of prolonged shock and lingering disbelief, and a large pot of tea was all that anyone could think of in the way of help. With Winnie's infant son asleep in his pram, they sat around the pot into the small hours. Introspective moments of silence were broken by verbal spasms of incredulity.

'How's Dad going to take this?'

The three daughters kept asking each other that question.

Chapter Eight

The following morning, the shocked typist carried to Mr Richards, the factory boss, a copy of her daily paper to let him see why Mrs Jones hadn't been at work yesterday and why she would never reappear. The Stop Press column announced that a Stockwell woman by the name of Hilda Jones had been found dead in her bath. That was all, but it was more than enough.

Mr Richards, who had Mr Burnside with him, drew a breath.

'Unbelievable,' he said.

'Let me see,' said Mr Burnside, and took hold of the paper, while the office typist looked on palely. He read the announcement, then breathed, 'Jesus Christ, her of all women.'

'Dying in her bath, a woman as healthy as that?' said Mr Richards.

'Lord, it must've been a weak heart and the water too hot,' said the typist, Miss Simmonds.

'Did she have a weak heart?' Mr Richards

asked the question of Mr Burnside. 'Did she ever mention she had?'

'Why ask me?' said Mr Burnside.

'Well, you had as much to do with her as anyone, she being the docket clerk,' said Mr Richards, 'and didn't I hear she'd just joined your drama group?'

'True,' said Mr Burnside, 'but I never discussed her state of health with her. I wouldn't have thought it necessary to, not a fine-looking woman like her.'

'I suppose a woman could faint in her bath if the water was too hot,' said Mr Richards.

'Yes, she could, sir,' said Miss Simmonds.

'And she wouldn't need to have a weak heart?' said Mr Burnside.

'No, she probably wouldn't, Mr Burnside,' said the shaken typist.

'Well, I'm damned sorry,' said Mr Richards, 'and I'll see to it that the firm sends a wreath for her funeral. Perhaps you'd like to represent the firm, Burnside?'

'Someone should,' said Mr Burnside.

'Thanks,' said Mr Richards. 'Meanwhile, I'll have to ring the Labour Exchange to see if we can get a replacement fairly quickly.' He shook his head. 'Poor bloody woman,' he said.

Miss Simmonds hesitated, then said, 'Did you know, sir, that Mrs Jones had just separated from her husband?'

'No, I didn't know,' said Mr Richards. 'Not my business, in any case, but I suppose it'll be as much of a shock to him as anyone.'

'I'm sure, sir,' said Miss Simmonds.

'I wonder now, could she have committed suicide if the separation was forced on her?' murmured Mr Richards.

'I couldn't answer that,' said Mr Burnside.

'But she didn't act or look or talk as if she was suffering,' said Miss Simmonds.

'True enough,' agreed Mr Burnside.

'People don't always show their innermost feelings,' said Mr Richards.

'That's true too,' said Mr Burnside. He rubbed his chin. 'Tragic,' he said. 'We'll miss her, and the drama group will be shocked.'

'Oh, I'm sure you thought a lot of her, Mr Burnside,' said Miss Simmonds, essaying a sidelong glance.

'We all did, didn't we?' said Mr Burnside, who could take or leave sidelong glances from pettifogging typists.

The post-mortem examination had been finished. The slab was cold, so was the body. The pathologist covered it up just as Detective Sergeant Tomlinson arrived.

'What's the verdict?' asked the CID man.

'Death by drowning.'

'Following a heart attack?'

'A reasonable assumption, Sergeant, but no, her heart was in first-class condition. She could have fainted and slid under, perhaps, but I can't say that that possibility is a fact.'

'We've probably got a suicide, then?' said Sergeant Tomlinson.

'That's for the coroner to decide when he's had all the relevant information. But certainly she drowned.'

'Then it's more a matter for the coroner than the police?' said Sergeant Tomlinson.

'I'm not so sure,' said the pathologist. 'There are slight bruises around her ankles. Look.' He lifted the sheet and Sergeant Tomlinson took note of faint marks around both ankles.

'Now how could they have come about?' he asked.

'Good question, Sergeant.'

Sergeant Tomlinson, a keen and incorruptible arm of the law, gave the point some thought.

'She wasn't touched until the ambulance team lifted her out of the bath,' he said, 'and I can't say I noticed those marks at that particular time. Would prolonged immersion in the water have temporarily reduced the signs of bruising?'

'Very possibly,' said the pathologist.

'Christ, you don't think she could have been tied up, do you?' said the CID sergeant.

'You're thinking of foul play? I wouldn't have said so. The marks would have been more definite, even allowing for the effects of immersion, and, in any case, there are none about her wrists or arms. Just her ankles. Worth a little thought, I suppose.'

'Yes, I'd say so,' said Sergeant Tomlinson, suspicions very much aroused, 'and I'll have to land it in Inspector Shaw's lap. Incidentally, I've just remembered, she had a tablet of soap in the bath with her.'

'That's news to me,' said the pathologist, 'but it's consistent with her deciding to take a bath, although not with any decision to drown herself, unless she had a sudden death wish.'

'Suicide on the spur of the moment? I don't go much on that, with or without any cake of soap,' said the sergeant as he left.

'You're talking about an enforced drowning?' growled burly Detective Inspector Shaw. 'On account of slightly bruised ankles? Reason? Motive? Method?'

'Haven't got a reason or motive yet,' said Sergeant Tomlinson, 'but method, sir? Held down in the bath?'

'That would mean two buggers, wouldn't it? One holding her ankles and one pressing her shoulders?'

'Might be on, sir, if the motive was a bit serious,' said Sergeant Tomlinson.

'A bit serious?' The growl was deeper. Inspector Shaw was noted for imitating irritable bears. 'I see. Two possible suspects make the motive a bit serious, do they? One would be enough to make it bloody serious to me. What're you offering me, might I ask?'

'Suspicion of murder, sir?'

'Don't make me cry for you, Sergeant.' Inspector Shaw regarded Tomlinson pityingly. 'All you're offering are faint marks around the ankles. Shoes, man, shoes.'

'Shoes, sir?'

'With ankle straps. Women wear them. They're fashionable. Go back to the flat and see if you can find the pair Mrs Jones was wearing that particular evening. They'll probably be on the floor of her bedroom. If they've got ankle straps, let the pathologist have a look at them. Then he'll let you know if the marks were caused by the straps. I don't want to be bothered by flights of fancy. I'm busy.'

'What?' Nell Binns goggled at Herbert. They were in the kitchen of her Brixton flat. 'Hilda's dead?'

'Drowned in her bath,' said Herbert.

'Gawd Almighty,' breathed Nell, 'you're standing there telling me that?'

'Be all the same if I was sitting down,' said Herbert.

'Herbert, I don't know how you can be so calm.'

'I'm not,' said Herbert, 'I'm out of my wits, I can tell you. It looks like it could have happened while I was on my way home from my evening with you. Well, the police said between nine and ten thirty. What time was it I left? Was it about nine thirty?'

'Was it a bit earlier?' said Nell.

'Might have been,' said Herbert. 'Anyway, the news was a real shaker, Nell, and still is, believe me.'

'Oh, you poor man,' said Nell, 'imagine the police bringing word of it to you at that time of night. You couldn't have slept a wink. Here, sit down, and I'll make us some Camp coffee, and you can talk to me about what the police told you.'

Herbert seemed to fold his firm frame limply. It put him into the holding security of a kitchen chair.

'I still can't believe it,' he said. 'I'm actu'lly on the way to my daughter Olive, but I stopped to call on you. Hope you don't mind, Nell.'

'Course I don't mind,' said Nell, and while she bustled about he recounted details of his conversation with the police. Nell was all shocked and astounded ears, but she produced two cups of hot coffee made from Camp, and then sat down with Herbert. He drank his coffee scalding. She talked to him, trying to console him, and of course, like others, she suggested Hilda had

had a heart attack. Herbert said it might have been that, but the police hadn't mentioned the possibility. Nell said well, a police doctor would find out fairly quick, wouldn't he? There'd be a proper examination, wouldn't there?

'Yes, I suppose so, yes,' said Herbert.

'Well, I'm sure it'll show something was wrong with her heart,' said Nell. 'But I can see that's no consolation, I can see you're sorely grieving, Herbert.'

Herbert, finishing his coffee, said, 'I'd better go, Nell, but it's helped a bit, talking to you.'

'Come in again this evening, if you want,' said Nell, 'you shouldn't be alone, not at a time like this.'

'Thanks,' said Herbert, 'you're a good woman, Nell, and a good friend too.'

Roger had taken the day off from his work to stay with Olive, who was a rag of a young woman after a sleepless night. They were expecting Herbert, both quite sure he would call since the police had said they were going to inform him of his wife's death and of who found her. Olive cried on his shoulder when he arrived, and Herbert gave her some embarrassed pats.

'It can't be helped, Olive, things like this do happen to people,' he said awkwardly.

'Old people, yes, they can sort of collapse in a bath, but not Mum, not when she was still such a healthy woman,' said Olive, 'not when she was still young compared to the old. Oh, if only she hadn't been by herself in that flat, if only you'd stopped her leaving you, which you ought to have, Dad. You ought to have stood up to her instead of standing aside.'

'No, your dad can't be blamed, Olive,' said Roger, 'he and your mum came to an agreement about the separation. They could have chucked things at each other and had an almighty row, but I don't think that would have stopped your mum doing what she wanted. I knew her well enough to know she liked having her own way.'

'All the same, she'd still be alive if Dad had put his foot down for a change,' said Olive.

'I'll take the blame,' said Herbert.

'No, I didn't mean that,' said Olive, red-eyed and pale.

'Nobody's to blame,' said Roger. 'Listen,' he said to Herbert, 'I'd go back home now, if I were you, because the police will probably have been told by now the exact cause of death, and I suppose they'll let the family know. If so, you're bound to be the one they'll call on, you're the nearest next of kin.'

'I ought to go and see Madge and Winnie,' said Herbert.

'I'll see to it that they come and see you,' said Roger. 'You must be as hard hit as anyone, and Madge and Winnie'll recognize that. You're done in. Go back home, and stay there for the time being.'

'Yes, that's best, Dad,' said Olive shakily, 'and I'll come and see you myself as soon as I feel a bit better.'

'Perhaps I'd better go back,' said Herbert, 'I don't want to be out if the police do call.'

'Yes, push off, old man,' said Roger, 'and if there's anything I can do any time, just let me know.'

'Thanks, Roger,' said Herbert.

After he'd gone, Roger said, 'He's a walking question mark.'

'What d'you mean?' asked Olive.

'He can't understand that it's actually happened,' said Roger, 'and he's asking himself all the time if it really did.'

'Well, I'm the same, I'm asking myself the same question over and over,' said Olive.

'I agree with what everyone else in the family thinks,' said Roger.

'What's that?' asked Olive tiredly.

'Heart attack,' said Roger.

'Yes, it's got to be that,' said Olive, refusing even to think about an act of suicide.

'I've just thought,' said Roger, 'the front door's still broken. It's open to anyone, so's the flat. Your mum had quite a few decent possessions, and there might be a bit of money around as well.'

'Oh, there wouldn't be a lot,' said Olive, 'except what's in her handbag. She kept all her real money in the Post Office Savings Bank.'

'And where's her savings book, I wonder?' asked Roger. 'Would you know where she kept it?'

'No, and who cares, anyway?' said Olive.

'Still, some petty thief could pinch her handbag and whatever little valuables she had by sneaking into the flat,' said Roger. 'I'd better go round, Olive, and at least get her handbag. And I ought to do something soon about getting the street door repaired.'

'All right, go and fetch her handbag, Roger,' said Olive, 'I can't get worried about her little possessions myself. Nothing seems important to me except her death.'

'You'll be OK till I get back?' said Roger.

'Yes, I'll be all right, but don't be long,' said Olive.

There was a uniformed constable guarding the damaged door by the side of the shop, a shop that sold pictures and picture frames. Roger, arriving, explained to the constable that he was the dead woman's son-in-law and had come to check up on her possessions. The constable, however, had a duty to ensure all such possessions remained intact and that entry was allowed only to authorized persons. Accordingly, he was dubious about allowing Roger entry, since there was no way of proving his relationship with the dead woman there and then.

Roger said that while it was jolly decent of the police to be keeping an eye on the place, he really was the unfortunate lady's son-in-law. In fact, he and his wife had been the ones who'd discovered her dead in her bath last night. He described the discovery in detail, and pointed out he himself had been responsible for telephoning the police. He gave the constable a description of Detective Sergeant Tomlinson, the investigating officer. The constable relaxed.

'Right you are, sir, you can go up, then,' he said.

The door that had been jemmied open by Roger showed splintered wood by the forced lock. Its damage was evident to any passer-by, and although it was closed it swung inwards as Roger pushed it. He stepped in, closed it again, and went up to the flat. The entry door wasn't locked and he went in. All three rooms were empty and had an air of brooding quiet. He didn't go into the bathroom. He made a careful survey of the kitchen and living room, both of which seemed undisturbed, and then went into the bedroom. He began a search of the dressing-table drawers.

A voice from the doorway startled him.

'Hello, what's the idea? My constable informed me a relative was here. Who are you and what're you up to?'

Roger swung round. Detective Sergeant Tomlinson eyed him suspiciously for a second, then he gave a nod of recognition.

'I know you,' said Roger, 'and you know me.'

'You're Mr Way, of course,' said Sergeant Tomlinson, 'you had the nasty experience of finding Mrs Jones.'

'Yes, I'm her son-in-law, you remember,' said Roger. He made a face. 'Or was, I suppose. I don't know, I'm still a bit out of sorts. I came to look for her handbag and to see if anyone had sneaked in. Well, it was on my mind, the possibility that the wrecked door meant the place was wide open to wrong 'uns, and my wife and I thought her mother's handbag and any little valuables might get pinched. I'd no idea a constable was on guard.'

'As a precaution, Mr Way,' said Sergeant Tomlinson. 'Incidentally, is that it, what you were looking for?' He pointed. 'The handbag there, on the bedside chair?'

Roger smiled faintly.

'Can't see for looking, can I?' he said. 'Shows I'm still in a state. It's OK for me to take it?'

Sergeant Tomlinson considered the request. He was still not in favour of a suicide verdict.

'D'you mind if I have a look at it first, sir?'

'What for?' asked Roger, picking up the hand-bag.

'Just a formality, sir,' said Sergeant Tomlinson, who had already seen what he himself had come for, a pair of shoes, with ankle straps, next to the bedside chair.

'Wait a bit,' said Roger, 'd'you know the cause of death now?'

'We know at the moment that she did drown,' said Sergeant Tomlinson, 'but not why. There's one or two loose ends.'

'What loose ends?'

'Oh, only the kind that need tidying up before the inquest,' said Sergeant Tomlinson. 'Shouldn't take long. Regarding the inquest, your father-in-law Mr Jones will be informed of the date. And so will you and your wife, sir.'

'Hold on,' said Roger, 'drowning means – well, suicide or a fatal heart attack, doesn't it?'

'That's for the coroner to say,' said Sergeant Tomlinson.

'There was nothing like a heart attack?' said Roger.

'It seems her heart was as sound as a bell, sir.'

'The family's not going to believe it was suicide,' said Roger. 'Still, if it looks that way—?'

'Very sad, sir,' said Sergeant Tomlinson.

'Could I ask why you're here yourself?'

'I'm doing what you might call a bit of the

117

tidying up,' said Sergeant Tomlinson. 'The handbag, sir?'

Roger gave it to him. Sergeant Tomlinson opened it. He also opened up an inner compartment, then turned the bag upside down and shook the contents out on the bed. Out came a compact, a handkerchief, a comb and various other little items indigenous to most women's handbags. He ran a well-trained eye over all of it.

'There's no purse,' said Roger.

'So I note,' said Sergeant Tomlinson, and wondered when it had gone missing and who had it now. 'Has someone sneaked in under the eyes of our constable?'

'I shouldn't think so,' said Roger.

'So where's the purse?' said Sergeant Tomlinson.

'You tell me,' said Roger, flicking glances here and there in hopeful search.

'Well, it's a fact that some women living alone like to keep their money out of sight. Let's see.' He crossed to the bed. The covering sheet and blanket were turned down at one corner, exposing part of the pillow. He lifted the pillow and revealed a purse and a brown envelope about six inches by four. 'There we are, sir.' He picked up the purse and handed it to Roger, then took up the envelope. There was something in it, something that might represent a clue to a policeman disbelieving of suicide. The envelope wasn't sealed and he took out what was in it.

'Well, look at that,' said Roger.

'I am looking, sir.'

'That's her Post Office savings book,' said Roger.

'Yes, so it is,' said Sergeant Tomlinson, leafing through it. He noted regular entries in the deposits column, and two recent withdrawals amounting to ten pounds. He made a guess that on leaving her husband, she'd treated herself. 'Savings aren't uncommon to some housewives.'

'No, but that book's valuable if there's much in the account,' said Roger, ready to take care of it. 'It's favourite with some petty crooks, getting their hands on Post Office savings books and fiddling withdrawals. I suppose my mother-in-law kept it in her handbag by day and under her pillow at night since moving here. I wouldn't keep a savings book in a handbag myself.'

'Nor would I, Mr Way, but neither of us is a woman,' said Sergeant Tomlinson. 'And your mother-in-law, by keeping it in an envelope as well, at least made sure it didn't show whenever she opened her handbag.' He looked over the collection of items again, but without any real interest. Whatever he might have expected to find to give him more food for thought, he'd found nothing. His suspicions were still fed by the marks around the deceased woman's ankles, which the pathologist thought odd, and which Inspector Shaw thought might have been made by ankle straps. Inspector Shaw might be right. 'Well, that little lot seems all right, Mr Way, though I suppose the savings book should be held by the nearest next of kin for the moment. The husband.'

'I'll see he gets it,' said Roger, taking the book and putting it into his jacket pocket.

'Um, what's in the purse?' asked Sergeant Tomlinson as an afterthought.

Roger opened it, and the CID man watched him count its contents, three pound notes, two ten-shilling notes and seven shillings and eight-pence in coins. The CID man thought that meant the deceased was pretty flush.

'Four whole quid plus seven bob and a bit,' said Roger. 'It would've pleased my father-in-law to know the separation hadn't put her into a hard-up state. Well, she had her job, in any case.' He returned the money to the purse, and then began putting everything back into the handbag, except for the savings book, safe in his jacket pocket.

'Just as well you came back, Mr Way,' said Sergeant Tomlinson. 'It would be a good idea, wouldn't it, to have the street door repaired pretty quick?'

'I'll see to it,' said Roger.

'Oh, when you do, let us have a spare key just

in case we need to do more tidying up,' said Sergeant Tomlinson. 'Don't touch anything in the bathroom.'

'Right,' said Roger. 'I'll get back to my wife now, I'm taking time off from my job to keep her company until she's over the shock.'

'Understood, Mr Way,' said Sergeant Tomlinson, and waited until Roger was out of the place before picking up the shoes. They were very nice shoes, of black patent leather. He looked them over, paying particular attention to the slender ankle straps. Then he dropped the footwear into a carrier bag.

Chapter Nine

The pathologist made an earnest examination of the shoes and their fashionable ankle straps.

'No,' he said eventually.

'Why not?' asked Sergeant Tomlinson.

'Because the straps are the wrong shape, Sergeant, and also not high enough. The marks describe a level circle around each ankle above the joint. The straps are angled downwards from the ankles below the joint.'

'Would you say, then, that the marks were more likely caused by gripping hands?' asked Sergeant Tomlinson.

'No, I wouldn't. They're not wide enough.'

'Cords, then?'

'No. I told you earlier, Sergeant, that the bruises aren't deep enough to point to tied ankles. Cord would have resulted in positive weals. But I'll admit I'm suspicious. That is, I will be if you or the coroner can find no reason why the deceased should have committed suicide.'

'I'll tell Inspector Shaw that,' said Sergeant Tomlinson.

'I see,' said Inspector Shaw, who looked as if he didn't see at all. 'You feel there's still a reason for an investigation into suspicious circumstances, do you?'

'It's a fact I do have a feeling, sir.'

'You can't wait for the result of the inquest?'

'That's not up to me, is it?' said Tomlinson.

'Are those the shoes?' asked the inspector.

'They're the ones.' Sergeant Tomlinson extracted the pair from the carrier bag and handed them to the inspector, who regarded them sourly.

'Well, they're a decent pair of shoes, I'll say that much, Tomlinson. But they've been ruled out, you said, so what am I doing holding them? You can return them. Here.' Inspector Shaw handed them back. 'I've seen the body while you've been out.' He then delivered some instructions that suggested he'd come round to puzzling about the faint ankle bruises himself. 'Listen, on account of your feelings, and on account of the deceased having left her husband, find out if she had a bloke on the side.'

'You mean – ?'

'She wasn't too old for an affair,' said Inspector Shaw. 'That might have been the real reason why she set up on her own. Women are deep,

Tomlinson, deep, even women over forty with twenty-five years of marriage behind them. Married women only a little over forty, in fact, sometimes try to make up for what they think they've missed. From my inspection of her corpse, I'd say Mrs Jones still had a good body.'

'I agree, sir.' Sergeant Tomlinson, of course, had seen the body as it lay in the bath.

'Get going, then.'

'Where do you suggest I start?' asked the sergeant, who knew he'd get a rollicking if he decided for himself and nothing came of it.

'Where?' Inspector Shaw growled. 'Where do you think, man? Among the people she worked with. Women talk to the people they work with, especially to other women. Then there are the daughters. Mrs Jones might have confided in them, or one of them. If you come up with anything, then I might take a hand myself. Until then, it's your job.'

'I'll take it on,' said Sergeant Tomlinson, twenty-nine, broad-shouldered, physically impressive, quick of mind, and in line for promotion.

'Have Constable Fry go along with you. D'you know Mrs Jones's place of work?'

'Yes, sir, Stockwell Tools Ltd.'

'Get going, then.'

'Right, sir,' said Sergeant Tomlinson, and left to pick up his colleague, Detective Constable Fry.

A brawl erupted in a Brixton pub, the publican himself being on the receiving end. At the delivery end was Muscles Boddy, whose manners and behaviour never improved. Just three customers were present, two of whom were looking the other way. The third was a newcomer. A fairly naive character, he couldn't understand why nobody was doing anything about what was going on. He couldn't do much himself, he was a shortie, a titch. So, unseen by Muscles, he slipped out and almost at once ran into what he hoped to come across, two uniformed constables on their beat.

That proved unfortunate for Muscles, who was only doing what he was paid to do to a recalcitrant client. Usually, he delivered his punitive assaults in quick time and without inter-ference, and was away before trouble arrived in the shape of the law. On this occasion, the early and unexpected appearance of two hefty bobbies not only flabbergasted him but caught him behind the bar putting his boot in. He was arrested, taken away, given a summary hearing at Lambeth Magistrates Court, and awarded twenty-eight days without the option of a fine. Muscles Boddy was too well known merely to have his wrist slapped.

Twenty-eight days upset him considerably. He complained bitterly about the prospect of being forcibly locked away from his friends.

'Miss you, will they, Muscles?' said an escorting copper on the way to Brixton Prison.

'Course they bleedin' will, you bugger,' said Muscles. 'They rely on me, don't they? To cheer 'em up and do 'em reg'lar good turns.'

'We know what kind of good turns. And what kind of friends. They end up in hospital.'

'You been misinformed,' said Muscles, lumpy countenance all gloomy undulations. 'I had a visit to a special friend all lined up for Sunday. Now you've been and messed it up.'

'Your special friend won't mind. Might save him a broken leg, in fact.'

'Don't come it,' said Muscles, 'I hate the lot of you, and I pertic'lerly hate you.'

'Why me?' asked the copper.

'I don't like your phizog. It ain't human.'

'Well, you're in luck, you won't see it for the next twenty-eight days.'

'I'll improve it for you one day,' said Muscles, who was at his gloomiest. Among other things, he'd proposed to call again on his friend Herbert on Sunday, just for a chat. He'd miss out on that. And then there was the fact that he knew he'd have to answer to his guv'nor for getting himself crimed when he came out. Not that he'd told the court exactly why he was sorting out the publican. But the bleedin' coppers knew, of course, and they'd be keeping a closer watch on his guv'nor, who wouldn't like it a bit.

'What's that?' asked Olive, returning to the living room after making herself a mug of hot Bovril. Roger was examining something.

'Eh?' He looked up. 'Oh, didn't hear you, thought you were still in the kitchen. Feeling better?'

'No, not much,' said Olive, 'but I hope this Bovril will help a little.' She sat down. 'Roger, what's that you've got?'

'It's your mum's savings book,' said Roger.

'I thought you'd only found her handbag and purse,' said Olive.

'Didn't I mention her savings book?' asked Roger.

'No, you didn't,' said Olive, 'so let me see.'

'It's—'

'Let me see.'

'Of course,' said Roger, and handed it to her. Olive opened it and looked at the current balance. It was quite a bit.

'Oh, well, it's not much good to poor old Mum now,' she said. She was unable at the moment to express any further interest, and she passed the book back to Roger.

'I'm glad I found it before any petty thief did,' said Roger. 'Can you believe that balance of eight hundred and eighty-three pounds?'

'Does it matter?' said Olive, still grieving. 'Who cares about it just now?'

'Well, even as things are,' said Roger, 'all that much money is still an eye-opener, Olive, especially as it's earning interest.'

'Is it?' Olive sipped the Bovril and sighed. 'Roger, I simply can't credit Mum taking her own life. Did that policeman say it was definitely suicide?'

'No, I told you he said it only looked like it, that we'll have to wait for the inquest,' said Roger. 'All the same, Olive, I think we're going to have to accept it. But God knows why she did it.'

'Yes, why should she, it doesn't make sense,' said Olive, 'especially as she kept saying she liked being a free woman, that she was already enjoying herself. That might not have been very fair on Dad, considering he felt he always did his best as a husband, but living her own life was what she wanted, so why should she commit suicide?'

'Beats me, Olive.'

'I'd rather she'd had a heart attack,' said Olive.

'Well, there's still a possibility she fainted,' said Roger, 'we both agree that could have happened. Christ, though, she had nearly nine hundred pounds savings. Look at all the monthly entries since 1911, one after the other and no withdrawals except two recent ones of five quid each.'

'What's there is all the money she saved out of her housekeeping allowance every year of her marriage,' said Olive flatly.

'Well, that's in your dad's favour,' said Roger, 'giving her the kind of housekeeping that enabled her to save this much in twenty-five years. It's an average of about thirty-five quid a year. No wonder the poor old bloke couldn't understand her walking out on him. D'you know how much housekeeping he gave her each week?'

'Roger, I can't get interested in this,' said Olive, 'but all right, it was two pounds five shillings.'

'As much as that?' said Roger.

'Well, Dad made a profit of about five pounds a week from his shop, and a lot more at Christmastimes,' said Olive. 'And he paid all the bills so as to make sure Mum could put more than a few shillings into her savings every month. And he put savings away himself for their old age.'

'Then she was a bit hard on him in the end, wasn't she?' said Roger.

Olive told him not to speak ill of the dead. She said her mum deserved extra housekeeping because of all she did for her family, and that she wouldn't have walked out if only she hadn't been taken for granted, and if Dad had been more sociable as a husband. Roger said he supposed her mother's savings would all revert to her father, unless her mother had made a will and given equal shares to everyone.

'Mum wouldn't have made any will,' said Olive, 'she never thought about anything like that. Only property owners and the gentry make wills, generally.'

'It'll all go to your dad, then,' said Roger.

'At the moment, Roger, I don't care what happens to it,' said Olive. 'I'm not good for anything except grief just now. You'll have to give me time to get over the shock before I can interest myself in Mum's savings.' However, she managed a few moments of concentrated thought, and came to the silent conclusion that if she did receive a share she'd open a savings account of her own with it. A savings account would guard against an empty domestic kitty, which Roger's spendthrift habits might bring about.

Madge and Winnie arrived then, wanting to talk and to mull repeatedly over everything, especially when told that according to the police their mother's death looked like suicide. That really got them going, and although Roger could understand it, the constant repetition of the same overworked questions and disbeliefs began to play on his nerves. So he brought the savings book up for discussion. Neither Madge nor Winnie were all that surprised by the recorded balance. They both said their mother was a good manager, and that she was able to save more each week when she started her part-time job a year ago. Roger said it all belonged to their father now.

'I don't see why,' said Madge, 'it all ought to be shared out.'

'Yes, so it ought,' said Winnie. 'It's what she'd have wanted.'

'I don't think money is what we should be talking about now,' said Olive, 'it's not the right time. I'm still hoping I'll wake up and find everything's just been a nightmare.'

'God, wouldn't we all like that,' said Madge, recovered enough to be her assertive self. 'But listen, I must say something about Mum's savings book. Don't let my father have it, Roger, not until we find out if he intends to divide the amount into fair shares.'

'Fair shares sound like a fair solution to me,' said Roger. 'You girls all had a special regard for your mother, and she appreciated that. You're all entitled to fair shares.'

'Roger, must you?' said Olive.

'Sorry, love,' said Roger.

'We can put that subject aside now,' said Madge.

'Actually,' said Winnie, 'the stars aren't right at the moment for money matters. Oh, Lord, and they couldn't have been right for Mum two nights ago. I still can't take it in.'

That, not unnaturally, brought the sisters back to their lamenting state, to a resumption of the sad whys and wherefores, with an emphasis on the fact that if only she had stayed with their father she would almost certainly still be alive.

Roger intervened to say their father had called earlier, but had been persuaded to go back home because he looked done in. Perhaps Winnie and Madge would go and see him sometime? Madge said they'd do that, of course they would.

'Well, I know one thing,' said Winnie, 'and that's that Mum didn't deliberately drown herself. She wasn't born under that kind of star.'

'Oh, leave off about stars,' said Madge.

'I expect it'll be called an accident,' said Roger.

Olive picked quickly and hopefully at that remark.

'Oh, d'you think she might've slipped, hit her head on the side of the bath and then fell in unconscious?' she said.

'She might, yes,' said Madge, 'but, look here, we can't keep on and on about what might have been. It's not doing us any good, and it's not getting us anywhere. Roger, did the policeman say anything definite at all?'

'Sergeant Tomlinson?' said Roger. 'About the cause? No, nothing definite, just that we'd have to wait on the inquest.'

'Well, the police ought to know something a bit definite by now,' said Winnie. 'I mean, if Mum did hit her head.'

'I don't think he thought anything like that happened,' said Roger.

'But it might have,' said Olive. 'You could go round to the police station and ask.'

'Yes, stop being negative, Roger,' said Madge.

'Roger's not being negative, just reasonable,' said Olive. 'All the same, go and ask, Roger.'

'All right,' said Roger. Although easy come, easy go as far as money was concerned, and not a stickler for principles, he had his good points, and was willing to humour his stricken wife.

'I'll come with you,' said Madge, 'let's go now.'

She and Roger went together. The desk sergeant at the station assured them that if there'd been any signs of a head bruise on Mrs Jones, it wouldn't have been missed during the post-mortem examination.

'Sure?' said Roger.

'Sure,' said the desk sergeant.

'Well, it just might have been missed,' said Madge.

'It might, but I don't think so, Mrs Cooper,' said the sergeant sympathetically.

'But you never know,' said Madge, 'and I'd like the doctor or surgeon or whoever did the examination to have another look.'

'Pardon?' said the sergeant.

'I do have a right to ask him to,' said Madge.

The sergeant realized argument wasn't the thing.

'I'll pass your request on, Mrs Cooper,' he said, 'and if you could come back tomorrow, I think I'd be able to give you an answer. Will that do?'

'Yes, all right,' said Madge, clutching at straws on behalf of the family. 'You can understand, I suppose, that none of us can believe it wasn't accidental?'

'I can understand, but, of course, I'm not at liberty to discuss it, Mrs Cooper.'

'No, I suppose not, and it's painful for me too, I assure you,' said Madge.

'You do have my sympathy, Mrs Cooper. A shock like that takes a long time to recover from.'

'Yes,' said Madge, 'I'm sure of that. Well, thanks, anyway, and I'll call in again tomorrow.'

That was all she and Roger could carry back to the others, the hope that an answer tomorrow would point to the possibility of an accident, which would be far more acceptable than suicide.

None of the daughters wanted to believe their mother had taken her own life.

Chapter Ten

Sergeant Tomlinson had a thought as he and Constable Fry left the station that afternoon. The thought made him suggest they should visit the Stockwell Road flat again.

'What's the idea?' asked Constable Fry. 'Aren't we supposed to be heading for the poor old girl's place of work?'

'There's something I want to find out first,' said Sergeant Tomlinson.

'Don't mind me or my aching feet,' said Constable Fry.

'I've got my own feet to worry about,' said Sergeant Tomlinson, who'd have liked the use of a police car. Inspector Shaw, however, had said do some old-fashioned plodding, too much use of cars is softening the force. Furthermore, he'd said, this isn't an emergency, it's a shot in the dark.

When they reached 25 Stockwell Road, there was a barrow parked at the kerbside, its painted boards advertising 'J.C. Meadowes – Carpenter – Stockwell Lane S.W.9'. The carpenter himself was at work, and about to take the damaged door off its hinges. The duty constable was standing by.

'Sorry, the bobby can't let no-one in,' said Mr Meadowes. 'Mr Roger Way was particular about telling me that.'

'We're police officers,' said Sergeant Tomlinson, and the carpenter looked them over. He nodded.

'That's different,' he said. 'Finding things out, are you, about the poor woman's accident? Mr Way told me about it. Imagine she finished up drowning. Talk about you never know what's going to hit you. Well, there we go, gents, the door's off.' Manhandling it, the carpenter rested it against the outside brick wall. 'You can go up now.'

'You're fitting a new lock when you've made the repair?' said Sergeant Tomlinson.

'Repair? That's a job for me workshop,' said the carpenter, 'and pricey too. And time-consuming. No, I agreed with Mr Way to fit a new door. There it is, in the passage.'

'Good,' said Sergeant Tomlinson. 'Got the keys for the lock?'

'A door lock ain't much use without a key, y'know,' said the carpenter. 'I've got three for that there new one.'

'Two spares? Let me have one. I'm Detective Sergeant Tomlinson of the Stockwell station.' The sergeant showed his card. 'You can take my word it's all right by Mr Way.'

'Well, if you say so, guv'nor,' said the carpenter. He dug into the pocket of his boiler suit, brought out three keys on a ring, released one and handed it to the CID man.

'Much obliged,' said Sergeant Tomlinson, 'you can let Mr Way know you've given me one, which I'll let him have in due course.'

'Fair enough,' said the carpenter.

The CID men climbed the stairs and went straight to the bedroom.

'Now what, seeing the key means you're thinking of coming here again?' said Constable Fry.

'Well, I'll tell you,' said Sergeant Tomlinson. 'It's assumed Mrs Jones was taking a bath before she went to bed. I don't suppose she intended to dress again. I suppose what she'd have put on after her bath was her nightdress. I don't recollect seeing it about. Nor did I see it when I lifted her pillow and uncovered the purse and savings book. So let's find out if she left it somewhere handy.'

'You've got a bee in your bonnet,' said Constable Fry.

'Yes, and it's buzzing,' said Sergeant Tomlinson, and crossed to the bed. The covering sheet and blanket were turned down at one corner, as before, showing part of the pillow. He lifted the pillow to confirm that, with the purse and savings book having been removed, there was nothing there. 'Don't women keep their nighties under their pillow?' he asked.

'Usually,' said Constable Fry. 'Lily does.' Lily was his better half.

'Well, Mrs Jones's isn't here, is it?'

'I can't see it, no,' said Constable Fry, 'but what I can see is that the bedclothes have been turned down. Was that to get at her nightie?'

'Or just to put her purse and savings book under the pillow?' suggested Sergeant Tomlinson. 'In any case, where is the ruddy nightdress?'

'Have you thought of trying the bathroom door? It might be hanging on the peg, ready to be put on.'

'Wouldn't we have noticed it when we were called out to investigate? And who'd use a nightdress damp with steam? But never mind that, take a look, Sidney.'

'That won't be too hard on me feet, Frank,' said Constable Fry, and went to the bathroom, while Sergeant Tomlinson moved around the bedroom. Back came Constable Fry. 'No luck, Sarge, no nightie, just an empty peg except for one of them thin waterproof bath caps.'

'Eh?'

'Fact. No nightie, only the cap, the kind some

women cover their heads with when they take a bath.'

'Well, ruddy hell, why wasn't Mrs Jones wearing it? Her head was bare.' Sergeant Tomlinson made a quick journey to the bathroom himself. He saw the cap on the peg. He looked around, and the bee in his bonnet buzzed louder. 'Something else,' he said.

'We've been here before, y'know,' said Constable Fry, 'so what's the something else that's on your mind?'

'Where's the ruddy bath towel?' asked Sergeant Tomlinson. There wasn't one, only a small hand towel hanging from a hook between the handbasin and the toilet.

'Listen,' said Constable Fry, 'this bathroom is as we left it.'

'I can see it is,' said Sergeant Tomlinson, 'and we should have made a note about no bath towel. But we were only interested in the bath and its corpse, and what looked like suicide or an accident. Now why didn't Mrs Jones put the cap on and bring a towel with her? And another thing, wouldn't she have worn some kind of a wrap or did she walk naked from the bedroom to here?'

'If she'd made up her mind to drown herself, she wouldn't have bothered with a wrap or a bath cap,' said Constable Fry. 'But I've suddenly got a bee in me own bonnet.'

'Listen, she'd left her old man, and we know from what he said himself and what Mr and Mrs Way said, that she was looking forward to a new and more exciting life.' Sergeant Tomlinson spoke firmly. 'No, I'm passing on suicide, so there's got to be a nightdress somewhere.' He went back to the bedroom. He pulled the covering sheet and blanket halfway down, but again only revealed the undersheet. 'Where the hell is it?'

'Any good suggesting she slept in the altogether?' offered Constable Fry.

'I'm not buying that, this is London, not the Sahara.' Sergeant Tomlinson opened up the wardrobe. It disclosed various garments, but nothing in the way of nightdresses or underwear. He advanced on the dressing table, and began to open its drawers. He found clean folded underwear in one drawer, and in the one below he found a pink nightdress on top of a white corset.

'That's it,' said Constable Fry.

'Is it?'

'Well, it's not an overcoat.'

'Don't let's get clever. Ten to one it's not the nightdress she was using. It's folded, it's clean, and uncreased. It's her spare.'

'You could be right,' said Constable Fry. 'So where's this week's one?'

'Is there an airing cupboard?' asked Sergeant Tomlinson. 'If so, she might have kept it there to put on warm each night.'

They discovered a small airing cupboard next to the bathroom, but it contained no nightdress. However, they did find two folded bath towels, the top one looking a little used. That's the one she would have taken to the bathroom, thought Sergeant Tomlinson. Now then, a drowned corpse, with the faint marks of a ringed bruise around each ankle. No bath cap or wrap worn, and no towel taken. And no nightdress visible. Was it an enforced bath? Had some lunatic got into the flat and jumped her at the moment she was fully undressed? If so, she'd have screamed and struggled. The flat overlooked the road, and someone could easily have heard the screams. And a violent struggle would have left its marks on her. He'd bet she was a strong woman: she was no little weakling – she had a fine physique. She wouldn't have gone quietly unless she'd been knocked out. But, in that case, the pathologist would have found traces of the blow.

And when it came down to the possibility of a lover, what reason would he have had to forcibly drown her? If there was a reason, if he had committed the crime, he'd done it in a way to make it look like suicide, a spur of the moment suicide after she'd got into the bath and picked up the soap.

He discussed the ifs and buts with Constable Fry. Sidney Fry wasn't exactly an imaginative plainclothes copper, but he could work a few things out.

'You know what we've got, don't you, Sarge? Pointers, but nothing else, not unless we can turn up a suspect, which would be a bloke with a motive. Such as her old man.'

'And what would have been his motive?' asked Sergeant Tomlinson.

'Blind fury. Seeing she dumped him, he could have told himself he had justifiable cause to drown her. Didn't you get the impression he was sweating a bit when we were talking to him? As if he was realizing an act of blind fury could land him in the dock?'

'It's a point,' said Sergeant Tomlinson. 'I wonder, did she have a lover? If she did, and Herbert Jones found out after she'd left him, that on top of having been dumped might've set him well alight.'

'Blazing,' said Constable Fry. 'And let's see, if he's as useless as a doorpost to a woman, then I don't suppose he's too bright generally. A cleverer bloke would've put the bath cap on Mrs Jones, and left a towel in the bathroom after drowning her.'

'He said he was with a friend that evening, remember?' Sergeant Tomlinson was thinking, thinking.

'Told you we ought to have checked on that,' said Constable Fry.

'I think we'd better do that now,' said Sergeant Tomlinson. 'I don't fancy presenting Inspector Shaw with what we've got if it doesn't include a check on Jones's alibi. But what we have got does make a call on Mrs Jones's place of work secondary at the moment. Not that I'm completely sold on what looks obvious, that Jones did away with his wife in a fit of blind rage.'

'You having second thoughts already?' said Constable Fry.

'Well, I think I'll allow for alternatives,' said Sergeant Tomlinson, tipping his hat back as if to let air cool his furrowed brow. 'All the same, let's find out if Jones is at home before we go back to the station. Listen, Sidney, how did we miss the marks around her ankles?'

'Easy,' said Constable Fry. 'She was right under the water, and the bath was as full as it could be. The tap was trickling, the water wasn't crystal clear and the body was a mite blurred. Seeing she was obviously as dead as a drowned sheep, we left it to the ambulance crew to get her out. They had a blanket over her in no time. You and me, we'd only have been interested in looking her over if there'd been clear signs she'd been knocked about.'

'Maybe, but I think at the time we took the possibility of an accident or suicide too much for granted,' said Sergeant Tomlinson.

'You can say so now,' said Constable Fry, 'but

at the time there was nothing to make us think there were suspicious circumstances.'

'That's true,' said Sergeant Tomlinson, 'and it's a fact that it wasn't until I was listening to Jones telling us how he'd been treated after twenty-five years of marriage that I started to think there might be more in that bathroom than met the eye.'

'Very upset husband and, all of a sudden, a dead wife,' said Constable Fry. 'Made us both think, didn't it?'

'Well, let's see if we can satisfy ourselves,' said Sergeant Tomlinson, and they left.

Chapter Eleven

Herbert was in. He wasn't surprised to see the CID men.

'Been expecting you,' he said, letting them in.

'Well, here we are, then,' said Constable Fry.

'You're going to tell me the cause of death?' said Herbert, taking them into the living room.

'Your wife drowned, sir,' said Sergeant Tomlinson.

'Well, I know that, don't I?' said Herbert, as tidy-looking as ever but showing strain. 'I meant what caused her to drown?'

'We can't say, Mr Jones,' said Sergeant Tomlinson. 'It's the coroner who'll deliver the verdict after the inquest has presented him with all the facts. But, from our point of view, there are one or two things to clear up.'

'Tidy up, you might say,' said Constable Fry. 'Like there's yourself, Mr Jones. The coroner'll want to know where you were at the time. I think you said with a friend, didn't you?'

'Oh, we're back to that, are we?' said Herbert.

'Back to what, sir?' asked Sergeant Tomlinson.

'To me,' said Herbert.

'It's a formality, y'know, sir,' said Constable Fry.

'I've heard about formalities,' said Herbert.

'We live with them every day ourselves,' said Sergeant Tomlinson. 'But we do have to tie up loose ends.'

'I'm a loose end?' said Herbert.

'Hardly, sir,' said Sergeant Tomlinson with a slight smile. It made him look more like Herbert's best friend than a policeman. 'As a matter of routine, we'd simply like to establish exactly where you were on the evening in question. So could you give us the name and address of your friend?'

'I'll be pleased to,' said Herbert, and gave Nell's name and address, which Constable Fry noted down. 'That's only a few minutes' walk from here. Oh, and give a double knock, her flat is upstairs.'

'Much obliged, sir,' said Constable Fry, 'that's all we wanted.'

'Fair enough,' said Herbert. 'And all I want is to know if my wife drowned because of a heart attack or because of some kind of collapse. It's got to be one or the other.'

'Well, sir,' said Sergeant Tomlinson, 'as I told your son-in-law, Mr Way, earlier today, the post-mortem showed her heart was sound, which could mean there was no obvious reason for a sudden collapse.'

'Bloody hell,' said Herbert, 'what you're saying could mean my poor old Hilda could have committed suicide. Not that I can believe it, but what else is there?'

'Good question, Mr Jones,' said Constable Fry.

'Well, we'll just make this routine call on Mrs Nell Binns, sir,' said Sergeant Tomlinson. 'Oh, and thanks for being helpful.'

'It's the inquest next?' said Herbert.

'That's right, sir,' said Constable Fry, and Herbert saw them out.

When they had gone he went into the kitchen and put the kettle on. He felt he needed some hot strong tea.

When he'd had it, he'd take a walk and call on Nell.

'You're what?' said Nell, having come down from her flat to answer a double knock on the front door.

'CID, Mrs Binns, from the Stockwell station. I'm Detective Sergeant Tomlinson, and this is Detective Constable Fry.'

'Well, thank you, I'm sure, and you look all right,' said Nell. 'Respectable, I mean. Me neighbours don't take much notice of respectable callers. It's the other kind that makes them talk.

Anyway, what can I do for you?' She had a good idea, of course, of why they had come.

'It concerns Mr Jones, Mr Herbert Jones – '

'Oh, you'd best come up,' said Nell. She took them up to her flat of three rooms, and into her living room, very neat, spruce and homely, with some potted plants on the wide window ledge. 'You can sit down, gents,' she said. They seated themselves. Nell brushed her skirt and sat down herself. 'Here we are, then,' she said, 'what d'you want to know about Mr Jones, poor man?'

'You're aware of his wife's death?' said Sergeant Tomlinson.

'Yes, and I was never more shocked,' said Nell. 'I expect Herbert – Mr Jones – has asked the same question, but did his wife have a heart attack in her bath?'

'No, the post-mortem examination showed her heart was sound,' said Sergeant Tomlinson, not for the first time that day.

'Was it suicide, then?' asked Nell.

'We can't say at the moment,' said Constable Fry.

'It's a bit of a mystery, then, is it?' said Nell. 'I knew Mrs Jones fairly well, although she hadn't visited the shop much these last two years. Oh, I worked in Mr Jones's shop for a good long while, I expect he's told you that. Anyway, his wife always looked very healthy, like, and I never thought she'd come to a mysterious drowning in her own bath, poor Hilda. It's been in the local weekly paper that come out this morning, but of course I already knew about it from Mr Jones, and I never saw him more upset. It's hard on him, coming at a time when he'd just sold his shop.'

'We understand he was with you on the night of his wife's death,' said Sergeant Tomlinson.

'Yes, so he was,' said Nell, 'and that's what really upset him, that he was here, spending a friendly time with me, when it happened. It made him feel guilty, made him feel that if only he'd gone to visit her that evening, she'd still be alive. I expect you know they were separated, that she'd moved out last Monday week, and that upset him as well. He did say he thought about going to see her, to find out how she was getting on, and now, of course, he wishes he'd gone that evening instead of being here with me.'

'You and Mr Jones are close friends?' said Constable Fry.

'Yes, course we are,' said Nell, too sensible a woman to dissemble. 'It comes from all the years I worked with him in his shop.'

'Mrs Jones didn't mind that?' said Sergeant Tomlinson.

'Beg your pardon?' said Nell.

'Mrs Jones didn't mind your close friendship with her husband?'

'Here, wait a minute,' said Nell, bristling, 'I

hope you're not making insinuations. Mr Jones is an upright and straightforward gent, and I'm a respectable widow. Like I've just said, I worked for more than a few years in his shop and we got on very nice together, but that's all. I don't want no-one being suggestive, if you don't mind. When poor Hilda left him, he needed someone to talk to, someone that could understand why he was so upset. I don't have to excuse meself for trying to cheer him up, nor for giving him me sincere sympathy when he told me what had happened to Hilda. If you think she left him because of me, and that she drowned herself on that account, you can think again, and I don't mind telling you so. There wasn't ever anything between me and Herbert except a nice friendship.'

'We simply want a clear picture of circumstances immediately prior to the unfortunate happening,' said Sergeant Tomlinson. 'Could you tell us how long Mr Jones was with you on the evening in question?'

Nell was no simpleton. It was obvious to her that these policemen were after something, probably something to do with Herbert because he'd been a wronged husband. Well, she wasn't going to say anything that would make them suspicious of him. Herbert would never lay a finger on any woman, not even on Hilda who'd said such terrible unkind things to him.

'I should think he was here most of the evening, from about half past eight,' she said. She paused. 'About what time did the police doctor say Mrs Jones died?' she asked, as if Herbert hadn't already told her.

The CID men looked at each other.

'If Mr Jones was with you most of the evening, can you say exactly what time he left?' asked Constable Fry.

'No, not exactly,' said Nell. 'I know I've got a mantelpiece clock, as you can see, but I don't look at it unless I need to know the time. I'd say that Herbert – Mr Jones – could've left sometime between ten and eleven. What I do know exact is that I went to bed just about eleven, which couldn't have been long after he'd gone.' Nell was being protective, simply because she was never going to believe Herbert had anything to do with his wife drowning.

Constable Fry thought the questions should have been asked of this witness immediately after they'd first talked to Jones about his wife's death, and before he'd had a chance to call on his lady friend. But at that time the police had no reason to begin an investigation into suspicious circumstances. Suspicious circumstances weren't evident then. But they were now.

Sergeant Tomlinson regarded the lady thoughtfully.

'Well, thanks for your time and your help, Mrs

Binns,' he said. 'Sorry to have bothered you.'

'Oh, don't mention it, I'm sure, you've both been nice and polite,' said Nell, altogether a very pleasant woman and disinclined to think ill of anybody. She'd shocked herself at what she'd thought of Hilda after her treatment of Herbert.

She saw the CID men out and said goodbye to them with a smile. Sergeant Tomlinson returned the smile, and she thought what a likeable man he was for a policeman. Most policemen, even the nice ones, could be very po-faced at times.

Inspector Shaw sat thinking. Tomlinson and Fry stood looking. Their interest in his ruminations made them search his broad countenance for signs of encouragement. But he hardly moved a muscle, and there was not even the slightest twitch as he finally glanced up at them.

However, he did say, 'I think there's the makings of a case.'

'You're taking charge, sir?' said Sergeant Tomlinson.

'Am I? I don't think so, I'm up to my eyes as it is, and you're doing well enough, Sergeant. So you can see this case through to the finish, if there's definitely a case. Up to you to get the evidence. It'll help your prospective promotion.' Inspector Shaw consulted his watch. 'The day's running away, I see, but there's still enough time for you to start getting your teeth into the case.'

'Right, sir,' said Sergeant Tomlinson.

'The bath towel, that's the main pointer,' said the inspector. 'Who takes a bath without having a towel handy?'

'Only forgetful old ladies or absent-minded inventors,' said Sergeant Tomlinson.

'Inventors?' said the inspector.

'If you know what I mean,' said Sergeant Tomlinson.

'Was Mrs Jones an inventor?' asked Inspector Shaw.

'A factory office clerk,' said Sergeant Tomlinson.

'Well, then?'

'Yes, do factory office clerks take a bath without a towel handy?' said Sergeant Tomlinson. 'No, I wouldn't think so, sir.'

'They're like the rest of us,' said the inspector. 'As for the nightdress that can't be found, you've got some thoughts about that, haven't you?'

Sergeant Tomlinson smacked himself on the forehead.

'I have now,' he said. 'Yes, of course. She was wearing it at the time, and it was taken off her.'

'Before or after she got drowned?' said Constable Fry.

'What do you think, Tomlinson?' asked the inspector.

'I think that if it had been pulled off her before, it would later have been put back in its

153

natural place, under the pillow,' said Sergeant Tomlinson. 'Taken off after she was forced into the bath, it would have been soaking wet, and that would have meant having to disappear with it.'

'Someone's got a wet nightdress somewhere, unless it's been destroyed or hung out to dry,' said Inspector Shaw. 'Now then, Sergeant, go back again to the flat. Take Stebbings with you and have him collect what fingerprints he can find. Tell him to concentrate mainly on the bedroom and bathroom. He'll probably find any amount of the deceased's, but what you need are someone else's. By the way, what's the husband do?'

'Not much at the moment,' said Constable Fry, 'he kept a corner shop, but he's retired from that.'

'Has he?' asked the inspector. 'When did he retire?'

'Not long after Mrs Jones left him,' said Constable Fry.

'Sounds like a case of the angry sulks,' said the inspector. 'Mrs Binns is sure, is she, that he was with her up to about half ten?'

'Not sure, no,' said Constable Fry. 'She pointed out that she didn't consult her clock, so she made a guess at the time in question.'

'Well, I suppose a close lady friend of Jones's wouldn't want to quote the wrong time,' said the inspector drily. 'Have either of you got the impression that they were a lot more than close?'

'Personally, no,' said Sergeant Tomlinson.

'I'm a suspicious type meself about a close friendship when the woman's a widow and the man's not his wife's favourite bloke,' said Constable Fry.

'We could call Jones the obvious suspect, but for my liking he's a bit too obvious,' said Sergeant Tomlinson.

'You've got likings, have you?' said Inspector Shaw. 'That's dangerous. It can lead to catching a dose of intuition, which is a woman's complaint and nothing to do with tried and tested police work. Anyway, why is Jones too obvious?'

'Well, if he's got any sense at all, he'd have known he'd be the first one we'd look at if we started to ask ourselves questions,' said Sergeant Tomlinson. 'He'd have known we'd find out he had cause to be furious with his wife. My guess is he'd have done a runner by now, if he'd been guilty.'

'Was he furious?' asked Inspector Shaw.

'Well, you've got all the details, sir, about how she walked out on him after twenty-five years of marriage,' said Sergeant Tomlinson.

'On top of which, she told him he was a boring old bugger and about as useful as a doorpost,' said Constable Fry. 'That must've got right up his nose, sir.'

'I see,' said Inspector Shaw, 'you're after a crime relating to injured feelings, Fry, and Tomlinson's after something else.'

'Something not so obvious,' said Sergeant Tomlinson.

'Mystery geezer?' suggested the inspector.

'Worth making inquiries, sir,' said Sergeant Tomlinson.

'Fair point, Sergeant,' said Inspector Shaw. 'Help yourself to a good start by getting Stebbings on the track of fingerprints, and keep an open mind as far as Jones is concerned. Keep me informed on progress.'

The new door was in place, and Sergeant Tomlinson used the spare key to open it. The time was nearing five o'clock as he went up to the flat with Detective Constable Stebbings, the fingerprint specialist. They made for the bedroom. Entering, they stopped short. A very attractive young woman, stylishly dressed, was sitting on the edge of the bed.

'Mrs Way?' said Sergeant Tomlinson, recognizing her.

Olive looked at him, her fine grey eyes a little hollow.

'Oh, you're Sergeant Tomlinson,' she said.

'Can I ask why you're here, Mrs Way?'

'It's my mood,' said Olive, 'I felt I just had to come and do some thinking about my mother leaving my father to live in this place, which isn't very much compared to their house in Brixton. I haven't done much clear thinking, though, everything's still going round and round in my head, and all I can do is ask myself why she's dead.'

Sergeant Tomlinson felt a twinge of pity, pity of a very human kind. He knew she was the dead woman's youngest daughter, the daughter who, with her husband, had found the immersed corpse.

'We're asking ourselves the same question, Mrs Way,' he said.

'We all hate the thought that it might have been suicide,' said Olive, 'we'd all rather it had been a sudden heart attack. I'm sorry I was in such a state at the time, it must have been very embarrassing for you.'

'Not a bit, Mrs Way,' said Sergeant Tomlinson. Constable Stebbings looked from one to the other. Olive came to her feet and walked to the window, seeming to be lost in thought. 'I don't see how you could have taken it calmly.'

'I'm calmer now, at least,' said Olive, turning to face the men. 'Roger – my husband – has been a help. You saw him again here, didn't you?'

'Yes, he was looking for your mother's handbag,' said Sergeant Tomlinson. 'And we had one or two things to tidy up.'

'Why are you here again?' asked Olive.

'Oh, to make sure there's nothing we've missed.'

'What could you have missed, then?' asked Olive.

Sergeant Tomlinson hesitated, then said, 'Mrs Way, would you know where your mother kept her nightdress?'

'Under her pillow,' said Olive. 'Why d'you ask?'

'It's one of those things that needs tidying up,' said Sergeant Tomlinson. Olive looked at his colleague, a question in her eyes. 'This is Detective Constable Stebbings, Mrs Way.'

With a faint smile, Olive said, 'Oh, is he the tidying-up expert?'

'After a fashion, Mrs Way,' said Stebbings.

Olive, now regarding Sergeant Tomlinson a little wistfully, said, 'I wish you could find my mother had some kind of accident that led to her being drowned.'

'Mrs Way, perhaps we'll find exactly that.'

'Thanks, you're very kind,' said Olive. 'I'd better go now, I'd better get back to my husband. He doesn't know I came here, he'll think me morbid. I told him I just needed some fresh air and to do some thinking. Oh, if you want any more information on my mother before the inquest, you can always come and ask.'

'I'll remember that, and thanks,' said Sergeant Tomlinson.

'Do you know the date of the inquest?' asked Olive.

'No, not yet, but you'll be advised, of course.'

'Yes, I see.' Olive walked to the door. Sergeant Tomlinson stood aside, then accompanied her to the door of the flat. He opened it for her. She glanced at him, and he thought what exceptionally fine eyes she had, even if they were rimmed with strain and sleeplessness. 'Goodbye, Sergeant.'

'I'm damned sorry about everything, Mrs Way.'

'Are you?' The faint smile showed again. 'That helps, coming from a policeman. I need policemen to be kind to me at the moment.'

'That's not very much to ask,' said Sergeant Tomlinson.

'Did you always want to be a policeman?' asked Olive.

'A kind one?' he said, and again came her faint smile.

'If you like,' she said.

'Well, let's say even when I was at Wilson's Grammar School and most of my friends were thinking of more elevated careers, I wanted to join the force in due time.'

'Well, I hope you become Chief Inspector Tomlinson,' said Olive. 'That's fairly elevated, isn't it? Goodbye again.' She put out her hand.

He took it, and lightly pressed it. Her fingers were cold, but they lightly responded.

'Goodbye, Mrs Way.'

Olive left and he returned to the bedroom. Stebbings was already busy with his brush and powder. He glanced over his shoulder.

'Nice young woman,' he said.

'Yes, the dead woman's youngest daughter,' said Sergeant Tomlinson. 'She and her husband were the ones who found the body.'

'No wonder she's under strain,' said Stebbings.

'Yes, and I feel for her,' said Sergeant Tomlinson, and thought about her, so strangely wistful once or twice, like a young waif hoping for magical surprises on Christmas Day. He shook himself, thought about the nightdress, and went down the back stairs to the yard. There, he examined the contents of the dustbin. Everything seemed to be in it except a nightdress. Well, there'd been a faint chance it might have been rolled into a ball and buried in the bin.

He returned to the flat, where Stebbings told him he was acquiring an interesting collection of prints.

They went back to the station eventually. Inspector Shaw, however, had left. Stebbings went to the mortuary to take the fingerprints of the dead woman. Sergeant Tomlinson went home, to his quarters. He was still a bachelor, although he knew a few ladies who were always ready to be taken out, but not too ready to marry a policeman whose duties were demanding and whose homecoming times were accordingly unreliable.

Chapter Twelve

'You went to the flat?' said Roger.

'Oh, I just found myself there,' said Olive. 'I suppose it was a kind of morbid magnet, and, when I got there, I felt I wanted to sit and try to work out why Mum – well, why.'

'It's something none of us can work out,' said Roger.

'But there has to be an answer,' said Olive.

'It'll come out at the inquest,' said Roger.

'Oh, that CID sergeant turned up again, with a colleague,' said Olive. 'To finish tidying up one or two things, he said.'

'Sergeant Tomlinson?' said Roger.

'Yes,' said Olive.

'I don't trust that tidying-up business of his,' said Roger, 'and I don't trust him too much, either.'

'Why?' asked Olive.

'I think he's after making a meal of things,' said Roger.

'I think he's only trying to find out if there's a reasonable explanation for Mum's death,' said Olive.

'Don't you believe it,' said Roger. 'He's a policeman, he's not after a reasonable explanation, more like something he can really get his teeth into.'

Olive stared at him.

'What d'you mean, Roger?' she asked.

'Did he say anything to you apart from tidying up, Olive?'

'No,' said Olive. 'No, wait, he asked me where Mum kept her nightdress, so I told him under her pillow.'

'Did he look?' asked Roger.

'No, not then. Not while I was there. He simply said it was one of the things to be tidied up.'

'He's fishy,' said Roger.

'I don't think so,' said Olive. 'I think he's a rather nice man.'

'He's a policeman, and he's fishing,' said Roger.

'You said fishy a moment ago, Roger.'

'Well, one word leads to the other,' said Roger.

'Roger, what're you on about exactly?' asked Olive.

'Oh, nothing very much, Olive, just that the police have got their own way of looking at things. Are we going to try to eat some supper this evening?'

'Yes, all right,' said Olive, 'and later on I'm going to try to get a good long sleep without any bad dreams. I hope Dad does too. I'm sure he's suffering because he let Mum have her own way the one time when he knows now he shouldn't have.'

Herbert walked round to see Nell that evening. Her welcome was a warm and very friendly one. So he gave her a kiss on her smooth cheek.

'Now, Herbert, should you?'

'Just by way of a greeting, Nell.'

'Pleasure, I'm sure,' said Nell, 'and you're beginning to look a bit better. I never saw you all haggard before, like you were the morning after the police told you about Hilda. Well, sit yourself down, and I'll make us a pot of tea. Oh, the police called on me this afternoon, did you know?'

'They called on me first,' said Herbert, seating himself in a fireside armchair. 'They asked for your name and address, saying they wanted to see you about our time together that evening.'

'Yes, and they told me they had to get things clear about the circumstances, specially as Hilda didn't die of any heart attack,' said Nell. 'I suppose – well, I don't know what I suppose.'

'Myself, I suppose they were thinking I might have drowned Hilda on account of the way she walked out on me,' said Herbert, frowning.

'Well, I don't think much of that sort of thinking,' said Nell tartly. 'It's disgusting and silly as well. I told them you were here most of the evening up to some time between ten and eleven.'

'I can't remember the exact time I did leave,' said Herbert.

'Well, that's what I told the policemen, that I couldn't remember the exact time,' said Nell.

'I appreciate that, Nell,' said Herbert. 'You're not just a good woman, you're a good friend as well.'

'Well, good friends should stick together, shouldn't they?' said Nell. 'You've had enough troubles to be going on with, Herbert, you don't want more. I'll put the kettle on now.'

They were sharing the tea a little later, as well as some of Nell's home-made cake. It pleased her that Herbert hadn't let Hilda's death get him right down in the dumps. He was sad about everything, of course, but he wasn't all grey and brooding. Although he felt he was a bit to blame for Hilda's death, he was standing up to things, like a real man should. In fact, the happenings had changed him for the better, really. He'd always seemed like a man who didn't need company, which was probably one of the reasons why he hadn't had a very talkative relationship with his wife. Still, most women accepted that men just weren't as conversational as they were.

Men spent a lot of time thinking about politics and inventions and how to make money.

Anyway, it pleased Nell that he was a bit more outgoing and showed interest in her little stories about her life before she was widowed. She didn't have any children. She pointed out quite frankly that her late husband's serious war wound, which happened in France when they'd only been married a month, was responsible for that. But he'd made up for it by being a real love, and they'd had some happy times together.

'Well, you sort of spread happiness, Nell,' said Herbert. 'Not having children hasn't made you sour. People like you are worth a lot to mankind.'

'Well, bless me,' said Nell, 'what a cultivated thing to say, worth a lot to mankind.'

'Cultivated?' said Herbert.

'Yes, like you were very educated,' said Nell. Herbert smiled. 'That's it, put a smile on, Herbert. Life's treated you hard lately, and I like a man that can stand up to the kind of knocks you've had. And nothing's going to bring poor Hilda back.'

'It's hard to believe she's gone,' said Herbert.

'You'll get over it,' said Nell, 'specially as you'd already lost her. Well, you had, the day she walked out on you.'

'You're probably right,' said Herbert, 'she probably wouldn't have come back ever, but I'd still like to know exactly how she came to die in her bath.'

'Oh, won't you have to wait for the inquest to find out?' asked Nell.

'It looks like it,' said Herbert. 'By the way, about your uncle – '

'Oh, I went and saw him and put that off for a bit,' said Nell. 'Well, you need a friend just now more than he needs a housekeeper. You've always been a friend to me, Herbert. All that nice relationship we enjoyed in the shop means a lot to me. It helped to keep me going and it more than paid me rent. And it told me you're a kind man, even if you didn't say a lot. So I'm not going to housekeep for me uncle yet. I want to do more thinking about it.'

'Well, I appreciate having you around to talk to,' said Herbert. 'Did you know you dress very nice, Nell?'

'It's pleasing to hear you say so, I'm sure,' said Nell. 'I don't have much to spend on clothes, so I take care with what I do buy. You dress very tidy and respectable yourself, and that must've pleased Hilda a bit.'

'More like she saw me as a doorpost in a suit,' said Herbert.

'Oh, Lor',' said Nell, and put her teacup back in its saucer with a rattle.

'What's wrong?' asked Herbert.

'You saying what you did. It nearly made me forget respect for the dead.'

'Did it?' said Herbert.

'Yes, it nearly made me laugh,' said Nell, 'and that would've been disrespectful, wouldn't it?'

'Oh, I don't know,' said Herbert, 'it's not like chortling at a funeral. Now that would be very disrespectful.' He sounded so droll that Nell smiled, even if it was Hilda's funeral they were both thinking about.

'Well, somehow we've cheered up a bit,' she said.

'Nell, let's talk some more,' said Herbert.

'I'll be pleased to,' said Nell.

'Good,' said Herbert.

They talked some more, and in quite earnest fashion, until they were interrupted by a double knock on the street door.

'That's someone for me,' said Nell, getting up. 'Probably me neighbour Mrs Parsons. She's always popping in to borrow some tea or sugar.'

It wasn't Mrs Parsons, however. It was Madge and Winnie. They asked if their father was here. Nell said yes, he was, and she also said how terrible sorry she was about their mother's death. Would they like to come up and see their dad? He'd suffered shocking hard blows just recent, poor man.

'Yes, that's why we've come, to see how he is,' said Winnie.

'It's all very sad,' said Nell, 'you must be suffering yourselves.'

'Very much, Mrs Binns,' said Madge.

'Come on up,' said Nell kindly, 'I've been doing what I can to help your dad in his grieving.'

They went up, and Herbert came to his feet when he saw his daughters.

'Nice of you to come,' he said, and Madge and Winnie fell on him then. Awkwardly he patted their shoulders. 'Know how you feel,' he said, 'it's hard for all the family.'

Madge eyed him in moist sorrow.

'We called at the house first,' she said, 'but as you weren't at home, I thought you might be here.'

'I'm needing someone to talk to these days,' said Herbert.

'Yes, we can see you've got someone,' said Winnie.

'You both know Mrs Binns,' said Herbert. 'She's an old friend.'

'Yes,' said Winnie.

'How are you girls?' asked Herbert.

'Awful,' said Madge.

'Oh, I'm so sorry for all of you,' said Nell, sympathetic enough to ignore slightly cold shoulders. 'It must be very hard to bear.'

'It is,' said Winnie.

'I still can't believe it,' said Madge.

'Mum of all people,' said Winnie.

'Yes, of all people,' said Herbert sombrely.

'We're not interrupting, are we?' said Madge.

'You can't think you are, not at a time like this,' said Herbert. 'I've been wanting to see you and Winnie. Olive and Roger have been to see me.'

'Yes, we know,' said Winnie.

'Sit down, everyone,' said Nell, 'and I'll make a fresh pot of tea.'

'It's all right,' said Madge, 'we—'

'They'll have some tea, Nell,' said Herbert, and Nell went into the kitchen, leaving him to his daughters.

'We had to come and see how you were bearing up, Dad,' said Winnie.

Herbert said it was a shaker of a lasting kind, and that it was going to take a long time for all of them to get over it. He'd had the police call on him again, but they hadn't been able to say exactly what caused their mother to die like she did.

Madge said it just had to be something like a heart attack, except the police had told Roger no, that her heart was sound.

'So Winnie and I thought perhaps she fell and hit her head as she got into the bath.'

'Wouldn't there have been a bruise?' asked Herbert, neat shirt cuffs peeping, suit tidy-looking, and his mane of hair well brushed.

'Madge went round to the station with Roger to ask the police about that,' said Winnie.

'We didn't get any satisfaction,' said Madge. 'The sergeant there thought a bruise wouldn't have been missed during the examination, but he's going to make enquiries and let us know tomorrow.'

'Still, wasn't there any suggestion that your mum might've drowned by some sort of accident?' asked Herbert.

'As far as I know, the police haven't made any suggestion like that,' said Madge. 'Roger mentioned they weren't certain about anything, and that we'd all have to wait for what comes out at the inquest.'

'Yes, I suppose we must,' said Herbert, 'and I suppose we've got to make certain arrangements.'

'What arrangements?' asked Madge.

'Well, it's got to be mentioned,' said Herbert, 'it's – ' He fell silent and tugged self-consciously at his tie.

Winnie and Madge looked at each other.

'Dad, what's got to be mentioned?' asked Madge.

Herbert cleared his throat.

'Your mother's funeral,' he said.

Madge bit her lip and Winnie sighed.

'I don't know when's the right time for a funeral, I haven't looked at any stars lately,' she said, and she and Madge sat down as Nell came in with the tea tray.

'Here we are,' said Nell, setting the tray down on a table. She poured the tea and handed round the cups and saucers.

Winnie told Herbert that the family didn't want him to take on the worry of arranging the funeral. Madge said the husbands would to see to everything, and that she'd do the funeral breakfast herself. Winnie said she'd help, and that their dad needn't do anything except order his own special wreath for the occasion.

Nell recognized that Madge and Winnie were leaving her out of the conversation. It was obvious they didn't approve of their father being here with her. It didn't upset her, she knew they were their mother's daughters, and that only Olive had any kind of a soft spot for him. She let them talk away and didn't attempt to butt in. Herbert took all they had to say in his quiet way, and only offered a few apologetic words when Winnie said he shouldn't have let their mother go and live by herself in that flat.

'Sorry about that, Winnie.'

The sisters didn't stay long after they'd finished their tea. Madge told Herbert it was a relief to know he wasn't actually ill with shock, and Winnie echoed that. Madge asked if there was anything he wanted doing. Herbert said he was managing all right at the moment, that he was taking his washing to the laundry and getting on fairly good terms with the gas cooker.

Of course, he said, they were only very little things compared to everything else.

Madge and Winnie said goodbye very politely to Nell, and it was Herbert who went down to the street door with them and saw them off.

'You'll have to keep in touch, Dad,' said Madge.

'I know,' said Herbert, 'we've all got to keep in touch, and we'll all have to go to the inquest. Anyway, thanks for coming to see me, and take care of yourselves.'

'Are you going home now, or staying here all night?' asked Madge bluntly.

Herbert took that without flinching.

'I'll be going home soon,' he said, and they said goodbye to him then. He went back up to Nell.

'They didn't like you being here,' she said.

'Natural under the circumstances, I suppose,' said Herbert.

'Never mind, it still did you a bit of good to have them come and see you,' said Nell.

'Glad you think so,' said Herbert.

'I do,' said Nell.

'Goodnight, then,' said Herbert.

'Goodnight, Herbert.'

On their bus ride back to Streatham, Winnie said to Madge, 'I wouldn't like to think Dad has taken up with that woman.'

'If he has,' said Madge, 'he's a lot deeper than I ever realized.'

'I suppose you never know with these quiet men,' said Winnie, 'even with one's own father. I was shocked finding he was with Mrs Binns only a few days after Mum passing on.'

'And he wasn't at all embarrassed,' said Madge. 'I meant to ask him about Mum's savings, but decided not to in front of Mrs Binns.'

'Still, he can't do anything with the savings while Roger's got the book under lock and key,' said Winnie.

'Dad couldn't even if he had the book,' said Madge. 'Mum's savings have to be legally released to him. But it's better for Roger and Olive to keep the book for the time being, just in case.'

'Don't forget to go to the police station tomorrow to find out if there were signs of Mum falling and hitting her head,' said Winnie.

'I won't forget,' said Madge.

'I know I keep on saying it, but I'll never believe she committed suicide by drowning herself,' said Winnie.

'It's the last thing she'd have done,' said Madge.

'Yes, she wasn't born under that kind of star,' said Winnie.

'Do you take stars to bed with you?' asked Madge fretfully.

'No, I've got Victor,' said Winnie. 'How about you with your cats?'

'Don't be funny,' said Madge, 'I'm not in the mood.'

Chapter Thirteen

Inspector Shaw pored over fingerprint specimens the following morning.

'There's any amount of the dead woman's prints, sir,' said Constable Stebbings.

'Don't state the obvious,' said Inspector Shaw. Although he'd put Sergeant Tomlinson in charge of the case, he didn't mean to be left out of it. 'Tell me who the others belong to.'

'No idea yet,' said Stebbings. 'There's a variety.'

'How long did you say she'd been living there, Sergeant Tomlinson?' asked the inspector.

'Since last Monday week,' said Sergeant Tomlinson.

'Then I don't suppose she'd done a lot of entertaining. Find out from her daughters if any of them visited, and ask if they'd like to be fingerprinted, anyway. And you'll have to get prints from Jones himself. I've got a feeling we might find some of his among these specimens.'

'Does that mean—' Sergeant Tomlinson

checked and decided not to ask if that meant the inspector was experiencing a spot of intuition and also an inclination to take charge, after all. 'Does it mean going to see Jones again, sir?'

'Sometime today or tomorrow,' said Inspector Shaw. 'First let's try to eliminate the possibility that Mrs Jones had a lover. Go to her place of work. You might pick up the right kind of gossip there.'

'Eliminating a lover puts Jones in the frame?' said Sergeant Tomlinson.

'It could, and never mind if you think it too obvious,' said the inspector. 'Get going, Sergeant.'

Sergeant Tomlinson smiled wryly, knowing his immediate superior was going to be breathing down his neck.

Miss Simmonds, the typist, knocked and entered the boss's office.

'Yes?' said Mr Richards from his desk.

'There's two policemen who'd like to see you, sir.'

'They're after checking on my criminal record, are they, Miss Simmonds?' said Mr Richards.

'I should hope not, Mr Richards.'

'All right, send them in.'

Sergeant Tomlinson presented himself in company with Constable Fry. They were making inquiries concerning the death of Mrs Jones, he said.

'What kind of inquiries?' asked Mr Richards, mystified.

'Formal inquiries, sir,' said Sergeant Tomlinson, his impressive self making its mark on the factory boss.

'I understood the unfortunate lady was found dead in her bath,' said Mr Richards.

'So she was, sir.'

'Heart attack?' said Mr Richards.

'Did someone tell you that, sir?'

'I think it's a rumour going round the factory,' said Mr Richards.

Sergeant Tomlinson said he was trying to satisfy himself about one or two things, and would like permission to interview anyone who had worked close to Mrs Jones. Mr Richards said that would be the typist and the invoice clerk. Mrs Jones had shared an office with them. Tomlinson said he'd like to interview them one at a time, and in private, if possible. Mr Richards asked if he wanted to interview them at their homes or here in the factory. The CID sergeant said he'd appreciate here and now, if Mr Richards had no objection to their work being interrupted. Mr Richards offered immediate use of his office, as he needed to talk to the foreman of one of the workshops, anyway.

'Very obliging of you, sir,' said Sergeant Tomlinson.

'Highly convenient,' said Constable Fry.

'I'll call in the typist, Miss Simmonds, first,' said Mr Richards, and did so. Then he left the young woman with the CID men. Miss Simmonds, in her late twenties, appeared neat and efficient in a white blouse and bow tie. She was quite personable in her looks, her high cheekbones nicely symmetrical.

'What d'you want to see me about?' she asked Sergeant Tomlinson.

'About Mrs Jones,' he said.

'Oh, that poor woman,' said Miss Simmonds.

'Yes, very sad,' said Sergeant Tomlinson. 'We'd like to know if she ever talked to you about her private life.'

Miss Simmonds seemed pleased to be invited to talk, and at once said Mrs Jones often spoke to her and to Miss Taylor, the invoice clerk, about her family. She always said nice things about her three daughters, but wasn't very complimentary about her husband. She once said that he'd never properly come alive from the day he was born, except where his shop was concerned. Sergeant Tomlinson thought that since he was the father of three daughters he must have woken up three times during his married life. Miss Simmonds said Mrs Jones always seemed a very alive person herself, and had told her and Miss Taylor several weeks ago that, as all her daughters were married and settled, she was going to leave her husband before she turned into a sort of cabbage. She was very set on that, and of course it had happened in the end, and she'd said several times since how happy she was as a free and independent woman. It was an awful shock to hear she'd died in her bath.

'Um, did she speak about friends sometimes?' asked Sergeant Tomlinson.

'She spoke about her neighbours sometimes,' said Miss Simmonds, 'and what a blessing it was to have them to talk to. She said her husband hardly ever talked himself, and hardly ever listened, either.'

'D'you know if she had any men friends?' asked Constable Fry.

'She never mentioned any,' said Miss Simmonds.

'I suppose even as a lively woman, she didn't strike you as the kind who'd have broken her marriage vows?' said Sergeant Tomlinson.

'I wouldn't know about that,' said Miss Simmonds.

'Well, thanks, that's all, Miss Simmonds,' said Sergeant Tomlinson. 'Would you ask Miss Taylor to come in?'

Miss Taylor was twenty-one, thin and earnest-looking. She said she was surprised that the police had come to ask questions, because she thought Mrs Jones had simply suffered a heart attack while taking a bath.

'Not quite,' said Sergeant Tomlinson, who

wondered how many more times he'd have to listen to people talking about a heart attack. It was putting him off the subject of cardiac arrest. 'Could you tell us what you know about her private life? That is, did she confide in you?'

Miss Taylor said Mrs Jones didn't actually confide any secrets, she just came out now and again with talk about her family. She liked talking about her daughters and their marriages. She had said her own marriage would have been a mistake if it hadn't given her three nice daughters. Her husband was a sort of nothing, she said once. Sergeant Tomlinson asked about the possibility that Mrs Jones made up for that by having a special man friend.

'She was a married woman,' said Miss Taylor a little huffily.

'Not happily married, though,' said Sergeant Tomlinson.

'Thought her old man a bit of a stuffy codger, didn't she?' said Constable Fry.

'But she was still a married woman,' said Miss Taylor, looking offended.

'So there was never any suggestion of – um – an affair?' said Sergeant Tomlinson.

'She'd lately joined the Stockwell Amateur Dramatic Society,' said Miss Taylor, 'and it seemed to me that that was all she wanted in the way of outside interests. She never ever said anything about having a special man friend.'

'Thank you, Miss Taylor,' said the sergeant.

'I can get back to my work now?' said Miss Taylor.

'Yes.'

Miss Taylor left.

'You satisfied?' asked Constable Fry.

'Are you, Sidney?' asked Sergeant Tomlinson.

'Well, what about a special bloke in the drama society?'

'That's a hell of a long shot,' said Sergeant Tomlinson, 'especially as neither Miss Simmonds nor Miss Taylor ever got the impression that Mrs Jones was interested in other men. That puts a dent in my suspicions about an unknown bloke. I suppose I've got to face the fact that although Jones looks too obvious to me, he did have a bloody good reason for at least giving his wife a smack in the mouth.'

'That and a bit more,' said Constable Fry.

'On the other hand, she might have had a good case,' said Sergeant Tomlinson.

'What's a good case?' asked Constable Fry.

'Twenty-five years with a block of wood, you dummy. All the same, even a block of wood can catch fire. That's something we've already considered.'

'And which I think is a genuine pointer,' said Constable Fry.

Mr Richards returned, curious about what these policemen were after exactly. Good God, were they delving into suspicious circumstances?

'Finished, Sergeant?' he said.

'Yes, and I'm obliged for your co-operation,' said Tomlinson.

'Has it helped?' asked Mr Richards.

'To a certain extent.'

'Well, if it's of interest to you,' said Mr Richards, 'our factory manager, Mr Burnside, might also be helpful. He knew Mrs Jones well. He had a lot to do with her in her work, and he helps run an amateur dramatic society which she recently joined. I presume you're trying to find out something about her social life, that you're not happy about the way she died. There was a notorious case once, wasn't there, concerning a man called Smith who married three times and all three brides suffered a mysterious death in the bath.'

'Very interesting case, I believe,' said Sergeant Tomlinson, 'but well before my time, of course. Let's see, Miss Taylor also mentioned that Mrs Jones joined an amateur dramatic society.'

'The Stockwell group,' said Mr Richards. 'Mr Burnside's the director.'

'Is it possible to talk to him while we're still here?' asked Sergeant Tomlinson.

'That's no problem,' said Mr Richards, and phoned through to Mr Burnside, who arrived a minute later from his own office. He was carrying a black ebony ruler. Handsome bloke, thought

Sergeant Tomlinson. Getting on a bit, but still looked energetic as well as distinguished.

'Hello, what's all this?' asked Mr Burnside.

Sergeant Tomlinson introduced himself and his colleague, and told the factory manager they were making inquiries concerning the late Mrs Jones. Mr Burnside's alert expression changed to a rueful grimace.

'Can't believe that lady died the way she did, in her bath,' he said, and grimaced again, like a man disgusted with the indiscriminate hand of fate. 'She enjoyed being alive.'

'But she didn't, apparently, enjoy being married,' said Sergeant Tomlinson. 'That is, not to Mr Jones.'

'Never knew the fellow,' said Mr Burnside, 'but she did mention he was a stick-in-the-mud. She left him, didn't she? Out of boredom, I believe.'

'She confided in you?' said Sergeant Tomlinson.

'Only to the extent of saying twenty-five years of marriage were more than enough for her,' said Mr Burnside, lightly smacking one hand with the ruler. 'I didn't go into it with her. We had only two common interests, our work and amateur dramatics. She was so keen about the dramatics that I invited her to join the society, the Stockwell Amateur Dramatic Society. She enrolled a few days after she left her husband.'

Mr Burnside tapped his chin with the ruler. 'Incredible that she's dead,' he said, frowning.

Still interested in the possible existence of another man, Sergeant Tomlinson asked, 'Did she know any members of your society before she enrolled?'

'Not to my knowledge,' said Mr Burnside. 'Certainly, when she enrolled, she never mentioned she knew anyone there. But I'm not able to give you a definite no. People's private lives are their own affair as far as I'm concerned. I know nothing about the private life of Mrs Jones, apart from her interest in amateur dramatics. Is there something about her death that needs investigating? Here, we all thought it must have been a heart attack.'

'Point is, sir, we need a fair bit of information about her for the inquest,' said Constable Fry.

'It wasn't a heart attack, then?' Mr Burnside looked curious. So did Mr Richards.

'Her heart was as sound as a bell,' said Sergeant Tomlinson. 'That's put us in the position of having to establish certain facts, sir. I take it Mrs Jones never dropped a hint to you that made you feel her reason for leaving her husband wasn't solely to do with his faults?'

'Was there another man, you mean?' said Mr Burnside. 'I've no idea. There might have been. Although she was over forty, she was still a good-looking woman, and might have been an asset to the society. When's the inquest, by the way?'

'In a week or so, probably,' said Sergeant Tomlinson. 'Well, I think that's all, Mr Burnside.'

'You've made me curious,' said Mr Burnside.

'I share that feeling,' said Mr Richards.

'So do we,' said Sergeant Tomlinson. 'We don't have many cases of healthy women drowning in a bath.'

'Not the sort of thing that happens every day,' said Constable Fry.

'Just as well,' said Mr Burnside, 'or women would stop taking baths.'

Sergeant Tomlinson thanked the men for their help and co-operation, and he and Constable Fry left.

'What the devil was that all about?' asked Mr Burnside.

'My guess is that they're investigating suspicious circumstances,' said Mr Richards.

'Not foul play, for God's sake,' said Mr Burnside.

'Well, why else would they come here asking questions?' said Mr Richards. 'From those they asked of you, I'd say they were trying to find out if Mrs Jones had a side to her social life that her husband probably didn't know about.'

'Mrs Jones? Rubbish,' said Mr Burnside.

In the general office, Miss Taylor was buzzing with curiosity about the questions the police had asked. She thought it meant there was something suspicious about the death of Mrs Jones, and she said so to Miss Simmonds. Miss Simmonds told her she was letting her imagination run away with her.

'Well, perhaps I am,' said Miss Taylor. 'Anyway, even if I wouldn't want to say so, I sometimes thought Mrs Jones a bit deep, didn't you?'

'I wonder exactly what Mr Burnside thought of her?' mused Miss Simmonds. 'They were jolly friendly at times.'

'That's not something we ought to talk about,' said Miss Taylor.

'Of course not,' said Miss Simmonds. 'We don't want to get Mr Burnside into trouble.'

The absence of a bath towel, the unworn bath cap and the missing nightdress had enabled Sergeant Tomlinson to convince Inspector Shaw it was worth looking at the possibility of murder. Inspector Shaw said he didn't like that word, and never had. It was only a possibility, said Sergeant Tomlinson who, after the factory interviews, hadn't changed his mind about Mrs Jones. He still doubted that she'd left her husband solely because she had had enough of his wooden image. Many husbands were dull and boring, and more than a few wives overdid their prattle. But the great majority did not walk out on each other. They soldiered on. Mrs Jones, however, had become one of the exceptions, and in leaving her husband she had perhaps made the fatal mistake of letting him know too crushingly that she had no time for him. Accordingly, if she had died by enforced drowning, the first reaction of any policeman would be to point himself at her better half as the most likely suspect.

But Sergeant Tomlinson wasn't going to discount the possibility of another man, a man who represented the final reason for Mrs Jones's wish to be free and independent.

On receiving the report of the factory interviews, Inspector Shaw put some questions.

'What did you make of the office women and the factory manager?' he asked.

'The women didn't offer much in the way of anything we didn't already know,' said Sergeant Tomlinson, 'but I couldn't see they had any reason to hold anything back. Unless – ' He paused.

'Well?' said the inspector.

'The factory manager,' said Sergeant Tomlinson.

'What about him?'

'Likeable bloke,' said Constable Fry.

'So's my milkman,' said the inspector.

'Burnside helped Mrs Jones to enrol in the dramatic society I mentioned,' said Sergeant Tomlinson.

'Was there something fishy about that, then?' asked Inspector Shaw.

'Not as far as I know,' said Sergeant Tomlinson, 'but it could have meant they were on very friendly terms, friendlier than he cared to admit.'

'That sounds like wishful thinking on your part, Sergeant,' said the inspector. 'Is the bloke – what did you say his name was?'

'Burnside.'

'Is he married?'

'I've no idea,' said Sergeant Tomlinson.

'Didn't you ask? No, you didn't, did you?'

'Well, married or not, women could still fancy him,' said Sergeant Tomlinson, 'especially a woman who had no fancy for her old man.'

'Yes, handsome bloke,' said Constable Fry, 'with middle-class articulation, you might say.'

'I wouldn't,' said the inspector. 'What's it mean?'

'Educated way of talking, sir. Some women go for that.'

'Like the unfortunate deceased?' said Inspector Shaw. 'You're trying to convince yourself she fancied Burnside?'

'I'm just offering information, sir.'

'Someone talking educated is information, is it?' said the inspector.

'Not quite, sir,' said Sergeant Tomlinson. 'I think Constable Fry is only suggesting Burnside might have been the type to impress Mrs Jones. Certainly, he could have been friendlier with her than he let on.'

'Just because he helped her enrol with the dramatic society?' said Inspector Shaw. 'It's another shot in the dark. Still, it won't hurt to find out if he's married and to get hold of his fingerprints. If he's been at Mrs Jones's flat at any time, they might match some of those that Stebbings found. But don't make him suspicious, or he might come up with a cast-iron alibi for the evening in question. I don't like cast-iron alibis, they get in the way.'

'Get hold of his fingerprints?' said Sergeant Tomlinson. 'Behind his back? That'll be easy, I don't think.'

'Up to you,' said Inspector Shaw. 'This afternoon, go and see Mrs Olive Way. Of the daughters, her address is the only one we have. Let her know we need fingerprints to clear the way to a satisfactory solution of her mother's death, those of herself, her husband, her sisters and their husbands. They've probably all visited Mrs Jones's flat. Ask her if she'll arrange for all of them to come to the station.'

'Could I get Constable Fry to do that, sir?' asked Sergeant Tomlinson.

'Why?'

'I'm feeling particularly sorry for Mrs Way.'

'Don't give me that sort of stuff,' said the inspector. 'You know her well by now. You go. Constable Fry can stay here and write up the notes of the factory interviews. As for Mr Jones, I think I'd like to take a look at him myself. Stebbings and his fingerprint equipment can come with me.'

'Are you taking charge, sir?' asked Sergeant Tomlinson.

'It's still your case, Sergeant, I've got too many other things on to do more than give you some help.'

Well, if it's my case, thought Sergeant Tomlinson, I'll have to watch that the clever old fox doesn't make the arrest, if that's what the investigation comes to eventually. To keep my end up means I've got to be right in assuming Mrs Jones didn't commit suicide, didn't drown herself by accident, but was held down under the water either by her husband or some unknown geezer. The inspector did point out originally that it looked like a two-man job, but somehow I can't go along with that.

Chapter Fourteen

'Sergeant Tomlinson?' The faint smile showed on Olive's face as she beheld the CID man on her doorstep.

'Sorry to bother you again, Mrs Way.'

'I hope it won't be a bothersome bother,' said Olive.

'I hope so too.'

'There's only me,' she said. 'My husband Roger is back at work. I've managed to recover and to cope with all that's on my mind. So do come in.'

He entered, taking off his hat and closing the door for her. She led the way into the cheerful-looking living room, where they faced each other, Olive's expression of an enquiring kind, while he looked hesitant. He was, in fact, extremely reluctant to harass her in the matter of fingerprints.

'Not more bad news, is it?' she said quietly.

'No, not at all,' he said reassuringly, 'it's just

that we're still trying to get a clear picture of circumstances.'

'I think you mean you're trying to find out if my mother's death wasn't an accident,' said Olive.

'What makes you say that?'

'You do,' said Olive, 'you and your frequent appearances.'

'Does it upset you, an inquiry into the circumstances?'

'Yes.'

'I'm sorry,' said Sergeant Tomlinson.

'Oh, I'm not being accusing,' said Olive. 'You can begin bothering me again. What do you want to ask me?'

He explained that he required to know who might have been with her mother that evening. Various fingerprints had been found, and it was necessary to determine whose they were. Olive, still quiet, said she understood, and could say that she and Roger had been there that evening, had visited before, and so had her sisters, but not their husbands. If anyone else had visited, that was outside her knowledge. Sergeant Tomlinson asked if she could arrange for herself, her husband and her sisters to call at the station and be fingerprinted. Olive said yes, very well.

'Well, thanks,' said Sergeant Tomlinson in relief.

'It didn't hurt too much, having to ask me that?' said Olive.

'Not too much.' He gave her a smile.

'You're a very human policeman,' she said. 'Would you like a cup of tea? I was just going to make one.'

'I won't say no, Mrs Way.'

'Then sit down, while I put the kettle on,' said Olive.

Over the tea, he found her composed and resilient, much as if she had forced herself to come to terms with the tragedy. The haunted look had gone from her fine eyes. She spoke of her mother and father without any hint of breaking down. She was rueful, not tearful. He suspected she had shed an ocean at some stage, but she was in courageous control of herself now. She said how very silly it was of her parents to have come to a parting of the ways, that both of them had been old enough to realize they should have talked their way through their differences. Sergeant Tomlinson wanted to suggest it perhaps wasn't those differences that had caused the break, but something else. An affair. But he kept quiet, of course.

'Heavens,' said Olive after a while, 'I'm doing all the talking, and being tedious, probably.'

'Don't you believe it,' he said, 'but I'd better push off now. Can't thank you enough for the tea.'

'Have you seen my father since you last saw me?' she asked.

'Yes.'

'Is he bearing up?'

'He's a solid man, Mrs Way.'

'Too solid for Mum,' said Olive, then winced a little. 'It's still incredible,' she said, and he thought she looked wistful again, as if she would have given much to recapture the calm of unworried days.

'We'll see you and your husband and sisters at the police station as soon as you can arrange it?' he said.

'Fingerprints? Oh, dear,' she said. 'Yes, I'll do the arranging. Roger will help to get us all there together.'

'That'll be a great help, Mrs Way.'

'I still hope you'll find it was an accident. Goodbye again, Sergeant Tomlinson.'

'Well?' demanded Madge of the desk sergeant.

'Ah, yes,' he said.

'Yes what?' said Madge, who had fought all her demons and come out on top. She was almost aggressive in her approach.

'Your enquiry concerning the post-mortem. Miss – '

'Mrs Mrs Cooper.'

'Ah, yes. Mrs Cooper. Right. I can confirm no head bruises were found, no signs that the deceased had a fall.'

'Are you positive, Sergeant?'

'The pathologist is, Mrs Cooper, and he's not known for making mistakes. It wouldn't do, y'know, for anything to be overlooked during a post-mortem examination.'

'Then how did my mother come to drown in her own bath?'

'Ah, well – '

'It's not ah well.'

'I mean it's not for me to say, Mrs Cooper, it's for the coroner.'

'Don't you police know anything?'

'I can't say.'

'Sergeant, you're useless.'

'That's what me wife tells me occasional, Mrs Cooper.'

'Your wife is very discerning, then. Good afternoon.'

Herbert was not amused by the visit of Inspector Shaw and Constable Stebbings, but neither was he put out. He accepted the inspector's explanation that it was necessary to establish certain facts, which meant they wanted to find out who had visited the flat and could do so by examining fingerprints.

'Well, I didn't visit,' said Herbert, 'I had to wait to be invited.'

'You mean your wife discouraged you from arriving uninvited?' said the inspector.

'Yes, I do mean that,' said Herbert.

'She didn't give you a key?'

'No,' said Herbert, and the inspector thought that pointed to the possibility that his wife didn't want to risk him turning up at a time when he wasn't welcome. When she had someone with her?

'Do you mind being fingerprinted, Mr Jones?'

'I'll mind if it means I'm suspected of doing what I'm not capable of doing,' said Herbert. 'It's not in my nature to be violent. Never hit a woman in my life, nor wouldn't, nor couldn't. If I'd wanted to get my own back on Hilda for what she did to me, which ruined my self-respect, I'd have chosen my own way, which wouldn't have cost her her life.'

Here was a man, thought Inspector Shaw, who according to Sergeant Tomlinson had been seen by his wife as an inarticulate lump, but who had just come out with a bellyful of words and made each one count. Not that his protestations of innocence could be taken at face value. He was probably deeper than his wife had thought. Quiet men could be dangerous men. Mrs Binns had given him an alibi. What was that worth? On the other hand, exactly why didn't his wife want him to turn up unless she invited him?

Sergeant Tomlinson's feeling that there was another man in the frame seemed to make a little more sense now.

'I appreciate all you say, Mr Jones, and I hope you appreciate we're simply trying to work things out for the benefit of all concerned.'

'You can have my fingerprints,' said Herbert, 'and if it won't take too long I'll have time for an afternoon walk.'

It didn't take long at all, after which the inspector left with Stebbings, and Herbert took his walk. Round to Nell's.

'What a liberty, Herbert,' she said, when told the police had fingerprinted him. 'Well, blow them, I say. They're being terrible suspicious, which is daft considering I told them you were with me. Would you like a nice cup of tea?'

'Yes, I would, Nell, thanks.'

'Oh, you're very welcome, Herbert.'

'So Mum definitely didn't have a fall as she was getting into her bath?' said Olive.

'If she did,' said Madge, who had called to give Olive the negative answer from the police, 'there weren't any bruises.'

'So it really does look like suicide?'

'It might look like it, but nobody who knew Mum is going to believe it,' said Madge. 'Hell, if I have to say that one more time, I'll go cuckoo.'

'It simply must have been some kind of accident,' said Olive, and then told her sister of Sergeant Tomlinson's request for fingerprints.

Madge took a poor view of that, saying the police were out of their minds. Olive said she thought the police had an idea that the death wasn't an accident.

'That's horrendous,' said Madge, 'I can't even put words to the implications.'

'Try,' said Olive.

'My God,' said Madge, 'if they should want Dad's fingerprints too, think what that means.'

'It means they want to find out if his finger-prints are in the flat,' said Olive, and Madge stared at her.

'What are they after, for God's sake?' she asked,

'That someone drowned Mum in her bath,' said Olive.

'Did that swine of a Sergeant Tomlinson say so?' demanded Madge, horrified.

'No,' said Olive, 'and I don't think he's a swine. He was embarrassed in having to ask me to arrange for us to be fingerprinted.'

'Embarrassed?' Madge was caustic. 'Is there such a thing as a policeman suffering embarrass-ment?'

'Well, there's Sergeant Tomlinson,' said Olive.

'Olive, don't talk like a crazy woman,' said Madge. 'You're not accepting this implication that Mum's death wasn't an accident or, at the worst, suicide, are you?'

'I've just told you it must have been an accident,'

said Olive, 'and I'm not accepting anything else until the inquest.'

'Why are you so calm about it?' asked Madge. 'I'm seething.'

'I don't actually feel calm,' said Olive, 'I feel lost. Madge, I think Mum was having an affair.'

'What?'

'I've thought and thought about how determined she was to leave Dad and live her own life,' said Olive. 'Dad may have been a quiet and unexciting husband, but he never let her down, and as our father he never let us down, either. We were all a bit hard on him when we went along with Mum's complaints, we all told him he was the one mostly at fault. But I still felt Mum was out of order, that it was a bit much walking out on him the way she did. Now I think it was because she was having an affair, which could have been the main reason why she wanted her own place.'

'Having an affair?' said Madge. 'Mum, at her age? She was over forty.'

'But very well preserved, and still attractive,' said Olive.

'How can you think such things about your own mother?' asked Madge furiously.

'Only because I've given everything a lot of thought,' said Olive. 'Why, for instance, did she make it clear to Dad that he was never to visit her unless she invited him? Dad must have considered that the final insult. It was like being treated as a servant.'

'My God,' breathed Madge, 'are you trying to say that that made him mad enough to – to –'

'No, I'm not,' said Olive, 'because I don't believe Dad would ever get as mad as that. What I am saying is that because Mum didn't die from a sudden heart attack, the police are wondering exactly how it happened and looking suspiciously at Dad.'

'Did he have a key to the flat?' asked Madge.

'You know he didn't,' said Olive, 'you know Mum told us she wasn't going to give him one. That's another thing I've thought about, and it seemed to me it was another way of Mum making sure that, if Dad did turn up at any time, he couldn't actually get into the flat.'

'Olive, you're off your head,' said Madge. 'It must be the shock, it's made you lose your senses. Well, you were the most upset of all of us. For God's sake don't talk like this to Winnie, she'll faint. Look, we'll all go along to the police station tomorrow afternoon, Saturday, when Roger is home from his job, and after that we won't give the police any more help or co-operation. Let them work on the basis that it was some kind of accident. You're not to talk to Sergeant Tomlinson any more, is that clear?'

'I'll help Dad in any way I can,' said Olive,

'even if it means I'll have to put up with Sergeant Tomlinson calling every day.'

'Well, if he calls on me and Brian,' said Madge, 'he'll hear things he won't like.'

'That won't help,' said Olive.

'It'll help me, I'll tell you that,' said Madge. 'I'm going to see Winnie now, to let her know about the fingerprinting, and I just hope she won't be stargazing in the same way that you've been dreaming.'

'Request from Muscles Boddy,' said Warder Phillips to Chief Warder Brookes of Brixton Prison.

'What request?'

'To be let out for the evening.'

'Eh?'

Warder Phillips grinned.

'Says he's got to play in a darts match.'

'Is that a fact?'

'He missed out on the last one, he says, and he's sweating on making this one.'

'Don't make me spit iron filings,' said Chief Warder Brookes. 'Let him sweat.'

Inspector Shaw and Sergeant Tomlinson compared notes. The inspector's concerned his interview with Herbert Jones, which had revealed the man to be quietly but intensely resentful of his late wife's treatment of him. Yes, he could have been angry enough with her to consider doing her in. Another point to consider was that much of what he said emphasized a determination on the part of his wife to keep him out of her new way of life. Why? Because she was carrying on with some other bloke? Now, who was the more likely to do her in, a wronged husband or a lover with a mental kink who got some kind of queer satisfaction from drowning a woman in her bath?

'Have you stopped thinking it took two persons?' asked Sergeant Tomlinson.

'All right, I'll go along with one,' growled the inspector. 'Two would have been a bit of a crowd.'

'I can't help thinking a woman with an unexciting husband and a starved body might go off her head and take a lover,' said Sergeant Tomlinson.

'Along with her own flat?' said the inspector.

'Just a thought, sir.'

'Fair, Sergeant, fair. I'll accept the possibility that she kept open house for a lover while making sure her husband couldn't walk in on her.'

'Well, I favour that myself,' said Sergeant Tomlinson.

Inspector Shaw pointed out it was possible that, when she told her husband in no uncertain terms why she was leaving him, she could have included a confession that she had a lover.

Sergeant Tomlinson suggested she'd have kept quiet about that, otherwise her husband would have mentioned it during one of the interviews, wouldn't he? And she wouldn't have wanted her daughters to know. She seemed to have had a good relationship with them, the kind she'd have wanted to preserve. Her youngest daughter Olive certainly wouldn't have liked being told, and her mother wouldn't have wanted her to find out. He'd bet she hadn't been given a key, nor her sisters.

'Are you talking about Mrs Olive Way?' asked Inspector Shaw.

'Yes.'

'The daughter you weren't keen to interview about fingerprinting?'

'Yes,' said Sergeant Tomlinson.

'Are you soft in the head about her, Sergeant Tomlinson?'

'No, sir. I simply feel sympathetic.'

'Don't be bloody silly, man. What happened during your interview with her?'

'Nothing spectacular,' said Sergeant Tomlinson. 'She agreed without any fuss to arrange for herself and her husband, and her sisters, to come along to the station to have their fingerprints taken.'

'When?'

'As soon as possible.'

'You didn't suggest to her that we're very

interested in the possibility of murder?' said Inspector Shaw.

'Was I supposed to?' asked Sergeant Tomlinson.

'Did you mention it?'

'No. But she guessed we're not satisfied that it was suicide or accidental drowning. It upset her without making her break down.'

'Perhaps that young lady knows more about her mother's social life than you think,' said Inspector Shaw. 'Now, what about that factory manager, name of Burnside? Have you found out if he's married or not?'

'Not yet, but would it make any difference, one way or the other?' said Sergeant Tomlinson. 'I mean, either he was the lover or he wasn't.'

'I like to know everything, and so should you,' said Inspector Shaw. 'Get hold of his fingerprints tomorrow. Use your initiative. You've got your share of that.'

Sergeant Tomlinson asked what had happened concerning the fingerprints taken of Herbert Jones. Had they matched any found in the flat? Inspector Shaw sat up, came to his feet, walked to the door of his office, opened it and bawled for Stebbings. A relay of shouts took place, and Stebbings appeared after a while.

'Want me, sir?' he asked.

'I want the results of the check on Jones's fingerprints, don't I?' growled the inspector.

'I was about to come and see you,' said Stebbings. 'I wasn't able to match them with any found in the flat proper, sir.'

'What the hell d'you mean, the flat proper?' asked the inspector.

'Around it, sir. There's none of Jones's finger-prints on the furniture, door handles and suchlike,' said Stebbings. 'But I did find some on the luggage trunk that stood beside the bedroom wardrobe. I've just matched them with those we took from him.'

'The luggage trunk?' said the inspector.

'Yes,' said Stebbings.

'Is that helpful?' asked the inspector.

'You tell me, sir,' said Stebbings.

'It's not too helpful,' said Sergeant Tomlinson. 'We couldn't make a case out of prints on a luggage trunk. They could easily have been there before the trunk arrived at the flat.'

'My advice to you, Sergeant, is to hang on for the time being to the fact that they were there,' said Inspector Shaw.

'If we're going to produce a decent case against Jones, we've got to place him at the flat on the evening in question,' said Sergeant Tomlinson. 'I put it to you, sir, fingerprints on a luggage trunk would add up to sweet Fanny Adams in court, wouldn't they?'

'Damn it, man, you've either got to eliminate him from your inquiries or go for him,' said

Inspector Shaw, his familiar growl roughing up his tonsils. 'Eliminate him, and that leaves you looking for your unknown party. Or with the unfortunate party, the woman who took a bath, forgot to put her bath cap on, forgot to take a towel with her, mislaid her nightdress and was subsequently found drowned. Which points to premeditated suicide, or would do if there hadn't been a tablet of soap in the bath with her.'

'And if she had good reason for suicide,' said Sergeant Tomlinson. 'Oh, well, outside of her husband, a possible unknown party might get to be known if I can dig deep enough.'

Chapter Fifteen

'Roger, I'm going to see Dad,' said Olive after supper that evening.

'Good idea,' said Roger. 'I expect the old boy's well down in the dumps. Like me to come with you?'

'No, you put your feet up and listen to the wireless,' said Olive.

'By the way,' said Roger, 'find out if your dad has got to be fingerprinted, the same as us and your sisters.'

'Yes, it's food for thought, isn't it?' said Olive.

'Not the kind I like,' said Roger. 'Still, if it's going to help the police make up their minds about what might have happened just prior to your mother taking her bath, who's grumbling?'

'I'm wondering, not grumbling,' observed Olive, who had kept to herself most of what she had said to Madge. 'And I'll ask Dad if the police want his fingerprints too. I should have asked Sergeant Tomlinson while he was here.'

'That bloke's turning into your shadow,' said Roger. 'Talk about a dogged copper, he's that all right.'

'Perhaps dogged coppers get the best results,' said Olive, putting her hat on. 'Well, I'm off now, Roger.'

'Give my regards to your dad,' said Roger, relieved that Olive had recovered so well from the terrible shock, and saying nothing about where he thought fingerprinting was leading. 'Tell him I'm on his side.'

'He'll appreciate that,' said Olive. She gave her husband a kiss and left.

When Herbert answered a knock on his front door and found his youngest daughter on the step, he smiled.

'Well, this is pleasing, Olive.'

'How are you, Dad?'

'All the better for seeing you,' said Herbert, and stepped aside as she entered. 'You don't shout me like Madge does.'

'Now, Dad, Madge doesn't shout, she's just got a strong contralto voice,' said Olive, and kissed him.

'Then there's Winnie and her thing about stars,' said Herbert.

'You're bucking up a bit, aren't you?' said Olive, going into the living room with him.

'Well, Olive, no-one can say I wasn't fond of

your unfortunate mum,' said Herbert, 'nor that her death didn't poleaxe me. But knowing, as I do now, that I didn't mean very much to her, except as someone providing her with house-keeping money, I can't sit and grieve over her. I'm sorry her life got cut off only a short time after she'd begun to properly enjoy herself, and I'm sorry for her generally, as I would be for any woman who had to pay as she did for being free. But I hope you'll forgive me, Olive, for the limitations of me grief.'

'Dad, none of that could be called nice,' said Olive.

'Sorry about that,' said Herbert.

'And after all these years of being a quiet man, you've begun to make speeches,' said Olive.

'Sorry about that as well, Olive. Has what I've just said hurt your feelings?'

'Yes, Dad. I'm still grieving for Mum myself, even if you aren't.'

'Well, you would be, Olive, you've always been a nice caring girl,' said Herbert.

'Even if I did take you for granted as a provid-ing father?' said Olive with a little smile.

'Could you forget I said that?' asked Herbert.

'I understood why you did at the time,' said Olive, thinking he was still quite personable. It was strange, that, her mother so well preserved in her looks and her father still a fine figure of a man, yet they didn't have enough in common to prevent the separation, a fatal separation. 'Dad, have the police asked for your fingerprints?'

'They took them earlier today,' said Herbert.

'Did you ask them why?'

'Didn't need to, Olive, did I?' Herbert frowned. 'It's obvious they suspect I could have done it.'

'Done what?' asked Olive painfully.

'Seen your mother off for doing me down after twenty-five years,' said Herbert.

'Dad, oh my God, don't talk like that,' breathed Olive.

'That's what they're after, Olive, death in suspicious circumstances, as is said, with me as the prime suspect.'

'Well, I don't believe it,' said Olive, 'and I certainly don't believe you'd ever think about even harming a cat. You're not to speak like that. You didn't ever go to the flat, did you?'

'I wasn't ever to go unless your mum invited me,' said Herbert. 'Would you like a cup of Camp?'

'I'll make it,' said Olive.

'No, you won't. You do your share of chores, looking after Roger,' said Herbert, 'and you've had a bad week. You sit down and I'll see to it. I like it that you're here.'

'It's so strange, the way you've come out of your shell, Dad.'

'Well, I had to, didn't I, the day your mum left

and no-one was talking at me. I didn't like the silence. You know how everyone is comfortable with what's familiar. Won't be a minute with the coffee, Olive.'

Over the coffee, Olive came out with the information that her mother's savings book had been found in the flat. Herbert said he was glad to hear it, that he didn't want it to be wandering about for anyone to pick up. Olive said the savings were very high, amounting to nearly nine hundred pounds. Herbert said that proved what he'd always thought, that her mum had been a very good manager and able because of that to put money regularly into her Post Office account. Pity she hadn't lived to enjoy it, he said. Olive said she supposed it all belonged to him now.

Herbert shook his head.

'I don't want it,' he said.

'Dad?' said Olive.

'Having sold the shop, I'm not in need,' said Herbert. 'When the legalities have been sorted out, I'll see to it that you girls each get an equal share.'

So much, thought Olive, for Madge's insistence on keeping the thing dark from Dad, and Roger's agreement to that.

'You could have your own share, Dad,' she said. 'After all, I daresay the best part of the amount has come from you over the years.'

'No, once I handed your mum's allowance

to her every week, it was hers,' said Herbert, 'never mind where it came from. Fair's fair in a marriage, Olive. There's just one thing. I'd want each of you girls to start your own savings accounts, to have money that was all your own, like your mum had. It's good for women to have something at the back of them. That doesn't mean I've got anything against Roger or my other sons-in-law, only that I'd like all you girls to regard the money as your own. What d'you think?'

'I think I'm sad that you and Mum parted in the way you did,' said Olive, eyes just a little moist.

'All over now, Olive,' said Herbert. 'I've had my say about all that, and more than once these last two weeks, and that's the end as far as I'm concerned. I'll just remember her from now on as a good wife to me and an affectionate mother to you girls. I don't suppose any man could ask for more in a whole twenty-five years.'

Olive let go a few tears then, which embarrassed Herbert very much.

'Hello, love, how did it go?' asked Roger when Olive arrived home.

'Oh, the police took Dad's fingerprints today,' said Olive. 'He thinks they've got some idea that fingerprinting the whole family is going to clear up any mystery.'

'I bet they've got that idea all right,' said Roger. 'Is your dad worried at all?'

'Well, you know Dad, solid as the Rock of Gibraltar,' said Olive.

'Pity your mum wasn't an admirer of the Rock of Gibraltar,' said Roger.

'Roger, that remark was out of place,' said Olive.

'Well, excuse me, sweetie,' said Roger, 'but we could have a little bit of light relief now and again, couldn't we?'

'I'm dreading the funeral,' said Olive.

'Yes, when are the police going to release the body to the undertakers?' enquired Roger.

'We'll ask tomorrow, at the station,' said Olive.

'By the way,' said Roger, 'did your dad think to ask about your mum's savings book?'

'No, he didn't ask,' said Olive.

'Well, that helps us to keep quiet about it,' said Roger.

Madge and Brian were with Winnie and Victor, and Madge was carrying on furiously about all Olive had said to her in the afternoon. Winnie said as soon as it was dark she'd go and look at the stars. Brian asked what good that would do, and Winnie said it would make her feel more at peace with things. Victor said it wouldn't alter the fact that something odd was running about in the minds of the police. Madge said they want their heads examined, then, and as for Olive, she's gone strange. The sooner the inquest is over, she said, the better for everyone.

Sergeant Tomlinson entered the factory at ten the next morning. He avoided the general office with a sign inviting callers to knock. Running into a man in overalls, he stopped him.

'Where's Mr Burnside's office?' he asked. 'I need to see him.'

'Turn left just up there,' said the factory worker, 'and his is the first office on the right.'

'Ta,' said Sergeant Tomlinson, hatless and in a well-worn suit. 'By the way, is he married?'

'Hold on, what d'you want to know for? Got a sister who's looking for him?'

'You could say it's more to do with insurance than my sister.'

'Well, he ain't married, I can tell you that. Except to his amateur dramatics.'

'Not my line of country,' said Sergeant Tomlinson, and went on before the worker became curious about him. He found the office. It was marked 'FACTORY MANAGER'. He knocked, opened the door, and put his head in. The office was empty. He went in. He was out again in a matter of seconds. On his return to the station, he handed Constable Stebbings a black ebony ruler and told him to test it for fingerprints.

Then he went to see Inspector Shaw, to put him in the picture.

Growls were heard.

'You did what, Sergeant Tomlinson?'

'Used my initiative, sir.'

'You were well out of order. You don't enter private premises or business premises in order to do a bit of thievery, you announce yourself and ask for what you want.'

'My mistake, guv, but I thought you recommended doing it on the quiet,' said Sergeant Tomlinson. 'The idea being not to put Burnside on his guard.'

'I don't recall recommending an action that's against lawful procedure,' said Inspector Shaw.

'It seemed too good an option to turn down,' said Sergeant Tomlinson.

'If there's a complaint, don't expect my support,' said the inspector with another growl. 'Just phrase your report with care. So, Burnside's not married and you've brought back one of his rulers. Pleased with yourself?'

'Not yet,' said Sergeant Tomlinson. 'I'm waiting on Stebbings.'

The wait wasn't long. Stebbings arrived speedily.

'Well?' said the inspector.

'Prints on a certain ruler, sir, match several found in the flat.'

'Were any of those found in the bedroom?'

'Yes, a set of three prints on the mantelpiece,' said Stebbings. 'Might've got out of the bed feeling a bit weak, and held onto the mantelpiece for a couple of secs.'

'That's all your own work, that theory?' said the inspector.

'Yes, all my own work, sir,' said Stebbings.

Sergeant Tomlinson thought developments were suddenly working in favour of Herbert Jones. If they cleared him, his daughters would be spared more trauma.

'So Burnside visited Mrs Jones, and has been in her bedroom,' mused Inspector Shaw. 'Well, there are no signs that Jones was ever there, if we forget about the luggage trunk, and that puts Burnside in the lead. The factory operates on Saturday mornings, I suppose. Go down and commandeer a car, Tomlinson, and wait for me. Stebbings, you'll come as well.'

The old goat, thought Sergeant Tomlinson, he's taking over after all, never mind that it's my teeth that have been stuck into the roughest side of the investigation.

Five minutes later they were driving to the factory, and shortly after their arrival the inspector and Sergeant Tomlinson received permission from a wondering Mr Richards to interview Mr Burnside in the factory manager's office, while Stebbings remained in the car, his equipment with him.

Mr Burnside wasn't in the least happy at being asked to answer a few more questions, or to know that one of the CID men was a detective inspector.

'Damn it,' he said, 'what's the idea?'

'Something's come up, sir,' said Sergeant Tomlinson.

'And what's that?'

'Nothing we can't clear up with a little help, Mr Burnside,' said Inspector Shaw.

'And quickly, I hope,' said Mr Burnside. 'I'm busy.'

'Sorry and all that,' said Sergeant Tomlinson, 'but did you ever visit Mrs Jones after she moved into her flat in Stockwell Road?'

Mr Burnside, looking irritated, said, 'I saw her home after her first evening with the society.'

'Did you go up to the flat with her?' asked the inspector.

'No.'

'There was no occasion when you were in the flat?' said Sergeant Tomlinson.

'None.'

'You're sure, sir?' said Sergeant Tomlinson.

'Of course I'm sure.'

'That's odd,' said the inspector.

'Odd? Why?'

'We found your fingerprints here and there, sir,' said Sergeant Tomlinson.

'Bloody rubbish. You can't know they're mine.'

'Well, to confirm it, would you mind if we took yours now, sir?' said the inspector. 'It can be done here, or at the station.'

'Now look here,' said Mr Burnside, 'what's the point, anyway? What have I got to do with what happened to Mrs Jones, whether I visited her or not?'

'Well, you'll understand we'd like to know if anyone was with her on the evening she was found drowned in her bath,' said Sergeant Tomlinson.

'Why?' Mr Burnside wasn't giving an inch.

'We've reason to believe her death wasn't by suicide or accident,' said the inspector.

'Never heard such rot,' said Mr Burnside. 'Push off.'

There was a knock on his office door, and Mr Richards put his head in.

'Could you spare a moment, Inspector?' he asked.

'Take them both away,' said Mr Burnside, 'they're off their heads.'

'I don't think I can do that,' said Mr Richards, 'just hang on.'

His head withdrew and Inspector Shaw joined him in the corridor.

'Something to tell me, Mr Richards?'

'Miss Taylor, our invoice clerk, has,' said Mr Richards, 'and she'd like to talk to Sergeant Tomlinson in private. She heard Mr Burnside was being interviewed again. She's in my office, and particularly asked for your sergeant.'

'I'll send him along,' said the inspector.

'If you could hurry things up, Inspector, I'd appreciate it. There's a buzz going round the factory.'

'We'll do our best, sir,' said Inspector Shaw.

Miss Taylor, waiting for Sergeant Tomlinson, looked nervously at him when he arrived.

'Oh, good morning, Sergeant,' she said.

'Morning, Miss Taylor. I believe you want to talk to me.'

'Well, yes, I do, I feel I must,' she said.

'Go ahead,' he said encouragingly, 'I'm listening.'

Miss Taylor said she and Miss Simmonds both knew Mr Burnside had been thick with Mrs Jones, but hadn't wanted to get him into trouble, not when the poor woman had died like that, in her bath. Miss Simmonds especially didn't want to say much about Mr Burnside, as she had a soft spot for him. In fact, she'd been a bit jealous of Mrs Jones, even if she was over forty. Anyway, the day before Mrs Jones died she spent quite a bit of time looking through some files. Miss Simmonds asked her what she was doing, and she said just a bit of checking. Well, said Miss Taylor, the files contained copies of dockets, factory order dockets, and the way Mrs Jones went through them made her curious, especially as Mr Burnside was in the habit of getting Mrs Jones to make out dockets for orders he received over the phone. Or said he did. Miss Taylor then remembered they were usually for a firm called Timms, so because she was curious she did some checking herself, and soon realized there wasn't one copy of any of those dockets on either file, which meant no invoices had been made out against them. Invoices were usually made out the day after the docket copies were placed in her in-tray by Mrs Jones. There were always a lot, and Miss Taylor said she simply never noticed that dockets for Timms weren't among them. There were so many firms and every kind of name. But once she'd done her own checking of the files, it did occur to her that she'd never made out a single invoice for any Timms orders during the last few months.

She spoke to Mrs Jones about it the next day, and Mrs Jones said not to worry, she'd sorted it out with Mr Burnside, and he was going to put things right.

'Why didn't you mention this to me when I interviewed you yesterday?' asked Sergeant Tomlinson.

'Oh, just because I didn't want to get Mr Burnside into trouble,' said Miss Taylor, 'he's always been very nice and helpful. Miss Simmonds felt the same. Well, I told her what I'd found out, and she'd said to keep it to ourselves. Mind, that day, the day after, Mr Burnside seemed to be as dark as thunder, but Mrs Jones looked pleased with herself. It was awful later on to realize it was the last day of her life.' Miss Taylor went on to say she'd been worrying about it since she'd been interviewed, and when she heard Mr Burnside was being interviewed again, she decided she had to speak out. Miss Simmonds didn't want to, she still didn't want to get Mr Burnside into trouble.

Sergeant Tomlinson reflected. Burnside had been doing some fiddling and Mrs Jones had found out and spoken to him? It made him as dark as thunder? Had he decided to silence Mrs Jones? Would he do that just to make sure she didn't talk about some petty fiddling of his?

'Well, I'm obliged to you, Miss Taylor.'

'Have I done right?' asked the nervous invoice clerk.

'Of course you have. Just one point. When you spoke about Mr Burnside being thick with Mrs Jones, d'you know how thick?'

'Pardon?'

'Bluntly, Miss Taylor, were they having an affair?'

'Oh, I really don't know about that,' said Miss Taylor, slightly flushed. 'Is – is it all getting serious, Sergeant?'

'It's something that needs clearing up,' said Sergeant Tomlinson. 'Thanks very much for your help, I really am obliged.'

He returned to the factory manager's office. Mr Burnside was sitting at his desk, looking like a man whose patience was being sorely tried. Inspector Shaw glanced at his sergeant and nodded to let him know he could have the floor.

'Now what?' said Mr Burnside.

'Have you decided to let us fingerprint you, sir?' asked Sergeant Tomlinson.

'All right, get on with it,' said Mr Burnside.

'Get Stebbings, Sergeant,' said the inspector, and Tomlinson left the office to go and wake up Stebbings.

'I really don't know what you expect to get out of this farce,' said Mr Burnside.

'A few facts,' said Inspector Shaw.

'Concerning what?' asked Mr Burnside.

'The death of the late Mrs Jones, a friend of yours, sir. Can I assume she was a close friend?'

'You can assume what you like, it won't get you anywhere,' said Mr Burnside. 'You're barking up the wrong bloody tree if you think I was responsible for her death. Can't you people get it into your thick heads that it must have been an accident?'

'Like a fainting fit that made her fall into the bath?'

'Sounds feasible to me,' said Mr Burnside. 'She was a well-built woman.'

'You'd know that for sure, sir?' said the inspector.

'I'm not answering that.'

Sergeant Tomlinson returned with Stebbings in tow. Mr Burnside was silent as he watched Stebbings lay out his equipment.

'Might I have your full name and address, sir?' asked Stebbings.

'Rupert John Burnside, 14 Stockwell Park Crescent.'

'Thank you, sir.'

Mr Burnside lapsed into silence again as he submitted to the fingerprinting process, and merely looked sardonic when Stebbings compared results with existing specimens. The constable took his time before giving a nod of satisfaction.

'They match?' said Sergeant Tomlinson.

'Yes, they do,' said Stebbings.

'Well, then, Mr Burnside, here's one fact,' said the inspector. 'You did visit Mrs Jones in her flat.'

'So?' said Mr Burnside.

'Having an affair with her, were you, sir?' suggested Sergeant Tomlinson.

'I don't consider that any business of yours,' said Mr Burnside. 'In any case, can't you understand I've been trying to protect that dead lady's reputation? You'd like her family to know we made love, would you? What purpose would that serve except to give her husband and daughters a bitter pill to swallow?'

'I'd be sorry about that, sir,' said Sergeant

224

Tomlinson, 'but what it amounts to, as far as our inquiries are concerned, is the possibility you were with her on the evening of her death.'

'You mean I made love to her and then drowned her in her bath?' said Mr Burnside. 'That's stretching it a bit, even for you policemen. I'm not a psychopath.'

'Could I have a word, sir?' said Sergeant Tomlinson to the inspector.

'If it's necessary,' said Inspector Shaw, and withdrew, Sergeant Tomlinson following and closing the door behind him. 'Well, Sergeant?'

As tactfully as possible, Sergeant Tomlinson pointed out they were overlooking something, which was that Mrs Jones had spent that particular evening with Mr and Mrs Chance. That is, her daughter Winnie and her son-in-law Victor, who lived somewhere in Streatham. She hadn't left them until eight forty. She would have arrived home at about nine, and the time of death had been estimated between nine and ten thirty.

'So what's certain, sir, is that she didn't spend the evening with Burnside.'

'That's your problem, Sergeant.'

'But suppose the bugger was waiting for her? Let me tell you why he might have been.' Sergeant Tomlinson recounted what Miss Taylor had come up with in the way of highly interesting information. It meant Burnside might have decided to dump Mrs Jones. In her bath. Inspector Shaw didn't look too convinced. 'You don't think much of that, sir?'

'You're writing a detective story,' said the inspector.

'We might have a bit more than a story if we found a nightdress at Burnside's place.'

'Granted,' said the inspector, 'and even more if he hasn't got an alibi for the evening. One that covers him from nine until ten thirty.'

They re-entered the office. Mr Burnside gave them a glance of contempt.

'Whatever else you've now got on your minds won't help you,' he said. 'I'm not your man.'

'Well, maybe not, sir,' said Sergeant Tomlinson, 'but where were you between, say, nine and eleven on the evening Mrs Jones died?'

Mr Burnside smiled.

'Good question,' he said, 'the first good one. I was at the home of some friends, Mr and Mrs Worboys. Their daughter Felicity was also there. They're all members of the society. Felicity's our regular prompter, George Worboys in charge of props and his wife one of our leading players. I was with them from eight until eleven.'

Well, damn that, thought Sergeant Tomlinson, it's crashed a near certainty and put us back to Herbert Jones. If it's true.

Inspector Shaw chewed on his sergeant's collapsing hopes.

'We'll need to check on that,' he said.

'You're more than welcome,' said Mr Burnside. 'I'll give you their address, but you won't be able to interview them until Monday. They're in Brighton for the weekend, all of them, staying with friends.'

'Would you have the address of their friends?' asked Sergeant Tomlinson.

'Sorry, no,' said Mr Burnside. 'I'll have to wait as well, shall I, for this farce to be over?'

'It looks like it, sir,' said Sergeant Tomlinson.

'I see. Anyway, here's the address of the Worboys family.' Mr Burnside scribbled it on a slip of paper, which he handed to Sergeant Tomlinson.

'Thanks for that, Mr Burnside.'

'Good morning,' said Mr Burnside.

Chapter Sixteen

'Done in the ruddy eye,' said Sergeant Tomlinson on the way back to the station.

'Good and proper, if his alibi stands up,' said Stebbings. 'Specially if he pops down to Brighton to see the Worboys family and makes sure it does.'

'By asking a pretty dodgy favour of all three, mother, father and daughter?' said Sergeant Tomlinson. 'I've got an unpleasant feeling he doesn't need to.'

'You believed him?' said Inspector Shaw.

'I thought he made it difficult for any of us to disbelieve him,' said Sergeant Tomlinson.

'All the same,' said the inspector, 'get yourself round to see the Worboys family on Sunday evening.'

'Sunday evening?' said Sergeant Tomlinson.

'Tomorrow. Up to you, of course, Sergeant, it's still your case. I'd say Sunday evening would do nicely. Catch 'em just as they get back from

Brighton, while they've still got sand in their shoes.'

'Aside from the fact that I don't know what time they'll be back, there's not much sand at Brighton, Inspector. It's mostly all pebbles.'

'Well, hard luck for kids with buckets and spades, then,' said the inspector. 'Get to the house early in the evening, and wait for them, if necessary. Take Constable Fry with you. I'll be unavailable myself.'

So ought I to be, thought Sergeant Tomlinson, I'm supposed to be off duty tomorrow.

Roger arrived home at one o'clock from his morning's work and with a look of disgust on his face.

'What's wrong?' asked Olive.

'You may well ask,' said Roger. 'I've got to go up to Preston for three days. That's where our main works are, and there's a special project on. The blueprints relate to new railway construction in Burma. They need another draughtsman for a few days. I'll have to go up tomorrow to get in a full day on Monday, and I'm travelling back on Thursday.'

'Roger, that's four days,' said Olive.

'Yes, four days away,' said Roger, 'what a swine. Preston, of all places. It's not like Hyde Park. Wouldn't like to come with me, I suppose?'

'I would if it were Harrogate,' said Olive, 'there

are some lovely shops and hotels in Harrogate. But Preston? Have a heart, Roger.'

'Will you be all right here?' asked Roger. 'You could stay with Madge or Winnie, if you wanted.'

'I don't want,' said Olive, 'I'll be quite all right here.'

'What happens if – no, never mind.'

'Never mind what, Roger?'

'I was thinking of your mother's funeral,' said Roger. 'It's got to be soon, surely.'

'I expect it could still be delayed a little longer, until you get back,' said Olive.

'Well, I'd like to be with you,' said Roger. 'Let's see, we're going to the police station after lunch for the fingerprinting, aren't we?'

'Yes, we're meeting Madge and Winnie there at two fifteen,' said Olive.

'I've got to admire you, Olive, you've taken a bloody awful blow and come out of it still standing up.'

'I'm still hurting,' said Olive.

The police at the station were very polite, but the atmosphere was hardly cheerful for the visitors, and when Sergeant Tomlinson put in an apppearance to take charge of things, Olive looked grateful. Madge, however, took the opportunity to assert her right to express her disgust at what was going on behind the closed doors of the police station. Sergeant Tomlinson assured her nothing was going on that wouldn't be of benefit at the inquest. Madge responded to that by saying everything should be of benefit to the family and to her dead mother's good name. Brian was with her, having been asked by Madge to support her. Victor was outside, looking after his and Winnie's infant son in his pushchair. Victor was the more fortunate. Brian was rolling his eyes as Madge dressed Sergeant Tomlinson down for being so impertinent as to demand fingerprints.

'Just a formality, Mrs Cooper,' he said, 'and we're very grateful you're all here together. It won't take long.'

'You haven't been listening to me,' said Madge.

'I assure you, I'm a trained listener, Mrs Cooper, and we all understand your feelings.'

'What we all want is for you to understand my mother's death happened by accident,' said Madge.

'Which is what we're trying to prove,' said Sergeant Tomlinson with an agreeable smile, which at once caused Madge to tell him there was nothing to smile about.

'Madge, shall we get on with it?' asked Olive.

'Good idea,' said Roger.

'Good idea,' said Brian. 'I'll stand aside.'

'If I could only find my own star,' said Winnie, 'I think it would tell me all we need to know.'

'It'll drop on your head out of the sky one night, Winnie love,' said Olive.

'I object to all this,' said Madge, but gave in and the fingerprints were taken. After that, Sergeant Tomlinson saw them all out.

'Thanks a lot,' he said.

'It's all rot as far as I'm concerned,' said Roger, 'so try not to bother my wife any more, there's a good fellow.'

'My apologies for my calls,' said Sergeant Tomlinson.

'Apologies aren't necessary, Sergeant,' said Olive.

'There's one thing,' said Madge. 'When is my mother's body going to be released to the undertakers?'

Sergeant Tomlinson, who knew it wouldn't be released until the marks around the ankles had been satisfactorily explained, and the inquest over, said, 'It shouldn't be long now, Mrs Cooper.'

'It's absurd,' said Madge. 'Come along, Brian, let's get home to sanity.'

'And the cats, I suppose,' said Brian.

'I'm glad you care for them,' said Madge.

Goodbyes were spoken and a general departure effected.

The fingerprints matched various of those found in the flat, all of which had now been identified.

At one time or another, Madge, Winnie and Olive had all left their fingerprints. So had Roger, Hilda Jones herself, and Rupert Burnside. And so had Herbert Jones, but only on the luggage trunk. Nevertheless, in view of the possibility that Mr Burnside was going to be eliminated from inquiries, Sergeant Tomlinson had to turn his thoughts again on the deceased woman's husband. His daughters weren't going to like that. In a case like this, prolonged investigation could be bloody hard on a family, especially on young Mrs Olive Way.

Brockwell Park, expansive, sunlit and green, was a meeting place, a rendezvous, a playground and an escape from brick and stone. For Olive on Sunday afternoon, with Roger on his way up to Preston, it offered a slow pleasant saunter and a chance to reflect on the events of the past week. She thought about her mother, who had launched herself into the life of a free and independent woman and had had it taken away from her almost before it had begun. She thought about her father, who had failed himself as a man by not putting his foot down. But had he done that, had he failed, or had he made a splendid and selfless gesture in letting her mother go?

Reaching an empty bench, she sat down, absently watching parents and their children, young men with their young ladies, and energetic boys and girls dashing this way and that. A strolling man stopped, and his shadow fell across her. She looked up.

'Do you like the park too, Mrs Way?' asked Sergeant Tomlinson.

He was off duty, she could see that. He was casually dressed in tan-coloured slacks, brown sports shirt and brown shoes, and was without a hat. He looked a reassuring figure with his broad shoulders, his muscular frame and his pleasant smile.

'Where did you come from?' she asked.

'From my Stockwell police quarters,' he said. 'On Sundays, when I'm not on duty, I enjoy a walk in this park.'

'By yourself?' said Olive. 'Aren't you married, then?'

'I haven't met the right woman yet,' he said. 'Well, right for me as a policeman. They talk about a policeman's lot not being a happy one. The lot of a policeman's wife is a very trying one. Or so other policemen tell me.'

'Perhaps policemen's wives should persuade their husbands to change their jobs,' said Olive.

'Policemen get a bit rooted,' he said. 'Well, nice to have seen you, Mrs Way, enjoy the sunshine.'

'You don't have to run,' said Olive, 'you can do me a favour and sit down and talk to me, if you like.'

'But your husband, isn't he around?' asked Sergeant Tomlinson.

'At the moment, he's on a train to Preston,' said Olive. 'He's having to put in three days' work at his firm's main engineering works.'

'He's an engineer?'

'A draughtsman,' said Olive.

'I see.' Sergeant Tomlinson rubbed his chin. Olive smiled.

'It's against the rules to sit down with a married woman?' she said.

'It's against the rules to get drunk while on duty, but not to sit down with you,' he said, and he seated himself beside her. He detected a faint and very delicate scent. She was like that, he thought, a young woman of general delicacy.

'We don't have to talk about my mother or why you've taken my father's fingerprints,' she said.

'We don't, no, and I wouldn't be allowed to,' he said, 'that's definitely against the rules, but let me just say I admire your fortitude in the way you've stood up to everything. What recreations do you and Mr Way enjoy?'

'We have a little garden,' she said. 'He does the digging, the weeding and the lawnmowing, and I do the planting and the watering. I bring on flowers from seed. I'm not just the cook and bottle-washer. I think Roger and I have both been neglecting things lately. Just this last week, you know. But we'll get back to our routine before long. If we don't the weeds will sneak up on us and take everything over. Weeds run rampant in Brixton gardens, did you know that, Sergeant Tomlinson?'

'I think I've heard they do well even in the back yards of Walworth and Whitechapel,' he said.

'Pernicious, that's the word,' said Olive.

'They need smothering at birth,' said Sergeant Tomlinson.

'Oh, that's no good, they'll pop up through the smothering,' she said. 'You have to dig them out or pull them out.'

'Yes, so I believe,' he said. His parents, who lived in Clapham, had a garden. 'Well, then, is it a recreation or a chore, gardening?'

'Satisfying,' said Olive. 'And it's a bit creative, too. Do you have an interest outside your job?'

'Pencil sketching,' he said.

'Well, imagine that,' said Olive. 'I used to like painting with watercolours. I still do. I'm not very good, though. Are you good at pencil sketching?'

'I'm not famous,' said Sergeant Tomlinson, 'it's just a hobby.'

'What do you sketch?' she asked.

'Anything that takes my eye,' he said. 'How about your painting?'

'Oh, parks and ponds,' she said. 'You like sketching better than polishing your hand-cuffs?'

'I don't do much of that kind of polishing,' he said. 'Have you painted this park?'

'Not all of it,' she said, 'just parts of it. I don't think I could paint all of it all at once.' She smiled and sneaked in a question concerning the inquiry. 'Have you asked my father where he was last Tuesday evening?'

'Mrs Way – '

'You can tell me,' she said, 'I won't say anything.'

He shook his head at her, but said, 'A friend of his, a Mrs Binns, assured us he was with her until late.'

'I know Mrs Binns,' said Olive, 'she worked for several years in his shop. She's an honest woman. So that's all right, then. About where my father was, I mean.'

'Discussion closed, Mrs Way.'

'Still, thanks for telling me,' said Olive.

'Unofficially, of course,' said Sergeant Tomlinson.

'Is that what they call off the record?' asked Olive.

'You could say so. But the investigation isn't over yet, I'm afraid. Would you like a cup of tea at the refreshment rooms?'

'I would, but I won't, if you don't mind,' she said.

'Understood,' he said. 'Well, I'll be on my way now.'

'Thanks for our little talk,' said Olive. 'Good-bye again.'

'Good luck, Mrs Way,' he said, and left.

Olive departed herself after he had disappeared. With Roger away and the house empty, she took a bus ride to see her father. He opened the door to her knock, presenting himself to her in his shirt, tie and trousers. Since he was rarely seen without his jacket and waistcoat, Olive said, 'You're looking very casual, Dad, and on a Sunday too.'

'Well, I'm feeling a bit free and easy, Olive,' said Herbert as she stepped in. He gave her a kiss and added, 'You're looking nice yourself. Pleasing to have you call. Where's Roger?'

'He's gone up to Preston, to the firm's main works for a special job,' said Olive. 'He'll be away till Thursday.'

'Well, I'm glad you came,' said Herbert, 'I'm just about to have my Sunday tea. Stay and have some with me. Later on, I'm going to take Mrs Binns for a Sunday evening walk.'

'You're getting very thick with that lady,' said Olive.

'She's been a very good friend to me since your mother passed on,' said Herbert. They entered the kitchen. A loaf of bread and its board stood on the table, together with a dish of butter. 'I hope it doesn't hurt you, Olive, to have your mother mentioned in the same breath as Mrs Binns.'

'It's your own life, Dad,' said Olive. 'I'll stay and have tea with you. What are you going to give me?'

'Some nice bread and butter, a soft-boiled egg, some blackcurrant jam, and some scones fresh from the bakers yesterday,' said Herbert.

'Well, that's nice enough for you to have invited Mrs Binns,' said Olive.

'She's gone to see that uncle of hers today,' said Herbert, 'and won't be back till about half six.'

'The uncle she's going to keep house for?' asked Olive.

'That's the one,' said Herbert, omitting to say that Nell now had different ideas.

'I'll do the tea,' said Olive.

'I can manage,' said Herbert.

'No, let me, I'd like to,' said Olive, 'we all owe you something.'

'Nobody owes me anything,' said Herbert.

'We all turned into Mum's girls,' said Olive, 'we forgot we had a dad.' She could have pointed out that he'd been more like the Invisible Man than a husband and father, but hadn't the heart to.

'That was all my fault,' said Herbert, 'I did too much reading and hardly any talking. I've come to realize I wasn't any real company for your mother. Now it's too late to make it up to her.'

'Don't let's discuss painful things, Dad,' said Olive, 'just let me get the tea.'

Herbert gave in, and Olive prepared the tea in a way that gave distinct appeal to its presentation. They ate it in the parlour, where the family had enjoyed Sunday tea for many years. Hilda had always insisted the parlour was the only proper place for tea on Sundays. Herbert actually chatted in easy style, and Olive's faint smile was an acknowledgement of how much he had come out of his shell. They avoided any mention of the tragedy and the police investigation until Olive suddenly asked a direct question.

'Did the police want to know where you were on the evening of Mum's death, Dad?'

Herbert frowned over a scone liberally laced with butter and jam.

'They did,' he said.

'Were you upset?'

'Yes, I ruddy well was,' he said, 'seeing it was obvious what it meant, and why they took me fingerprints later on.'

'It all means, doesn't it, that they suspect it wasn't an accident or suicide,' said Olive.

'They're up the pole,' said Herbert.

'Where were you, anyway?' asked Olive.

'With Mrs Binns,' said Herbert. 'Most of the evening,' he added casually. 'It's come to something, Olive, when people you've never seen before knock on your door and suggest you might've drowned your own wife. It's put me off

Brixton and Stockwell and everywhere else here-abouts. Don't let's spoil our tea talking about it.'

'No,' said Olive, 'but could I ask if the police went round to ask Mrs Binns to confirm you were with her?'

'They did that all right,' said Herbert, 'and she confirmed it. It's very pleasing, having a friend like her. Now, how are you and Roger getting along?'

'We haven't come to blows yet,' said Olive, 'we're nicely in tune.'

'Well, Roger's a bright bloke and easy-going,' said Herbert.

Too easy-going where money's concerned, thought Olive, but a man could have worse faults.

She stayed until six fifteen and then departed, leaving her dad free to take Mrs Binns for the promised evening walk. It seemed to Olive he had really come out of his shell and, as a widower, was finding early consolation in the company of a widow.

Meanwhile, Sergeant Tomlinson and Constable Fry had entered themselves in the register for Sunday evening duty. It was for the purpose of interviewing the Worboys family after their return from Brighton.

Chapter Seventeen

It was just after seven when a man, a woman and a young lady appeared at the entrance to Stockwell Park Crescent. The man was carrying a weekend suitcase, and so was the young lady. They walked into the crescent, talking animatedly. Reaching a house, they turned in at the gate. The woman used a key to open the front door, and they all entered. The door closed behind them.

'That's them,' said Constable Fry. He and Sergeant Tomlinson had been strolling up and down, waiting.

'You're getting perceptive, Sidney,' said Tomlinson.

'You're getting sarky, like the old man,' said Fry. 'Anyway, what now?'

'As I've suggested, give 'em ten minutes to make themselves at home.'

They continued to stroll. At the end of ten minutes, Sergeant Tomlinson knocked on the door. The man answered it. He was in his forties, with thinning hair and a friendly face.

'What can I do for you?' he asked.

'Mr Worboys?' enquired Sergeant Tomlinson.

'Yes, I'm Mr Worboys.'

'Sorry to bother you on a Sunday evening – '

'I'm sorry too, I've only just got back from Brighton, with my wife and daughter.'

'I'm Detective Sergeant Tomlinson of Stockwell CID, Mr Worboys, and this is Detective Constable Fry.'

'Well, pardon me,' said Mr George Worboys, 'but what are you doing on my particular doorstep?'

'We're making inquiries in connection with a certain matter that's come to our attention,' said Sergeant Tomlinson. 'Mind if we come in, sir?'

Mr Worboys said he minded to some extent, especially under the circumstances, which included the fact that he and his family were in need of a meal, but he would yield to the principle of helping the law. He took them into the parlour, quite a pretty room with its bright colours, and asked them to go ahead with their questions, although he hadn't the faintest notion, he said, of how he could help. Sergeant Tomlinson asked if he and his family were friends of Mr Burnside, prominent in the Stockwell Amateur Dramatic Society. Mr Worboys said yes, is this something to do with the society?

'No, not the society, sir,' said Constable Fry, 'just Mr Burnside.'

'Hello, what's Rupert been up to?' asked Mr Worboys.

'Does he get up to things, then?' enquired Constable Fry.

Mr Worboys laughed.

'Burglary, you mean?' he said.

'He's not known to us for that, sir,' said Sergeant Tomlinson, and Mrs Worboys came in then. A woman in her late thirties, she was tall and attractive, and Sergeant Tomlinson could imagine she had quite a stage presence.

'George, what's going on?' she asked.

'It seems the police are interested in asking some questions about Rupert,' said Mr Worboys.

'Mr Burnside? What kind of questions, for goodness sake?'

'Apologies for disturbing your Sunday evening, Mrs Worboys,' said Sergeant Tomlinson, 'but I'm sure this won't take long. Can you and your husband think back to last Tuesday evening?'

'Tuesday? Tuesday?' Mrs Worboys reflected, and her husband did some thinking. 'Yes, we can both remember Tuesday evening.'

'Heather's always good for remembering for both of us,' smiled Mr Worboys, 'but I fancy this time I can remember for myself.'

Their daughter Felicity, a pretty young lady of seventeen, put in an appearance, and of course she too wanted to know what was going on. These policemen, said her father, needed answers to some questions about Rupert Burnside.

'Rupert?' said Felicity.

'Well, the first question was about last Tuesday evening,' said Mrs Worboys, 'and if we could think back to it.'

'That's easy,' said Felicity.

'Were you entertaining a visitor?' asked Sergeant Tomlinson.

'Yes,' said Felicity.

'True,' said Mr Worboys.

'Mr Burnside,' said Mrs Worboys.

'How long was he here?' asked Sergeant Tomlinson.

'All evening,' said Mrs Worboys.

'Until eleven at least,' said Mr Worboys. 'Why d'you ask, Sergeant?'

'Just a formal inquiry, sir,' said Sergeant Tomlinson.

'Just a minute,' said Felicity, 'is it something to do with what happened last year?'

'What happening was that, might I ask?' enquired Constable Fry.

'Nothing that's of any importance now,' said Mr Worboys.

'It was a private matter, it concerned only the Stockwell Amateur Dramatic Society,' said Mrs Worboys, delivering her words with the practised clarity of an actress who could perform well for an audience. 'We're all members. So is Rupert. Mr Burnside. He's a leading figure, in fact.'

'What did you say happened?' asked Sergeant Tomlinson.

'We didn't say,' said Mrs Worboys.

'The fact is, the takings for one of our Saturday night performances sort of disappeared,' said Felicity, 'so we had to have a meeting about it. Well, it was a lot of money in its way, and a loss to our funds. No-one could work out how it disappeared, and we decided the bag had been stolen by someone who got backstage. Some outsider. We didn't call the police in, we didn't want that kind of a fuss, but has someone reported it to you? Are you wanting to see Mr Burnside about it, because he's our president?'

'The society wouldn't wish the matter to concern the police,' said Mrs Worboys firmly.

'It doesn't, I assure you, unless we're asked for our help,' said Sergeant Tomlinson, sounding as if he understood a nod and a wink were required at this point. 'We only wish to know exactly where Mr Burnside was last Tuesday evening.'

'But why?' asked Mrs Worboys.

'Yes, why?' asked Felicity.

'It's a matter under inquiry, but nothing like theft or burglary,' said Sergeant Tomlinson. His smile made the family relax. 'It was definitely last Tuesday evening that Mr Burnside was here, and until eleven at least?'

'Quite definitely,' said Mrs Worboys. 'We entertain him regularly, usually to discuss something concerning stagecraft.'

'He's our expert on stagecraft,' said Felicity.

'I'm sure,' said Sergeant Tomlinson, smiling again, although his uppermost feeling was one of frustration. 'He's invaluable to you?'

'Certainly,' said Mrs Worboys.

'Well, that's all. Thanks for putting up with us, and sorry again for interrupting your Sunday evening.'

'I'm still puzzled,' said Mr Worboys.

'We're always hoping that some puzzles will work themselves out,' said Sergeant Tomlinson. 'Goodnight, and thanks again.'

Mr Worboys saw them out.

'I'll have to tell Rupert Burnside you called,' he said.

'That's quite all right, sir,' said Sergeant Tomlinson.

'Will he be surprised?'

'Probably not. Goodnight.'

The CID men left.

Constable Fry said, 'Dead loss, that was, except it looks to me like Burnside has got a few taking ways.'

'Perhaps his tastes are expensive, Sidney.'

'Such as women? They're expensive.'

'I suppose he appeals to women,' said Sergeant Tomlinson. 'Perhaps he appeals to Mrs Worboys.

I thought she was slightly aggressive on his behalf. Perhaps, in fact, she knows who made off with the takings, or has had a good guess.'

'If he's been doing his employers down, I don't suppose he'd lose any sleep over doing the society down,' said Constable Fry.

'It seems to me, Sidney, that it might have seriously worried him, Mrs Jones finding out about him diddling the firm, since it might have led in a roundabout way to the society asking new questions about the loss of their takings sometime last year. But damn it, how can we fit him into the frame regarding the death of Mrs Jones now that he's got what looks like a cast-iron alibi?'

'It's put him right out of the running,' said Constable Fry, 'which is making me think it might've been an accidental drowning, after all.'

'Did she forget her towel and her bath cap by accident, then?' Sergeant Tomlinson sounded as if irritation had crept up on him.

'Don't ask me, you're in charge,' said Constable Fry. 'Still, how about suicide? She wouldn't have needed to bother with the cap or the towel.'

'I still don't go along with suicide,' said Sergeant Tomlinson. 'She had no reason to do away with herself, not if it's true she was enjoying her new life.'

'We're getting nowhere fast,' said Constable Fry, 'and the old man's going to lose interest.'

'I'm not,' said Sergeant Tomlinson.

'I've got to point out, then, that that'll put you back on the doorstep of Herbert Jones,' said Constable Fry.

'Well, sod that,' said Sergeant Tomlinson, grimacing.

'I'm beginning to have a feeling I'm playing second fiddle to three fat cats,' said Brian Cooper.

'Don't be absurd,' said Madge.

'Get 'em out from under my feet, or I'll boot them through the back door,' said Brian.

'How anyone can even think of being cruel to animals horrifies me,' said Madge.

'Listen, sweetie,' said Brian, 'animals are cruel to each other. Those bloody cats think nothing of tearing birds into a pile of feathers, and come to that, if Mrs Russell's dog could have its way, it would bite Pinky's head off.'

'That doesn't excuse human beings from being cruel to animals,' said Madge.

'Even your mother aimed a smack at your cats last time she was here,' said Brian.

'Yes, and look what happened to her,' said Madge.

'What, it served her right getting herself drowned in her bath?' said Brian.

'Brian, how dare you say a terrible thing like that?'

'You asked for it,' said Brian. 'It's time you got rid of those cats and had some two-legged kids.'

'Two-legged kids?' said Madge, disgusted.

'Babies,' said Brian. 'They're more human than cats.'

Getting ready for bed, Olive thought again how empty the house was without Roger. She even had a feeling it was vulnerable, so she made sure the front and back doors were double-bolted.

On Monday morning, Inspector Shaw refrained from growling when told that Mr Burnside looked to have a cast-iron alibi and therefore couldn't be placed at the scene of the drowning last Tuesday evening.

He simply said, 'I told you I don't like cast-iron alibis. They get in the way of a solution.'

'I don't know we can break it, guv,' said Constable Fry, 'not when both parents and their daughter were all positive.'

'It's your problem, Sergeant Tomlinson,' said the inspector, 'you'll have to do some plodding. That's if you're still feeling sure it wasn't an accident or suicide.'

'You're suggesting we plod about looking for someone who might have seen a person entering by that side door?' said Sergeant Tomlinson.

'Up to you, man,' said Inspector Shaw.

'A person with a motive for murdering Mrs Jones?'

'You've only got two possibles, Burnside and Jones,' said the inspector, 'and you've as good as eliminated Burnside. I'll give you until Thursday to finish the investigation, one way or the other. Get going.'

'So what now?' asked Constable Fry, as he and Sergeant Tomlinson left the station.

'Plodding, Sidney.'

'What about my feet?' asked Constable Fry. 'I did all my plodding in the uniformed branch, didn't I?'

'It's the luck of the draw,' said Sergeant Tomlinson.

'What kind of luck is that, might I ask?'

'Making an effort to find someone who can help us place a bloke at the scene of the crime,' said Sergeant Tomlinson.

'Might I point out we can't officially call it a crime yet?' said Constable Fry.

'It's that as far as I'm concerned,' said Sergeant Tomlinson, 'so start plodding.'

Herbert took a bus ride up West again, and this time he took Nell with him. She wore her best costume and hat. When they alighted in the Strand, Herbert preceded her so that he could give her his hand as she stepped off. She said he was a natural gent, and that although she still didn't want to speak ill of the dead, she felt Hilda had been too taken up with herself to realize what nice ways he had. Yes, she took you for granted, Herbert. Herbert said best if they didn't talk about poor Hilda, that she'd passed on in very unfortunate circumstances and to leave it at that. Nell said yes, all right, Herbert.

They walked along the Strand together, making quite a picture of a mature couple in their Sunday best on a Monday morning.

Meanwhile, Muscles Boddy, who considered himself a good friend to Herbert, was working out his porridge in Brixton Prison. He wasn't too happy about it, especially as no word of sympathy from his guv'nor reached him. Incarceration didn't lessen his dislike of the law. The law, he reckoned, could take liberties with a bloke who had a living to earn and friends to see.

He downed a fellow inmate for giving him lip, then trod on his breadbasket as well. Luckily, no warder noticed the incident, and the injured geezer lodged no complaint.

Muscles asked about remission.

'Remission on twenty-eight days, you berk?' said a warder.

'Ain't I a model prisoner, then?'

'So's my Aunt Fanny.'

'Sod your Aunt Fanny,' said Muscles.

Chapter Eighteen

Sergeant Tomlinson and Constable Fry spent Monday and Tuesday in Stockwell Road in an attempt to find someone who might have seen a man at the door leading to Mrs Jones's flat the previous Tuesday evening. They knocked on neighbouring doors. All kinds of people appeared in answer to their knocks, but none had any help to offer. Some said they were too busy to spend time in the evenings looking out of their windows to see what was going on, and others said they weren't in the habit of spying on their neighbours, thanks very much. Inevitably, there was the belligerent householder who said, 'So you're the bleedin' police, are yer? Well, bleedin' bug off.' It was a fact of life that people of a certain kind were of the opinion that a police force existed as an interfering nuisance and ought to be done away with.

In several cases, there were no answers to knocks, and that meant going back again, which in turn meant extra plodding, something that wasn't to Constable Fry's liking. Sergeant Tomlinson made him buy a packet of bath salts in which to soak his failing plates of meat.

Inspector Shaw tactfully refrained from criticism, remarking only that Sergeant Tomlinson was on the way to establishing that the police had no case. Sergeant Tomlinson said there was a case, he was damned certain of it. Well, time's running out, said the inspector.

'I need a little bit of luck,' said Sergeant Tomlinson.

'Hope it soon lands in your lap,' said the inspector.

On Wednesday, Madge, Winnie and Olive arrived at their father's house in response to postcard invitations to have a light lunch with him. Winnie brought her child, Herbert's grandson, and put him to sleep in his pushchair.

Herbert laid out a lunch of tinned salmon and salad, with bread and butter, with pineapple chunks and custard to follow. The pineapple chunks were also out of a tin.

'Who's going to make the custard?' asked Madge.

'It's made,' said Herbert. 'I did it, and it's keeping hot. I know you girls don't like cold custard.'

'Dad, are you turning into a cook?' asked Olive.

'I'm learning the ropes,' said Herbert. 'Sit down, all of you.'

They all sat round the kitchen table. The talk prior to that had all been about the police inquiries and what they could mean. Herbert had said it was best to forget what they could mean, as they wouldn't lead to anything. Your mother, he said, drowned accidental, and the police would come to realize that.

Now, as they began their meal, Winnie asked, 'Exactly why have you invited all of us, Dad?'

'You asked that when you arrived,' said Herbert.

'So did I,' said Madge, 'and, like Winnie, I'm asking again.'

'Yes, what's the reason, Dad?' asked Olive.

'What do Winnie's stars say?' asked Herbert.

'I couldn't see any last night,' said Winnie, 'it was cloudy.'

'Well, I'll tell you,' said Herbert. 'It's about your mother's Post Office savings.'

'Oh?' said Madge.

'Mum's savings?' said Winnie.

'Those that's recorded in her savings book,' said Herbert, and Olive contrived to look innocent, having kept to herself the fact that her dad intended the money to be shared out.

'Well, I think Mum would have wanted everyone to have some,' said Winnie.

'Definitely,' said Madge in her positive way.

'Well, we don't have to come to any argument,' said Herbert. 'I've got a letter on my person. It's a sort of document, actu'lly, made out by a solicitor. It's for Madge, she being the eldest, and it instructs her to see the savings are shared out equal between the three of you. I don't want any of it, it's all for you girls, and I'll give the document to Madge in the presence of you and Olive, Winnie, which'll make you and her witnesses to the handing over. The solicitor said it's always as well to be careful about money matters like these, so that there's no family arguments, which I hope there won't be among you girls. Equal shares suit you all?'

Madge and Winnie, taken aback, looked at each other. Olive smiled.

'There won't be any arguments, Dad,' she said, 'and we're all grateful. Madge and Winnie will tell you so.'

'Well, yes, thanks ever so much, Dad,' said Winnie.

'But don't you have to wait for the savings to be legally yours before you can share them out?' asked Madge.

'That's taken care of,' said Herbert.

'Well, I must say it's very generous of you, Dad,' said Madge.

'Yes,' said Winnie, 'and especially as we thought that if—'

'We won't talk about ifs and buts,' said Madge,

'it isn't respectful to Dad or to the memory of Mum.'

'Let's just be respectful to her savings,' said Olive with a hint of good-humoured satire.

'Well, your mother always treated her savings with great respect,' said Herbert with a smile. 'Lunch all right, is it?'

'I must say you've come out a lot, Dad,' said Winnie.

'I've had to, Winnie,' said Herbert. 'Mind you, it's one thing being a free man and another doing everything for yourself. I've been spoiled all these years. It's sad, y'know, your mother going off like she did and coming to such an unfortunate end. Still, it's no use harking back or letting our grief get too much hold of us. You're all looking very nice, I must say. Your cats all right, Madge?'

'You keep saying more in one go than you ever said in all your married years,' remarked Madge. 'As for my cats, they'll be missing me.'

'You sure?' said Herbert. 'Mrs Binns was telling me cats are sort of independent and can always take care of themselves as long as there's a few mice and birds around. Bit of a hard life for the birds, though.'

'And the mice,' said Olive.

Madge sniffed.

Before his daughters left, Herbert gave Madge the document in the presence of Winnie and

Olive, and they all read it. It bore the name and address of a Brixton solicitor, and it settled the matter of Hilda's savings.

'Keep in touch,' said Herbert.

'Of course, Dad, we'll see you lots,' said Olive.

'Don't forget the money's to be your own savings, and try to add to them like your mum did, so that you'll all have something behind you,' said Herbert. 'By the way, I might be going on a sea trip sometime.'

'A sea trip?' said Winnie.

'Yes, I might treat myself to some ocean breezes,' said Herbert. In company with Mrs Binns, he had visited the offices of a shipping company on Monday. 'I'm thinking serious about it.'

'Do it, Dad, enjoy yourself,' said Olive.

'Dad, you're getting quite adventurous,' said Madge.

'Well, I'm a free man,' said Herbert. 'So long now, all of you. '

Sergeant Tomlinson and Constable Fry were close to Herbert's home early that afternoon, trying to find out if any neighbour of his had seen him last Tuesday evening. They discovered one lady, a former customer of his shop, who had run into him in Saltoun Road at about half past eight. They'd said good evening to each other, and the lady had asked him jokingly if he was going out on the tiles. He said no, that he was going to call on Mrs Binns, the woman who'd worked for him in his shop, and who lived in Saltoun Road. The lady thought my, and her a widow too, did his wife know? Mr Jones, apparently, hadn't informed the lady his wife had recently left him.

The lady wanted to know why they were asking questions about him, and the CID men said it was a private matter, and the lady said well, Mr Jones was a sort of very private man.

'We're still up a bleedin' gum tree,' said Constable Fry after they'd parted from her. 'We can't place Burnside at the scene, nor Jonesy. Sarge, we've got nothing that means anything. Inspector Shaw's going to tell you to drop the case.'

Sergeant Tomlinson, not keen to accept that, said they'd have to hope for some positive clues to turn up before the inquest took place. Constable Fry said that that could happen on the day a cow jumped over the moon.

'Let's go one more time to Mrs Jones's flat,' said Sergeant Tomlinson. 'Let's see if we overlooked any kind of clue.'

'It'll be giving my feet a hard time,' said Constable Fry. Nevertheless, he accompanied his sergeant to Stockwell, and they let themselves into the flat with the spare key.

While Fry gave the living room and bathroom

a thorough examination. Sergeant Tomlinson concentrated on the bedroom and kitchen. Neither man found anything that had not been noticed before, although Sergeant Tomlinson did come across a bunch of flowers in a vase on the kitchen table, with a card propped against the vase. Curious, he read what was written on the card.

'Sorry, Mum. Love, Olive.'

Sorry? Strange, very strange.

He left the kitchen, giving the flowers another glance on his way. He bumped into Constable Fry. They compared notes. Neither offered the other anything in the way of a fresh pointer.

'It's like the old man says, we've got no case, then,' said Constable Fry.

'Which gets up my nose,' said Sergeant Tomlinson.

'Ten to one the coroner's going to conclude it's death by accident,' said Constable Fry, 'which'll mean my feet have been hurting for nothing.'

'We're both suffering,' said Sergeant Tomlinson.

They left.

At eight o'clock that evening, Olive answered a knock on her front door. Sergeant Tomlinson doffed his trilby hat.

'Good evening, Mrs Way, am I disturbing you?'

'Well, yes, you are, Sergeant,' said Olive, 'I'm listening to a play on the wireless.'

'Oh, sorry. Shall I go away and come back again?'

'No, not now you're here. But I'd like to know why you've called.'

'May I come in and tell you?'

'Very well,' said Olive.

The first thing she did in her living room was to turn off the wireless. The second was to invite him to sit down. The third was to touch her hair and lightly fluff it. Sergeant Tomlinson, seating himself, thought she looked charming in her summer dress, and quite at ease with herself.

'Mrs Way – '

'Yes?' Olive sat down opposite him.

'I was at your mother's flat again this afternoon.'

'Were you?' she said. 'Why?'

'In connection with completing our inquiries.'

'Oh, inquiries.' Her faint smile showed. 'I'm glad to hear you say they're nearing completion. Are you going to tell me what your conclusions will be?'

'We haven't arrived at any yet, Mrs Way.'

'I should think that's because you're looking for something that's not there,' said Olive. 'You should accept my mother's death was suicide or an accident.'

'There were one or two things that puzzled us,

though,' said Sergeant Tomlinson. 'What I want to say now is that I noticed you'd placed a vase of flowers on the kitchen table in the flat.'

'Oh, just as a gesture after she'd died,' said Olive.

'You left a card saying you were sorry, Mrs Way. Sorry about what?'

'It meant I was sorry that none of us, none of the family, did anything to stop her leaving my father, sorry that this led to her death, sorry that none of us were there at the time, which might have prevented the accident. I believe, you see, that it was an accident.'

'I see.' Sergeant Tomlinson was thinking about her husband, Roger Way, and how he had found him in the flat looking, so he said, for his mother-in-law's handbag, which happened to be plainly visible. Then there was the fact that although this very pleasant young woman had suffered physical collapse at discovering her mother's body in the bath, she had made a remarkable recovery within a day or so. 'I don't want to upset you, believe me, but could you tell me where you and your husband were on the evening of what you feel was an accident?'

'My word,' said Olive, eyes opening wide, 'aren't you a demon, Sergeant Tomlinson? And a shocker as well.' She shook her head at him. 'It's all very well, only doing your job, as they say, but really, making suspects of Roger and me is the giddy limit. Never mind, I forgive you, and can tell you Roger and I were working in the garden until dusk. Our neighbours were in their own garden, we chatted a bit with them, and when we'd finished our outdoor chores they invited us in to have a drink with them, which we did, and were with them until about ten thirty. Your next move is to go next door and check, I suppose. Knock and ask to see Mr and Mrs Gibson.'

Sergeant Tomlinson knew he'd arrived at another negative.

'No, I'll take your word for it, Mrs Way,' he said.

'That's very nice of you,' said Olive, 'and makes up a little for thinking dark thoughts of Roger and me, although I'm astonished you could have such thoughts. You actually suspected Roger and I might have contrived my mother's death? How utterly rotten of you, Sergeant. What would have been our motive?'

'I haven't the foggiest idea, Mrs Way, and can only apologize for being the heavy policeman.'

'At the moment, you look more like an embarrassed one,' said Olive. 'And you should be. I ought to be furious with you. I'm me, my mother's daughter.'

'So sorry to have upset you,' said Sergeant Tomlinson.

'It's cost you the offer of a cup of tea,' said Olive, and he rose from his chair.

'I think my best bet is to disappear,' he said.

'Yes, I think so too,' said Olive, and saw him out. 'There's nothing suspicious about my mother's death, you know. Goodnight, Sergeant Tomlinson.'

'Goodnight, Mrs Way.'

Chapter Nineteen

'That's it, then,' said Inspector Shaw the following morning.

'I still don't think it was suicide,' said Sergeant
Tomlinson.

'No?'

'Or an accident.'

'Look, man, if it was murder, you've eliminated
the only two possible suspects and found no
other, haven't you?' growled the inspector.

'I'll admit we can't place either of them at
the scene,' said Sergeant Tomlinson, who hadn't
mentioned his latest interview with Mrs Olive
Way. He felt he'd made a fool of himself.

'You can't place anyone else, either,' said the
inspector. 'Call it off. There's the obvious fact
that if she was going to commit suicide, she
wouldn't have bothered about a cap or a towel.
We can't offer the coroner anything to sub-
stantiate murder. Well, don't let it get you down,
Sergeant, I'm satisfied you conducted a thorough

investigation, but we've got nothing to justify any further inquiries.'

'Just one thing, sir,' said Sergeant Tomlinson, 'there's still no explanation for the marks around the ankles.'

'Didn't we decide they were made by shoe straps?'

'Dr Strang's opinion was no.'

'Some other explanation, then,' said the inspector, who'd lost interest. 'Inquiries closed. Sergeant, unless the coroner finds we've got some work to do, after all.'

Sergeant Tomlinson still wasn't happy.

Olive received a letter by the midday post. It was addressed in Roger's handwriting. He was due back home today. Had he written to tell her his return was being delayed?

She opened the letter and read it.

'Dear Olive,

'I'm afraid this is going to be a shock to you, and I thought it only fair to write instead of leaving you wondering what was happening. The fact is, I'm going abroad. I can't tell you where, and I'll have sailed by the time you get this letter. I'm going with two artesian well engineers who have formed a company, and have an overseas contract. But they need a draughtsman and more capital, and I'm providing the extra, seven hundred and fifty quid, in exchange for thirty-three per cent of the shares. Well, of course, I didn't have that kind of money, not until this morning when, after giving the Post Office proper notice in your mother's name, I cashed all her savings. Yes, I had to forge her signature on the withdrawal form. You'll think me a bloody bounder, I know, but I couldn't turn down the chance of a lifetime, and your family would never have loaned me your mother's savings. But I'll pay it all back as soon as this company is in handsome and expected profit, and then I'll ask you to come out and join me. Don't gnash your teeth and curse me, just bear with me. I couldn't tell you my plans as I know you'd have scotched any attempt on my part to cash your mother's savings. Sorry about giving you a new shock on top of the other, but it'll all work out fine for us in the end. Love, Roger.

'PS. I'll be writing from time to time, if poss.'

Olive stood rigid, then read the letter again, to make sure that her husband's infamy really was evident in black and white. She placed it on the table and examined the postmark on the envelope. Southampton. She walked on stiff legs to the bedroom. There she opened one of the bottom drawers in her dressing table, and turned over the items it contained. Her mother's savings book had been put beneath them. It was missing now.

She put her hat on, returned to the living room, placed the letter and envelope carefully in her handbag, then went out to the nearest public phone box. She called the Stockwell police station and asked to speak to Sergeant Tomlinson. She gave her name, and after a minute's wait she heard his voice.

'Mrs Way? Sergeant Tomlinson here.'

'I want you to come and see me immediately, Sergeant Tomlinson. I've something to tell you.'

'Something important, Mrs Way?'

'You can judge for yourself. It's very important to me, I can tell you that.'

'I'll be with you as soon as I can.'

'Come by yourself, please.'

'If you're going to make some kind of statement – '

'For this interview, I'd prefer to speak to you privately. Any statement can come later.'

'Very well, Mrs Way.'

When Sergeant Tomlinson arrived, she did not beat about the bush.

'It's my husband,' she said, her voice ominous.

'Your husband?' Sergeant Tomlinson regarded her with intense curiosity. Was she going to tell him the unbelievable about her husband? Her face was slightly flushed, and he had a feeling she was on fire.

'I find I'm married to a swine,' she said.

'Then I'm sorry, Mrs Way, but is that anything to do with the police?'

'It's everything to do with the police,' she said. 'He's stolen my mother's life savings. He's aboard some ship that I think sailed yesterday. I want him arrested and brought back.'

'Mrs Way—'

'Read that,' she said, taking the letter out of her handbag and thrusting it at him. He took it. 'Read it and see what he's done to me and the family.'

Sergeant Tomlinson read the letter. His first reaction was to wonder if Roger Way had murdered his mother-in-law in order to get his hands on her savings book. The book, yes, that was what he had really been looking for in the flat that day. He had obviously already searched the handbag and not found it there. But would he seriously have considered murder when there were other ways of getting hold of the book, the ways of a petty thief?

'Mrs Way, what was the amount of your mother's savings?'

'Nearly nine hundred pounds.'

'I see he mentions he needed seven hundred and fifty.'

'Yes,' said Olive, struggling to control her fury. 'Are you going to stand there and ask questions? Shouldn't you be telling me that you're going to check ship sailings and passenger lists immediately?'

'No, I don't think so, Mrs Way.'

'You don't think so?' Olive's flush deepened. 'Why don't you think so?'

'Because I doubt if he's aboard any ship.'

'But he makes it quite clear he is. I asked for you to come and see me so that as a humiliated woman I wouldn't have to suffer a whole roomful of police.'

'We wouldn't have sent a roomful, Mrs Way. I take it as a compliment that you asked for my help. Well, let me suggest to you that this letter is an act of deception. I don't mean that he hasn't withdrawn the savings, I'd say that's all too true. But the set-up. A newly formed company with a contract to sink artesian wells somewhere overseas needs a draughtsman and extra capital? How would a new and under-capitalized company have secured a contract? And how would your husband in a very short space of time have secured his place in that company and a place aboard a ship? He had no money to show until yesterday. He needed a passport, a ticket, and other things. Mrs Way, a company with an overseas contract could have raised extra capital quite easily.'

'Sergeant Tomlinson, are you telling me that, apart from the withdrawal of my mother's savings, that letter is a lie?' demanded Olive.

'I'm suggesting it is, yes,' said Sergeant Tomlinson. 'In fact, I'm suggesting your husband is still in this country, but that he's hoping you'll believe he's on his way to the moon. That is, somewhere far away. Is he fond of money?'

'Very,' said Olive, 'and he's never had enough of it. My God, the swine.'

'Do you want him found and charged, Mrs Way?'

'You feel sure he's still in this country, Sergeant Tomlinson?'

'I'd bet on it,' said Sergeant Tomlinson.

'Then, yes, I want him found and charged,' said Olive.

'Um – ' Sergeant Tomlinson hesitated.

'Um what?' asked Olive.

'There's no possibility that he was responsible in some way for your mother's death?'

'That again?' said Olive. 'You're a bulldog, aren't you? No, Roger may be a swine, but not of that kind. As I told you, he was with me from the time he came home from work that evening until we went to bed, and that includes the time we spent with our neighbours. I hope you find him before he's spent my mother's savings.'

'We'll circulate his description, and if you've got a photograph, that will help, Mrs Way.'

'Yes, I'll give you a photograph,' said Olive.

'Do you know where he was when he wrote

this letter?' asked Sergeant Tomlinson. 'That is, where was the stamp franked?'

'Southampton,' said Olive, and produced the envelope. The sergeant inspected the postmark.

'Southampton, yes, very appropriate,' he said, 'and it wouldn't have cost him much to get there and make you think of ships.'

'I'm going to have a drink,' said Olive, 'a strong one. Would you like something, Sergeant?'

'Not for me, Mrs Way.'

'You're on duty, of course.'

'Yes. I'll take the photograph and also this letter, if I may.'

She found a framed photograph. She took it out of the frame and handed it to Sergeant Tomlinson.

'There,' she said. 'You won't mind, will you, if while you're setting the wheels in motion, I get drunk?'

'I think you're overdue, Mrs Way, for that kind of medicine, but don't empty the bottle.'

'You're a sympathetic policeman, aren't you?'

'Sometimes,' he said. 'I'll see myself out, and I'll be in touch.'

'Go ride your horse, Sergeant, and let me know when my husband's been arrested,' said Olive.

'By the way,' he said, 'our inquiries concerning your mother's death are being called off, and her body will be released to the undertakers. Your father was told this morning.'

'Then why did you ask me a little while ago to confirm where Roger was that evening?'

'Forgot myself,' said Sergeant Tomlinson.

'It's your bulldog streak,' said Olive.

When he had gone, she poured herself just a little brandy. She steeled herself and drank it at one go. She made a face, then thought about telling her father and sisters of Roger's infamy. But instead of doing so, she went out into the garden and used a hoe. She took her fury out on the weeds.

It would have pleased her to know that the police at Stockwell were setting in motion the procedures that they hoped would lead to the apprehension of one Roger Way. The wheels began to turn, the Post Office Savings Bank department consenting to help in a check that would establish at which branch the withdrawal was made.

Sergeant Tomlinson was particularly active on Olive's behalf. It took his mind off the frustrations brought about by his stubborn belief that Mrs Jones's death was neither the result of suicide nor accident.

Herbert had enjoyed a nice lunch at Nell's flat. He'd also enjoyed another satisfying chat with her, during which Nell had remarked that he'd turned into quite a talking man.

'Well, y'know, Nell, looking back, I can't help thinking Hilda had good reason to see me as unsociable, though I wish she hadn't called me so many names in the end. I always thought it was best to let her do all the talking, she being the kind of woman who hardly ever stopped. Real gift of the gab, Hilda had. Anyway, I don't want you to find me unsociable, which I hope I'm not at this here moment.'

'Oh, you're very sociable these days, Herbert. It's been very nice listening to you, and being told just how you're arranging everything.'

'Yes, shouldn't be long now, Nell. Say in two or three weeks.'

'Lor', by then I won't know if I'm on me head or me heels, Herbert. And all them new clothes, goodness me, I'll look like a duchess.'

'You liked going round the shops with me, Nell?'

'Best time of me life, Herbert. Ain't you a love?'

'Well, I'm hardly that, Nell, but I pride myself I've never minded putting my hand in my pocket. Anyway, I'll be off now. See you again tomorrow.'

'All right, Herbert. Oh, and I want to say again I'm pleased you've heard from the police that Hilda's funeral can take place. I hope she rests in peace, poor Hilda, and it must be a relief to you that the police aren't going to fuss any more.'

'There'll be the inquest soon, Nell. Me and the girls will have to face up to that. Well, goodbye now, thanks for the nice lunch.'

'Oh, you're always welcome, Herbert.'

Gritting her teeth, Olive called on her father during the afternoon. Herbert was surprised to see her again so soon, but it didn't take him more than a minute to realize she was far from her usual self.

'What's up, Olive? Not still worried about things, are you? I've heard from the police that the undertakers can collect your mother's body.'

'Yes, I've heard too, Dad, from Sergeant Tomlinson,' said Olive. 'It's something different from that, something you'll hardly believe.'

Herbert listened as she talked to him at length about what Roger had done to her and the family. He was thunderstruck. Olive went on to tell him she'd spoken to Sergeant Tomlinson.

'Well, he's the right kind of policeman to talk to,' said Herbert.

Olive said Sergeant Tomlinson believed that most of what Roger had put down in his letter was a lie, that there was no company, no nothing except a rotten swine of a husband absconding with her mother's savings. Herbert asked if that was what Sergeant Tomlinson had called Roger, a rotten swine.

'No, I did,' said Olive. 'Sergeant Tomlinson is

sure he's still in this country. He's promised the police will do their best to find him and arrest him.'

'You're going to have him charged, Olive?'

'Yes,' said Olive.

'So you should, even if he is your husband,' said Herbert. 'Any bloke who does that kind of thing to his wife needs a dose of hard labour. Did I have a feeling once that Roger was easy come, easy go about money?'

'If you did, you were right,' said Olive.

'This needs thinking about,' said Herbert. 'I'll make a pot of tea and we'll talk some more.'

Over the tea, he pointed out that Roger's deed was even worse than he'd first thought. He had left Olive with nothing, with no housekeeping money coming in, and probably nothing with which to pay the rent. Was that so, was she broke?

'All I've got is what's in my purse,' said Olive, 'about twenty-five shillings.'

'No savings, Olive?'

'Savings? Don't make me laugh, Dad.'

'Didn't he give you enough so that you could put a bit aside each week?'

'No,' said Olive. 'He always seemed to be in debt.'

'Well, some marriages turn out to be a mistake,' said Herbert soberly. 'You've found yours out early, I found mine out after twenty-five years. At least, your mother did.'

'Don't go on about her, Dad,' said Olive.

'I was thinking about selling this house,' said Herbert. Actually, the landlord who owned adjacent houses had already made him an offer. 'I won't now. Well, you'll get notice to quit as soon as you can't come up with the rent, Olive. You can move in here, and bring your furniture. Say in a few weeks, when you've had time to get over this new shock and you're able to think straight about what you're going to do. I'll see you can pay your rent till then.'

'Dad, that's so good of you,' said Olive.

'Part of me obligation as your father,' said Herbert.

'Don't spoil it by saying that.'

'Let's say due to me paternal affection for you, then.'

'That's better.' Olive smiled wanly. 'I'll have to get a job.'

'Go back to being a typist?' said Herbert.

'I don't like the idea,' said Olive, 'I like growing flowers and having a house to look after.'

Herbert said he understood. Women, he said, had to look out for themselves if they wanted to do what best suited them. And there were always some men willing to go along with that in return for what women could do for them, such as putting their meals on the table regular and doing their washing. And other things.

'You get rid of Roger,' he said, 'and look out

for some other bloke, a bloke who'll give you a house and garden and a decent amount of housekeeping. But find out first if he'll put his hand in his pocket for you. You don't have to be in love with him, though you've got to like him. You've got to consider what you want and go for it, especially if you don't fancy being a typist day in and day out. You'll be happy enough, Olive, with a husband who'll give you what you want.'

'Dad, you're the surprise packet of the year,' said Olive, 'you're talking like a wise old owl instead of being as quiet as a mouse.'

'I've learned a lesson, I daresay,' said Herbert. 'Now, seeing you've been knocked for six and left with nothing, I'm going to give you fifty pounds. That'll keep you going for a few months, especially as you won't be paying any rent here, and I should think, if you use your noddle and get rid of Roger legal, you ought to have found the right kind of bloke in that time. What d'you think, will that look after your problems?'

'Dad, what can I say?' Olive looked emotional. 'Only that if Mum were still alive she'd realize she'd badly misjudged you. The poor dear paid for that, didn't she?'

'God rest her soul,' said Herbert.

'There's one thing I can do,' said Olive, 'I can keep house for you.'

'You could do something with the back

garden,' said Herbert, 'turn it into something a bit pretty, perhaps, while I'm on my sea trip.'

'Oh, I'll be pleased to,' said Olive. 'You're really going?'

'Yes, do me good, I thought, after what's happened,' said Herbert. 'Australia.'

'Australia?'

'It's a long way,' said Herbert.

'Australia, for goodness sake, you'll be away ages,' said Olive.

'I should think I will,' said Herbert. 'I'll leave you to look after things here. Mind you, don't let that stop you looking out for another bloke. And keep your fingers crossed that Roger gets nabbed before he's spent too much of your mother's savings. By the way, have you told Madge and Winnie about him?'

'Oh, Lord, I'm not going to like having to confess to them that I married a rotter, and that he's thieved Mum's savings,' said Olive.

'They're all right, they've got husbands to look after them,' said Herbert. 'I'll let you have the fifty pounds on Monday, but here's a couple of quid to keep you going till then.' He took two pound notes out of his wallet and handed them to her.

'Well, bless you, Dad, I'm not in a position to refuse,' she said.

'You'd better go and talk to Madge and Winnie,' said Herbert. 'Tell you what, I'll call for you this evening and we'll go together. I know you've got backbone, but you've got a bit of misery as well, so you need some support. I'll be with you about half seven.'

'Thanks, Dad, you're a brick,' said Olive.

'I take it that's one step up from a doorpost,' said Herbert.

Chapter Twenty

Madge was furious, of course. Brian was stupefied. Madge said Olive could have done a lot better for herself and the family by marrying a postman. Postmen had to be honest and reliable men. Herbert said he didn't think every woman asked a would-be husband if he was honest and reliable. Madge said Olive should have made sure the savings book was put where it couldn't be found. Herbert said Olive wouldn't have known she had reason to distrust Roger to that extent. Brian said it wasn't Olive's fault. All that money, said Madge, gone like a puff of smoke unless the police get it back. Olive said she was utterly sick about it, especially when she was still in shock about their mother. The police, she said, were releasing the body to the undertakers at last, and the inquiries were over.

'What with a thief in the family, and the funeral and inquest to attend,' said Madge, 'I'm not in a fit state for any more conversation.'

However, she did manage to say that cats didn't give a woman trouble as some men did. Brian muttered something uncomplimentary about all cats.

'Dad and I will go and see Winnie now,' said Olive, and she and Herbert left before Madge found new voice.

Winnie was aghast. Victor couldn't credit it. However, they refused to attach any blame to Olive or to suggest she ought to have kept her eye on Roger. They both gave her a great deal of sympathy, and both were pleased to know the police were going after her worthless husband. Winnie hoped they'd get most of the money back, and Victor said Roger ought to be boiled in oil for what he'd done to Olive. Finally, they expressed relief when told that Hilda's funeral could take place at last.

Herbert took Olive to her home and then insisted she ought to stay at his place for the night. Olive shed a tear or two at that point. She packed a few things and Herbert took her home with him.

The funeral took place the following Monday. The family attended, and so did certain relatives and some friends, including Mrs Nell Binns. Madge, Winnie and Olive were all in black, Herbert, Brian and Victor in sober grey. At the church service, the vicar spoke some gentle words of praise about the deceased, and besought the family to bear with their loss.

At the cemetery, Herbert watched sombrely as the coffin was lowered into the grave. It was a certainty, he thought, that Hilda never expected her life as a free woman to be as short as this.

Nell, standing apart from the family, thought what a shame for poor Hilda, coming to her end so sudden, and in her own bath too. Still, Herbert was standing up to the burial with a straight back and a lot of dignity. His girls looked very mournful.

Brian thought, well, there you go, mother-in-law, ruddy hard luck that your bath was an oversized one. As for your eldest daughter, I know now why she hasn't conceived, having dipped deep into one of her dressing-table drawers. I'll give her Dr Marie Stopes. I'll give her a surprise. No, not tonight, on account of this being the funeral day. Tomorrow night.

Madge herself thought the occasion a suffering one for all concerned. And it was a suffering made worse by what Roger had done. The swine ought to be hanged and given a burial of his own.

Winnie thought poor Mum, there must have been one of her unlucky stars hovering about that night.

Olive simply hoped that her unlucky mother would rest in peace.

A representative from the factory was present. Mr Rupert Burnside. And he thought what a pity, a body like yours, Hilda, along with all your hidden fires. Not many women of your age look no more than thirtyish when they're all undone. Damned if you weren't a positive eye-opener. Still, I think you'd have turned into a nuisance as time went on. Wanting to play the part of Lady Bracknell was your opening shot. Well, perhaps St Peter can find you a suitable part. As one of his full-bodied angels with a touch of the seven veils. Enjoy yourself.

The funeral breakfast took place at Herbert's home. Madge, Winnie and Olive had all helped in the preparation of food, but Herbert had turned down an offer from Brian and Victor to supply the drink. Good of you lads, he'd said, but it's up to me.

Nell kept a low profile. Well, she knew it wouldn't do to give the impression she was stepping into Hilda's shoes.

There were some awkward moments, occasioned by friends or relatives asking exactly how Hilda came to drown. Herbert got over that by saying to each enquirer that the family couldn't give an exact answer, and wouldn't be able to until after the inquest.

Nell, standing in the passage and talking to one of Herbert's neighbours, was closest to the front door when its knocker sounded. So she opened it. An impressive-looking gent in a grey suit and trilby was on the step. She recognized him.

'Here, excuse me,' she whispered, 'but you shouldn't have come on the day of the funeral.'

'Perhaps not,' said Sergeant Tomlinson, 'but I do have some news which I think Mrs Way would like to hear, despite the occasion.'

'You sure?' said Nell.

'Yes, I'm sure, Mrs Binns.'

'Oh, you recognize me, do you?' said Nell.

'Yes, you're a close friend of Mr Jones. Would you tell Mrs Way I'm here?'

'Well, I suppose I should,' said Nell, 'but you'd best stay there while I go and find her.'

She found Olive and whispered to her.

'Oh, I'll see him,' said Olive, and joined him on the step, with the door pulled to behind her. 'Sergeant Tomlinson, you've something to tell me?'

Because she was dressed in mourning black, Sergeant Tomlinson took his hat off in a gesture of deference.

'I know I might be interrupting a very private family occasion,' he said, 'but I was sure you'd want to know your husband has been found. In Torquay, at the Palace Hotel. A constable spotted him coming out of the hotel this morning, recognized him from his description and arrested him.

He's now at the Torquay police station. His room at the hotel has been searched and a large wallet containing exactly eight hundred pounds in notes was found. It's now in the possession of the police. There were also twenty-two pounds in his pocket wallet.'

Olive's mouth tightened for a moment, and her lashes flickered. She'd spent the last few days feeling utterly sick about Roger. That feeling was gone now, replaced by contempt.

She said, 'Yes, I'm glad you came to tell me, Sergeant, I would have wanted you to. Thank you.'

'Damned rotten for you, though, your own husband failing you so badly on top of your mother's death, Mrs Way. You've had a rough time and I feel for you.'

'How did you know I was here?' asked Olive.

'I went to your house and was told by your next-door neighbour you'd be at your father's after the funeral,' said Sergeant Tomlinson. 'I don't want to worry you, but could you and your father come to the station sometime and make an official statement on which we'll base our charge when we have your husband in our custody? He's being brought from Torquay under escort.'

'I don't wish to see him or to be near him,' said Olive. 'And why do you need my father?'

'We presume he has first claim on the money

286

unless your mother left a will in favour of some-one else.'

'Yes, I see,' said Olive. 'I'll speak to my father. My mother made no will. My father means my sisters and myself to have equal shares. I'll let you know about making the statement. Thank you again. Goodbye, Sergeant.'

'Goodbye, Mrs Way.'

'We've said a lot of those, it seems.' Olive's little smile came and went.

'A lot of goodbyes?' he said.

'Yes,' she said, and he smiled and left.

Not until all friends, neighbours and relatives had finally departed did Olive tell the family that Roger had been found and arrested in Torquay, where he'd been staying at the Palace Hotel.

'Good,' said Madge, vibrant with satisfaction, 'his crafty little ruse to make us think he was somewhere on the high seas didn't come off, did it?'

'His star fell out of the sky,' said Winnie.

'You saw it, did you?' said Brian.

'It was a figure of speech,' said Winnie.

'Sounded all right, though,' said Herbert.

'Olive, what about the money?' asked Madge. 'Did Sergeant Tomlinson mention it?'

'Yes,' said Olive. 'The Torquay police found eight hundred pounds in one wallet, and twenty-two pounds in another.'

'Well, that's a piece of glad tidings for you

girls,' said Victor, 'but the sod still managed to spend all of sixty quid living it up at the Palace Hotel in Torquay.'

'I expect he used some of it to pay off the kind of debts he always built up,' said Olive.

'Olive, d'you still want him put away?' asked Herbert.

'Must we talk about that when Mum's only just been buried?' asked Winnie.

'All the same, there's one point that ought to be mentioned,' said Herbert, 'which is, will Olive be able to charge Roger? Well, it's just occurred to me that she can't charge anyone for stealing money that didn't belong to her. I think I'd have to do it.'

'Sergeant Tomlinson asked if we could go to the station and make an official statement, Dad,' said Olive. 'He mentioned the money would be legally yours.'

'I'll talk to you a bit later.'

'Roger's got to be charged,' said Madge.

'Well, yes,' said Winnie, 'but I'd let Olive decide. She's the one who's been hurt the most.'

'That's my advice too,' said Brian.

'And mine, even if it's not my business,' said Victor. 'Leave it with Olive. That's if your dad agrees.'

'I'll do what Olive wants,' said Herbert.

He had a little chat with Olive later.

*   *   *

The following morning she appeared at the Stockwell police station and asked to see Sergeant Tomlinson. She spoke to him in an interview room. His eyebrows went up.

'Your father doesn't want to press charges, Mrs Way?'

'No.'

'Well, damn it, we—'

'I beg your pardon, Sergeant?'

'Damn it, I said, we had all the wheels set in motion, police up and down the country alerted, time and money spent, and your husband brought here all the way from Torquay. Dropping the charge is making a monkey of us, and I'm not sure we can do it, anyway.'

'Sergeant Tomlinson, are you shouting at me?'

'Nearly, but not quite, Mrs Way. I'm angry.'

'I'm sorry,' said Olive, 'but neither my father nor I want to appear in court and give evidence against my husband. Anyway, only my father can do that, isn't that right? Wives are excused, aren't they? My husband, Sergeant, is a worm and a snake, and I never wish to see him again, in court or anywhere else. He can go on his way to the devil, as far as I'm concerned.'

'On behalf of your father, you're asking the chief inspector here to let your husband off with a caution?' said Sergeant Tomlinson. 'He'll raise hell.'

'I'm sorry,' said Olive again. 'Will it mean embarrassment for you?'

'Embarrassment?' Sergeant Tomlinson fixed her with a glowering look. 'It'll mean I'll get a rocket that'll blow my head off.'

'Oh, I am sorry,' said Olive.

'Don't keep saying sorry. I suppose you realize your husband has already been charged?'

'Well, I hope that's frightened him to death,' said Olive.

'It has.'

'Good,' said Olive.

'Now look, Mrs Way, he's a cheap thief and an unpleasant one in what he did to you.'

'I know,' said Olive, 'but my father and I don't want to go to court.'

'Well, I'm damned if I could be as forgiving as that,' said Sergeant Tomlinson.

'No, I haven't forgiven Roger,' said Olive, 'and I don't think I ever will. I simply don't wish to have anything more to do with him.'

'It's an offence, wasting police time, Mrs Way.'

'Am I going to be arrested, then?'

'You should be,' said Sergeant Tomlinson, almost as growling in his mood as Inspector Shaw was on occasions. 'Your mind is definitely made up, is it?'

'Yes. I'm sorry, but—'

'If you say sorry again, Mrs Way, I'll catch fire.'

'Oh, I'd better just say goodbye, then. Will I see you at the inquest?'

'Yes.'

'Well, I hope you'll have forgiven me by then, Sergeant,' said Olive.

Sergeant Tomlinson managed the ghost of a smile.

'I think you can bet on that,' he said.

Subsequently he was forced to suffer a very awkward and harrowing session with the superintendent, who threatened to have Olive and her father arrested for wasting police time. Inspector Shaw helped to cool things down. In the end, there was no alternative but to drop the charge. The following morning, Roger Way was released with a severe caution.

Roger at once made tracks for home. Olive, anticipating this, had her father staying with her for a few days before she finally moved out. It was Herbert who confronted Roger when he arrived, and it was Herbert who delivered defamatory words, the kind of words of which neither his family nor his neighbours would ever have considered him capable.

Finally, 'And if you ever try to see Olive again, you bugger, you'll wish you'd never been born. On top of which, you'll find yourself in court, after all. Now get out of here before I knock your bloody head off.'

*   *   *

Muscles Boddy, fuming and fidgeting in Brixton Prison, heard from his guv'nor eventually, through the grapevine. The message was short and terse. You're fired. Muscles considered that the height of spiteful ingratitude. It put him into the position of needing the help of a friend.

Chapter Twenty-one

The inquest was held two days later.

The coroner listened to the pathologist expounding on the cause of death. Drowning, with no signs to indicate the deceased could have suffered a heart attack. Her heart, in fact, had been sound. There was, however, a faint bruise around each ankle, but the pathologist could not say how they came about.

Sergeant Tomlinson, representing the police, spoke next. He told the coroner that he and Constable Fry had been called to the scene by a Mr Roger Way, son-in-law of the deceased. Mr Way and his wife had discovered the body. Following that, inquiries had been made to establish whether or not suspicious circumstances obtained, by reason of the marks around the ankles, and the fact that the deceased had not been wearing her bath cap and had, apparently, not taken a towel with her into the bathroom. Further, her nightdress was missing. However, after an exhaustive investigation, the police could offer no evidence that the deceased had been forcibly drowned.

The coroner asked if he might put some questions to the husband. Herbert stood up, looking entirely respectable in a navy blue suit, white collar and black tie, his mane of hair as well brushed as ever.

'Mr Jones,' said the coroner, 'I understand you and your late wife had recently separated.'

'That's correct, sir,' said Herbert.

'You and your wife had been on bad terms?'

'No, never,' said Herbert.

'What, then, was the reason for the separation?'

'My wife felt that after twenty-five years of marriage, it was time to live her own life.'

'But you weren't on bad terms, you said?'

'No, but my wife considered life on her own would be – well, more entertaining,' said Herbert, and Olive bit her lip, Winnie made a face, and Madge fidgeted.

'Are you saying, Mr Jones, that your wife left you in order to be entertained?'

'Well, the fact is, I'm not very entertaining meself,' said Herbert, 'being a bit quiet and conservative in my ways, whereas Hilda liked things a bit lively.'

'For that reason, Mr Jones, you agreed to a separation?' said the coroner.

'I wouldn't say I agreed, sir,' said Herbert. 'It was more that my wife made up her mind to leave and she upped and went. It upset me considerable.'

'Did you quarrel with her at that point, Mr Jones?'

'No, I didn't, I don't like quarrels,' said Herbert, 'they're too disturbing and never make anyone feel better – well, that's my opinion.'

'I must ask you, Mr Jones, if your wife had another reason for leaving you.'

'Pardon?' said Herbert, upright, solid and square-shouldered.

'I'm suggesting, Mr Jones, that perhaps she was looking forward to being entertained by a third party.'

'A what?' said Herbert.

'Come, Mr Jones, it happens,' said the coroner.

'Not with Hilda, no, she wouldn't have done that to me,' said Herbert. 'She just meant that life gen'rally would be more entertaining without me.'

'I frankly find it difficult to believe that after twenty-five years of marriage a wife would leave her husband in the hope of finding life was a kind of circus,' said the coroner.

'Hilda liked a circus,' said Herbert, 'I took her to one once. But I'm refuting any suggestions that there was another man in her life.'

'Well,' said the coroner, 'you must have known

her better than anyone, Mr Jones, and on this point I therefore go along with your feelings. I come back to the separation. I can't help suspecting that after so many years this would have had a drastic effect on her emotions, whether it was instigated by her or not. I wonder, would any of your daughters care to say something? I believe they're all here.'

Madge stood up.

'I'm the eldest daughter, Mrs Madge Cooper,' she said.

'Yes, Mrs Cooper?' said the coroner.

'I'd like to say yes, that my mother was very upset,' said Madge. 'She naturally hoped my father would fight to make her stay.'

'Did she tell you that?' asked the coroner.

'Yes, in so many words,' said Madge. 'My sisters will confirm it.'

The coroner consulted a slip of paper.

'Mrs Winnie Chance?' he said, and Winnie stood up.

'Yes, my mother was in quite a state about Dad letting her leave, sir.'

'But she need not have left, surely?' said the coroner.

'It was her pride,' said Winnie, 'she didn't want to back down, she just wanted my father to let her know he couldn't do without her. But he had his own pride.'

Herbert was agape by now. And Brian and

Victor were dumb-founded about the way their wives had spoken about their old man.

Olive stood up.

'I'm Mrs Olive Way,' she said. 'It's quite true, my mother was very emotional about it all. She wouldn't let everyone know she was, but she confided in me and my sisters. But I don't think she wanted my father to oppose the separation. She made it clear to us that it was what she wanted, the chance to make a new life for herself.'

'Yes,' said Madge, 'but you know how it all upset her.'

'And how it grieved her,' said Winnie.

Herbert addressed the coroner. 'I wasn't aware my wife had regrets about leaving, it struck me it was more the reverse,' he said.

'Perhaps you mistook her attitude,' said the coroner.

'Excuse me, sir,' said Olive, 'there's nothing to be held against my father. He was shocked out of his mind by everything. I want you to know he was always a good providing husband to my mother and a quiet and affectionate father to us. He was very good and kind always, but not very outgoing, and my mother was restless at times.'

'But it was a shock to her that your father made no effort to repair the break?' said the coroner.

'Yes, very much of a shock,' said Madge.

'Did he ever go to see her after she moved into the flat?'

'No,' said Madge.

'That is correct, Mr Jones?'

'Yes,' said Herbert. 'But that was because she wanted me to visit only when she invited me.'

'Surely that showed her state of mind was unusual?'

'It didn't seem so to me,' said Herbert, 'but I know mine was. Well, after twenty-five years, I was hardly meself, was I?'

'Your elder daughters seem convinced your wife was in a distressed state,' said the coroner, and looked at Madge.

'Yes, she was,' said Madge positively.

'Yes,' said Winnie.

The coroner glanced at Herbert.

'And your youngest daughter,' he said, 'has declared that your wife was in a very emotional state.'

'She was in a state all right, and so was I,' said Herbert.

'Of course,' said the coroner. 'Thank you, ladies, and thank you too, Mr Jones. I don't think there's any necessity for further evidence.' He deliberated for a short while, then said, 'I find the deceased took her own life while the balance of her mind was disturbed.'

'Drowned herself?' breathed Brian to Victor.

'Off her head, poor old girl,' murmured Victor.

The court rose.

Outside in the street afterwards, Herbert, still looking as if he'd walked into a brick wall, regarded his daughters helplessly.

'What happened, eh, what happened?' he asked.

'Oh, short and sharp, Dad,' said Winnie.

'No going on and on, and round and round,' said Madge.

'Best thing, Dad,' said Olive.

'But your mother was never upset about leaving me, then or afterwards, I'll bet my life on it,' said Herbert. 'Look what you've done, you've made her a suicide, which I thought was the last thing any of you wanted to believe.'

'We didn't, of course,' said Madge, 'but we had a serious talk about it just before the inquest opened, and realized that if the coroner decided it must have been some kind of accident, the police would never have let go of trying to find out what, why and wherefore, and everything else. So we decided to help the coroner settle for suicide.'

'You and Winnie went for that, did you, with a little backing from Olive?' said Herbert. 'Well, thanks a lot. Mind, I'm not forgetting that Olive managed some kind words on me behalf, even if she did talk about her mother being very emotional about everything, which you all know she wasn't. Well, the result hasn't done me much good, it's left me looking as if I'm to blame for not bringing her back home. She'd never have come, anyway. You girls did it on me.'

'Only to get it all settled once and for all, Dad, really,' said Winnie. 'It was for your peace of mind.'

'Yes, really,' said Olive, 'and nobody will put any blame on you, Dad. Let's be glad it's all over, and that Mum's resting in peace. No more calls from the police, no more of that.'

'I know now why they made such frequent calls,' said Madge, frowning. 'I mean, did you all hear Sergeant Tomlinson say Mum wasn't wearing her bath cap and that there was no towel in the bathroom?'

'Yes, that helped to point to suicide,' said Olive. 'The coroner would have told himself she wouldn't have bothered. Lord, perhaps she didn't. Perhaps she really did let herself sink under.'

'Might I remind you again that none of you liked the idea of your mum committing suicide?' said Herbert.

'We still don't like it,' said Winnie, 'but it was the only verdict that would settle things.'

'Winnie's right,' said Victor.

'Yes, I'll go along with that,' said Brian. He was quite willing to, since something else needed his attention following a serious talk he had had with Madge, a talk that was intimidating enough to make her promise to dispense with the contraceptive measures recommended by Dr Marie Stopes.

'I'd have liked it if I'd been consulted,' said Herbert.

'You didn't get here in time,' said Madge.

'All over, Dad,' said Olive. 'Now you can enjoy your cruise to Australia.'

'Australia, for God's sake,' said Madge, 'it'll be like going round the world.'

'Lovely,' said Winnie, 'think of all the tropical nights and the stars.'

'Perhaps he'll find yours hanging about over Sydney,' said Victor.

'Oh, excuse me a moment,' said Olive. She had seen Sergeant Tomlinson. She broke away and detained him on his walk to a police car. 'Sergeant, is that satisfactory to you, a suicide verdict?'

Sergeant Tomlinson was tempted to say no, it wasn't. But that would have invited questions he couldn't answer. He could only have offered suspicions.

'Was it satisfactory to you, Mrs Way?'

'I don't think any of us wanted to believe that of our mother,' said Olive, 'but I couldn't see how the coroner could have given a different verdict.'

'Yes, it did seem like that,' said Sergeant Tomlinson. 'By the way, your father can collect that money now, if he'd like to call in at the station sometime.'

'I'll tell him,' said Olive.

'And now, I suppose, this is our final goodbye, Mrs Way.'

'Do you think so?' said Olive. 'But I'm going to divorce Roger, I have the right grounds, I'm told. So if you brought your pencil and sketch block, and I brought my watercolours, perhaps we could go to Richmond Park together next Sunday. That is, if you're not on duty.'

'Are you serious?' asked Sergeant Tomlinson.

'Of course,' said Olive, who, on her father's advice, was looking out for herself with the right kind of bloke.

'You're on, then,' smiled Sergeant Tomlinson.

'Oh, that's good,' said Olive. 'Goodbye until next Sunday, then. I'll be ready at two o'clock.'

'I'll call for you.'

'Suicide, would you believe,' said Nell a little later, when Herbert was taking her home. She'd sat at the back of the court, and had thought she might be called.

'Beats me, those girls of mine saying what they did,' brooded Herbert.

'Well, p'raps Hilda did tell them things she didn't tell you,' said Nell.

'They cooked it up, to get it over with,' said

Herbert. 'Oh, well, it's done now, and the blame's mine.'

'Oh, I wouldn't say that, Herbert, and anyone that knows you wouldn't even think it was. Mind, it was a bit queer, wasn't it, that Hilda didn't take a bath towel with her to the bathroom. No wonder the police got suspicious. It got me agitated when they asked me questions about you being here that evening. Still, I was able to think straight and tell them you didn't leave till late. It was late, wasn't it?'

'Late enough, Nell.'

'Yes. Lor', Herbert, now I can't think of much else but Australia.'

'Life on the ocean wave, we'll enjoy that, Nell, all the time it'll take to get there.'

'I hope I don't get seasick,' said Nell.

Chapter Twenty-two

Herbert invited his daughters to lunch again a few days later, and over the meal he announced he was taking Mrs Nell Binns to Australia with him.

'You're doing what?' said Madge.

'Taking Mrs Binns with me,' said Herbert, looking his usual formal self, but implying from his announcement that he was chucking respectability out of the window.

'Dad, you can't, it's not decent,' said Winnie.

'Well, it's not half bad,' said Herbert, 'considering we're going cabin class.'

'My God,' said Madge, 'you're actually sharing a cabin with her? That's disgusting.'

'I'll thank you not to talk like that,' said Herbert. 'We'll have separate cabins, which is only right and proper, like I've always done.'

'It's not right and proper when it's not paying respect to the dead,' said Madge. 'Mum would turn in her grave if she knew you were going on a sea trip to Australia with a widow.'

'Dad, it's far too soon for you to take up with any woman,' said Winnie.

'I think Dad sees himself as a free man,' said Olive, 'and I have to admit I now see myself as a free woman, even if it'll be some time before my divorce comes through.'

'Being a free man doesn't entitle Dad to make eyes at Mrs Binns so soon after Mum's death,' said Madge.

'I'm free to reward Mrs Binns for all the years she worked for me in the shop,' said Herbert. 'She was a great help to me every day she was there.'

'But the cost of taking her all the way to Australia,' said Winnie, 'that's being a lot too grateful, I should think, and so would most people.'

'Well, never mind about most people, Winnie, it's all arranged,' said Herbert. 'We're sailing from Southampton on Friday, and we're going there tomorrow, Thursday, by train and staying in a hotel overnight. Olive, you can move in here now, any day you like.'

'I will, Dad, thanks very much,' said Olive, who had delayed her move until her dad was on his way. She was appreciative of the prospect of living rent-free. She had applied for an office job with an insurance company, and was waiting to hear. Of course, if Sergeant Tomlinson became very fond of her, well, things might happen that would enable her to give up any job and grow roses again. 'I'll move in definitely at the weekend.'

'It'll make up a bit for what Roger did to you,' said Herbert. 'Mind, I'm still sore that all you girls laid it on thick with the coroner over your mother's feelings. It was news to me that she had those kind of feelings.'

'Dad, we're all sure it must have upset her that you just let her go without doing a thing to stop her,' said Winnie.

'Anyway, that's all over, and a good thing too,' said Madge. 'It's sad enough to know we've lost her, and that we've got the grief to bear. But you can't be grieving much yourself, Dad, if you're going to enjoy a cruise all the way to Australia with Mrs Binns.'

'What I'm grieving about is that twenty-five years of marriage didn't count for anything in the end,' said Herbert. 'It's my opinion your mother danced out of all that like a happy sixteen-year-old.'

'That's an unkind thing to say,' said Winnie.

'Bitter, I call it,' said Madge.

'Still, Dad was badly hurt,' said Olive.

'Best not to chew over it,' said Herbert. 'Let's leave it now and for ever.'

Later, when his daughters were departing, he wished them luck and said he'd send them a picture postcard each time the ship touched port. Madge managed to say a fairly friendly goodbye to him, Winnie a forgiving and affectionate one, and Olive gave him a hug and a kiss.

After they'd gone, Herbert checked that certain items necessary to his voyage were at the ready in the top drawer of the dressing table. Passport, tickets and immigration document.

Nell had her own passport and immigration document securely lodged in a new handbag. Herbert had been so good, buying her all kinds of clothes and accessories.

Muscles Boddy was released from Brixton Prison the following day, having served his twenty-eight days in fairly fractious fashion. He was enjoined by the chief warder to behave himself from now on.

'Do me a favour,' said Muscles, 'fall under a bus.'

He busied himself as soon as he was out of jail.

The SS *Pacific Star* steamed out of Southampton at seven in the evening, on the turn of the tide. By half past ten it was well on its way, heading for the Bay of Biscay. The night was refreshingly cool, the stars visible in the inky sky, and Herbert was on the promenade deck, contemplating the faintly perceptible wash of the ship from the

stern rail. He and Nell had enjoyed their first
dinner aboard, in the cabin-class dining room,
and Nell was now in her cabin. He'd taken her
down after she'd spent a little while on the deck
with him. She'd said she was a bit tired and
would like to prepare for her first night's sleep at
sea. Herbert had come up again, wanting to take
in lungfuls of the night breezes before turning in
himself.

Well, he thought, this is the life. What a
dinner, as good as a bloke could get at the Ritz,
he'd bet on it. And having Nell enjoy it with him
had been highly satisfying. Nell was a warm-
hearted and affectionate woman, that she was.
She'd make a warm-hearted and affectionate
wife once they were married. The wedding would
take place in Australia. The people at Australia
House had been nice and helpful, especially
when shown that he had enough funds to ensure
he would not be a liability as an immigrant. He
intended to buy a shop and its goodwill, and
run it with Nell for about ten years, say, and
then retire with her. Nell had been in agreement, saying it was best to have something
to do, like running a shop, instead of sitting
around and doing nothing. Herbert ought to
have some spare time to grow things, she said, if
they bought a nice little house with a garden.
She thought flowers probably grew lovely in
Australia, and perhaps oranges too. Imagine if

we could have an orange tree, she said. That, thought Herbert, was very promising kind of talk. She hadn't said anything about hoping he would be lively and entertaining once they were married, she seemed happy to take him on just as he was. Madge, Winnie and Olive, well, his intention to stay in Australia would come as a surprise to them, but there it was, he'd given them many years as a father, and didn't owe them anything, any more than they owed him.

He jumped as a beefy hand clapped his shoulder and a voice reached his ear.

'Hello, 'Erbert old cock, ain't leaving yer best friend in the lurch, are yer?'

He turned. The lights of the promenade deck silhouetted the large bulky figure of Muscles Boddy. Herbert gaped.

'Eh?' he said.

'I been looking all over for you, 'Erbert. Caught a train to Southampton this morning, didn't I, after finding out yesterday from a neighbour of yourn that you was off to Australia today. What a bleedin' chase I've had to catch up with yer. Lucky I found this was the only ship going to Ossie, or I might still be looking for yer. Saw you up here a bit ago with a lady, saw you go down with her, and then up you come again. Might I ask if the lady's a welcoming widow that you're taking with you all the way?'

'None of your business,' said Herbert.

''Erbert, I wouldn't like to think you was after buggering off without me.'

'Now look here – '

'Don't come the old acid, 'Erbert. We're friends, ain't we? And I done you a good turn, didn't I, like a friend should. I scratch your belly, and you scratch mine, that's fair, ain't it? Australia'll suit me fine. Well, I lost me job with the guv'nor on account of a couple of lousy coppers laying an unfair charge on me, which cost me twenty-eight days in Brixton, which got up the guv'nor's nose.'

'Well, hard luck,' said Herbert, recovering a bit, 'but it's nothing to do with me. As for doing me a good turn, what good turn?'

Muscles took a look along the promenade deck. There were a couple of people leaning on the rail at a distance that was well out of earshot, but the coolness of the sea breeze had sent most promenaders down to their cabins. He edged close to Herbert, and from the corner of his mouth came confidential words.

'Now then, 'Erbert old matey, you know what good turn all right, don't yer? I'll grant your ungrateful missus didn't get pushed under a bus, but all that bathwater did the trick very nice, didn't it?'

'What the hell d'you mean?' asked Herbert, stiffening.

'Don't you worry, 'Erbert, it's just between you and me, like we agreed. Remember we talked about how you needed a friend that would do you a good turn? Well, I done it.'

'Jesus Christ,' said Herbert, 'you drowned my wife in her bath, you bloody fiend?'

'Not me, 'Erbert, not me personal.' Muscles turned his head and took another look along the deck. The couple had gone. A little deep chuckle found its way up from his large chest, and he told Herbert then that he'd used the services of an old East End mate of his. Herbert listened paralysed as Muscles relayed details. He'd found Hilda's address on Herbert's mantelpiece, having entered the house by way of the kitchen window. He was a dab hand, he said, at opening kitchen windows. He begged Herbert's pardon for doing that off his own bat, but it was always best not to let the client know too much beforehand.

'Client?' said Herbert, shivering. 'What d'you mean, client?'

Muscles said when a job was being done for a friend, the friend turned into a client. Herbert pointed out in a strangled voice that he hadn't asked for any job to be done.

'I'm talking about a good turn, ain't I?' said Muscles. 'Same thing, y'know.' Well, he went on, having got the ungrateful wife's new address, he did a recce on the flat and soon found it was easy to get into the yard and through the back door. He informed his old mate, and told him what was required. See the lady off nice and quick, but don't draw blood, don't get messy. So his mate said right, and put himself under contract.

'Contract, what's that mean, you bugger?' asked Herbert hoarsely.

'It's a trade term, 'Erbert,' said Muscles. His mate reported to him after the job was done. He'd got into the flat when Herbert's wife was out, and having already thought of a nice quick and clean way to see her off, he filled the bath with water and waited. Out of sight, of course. When the lady returned, she undressed, then entered the bathroom in her nightie. Of course, as soon as she saw the bath was full of water, she bent over to pull the plug out. Which was just what Cabbage Ears was waiting for.

'Cabbage Ears?' said Herbert from out of his nightmare.

'Best not to give no names,' said Muscles. 'Anyway, 'Erbert mate, he was wearing thick fur gloves and not leaving no careless fingerprints around. He took hold of her ankles from behind and upended her. Down went her napper in the water, where it rested very convenient on the bottom. She was no problem at all, not with her napper taking her weight, and all he had to do was keep hold of her ankles, which he did, and as gentle as a baby, with just a finger and thumb round each one. Mind, she waggled a bit under the water, but only for a few ticks. Well, the surprise and the shock helped to make it nice and quick, which I fancied you'd be in favour of, eh, matey?'

'In favour?' breathed Herbert.

'Well, she had been yer wife for a good many years, 'Erbert, and I know you've got feelings,' said Muscles. 'Just a bleedin' pity she didn't appreciate you. Still, all's well that ends well, she's gorn now. Me friend, yer contract man, laid her out in the bath with a cake of soap, took 'er nightie off, and off he went with it. Didn't want to leave it on her, yer see. Might have looked suspicious. He took it home to his missus, and I daresay she hung it on her yard line to dry out. Of course, he met me in a pub later to let me know the job was done. Well, we had an appointment there, anyways, with the landlord at chucking-out time. By the way, I paid Cabbage Ears on your behalf. Forty quid.'

'What?' said Herbert, aghast.

'No, I told a lie, blowed if I didn't,' said Muscles. 'Forty-five quid. Well, five for travelling expenses.'

'Travelling expenses?'

'Give or take a bob or two,' said Muscles. 'Still, all that can come out of me share of what you sold yer shop for. Say a half-share, 'Erbert, as soon as we get to Ossie. I'm stowage aboard this here ship, by the way, I'm tucking meself down in that there lifeboat at night.' He pointed. 'I ain't exactly comf'table, but you bring me some rations each night when it's dark and I'll put up with the inconvenience. In Australia, I'll be the first off the ship, I know how to manage that, and I'll be waiting for you, old cock, for you and yer welcoming widow. And yer bank balance. Well, half of it.'

'You ought to be hung up on meat hooks,' breathed Herbert. 'I never at any time asked you to have my wife murdered.'

'Now then, 'Erbert, you didn't say no to me offer to do you a good turn, and when a friend don't say no, it means yes, don't it? Course it does.'

The ship was steaming on through the night, churning water, and Herbert was sweating all over. He turned to the rail, put his arms along it and stared down again at the pale wake. Muscles turned with him, put his elbows on the rail and dropped his large chin into his cupped hands.

'I've got you on my bloody back,' said Herbert.

'Course you ain't, 'Erbert, you got me for your best friend,' said Muscles, and chuckled again.

Herbert moved like lightning then to put

314

himself behind Muscles. He stooped, took hold of him by his ankles, and heaved upwards. Despite his size and his weight, Muscles parted company from the deck, and because his elbows were on the rail and he was caught completely off guard, he cartwheeled over the side. Herbert let go and there was a choking gasp of maddened panic as Muscles plunged down and hit the foaming wake.

Man overboard, thought Herbert, and turned to examine the promenade deck. It was empty. Well, hard luck on Muscles Boddy. A stowaway, he wasn't on the passenger list. He wouldn't be missed because his presence aboard hadn't been registered.

Herbert walked towards a companionway. A ship's officer appeared.

'A fine night, sir,' he said.

'There's an ocean of fresh air out here,' said Herbert, 'and it's been doing me the world of good.'

'And there's a lot more to come,' smiled the officer.

'I suppose there is,' said Herbert, 'it's a long way to Sydney. I'm turning in now. Goodnight.'

'Goodnight, sir.'

Herbert went down to his cabin.

The ship steamed on.

Muscles Boddy, having escaped being sucked

into the mincing machine of the propellers, was nevertheless dead from drowning. He had come to the surface, however, and was floating like a large porpoise on a gentle swell.

THE END

ESCAPE TO LONDON
by Mary Jane Staples

Austria, 1938. Anne watches in horror as Hitler's
tanks roll through the streets of Vienna, amid
crowds of cheering supporters. Her embittered
ex-husband, now a fervent member of the Nazi
cause, is among the cavalcade – he is burning with
hatred for Anne, seeing her as a symbol of the old
Austrian empire he once served. Then a chance
encounter with a British journalist leaves Anne with
a secret that must be smuggled out of the country,
and Anne knows that she must forsake her beloved
Vienna and flee with her children to Britain.

In a thrilling journey that will separate sisters and
brothers, parents and children, Anne and her family
escape to freedom, to dream of a reunion
in far-away London.

A gripping story from the well-loved author
of the Adams family novels

9780552151108

CORGI BOOKS

THE SOLDIER'S GIRL
by Mary Jane Staples

Pretty young Maisie Gibbs is a conscientious young
woman, though life is harder since both her parents
passed away. She is relieved when she finds a
position as a housemaid in Kensington, under the
watchful eye of the formidable housekeeper,
Mrs Carpenter, and she quickly settles in.

When she meets a handsome young soldier, she is
tempted to give him his marching orders. But
gradually Corporal Daniel Adams starts to win her
over. When tragedy strikes the Fairfax household,
Maisie is lucky she has Daniel to rely on – a
good sign of things to come?

A delight for fans of the Adams family – the
heartwarming story of Daniel and Chinese Lady.

9780552154444

CORGI BOOKS

532

'I'm here to ruin my reputation, Cade,' she announced firmly. 'With you.'

Stunned by that scandalous notion, Cade couldn't speak.

But Violet didn't seem to mind.

'I'm here to make some thrilling memories,' she went on, 'and maybe change my future while I'm at it. And we've already wasted a great deal of time, so…' perkily, she smiled '…shall we get started?'

AUTHOR NOTE

Thank you for reading THE HONOUR-BOUND GAMBLER! I'm so happy to share this story with you. I always fall in love with all my characters while writing about them, and Cade and Violet were no exception. They quickly found a special place in my heart—as did Tobe, Reverend Benson, Adeline, Judah…and even that mysterious rascal Simon Blackhouse!

If you enjoyed this story (and I hope you did!), please try another book in my *Morrow Creek* series. It includes MAIL-ORDER GROOM, THE BRIDE RAFFLE, and several others (including some short stories), all set in and around my favourite Old West town.

You can learn about all my books at my website: www.lisaplumley.com. While you're there you can also download a complete book list, sign up for new-book alerts, read sneak previews of forthcoming books, request special reader freebies, and more. I hope you'll stop by today!

Also, as always, I'd love to hear from you! You can send an e-mail to lisa@lisaplumley.com, 'friend' me on Facebook at https://www.facebook.com/pages/Lisa-Plumley/164790176872702, follow me on Twitter @LisaPlumley, or write to me c/o PO Box 7105, Chandler, AZ 85246-7105, USA.

THE
HONOUR-BOUND
GAMBLER

Lisa Plumley

First published in Great Britain 2013
by Mills & Boon, an imprint of Harlequin (UK) Limited.
Harlequin (UK) Limited, Eton House, 18-24 Paradise Road,
Richmond, Surrey TW9 1SR

© Lisa Plumley 2013

ISBN: 978 0 263 89834 7

Harlequin (UK) policy is to use papers that are natural, renewable and recyclable products and made from wood grown in sustainable forests. The logging and manufacturing process conform to the legal environmental regulations of the country of origin.

Printed and bound in Spain
by Blackprint CPI, Barcelona

When she found herself living in modern-day Arizona Territory, **Lisa Plumley** decided to take advantage of it—by immersing herself in the state's fascinating history, visiting ghost towns and historical sites, and finding inspiration in the desert and mountains surrounding her. It didn't take long before she got busy creating light-hearted romances like this one, featuring strong-willed women, ruggedly intelligent men, and the unexpected situations that bring them together.

When she's not writing, Lisa loves to spend time with her husband and two children, travelling, hiking, watching classic movies, reading, and defending her trivia-game championship. She enjoys hearing from readers, and invites you to contact her via e-mail at lisa@lisaplumley.com, or visit her website at www.lisaplumley.com

Previous novels by the same author:

THE DRIFTER
THE MATCHMAKER*
THE SCOUNDREL*
THE RASCAL*
MARRIAGE AT MORROW CREEK*
   (part of Holiday Temptation anthology)
MAIL-ORDER GROOM*
THE HONEY-MED BRIDE*
SOMETHING BORROWED, SOMETHING TRUE
   (part of Weddings Under a Western Sky anthology)

*Morrow Creek series

And coming soon from Lisa Plumley's historical Undone! eBooks:

WANTED: MAIL-ORDER MISTRESS

To John, with all my love,
now and forever.

Chapter One

❦

Morrow Creek, northern Arizona Territory
October 1884

"A gambler is nothing but a man who makes his living out of hope."

—*William Bolitho*

From the moment he saw the boy, dirty faced and shabbily dressed, Cade Foster knew he was in trouble. Darting a glance at the middling horse, wagon and foot traffic surrounding him in the territorial backwater he'd arrived at this afternoon, Cade frowned. He stepped sideways, intent on making a detour.

The little sharper moved in the same direction. "Wanna try your luck, mister? I got me a nickel says I'm luckier than you."

Unhappily distracted, Cade glanced down at the coin the boy brandished. It looked cleaner than all the rest of the urchin combined. From his grimy fingernails to his shabby shirt, the boy looked powerfully worse for wear. Unfortunately, he also looked a little like Judah. Maybe that's why Cade stopped.

The boy grinned, revealing a smile that jabbed at Cade's heart like a sterling-silver knuckle-duster. "Ain't nothing finer than a fast game of craps, sir." The boy, probably twelve years of age or a little more, extracted a pair of dice from his trouser pocket. With élan he shook them in his scrawny fist. "How 'bout we toss 'em over yonder, where it's quiet?"

He nodded toward the nearest alleyway. Hesitating, Cade squinted up the main street toward the two-story brick house that was his destination. All Morrow Creek's movers and shakers were expected to be at the benefit being held there tonight, during which the Territorial Benevolent Association Grand Fair would raise funds for a new public lending library.

"You got yer roulette, el Sapo, rondo, rouge et noir, faro, and vingt-et-un—" the boy rattled off the names of those popular games of chance the way most youngsters recited their

ABCs "—but for a fast win and real excitement nothin' beats craps, sir."

Transferring his gaze to the child again, Cade noted the boy's hollow cheeks and the dark smudges below his eyes. He saw the way the pint-size "sporting man" hunched his skinny shoulders against the autumn chill. He assessed the boy's nimble movements even as he listened to more of the imp's patter.

"If you roll those bones as ably as you talk," Cade interrupted, "I'd be a fool to strike a wager with you."

"You'd be a fool *not* to, you mean. It's just a nickel."

To a boy like that, a nickel was the difference between eating and going to bed hungry. Cade knew that more than most.

He also knew, with another proficient glance, that the dice the youngster jiggled were likely a pair of dispatchers—so named because they effectively "dispatched" their intended targets: suckers. Like all gambling men, Cade recognized the tools of a cheat. There was no other way to assure himself a square game.

Not that he ever expected to actually get one. Cade reckoned that every game he went up against was crooked one way or another. But if he ever wanted to find Whittier, he had to follow the gambling circuit. Tonight, at least a few of its members would be scouting for prospects—and showing off—at the Grand Fair. Once Cade made his way up the street to that big brick house, he'd have to do his best to impress them.

Winning was the only way to progress up the circuit—to make it to the high-stakes tables where men like Whittier wagered.

Not that throwing dice with this youngster would help Cade do that. He should have tried harder to go around him—regardless of the boy's resemblance to Judah. Now it was too late.

When Cade glanced up again, wondering if he could sidestep the kid without taking too hard a punch to his conscience, the boy was shrewdly studying his watch chain. Doubtless he was envisioning the expensive gold Jürgensen timepiece—a particular favorite of professional gambling men—that dangled at its tail…and wondering if he could win it.

Seeing no other choice, Cade nodded. He ambled to the alleyway with the boy leading the way. They set their wager.

"I'm in a hurry." Cade nodded. "Go on and roll."

Smartly, the boy refused. "Let me see your nickel first."

Obligingly, Cade produced a coin. On the verge of throwing it in their makeshift kitty, he frowned. "Tell you what," he said in a tone of studied carelessness. "A nickel's not much of a bet. I'll put up my coat in this bargain, too." He was happy to forfeit the damn thing if it would keep this urchin warm for the coming wintertime. That was the least his problematic conscience demanded. "Just to keep things interesting."

"Yeah?" The boy jabbed up his chin. His eyes gleamed with wanting Cade's warm coat, but his decidedly unchildlike sense of skepticism demanded more. "What do you want of mine, then?"

Cade thought about it. "I want those fine dice of yours."

Reluctantly, the scamp examined his pair of clinkers. He'd probably been earning all the sustenance he had with them. He appeared disinclined to part with them. But the kid would be better off without those cheaters in his hands. They'd only get him in trouble. Nobody was likely to keep the boy from earning some much-needed money with fast gambling—and truthfully, Cade wasn't inclined to try—but at least the practice could be made safer. With a keener pair of loaded or expertly shaved dice—like the pair Cade kept ready in his coat pocket, for instance—the boy's subterfuge would be less detectable. All Cade had to do was slip them to the little sharper, easy as pie.

If the morals of helping a child to cheat were supposed to have bothered him, Cade guessed he was past repentance. Because this boy reminded him of his brother—of those hellacious orphan trains the two of them had been shoved onto and the hopes they'd had crushed for all those long-ago months—and he'd be damned if he'd let one small boy shiver for the sake of his own need for a heavenly reward.

Besides, the boy's future marks weren't any concern of Cade's. Any man who would set out to purposely bilk a down-on-his-luck child at gambling deserved to lose a few coins. Cade wasn't that man. But the boy didn't know that and never would.

At the child's continuing reluctance to strike a weightier wager, Cade heaved a sigh. "No deal? Fine. I'm late already."

"Oh? You goin' to Miss Benson's gala benefit?"

"You stalling for time? It's an easy bet. Yes or no?"

The boy toed the dirt. He eyed Cade's coat. "Add in that nice watch of yours too, an' you got yourself a good wager."

Against all reason, Cade admired the boy's pluck. "I won this watch in the biggest game of my life. It's sentimental."

"You sayin' no? 'Cause I ain't familiar with sentiment."

If Cade had been a softer man, that admission would have broken his heart. As it was, he only sobered his expression, then shook his head. "You can't have my watch."

The boy shrugged. Appearing resigned, he shook his fistful of rigged dice. With elaborate showmanship, he yelled, "Hold on to yer britches then, sir! Here comes the first roll, gents!"

Too late, Cade realized they'd drawn a clump of onlookers. In the shadows cast by the setting sun, four strangers watched as the dice spewed from the boy's hand, rolled on the ground, bounced theatrically from the nearest lumber wall, then stopped.

A five-spot and a one-spot winked up. Another roll, then.

Cannily, the boy let himself lose the first several throws. All the while, he kept up an animated pitch—a talk meant to reel in Cade and keep him wagering even after he began losing. Such tactics were all part of the game—a prelude to the inevitable swindle after which the boy would walk away victorious.

If a grown man had tried such tactics on Cade, he wouldn't have been so patient. There was a reason he carried a derringer, two wicked blades and a surfeit of suspicion wherever he went.

As the alleyway grew darker and the dice rolled on, side bets sprung up among the spectators. Money rapidly changed hands; good-natured insults were traded along with the wagers. Cade wasn't surprised. In the West, gambling was as common as breathing. After all, what was mining if not wagering that you'd find more gold than dirt in the nearby hills? Compared with wielding a pickax, pitching dice was hardly backbreaking.

As the dice rolled again, a sharp breeze whirled into the alleyway. The boy shivered. So did Cade. He'd upped the ante on their wager several times already. Now it was time to end this.

"My turn." Cade accepted the dice. Deftly, he switched them for the pair from his coat pocket. He rolled. Then he swore.

Exactly as he'd planned, he'd lost everything.

"I won! I won!" the kid crowed. "I get your coat, mister!"

The boy's eyes shone up at him. In that moment, Cade didn't mind that he'd made himself late for the Grand Fair. Then the urchin deliberately schooled his expression into his previous toughness, Cade remembered that he was a hard-nosed gambler who was in town only long enough to find the man he'd hunted through several states and territories...and the world righted itself.

"Tough break," a bystander commiserated. "You was just coming back, mister. You ain't got no kind of luck, do you?"

At that, Cade grinned, pinned by an unexpected sense of irony. This time, with the boy, he'd lost on purpose. But he *hadn't* enjoyed his usual run of good luck lately—that was true.

In fact, if his current unlucky streak continued, Cade didn't know what he'd do. He was *so* close to finagling a way into the high-stakes gambling circuit he'd been chasing. He desperately needed to keep up with that league of professionals.

It was the only way to find Whittier. He ran with that circuit; if not for his vaunted appearances at the table, he might as well have been a ghost. The minute rumors had flown that he'd been spotted here, in Morrow Creek, Cade had pulled foot for the town, too, hoping to catch up with him.

Besides, Cade had already tried everything else he could think of to track the man. His more legitimate search methods had turned up nothing.

"Well, it's like I always say," Cade told the bystanders, "if you must play, decide upon three things at the start—the rules of the game, the stakes…and the quitting time." As he spoke, he slipped off his overcoat. He dropped it, covertly divested of all the items he wanted to keep, on the boy's shoulders. "Now it's quitting time."

"What? You ain't even gonna try to win your money back?"

"Not tonight." Cade turned away. Behind him, he heard two awestruck whistles and several gruff, gossipy murmurs. Whoever said women were the only ones with flapping jaws was dead wrong.

"Hell! I'd say we got ourselves a new sporting man in town, boys!" one of the local men said with a chortle. "And he's droppin' money like he's got holes in his pockets, too."

The urchin ignored the chattering men. He chased down Cade, the oversize coat trailing on the ground behind him, then tugged at his suit sleeve. "Hey, mister! I know I won and all, but...I don't reckon you meant to leave *this* behind. I found it in your coat pocket."

He held up a wad of greenbacks, fastened with an ivory clip, which Cade had won off a cotton merchant down South.

Cade *had* meant to leave that money with the ragamuffin. He didn't have much use for his winnings—aside from their ability to stake his reputation, admit him into the elite high rollers' circle and eventually get him invited into their next private faro tournament. If he was lucky, that's where he'd find Whittier. Cade had already skimmed off a sufficient quantity of cash for his own incidentals. He had a fair bankroll set aside at his hotel. And there was always his benefactor, Simon Blackhouse, to rely on if he needed more funding, too.

But what concerned Cade now wasn't his own well-being. Because behind the boy, out of sight of his stupefied gaze, all those onlookers stared at Cade's carelessly lost money with hungry eyes. Surely they wouldn't actually *steal* from a *child*?

Cade didn't know. All he knew was that

some things—not many, in his experience, but some—weren't wagering material.

"You show me how to get to the Territorial Benevolent Association Grand Fair," Cade said, "and you can keep it all."

Wide-eyed, the boy nodded. Quick as a wink, he shoved the wad of cash down his pants for safekeeping. "For this much scratch I'll take you there myself! But I ain't stayin'. I done heard of kids bein' lured in by Miss Benson and then they ain't never seen again! I don't want no reformer gettin' ahold of me."

Cade only shrugged. "I don't care much for those do-gooder types myself." He started walking, with the boy eagerly dogging his every booted step. Something about the urchin's sudden devotion bothered him, but Cade shrugged that off, too. "Give me a bottle of mescal, a pretty girl, a fair hand and a chance to square off against Lady Luck, and I don't need much else."

The boy skipped ahead, belatedly taking the lead as he'd agreed to do. He pointed to their destination. "The fair's up yonder at that ole' brick house." He eyed Cade. "You fixin' to steal all the raffle money for the new library or somethin'?"

"Nope. I've never stolen anything in my life.

I've never had to, and I'm not starting now."
Speaking in all honesty, Cade leveled his gaze
on the house. Morrow Creek residents came
and went in all their meager territorial finery.
Music and lights spilled from inside, foretell-
ing exactly the frolic he expected. "I'm here
for something even better than raffle money."

The boy scoffed. "*Nothing's* better than
money."

"At least one thing is," Cade disagreed.

At that, the boy made a disgusted face.
"What? *Love?*"

Cade laughed. "Nope. Not love."

He wasn't even sure what love was. He cared
for Judah; that was true. Everyone else he kept
at arm's length for good reason.

"If it ain't money, and it ain't love, then what
is it you're after?" the child demanded to know.

"Answers," Cade told him. "I want answers."

Then, for the fourth time in as many months,
he headed toward the celebration he hoped
might change his life...all over again.

Standing at the edge of the boisterous Territorial Benevolent Association Grand Fair
with her toes tapping and her arms full of dis-
carded shawls, wraps and overcoats, Violet
Benson felt like nothing so much as a human

coat hanger—a coat hanger who wanted desperately to join in the fun.

All around her, the finest and largest house in all of Morrow Creek was packed to the gills with revelers. Her friends and neighbors were dancing, drinking and trying their luck at the evening's games of chance, including the fancifully painted wheel of fortune donated by Jack Murphy. Now that the device wasn't situated in his saloon, even the ladies felt free to place bets. Violet hadn't yet done so herself, but she thought she might later if she ever divested herself of her burden.

"Oh! Violet! How nice to see you!" One of her longtime friends bustled over, all smiles. "Are you collecting wraps? Here—take mine." She flung off her lace shawl, then added it to the pile in Violet's arms. "You're so kind. Thanks so much!"

"You're welcome." Rearranging the wraps, Violet glanced at her friend's dance card. A number of gentlemen's names adorned it already. "My, look at your card! Aren't you popular tonight."

"Yes!" Her friend beamed. "My card is almost full already, and I've only just arrived. But *you* must be in demand, too!"

In unison, their gazes dropped to the dance

card at the very tips of Violet's fingers. She hadn't even claimed it by printing her own name in the designated space at the top yet. She'd been too busy fancifully perusing her card's many blank *partner* spaces—imagining lots of suitors writing in their names with the small ribbon-attached pencil—when the first partygoer, another friend, had assigned her his overcoat for safekeeping.

Unfortunately her dance card remained conspicuously empty.

"Well—" her friend offered a cheering grin "—don't worry. It's early yet. Partners will be clamoring for you later on!"

Gamely, Violet grinned back. They both knew that wasn't likely. As far as people in Morrow Creek were concerned, Violet—the minister's plain-featured daughter—was better suited to doing good works than enjoying good times. Eventually, Violet reasoned, she would adjust herself completely to that fate.

In the meantime, she couldn't quit tapping her toes. The latest song was a fully frolicsome one, and she loved dancing.

"Look! I see Adeline Wilson and Clayton Davis!" her friend exclaimed. "I must congratulate them on their engagement."

Just like that, Violet was left alone again,

stuck pinning up a wall with her shoulder
blades and pining for a chance to dance. She
watched as her very best friend, Adeline Wilson, gracefully accepted a fresh dose of congratulations, appearing typically beautiful
and amiable all the while. Everything that Violet was *not*, Adeline *was*: pretty, dainty and
sought-after.

But Violet possessed her own good qualities, she reminded herself staunchly. She was
kindhearted, brave and intelligent. She was effective in her charity work. She was clever. She
truly enjoyed doing good works. She had many
close friends, as well.

So what if she had an empty dance card?
That didn't matter.

Except it *did* matter, Violet admitted to herself as she heaved a resigned sigh and went to
put away all those bundled overcoats. In her
heart of hearts, it mattered a great deal. Worthy pursuits were rewarding, that was true; but
so was dancing!

There was nothing to be done about her
empty dance card now, though. Nor was there
any point in torturing herself with it any longer. Almost to the cloakroom, Violet tossed her
dance card toward a nearby trash bin.

Likely there were several helpful tasks

she ought to be doing anyway, and there'd be cleaning up to do later, too.

She should concentrate on practical matters, just as she always did…and leave the daydreaming to women like Adeline—women who stood a chance of having their fantasies come true.

At the conclusion of his initial assessment of the Territorial Benevolent Association Grand Fair, Cade noticed the woman who tossed away a dance card. With nimble movements, Cade snatched the card from midair. He was surprised to see it was empty. But empty or full, that didn't matter for his purposes.

A man never knew when an accoutrement of belonging someplace, like a dance card, would come in handy. With a cursory glance at the primly dressed woman, Cade pocketed it. It might prove useful as an introduction to a conversation later.

He didn't know anyone in Morrow Creek; except for his sponsor, the notoriously private Simon Blackhouse, Cade was alone. That's why he'd made it a point to perform his usual analysis with extra caution, identifying every entrance and exit and cataloging every potentially dangerous character in attendance. A man couldn't be too prepared. As Cade patted down his pristine suit coat pocket, assuring himself the empty dance card was secure, he reminded himself a man couldn't be too vigilant either. In his line of work, surprises could be deadly.

Despite his expectations, though, it seemed the Grand Fair was nothing more than an ordinary rural raffle. On the stage across the ballroom, a wire cage held the raffle entries, ready for the drawing. A locked cash box stood beside it; foolishly, there was no guard in the vicinity to protect its contents. Near the refreshments table, partygoers bid on cakes and pies and other wholesome goodies. Banners and bunting hung gaily from the rafters. Gullible townspeople danced blithely beneath them.

To Cade's jaundiced eye, the whole place seemed improbably virtuous. But no place was *that* good. No *person* was that good. Hell, even that mousy woman with her armful of coats and her downcast gaze probably had scandalous secrets to tell.

Cade simply needed to look closer. If he did, he knew he'd find the bad behavior he expected—and along with it, the inevitable wagering that he hoped would lead him to the elusive Percy Whittier—professional gambler, runaway family man and odds-on favorite to win the upcoming private faro tournament.

Unless, of course, Cade got to Whittier first.

And that's exactly what he'd promised to do.

Another circuit of the Grand Fair later, after a few informative chats, some flirting and a bolt of whiskey, Cade found it: his first proper game of chance in Morrow Creek.

It was time to get to work.

Sliding in place between a dandified farmer—whose Saturday night shirt couldn't disguise the grime of Friday's labor—and a soberly dressed minister, Cade flexed his fingers. He offered his most charming smile. Then he hoped like hell his unlucky streak was at an end, because he needed a win.

Chapter Two

As typically happened at parties, Violet found herself at the spinsters' table in short order. She'd already made the rounds of the gala's volunteer helpers, offering her assistance wherever it was needed. She'd sat in with a fiddle for one of the musicians' simpler songs at the horn player's urgings. She'd also earned hearty laughs among the members of the ladies' auxiliary club with her anecdotes about baking apple-spice jumbles as her contribution to the Grand Fair bake sale. Now she was earnestly engaged in boosting the spirits of her fellow wallflowers. She simply couldn't stand seeing anyone unhappy.

"Even if we *don't* do any dancing tonight," Violet was telling the women nearest her, "that doesn't mean we have to abandon the notion of fun altogether! The evening is still young. Besides, I'm having a wonderful time talking with you!"

The town's most outspoken widow, Mrs. Sunley, snorted over her glass of mescal. "That's very kind of you, Miss Benson. But *I'd* prefer to trot around in the arms of a handsome young buck."

Everyone tittered. Mrs. Sunley typically spoke her mind, sometimes to the point of impropriety. Privately, Violet admired her for it— and for her enviable sense of independence, too. Most likely, her own future would be similar to Mrs. Sunley's, Violet knew—save the aforesaid marriage to begin it, of course.

"That would be delightful, Mrs. Sunley," Violet agreed, "*if* there were any handsome new 'young bucks' here in town."

"Oh! But there *is* a handsome new man in town!" one of the wallflowers said. "We were talking about him earlier!"

At that, everyone launched into a spirited dissertation of the mystery man's rugged good looks, sophisticated suit and rakish air of *je ne sais quoi*. One woman described his smile ("It made me dizzy! I swear it did!"); another rhapsodized over his masculine demeanor ("My brother, Big Horace, looked like a wee girl standing next to him!"); a third waxed lyrical about his elegant manners ("Yes! He *bowed* to me, just like a gentleman in a *Harper's Weekly* story! I almost swooned on the spot!").

"I think he must be here for the private faro tournament," one woman confided in hushed tones. "I heard from my Oscar that all the finest sporting men are coming to town to participate."

Everyone nodded in approbation. Out West, professional gamblers were accorded a great deal of respect, especially when they were winning. Even Jack Murphy, one of Morrow Creek's most reputable citizens, employed professional sporting men to run the tables at his saloon.

"I'll bet he's a big winner!" someone said, still prattling on about the mysterious stranger. "He certainly looked it, with that self-assured air he had. And those *eyes*!"

The women all sighed with romantic delight. Even curmudgeonly Mrs. Sunley fluttered her fan in a coquettish fashion. The gossip went on, but Violet couldn't help laughing.

"Gambler or not, no man is *that* fascinating," she insisted. "In my experience, men are usually clumsy, smelly, unable to properly choose their own neckties and in dire need of moral rehabilitation—which my father is always happy to provide."

"You've been meeting all the wrong men," a friend said.

"Or all the right ones," Mrs. Sunley put in with a knowing grin. "The most interesting men need a little reforming."

Tactfully, no one mentioned that it didn't matter which men Violet met. With a few notable and short-term exceptions, most men hadn't seen her as a potential sweetheart; instead, they'd usually approached her for an introduction to the beautiful Adeline Wilson. Now that Adeline was officially engaged to Clayton Davis, even that role had become obsolete.

As everyone belatedly pondered that dismal realization, silence fell. All the wallflowers exchanged embarrassed glances. Violet studied her still-tapping toes, wishing she didn't make people feel so awkward. Another friend cleared her throat.

"Speaking of moral rehabilitation," she said into the uncomfortable silence, evidently hoping to end it quickly, "where could I find your father? I have something to discuss with him. I saw him earlier, but he seems to have disappeared."

"He has?" Newly concerned, Violet bit her lip. All thoughts of the dazzling, wholly unlikely new mystery man—and her own unpopularity with such men—were forgotten. At an event like this one, chockablock with wheels of fortune, raffle tickets and—undoubtedly—backroom wagering, there was only one place Reverend Benson would likely be found. "Don't worry. I'll find him," she told her friend. "I'll ask him to speak with you straightaway."

Then, scarcely waiting for her friend to acknowledge her offer, Violet excused herself from the wallflowers' circle. She suddenly had a mission more important than consoling her fellow nondancing, non-sought-after companions: finding her father before he did something foolish.

Cade was down almost three hundred dollars when the first of his gambling companions quit. In disgust, the man hurled down his cards. His chair scraped back. "You keep 'em. I'm out."

The other men at the table protested. Cade did not. After a little conversation, a little gambling and much careful observation, he knew the man's retreat had been inevitable. Like the grubby farmer and the soft-handed minister who remained at the table, the man had been in over his head. All the same, Cade had the good sense and the good manners to keep his gaze fixed on the baize-covered table, tabulating the money in the kitty.

His unlucky streak had not yet ended. Nothing less than an impressive win would get him invited to the private, high-stakes faro tables where he expected to find Percy Whittier and to make him pay for his sins. With so much at stake, Cade couldn't relax. He couldn't quit. He couldn't fold. He could only focus on the game with the same taut intensity he always employed.

The departing man opened the back room's door. The lively sounds of the Grand Fair's music and dancing swept inside. So did the earthy, aromatic scent of Kentucky's finest tobacco.

Nostrils flaring, Cade looked up.

He knew that blend. Its fragrance was melded with his earliest memories. It was forever tied to loneliness and loss…and to questions he'd never been able to find the answers to.

It was the signature blend smoked by Percy Whittier.

Frozen in place, Cade stared blindly at his

cards. Could he be this lucky? He'd believed the rumor had been true. He'd believed Whittier was in Morrow Creek; otherwise, Cade wouldn't have come there, with or without Simon Blackhouse's aid. But to find Whittier by chance this way, *tonight*...

It defied the odds laid in by even the most hopeful gambler. And Cade had never been hopeful.

Hope was for people who fooled themselves into forgetting the truth: that life was short, fickle and cruel. More than anyone, Cade knew better than to put his faith in long odds. Doubtless, he told himself as he went on studying his hand, many men smoked that particular Kentucky blend, not just Whittier.

An instant later, a burst of raucous fiddle music restored his usual sense of purpose. What was he doing just sitting there?

Anyone looking at him would have thought Cade didn't *really* want to find Whittier. The notion was daft. He might not be hopeful, Cade reminded himself, but he *was* determined. He'd made promises to Judah. He intended to keep them or die trying.

"I'm out, too." Heart pounding, Cade made himself stand. He schooled his face in an impassive expression, needing to hide the damnably naive hopefulness he felt. The answers he needed felt tantalizingly close. "Night, all. Good luck, Reverend."

Startled, the minister glanced up. He couldn't have known that Cade had already taken pity on his foolish wagering and slipped him an "improving" card when everyone else had been watching their easily defeated companion leave the game. But Cade knew it. He hoped the minister took the boon and quit, too. Otherwise, the way he'd been wagering, he'd lose for sure.

Cade hadn't wanted to let that happen. Not because the minister was a holy man; Cade didn't have much use for preaching. But according to their chin-wagging, the widowed minister had a daughter—as it happened, the same mousy woman who'd tossed away her dance card—and Cade hadn't wanted the man's family to pay for his witlessness.

Giving the minister that improving card had meant setting back his own game, Cade knew. But he'd had faith he could regain his edge. The hapless holy man didn't have the same advantage.

The door creaked. Through the slowly narrowing gap in the doorway, Cade glimpsed swirls of dancers, a wisp of smoke...and the profile of a cigar-smoking man. Was it really Whittier?

Cade couldn't be certain. In Omaha, he'd spooked Whittier with a too-aggressive pursuit. He'd lost him for weeks. Now Cade had to be smarter. Otherwise, he might ruin his advantage.

As far as he knew, Whittier didn't know Cade was still in pursuit of him. Cade meant to keep it that way...until he caught up altogether.

"Don't forget our weekly game at the Lorndorff!" one of the men called from behind him. "We can always use one more man."

"'Specially a losing man!" Another yokel gambler guffawed.

Too intent to argue with their wrongheaded assessment of his skills, Cade raised his hand in acknowledgment of their invitation. It wasn't quite the wagering offer he needed, but he reckoned it was a start. From here, word of his ability would travel upward to the elite circuit and eventually—he hoped—garner him an invitation to those sought-after tables.

Decisively, Cade slipped into the giddy fray of the Grand Fair. He was almost close enough, he saw, to identify Whittier for certain. With only a faded tintype and his own hazy memory to go on, it was hard to tell. But the smell of the man's distinctive tobacco blend tantalized Cade with its nearness.

He needed a plan. The moment he saw the minister's daughter—no longer burdened with overcoats—determinedly on her way to the back room, Cade hit upon one. This time, he would keep his distance from Whittier until the moment was right. This time, he would be smart. This time, he would win.

In the meantime, he had to get a little closer. So...

"There you are!" Smiling, Cade pulled the woman into his arms, keeping Whittier in sight. "You're missing our dance!"

"Oh no I'm not!" the woman said. "I'd never miss a dance!"

Then, to Cade's immense relief and improbable good fortune, the woman allowed him to dance them both into the frolicsome melee... straight toward the spot where Cade had last glimpsed his quarry.

This must be what it felt like to fly, Violet thought as the handsome stranger whirled her around the dance floor. Guided by his strong arms and innate dexterity, she nearly laughed.

This was what she'd been wanting all night.

This...and maybe more.

Enchanted, Violet gazed up into the stranger's arresting face. Clearly, this was the man who'd had all the town's wallflowers aflutter. Indeed, as she examined his wavy dark hair, piercing blue eyes and impeccably arrayed features, she *did* feel a bit dizzy. A bit bedazzled. A bit swoony.

He was…*perfect*.

He delivered her an abashed smile. "Thank you for letting me sweep you away just now. I'm in your debt, Miss…?"

"Benson. Violet Benson." Beset by her rapidly galloping heartbeat, Violet sucked down a breath. She executed another turn in the dance. This had to be some sort of mistake, but she'd be jiggered if she'd miss this opportunity to kick up her heels. Politely, she asked, "And you are?"

"Cade Foster. I'm very pleased to meet you, Miss Benson."

Hearing her name on his lips made Violet feel downright light-headed. How did he manage to make her ordinary name sound so extraordinarily intimate? So intriguing? So… wonderful?

On the verge of asking him exactly that question, Violet stopped herself. Instead she blurted, "You're new in town."

It was not a smooth entrée to further conversation. But a person would not have guessed as much to look at Cade Foster's appealing smile—a smile that engaged twin dimples in his cheeks.

"Not anymore." He tightened his hand on hers, sweeping them both in an elegant arc across the room. "In your company, Miss Benson, I suddenly feel quite welcomed to Morrow Creek."

Goodness, he was charming. And he was charming *her*! Awed by the realization, Violet prayed her feet wouldn't lose all sense of rhythm. She glanced downward. Blessedly, her feet seemed to be keeping up very well…even while the rest of her dithered.

"Well, I have that effect on people," she confessed. "My friends say I'm a veritable one-woman hospitality committee. Probably owing to all my charity work. You see, I do a great deal of volunteering among the destitute, the sick, the needy—"

"They're fortunate to have you. As am I, tonight."

"Oh. Now you're teasing me."

"Not at all." Mr. Foster danced them both near the raffle cage and its attendant cash box.

"I'm enjoying you. I think you're enjoying me, too—at least if your smile is any proof."

Caught, Violet tried to tamp down her wide, telltale smile. But it was no use. It was simply too delightful to be *flirted with* this way! Especially by such a dashing man. Also, she couldn't help noticing that several conversations had quit at the edge of the dance floor. A few dancers had even slowed to gawk. The whole place, it seemed, was fixated on Violet and her gallant dance partner. The sensation was altogether novel.

She, Violet Benson, was the center of attention!

This must be what her friend Adeline experienced every day.

Encouraged by that realization, Violet gazed up at him. "My smile doesn't prove a thing about my supposed feelings for you, Mr. Foster," she said in her most coquettish tone. Until now she had only employed that tone in her imagination. It felt much more fun in truth. "I always smile when performing a good deed. It makes me happy to lend a hand to those in need."

Mr. Foster appeared dumbfounded. "Charity? You're likening *me* to a charity case?" He raised his eyebrows. "I assure you, Miss Benson, I do not need help. Not from you or anyone else."

"Are you sure?" Violet angled her head, studying him. "When you first invited me to dance, I felt sure I detected a certain air of...desperation about you. I know it sounds strange, but—"

He stumbled. For an instant, they both lost the cadence of the dance. Then his hand closed more securely around hers, they both recaptured the necessary steps, and Violet reconsidered.

Undoubtedly, Cade Foster had never been desperate for anything in his life. He seemed the sort of man for whom everything fell into place, lickety-split. Still, during those first few moments, she had definitely felt...*something* from him.

Something, if not desperate, then very, very needful.

"You move very well, Miss Benson." Cade Foster presented her with his flawless profile. If he noticed the avid stares and gossipy whispers directed their way, he gave no sign of it. "The men in town must be bereft that you threw away your dance card."

She gawked at him, all thoughts of his potential desperation forgotten. "You saw that? You saw…me?"

"Of course I did." Mr. Foster glanced sideways. He frowned. "Why did you do it? Why did you throw away your dance card?"

Still enraptured with the notion that she might *move well,* as he'd said, Violet felt a shiver race through her. *He* was the one who moved well—the one who danced with effortless poise. Cade Foster's skill was to make his partner seem equally adept.

Doubtless he possessed several similar talents…all of which would be scintillating and assured and unlikely to be shared with Violet beyond this night and this dance. Maybe that's why she let herself fling her usual caution to the wind.

"Why did I throw away my dance card? The answer to that question, Mr. Foster, will cost you another dance."

He smiled, seeming impressed. "You're bold. I wouldn't have expected that from a self-confessed do-gooder."

"I prefer 'aid worker.' And a straight answer."

Mr. Foster laughed. "And bolder still." He twirled her as the last flourish of music played.

He glanced sideways, then muttered a swear-word under his breath. "But I have to refuse."

"Why?" Violet kept her tone light. "Are you afraid I might save you with a dose of well-placed charity work?"

"No." Inexplicably, he paled. "I'm beyond redemption."

His voice sounded fraught. Troubled, Violet dared to touch his shoulder. "I'm sorry. I was being flippant. I didn't mean—"

"Take this." As the next dance began, Mr. Foster gave her something: a dance card. *Her* dance card. "You'll be needing it."

Violet boggled at it. How had he come to possess her dance card? "I don't need it. There was a reason it was empty."

He didn't seem to hear her. "Thank you for the dance."

"We could have another. I still haven't answered your—"

"Your father is headed to the mescal booth to celebrate his recent win at cards." Mr. Foster nodded. "I'm guessing you'll want to intercept him before he gets two fistfuls and a snort."

Her father? Winning and drinking? But how could Mr. Foster possibly have identified both the Reverend Benson *and* his worst foibles, all in a single glance? Confused, Violet turned.

It was true, she saw. However unaccountably, Cade Foster had summed up the situation. Papa did appear to have won.

He also appeared to be intent on memorializing his victory at the gambling table by pickling himself in locally brewed liquor. Her father, although devout and bookish by nature, had never refused a whiskey. He considered it a fair restorative.

"Next time I see you, you'll be overrun with suitors." With another beguiling smile and a touch of her hand, Cade Foster bowed to Violet. He didn't seem to realize how preposterous his statement really was. "I'm happy to have danced with you first."

Violet didn't have time to elucidate matters to him. Nor did she want to. Cade Foster had enjoyed dancing with her! Why should she spoil that by telling him that she typically spent more time decorating for parties than dancing at them?

"Thank you very much. I'm happy to have danced with you, too!" Eagerly, she nodded. "But now I really must dash!"

Then, with Cade Foster's enthralling features still dancing in her mind, Violet picked up her skirts and went to do her duty. Her turn at being belle of the ball was over. For her it was back to everyday existence—without the pleasure of a man's hand in hers to help guide her through...or to share her smiles.

"Papa!" she cried an instant later. "What have you done?"

"Violet, my dear!" Her father embraced her happily. "You're just who I wanted to see. Look! I won fistfuls of money!"

"Oh, dear." Nibbling her lip, Violet swept her father's winnings with a chary look. Probably he would add them to the collection plate on Sunday, but until then there was always the chance he would wager most or all of it. She didn't approve of gambling, but it seemed to give Papa a happiness he'd lost since the death of her poor mother years ago. "Congratulations!"

"That's my girl!" He kissed her cheek, then delivered her a quelling frown. "But shouldn't you be conducting the drawing?"

The drawing. She'd forgotten about the raffle entirely. As organizer of the gala, Violet was responsible for determining the winner and for delivering the money raised to the committee.

"Yes! I was just about to do that." Reminded of her pressing duties, Violet sighed. Dancing had been *so* much nicer!

Turning back for one last compelling look, Violet glimpsed Cade Foster striding through the dancers. He was leaving her behind just as abruptly as he'd swept her into the dance.

It was only too bad, Violet thought as she watched him go, that she'd had a taste of flying with him at all. Now she knew, for the first time ever, exactly what she'd been missing in her life.

Strangely enough, it had taken an enigmatic and downright captivating man to show her the truth: she *needed* to fly. Perhaps recklessly. Perhaps foolishly. But regularly and soon, preferably with a companion by her side. But... how?

Chapter Three

Seated across the table from Cade in his suite at the Lorndorff Hotel, Simon Blackhouse smiled. That's how Cade knew something significant was afoot. Blackhouse never smiled, not while there were cards in his hand or dice within his reach. Blackhouse took gambling as seriously as he did nothing else.

"What's the matter with you? Are you drunk?" Cade peered out the hotel suite's lavishly curtained window. A slice of autumnal blue sky greeted him. "It's only ten in the morning."

"I'm not drunk. I'm *thinking*."

"Aha. That explains it." With sham concern, Cade leaned nearer. "You're new at making an effort with things, so I should probably warn you—*thinking*, once begun, is hard to stop."

"Very funny." Unperturbed, Blackhouse smiled anew at his cards, making Cade feel doubly wary. "I can't help it if things come easily to me," his sponsor argued. "It's in my nature."

"It's in your inheritance." Cade gestured. "New game?"

With a murmur of agreement, Blackhouse rounded up the cards. He dealt. For a while, the only sounds were the ticking of the mantelpiece clock and the shuffling of cards.

At the conclusion of their game, Blackhouse smiled again.

"That's the fourth game straight you've won today." He studied Cade from over the tops of his losing cards. "You know what this means, don't you? Your unlucky streak has ended."

Cade wasn't so sure. "If I were playing a *skilled* gambler—"

"You'd still win," Blackhouse told him, ignoring his genial gibe. "You're the luckiest son of a bitch I've ever known." With his shirt half buttoned and his suit coat askew, Blackhouse seemed the very picture of privileged, happy-go-lucky young bachelorhood. "Aside from myself, of course. I'm damnably lucky, too." Appearing characteristically pleased by that, he lit a cheroot. He gazed at Cade through its upward-curling smoke. "What happened? Did you bed a Gypsy who broke the curse?"

"I wish it had been that simple. I would have done that months ago." It had been almost that long since he'd had a break in his search for Percy Whittier. Last night hadn't changed much in that regard. Cade had lost sight of Whittier while dancing with Violet Benson. Although he'd tried not to be, he'd been distracted by her—especially by her too-astute claim that he'd appeared desperate. *Desperate!* "I'm afraid the only woman I've been with lately was a naive reformer. She threatened to 'save' me." Cade shuddered at the remembrance. "I can't stand do-gooders. They remind me of orphan trains and foundling homes."

"So?" Blackhouse arched his brow. With nimble fingers, he scooped up the playing cards. "I've established a few foundling homes myself. They're not all bad." As though considering those altruistic efforts—along with the prestigious family name and attendant family fortune that had facilitated them—Blackhouse paused. He shook his head, then shuffled expertly. "A Rom woman would have been wilder," he alleged, grinning again.

Disturbed by the return of that grin, Cade

frowned, uncomfortably reminded that he didn't truly know Blackhouse well enough to discern his intentions but had to trust him anyway.

Although charming, wealthy and advantageously footloose—with a private luxury train car and a loyal valet to prove it—Blackhouse was nonetheless a mysterious figure to Cade. They had met at a poker table in San Francisco and had become friends (of a kind) while outlasting every other player at the table. When Blackhouse had unexpectedly offered to finance Cade's search for Percy Whittier, Cade had cautiously agreed. He hadn't had the stakes to continue alone. Likely, Blackhouse had known that and had decided to exploit it…for whatever reasons.

He still didn't know what Blackhouse's interest in Whittier was. Knowing Blackhouse, it was something frivolous. All Cade knew was that Blackhouse had the money, Cade had the tenacity, and between them they could bring Whittier to heel.

"I don't have time for *any* women," Cade said. "Rom or not." He told Blackhouse about spotting Whittier at the Grand Fair and about losing him during the dance. "He must still be in town."

"Yes. Faro is his game. He'd be unlikely to miss the tournament." Agreeably, Blackhouse cut the cards. He arranged them on the table between them, then nodded cannily at Cade. "Go ahead. Choose four. If you pick out all the aces, I'll lay out an extra thousand for tonight's gaming. And maybe lend you my overcoat, too." An amused look. "You seem to have lost yours."

Cade didn't take the bait. He didn't want to discuss giving his warm overcoat to the grimy-faced child sharper in the Morrow Creek alleyway. "I don't need any more of your money." *Not yet.* "Besides, the odds of choosing all four aces in a row are—"

"Inordinate. I know. That's the point." With a leisurely gesture, Blackhouse summoned Adams, his valet. "Do it."

"Fine." Exasperated, Cade flipped up four cards.

In short order, a queen and three aces stared up at him.

"See? Just as I thought." Blackhouse pointed. "Not all four aces, that's true, but still a good enough draw to prove I'm right. You should be delighted." Yawning, Blackhouse selected a postmarked envelope from the silver tray that Adams offered him. He tossed it in front of Cade. "By the way, this letter from your brother arrived this morning. I hope Judah is well?"

Cade nodded, still boggling at his chosen cards. Turning up three aces was unbelievable. "His leg should be almost healed by now." Distractedly, Cade frowned. "You must be double dealing."

Blackhouse scoffed. "I'm not double dealing. I'm not trimming cards. I'm not even wearing a holdout, despite my enthusiasm for collecting such things." He spread his arms, showing he was free of mechanical cheating devices. "It's *you,* Foster. Just you. Your usual good luck has clearly returned."

Dubiously, Cade regarded the cards. Like most sporting men, he believed in superstition. It was foolhardy and unreasonable not to. A man needed all the breaks he could get. But *this…*

"I think it must be your reformer who did it," Blackhouse opined. "She's your lucky charm. That's the only explanation."

Lucky charm. Cade could use one of those, especially now.

Still filled with disbelief, he scowled at the cards. He didn't want to agree with Blackhouse. He didn't want to believe in luck alone. But with no other leads readily available….

"Well, there's only one way to find out, isn't there?" Cade asked. "That's to find my 'lucky charm' and see what happens."

Then he threw on a necktie, grabbed his suit coat and hat, and went in search of his very own private do-gooder and (potential) good-luck charm.

God help him, he seemed to need her.

When Violet glimpsed the town newcomer, Cade Foster, from across the room at the charity kitchen she'd organized with the help of Grace Murphy and her ladies' auxiliary club, she knew she had to be imagining things… which wasn't altogether surprising, given how preoccupied she'd been since yesterday.

All afternoon long, even while ladling up soup and passing out bread donated by Molly Copeland's popular bakery, Violet had relived last night's dance at the Grand Fair. She'd recalled Cade Foster's smile. She'd remembered his features. She'd contemplated his intriguingly muscular personhood and sighed over his eyes. She'd even envisioned herself seeing him again.

So a part of her wasn't at all surprised to

catch sight of him there. The rest of her knew that she should pinch herself—especially when Cade Foster spied her, raised his hand in a masculine greeting, then determinedly headed in her direction.

"Yes!" someone whispered nearby. "It's definitely *him*!"

"Did you see them *dancing* together?" someone else added.

"I saw her *leave him* standing heartbroken on the dance floor!" a third gossip added in breathless tones. "Imagine that! Plain Violet Benson, the minister's daughter, having the cheek to turn her back on a man who's willing to dance with her!"

Well. Being the subject of such vaguely uncharitable gossip took some of the fun out of things, Violet thought. That was a new and unwelcome experience for her—one she'd helped Adeline through a time or two, though. Besides, she retorted to herself silently, she hadn't left Cade on the dance floor. She'd gone to fetch her father—it was an entirely different thing. Tightening her hold on her soup ladle, she went on watching Cade approach.

Plainly, he was close enough to hear everything her fellow helpers were saying, Violet realized. Because almost imperceptibly, he angled his head toward that chatty clump of gossips, flashed them a brief but brilliant grin, then kept right on going.

Collectively, the three women swooned. For herself, Violet only stood there with her ladle at the ready. *This,* she realized with another flutter of excitement, might be her chance to fly!

Cade Foster might be her chance to dance through *every* part of her life—her chance to have some *fun.* It was exactly what she'd yearned for at the Grand Fair last night. Violet certainly didn't have much to lose by trying something new. So that's exactly what she meant to do—beginning right now, with Cade.

Maybe the local men hadn't been able to glimpse Violet's charms past Adeline Wilson's dazzle, it occurred to her, but Cade had. That made him special. That made him worthy of joining her in her newfound quest to spread her wings.

At least that way, when she was Mrs. Sunley's age, Violet reasoned, she'd have some thrilling memories to look back on.

Oblivious to her hasty decision making, Cade reached her.

"You're a difficult woman to find." This time, his smile touched *her* alone, leaving aside her sharp-tongued cohorts. "I've been to the jailhouse, Dr. Finney's medical office, your father's church and the schoolhouse—I was told you sometimes volunteer with schoolmarm McCabe. And now here you are in the very last place I thought to look."

"Well, you always find everything in the very last place you look, don't you?" Violet couldn't help staring. She felt defenseless against his charisma, spellbound by his voice, fascinated by his just-for-her smile. With Cade Foster inside it, her charity kitchen suddenly felt much too small and meager. "If you kept on searching after that it would be silly."

Cade Foster blinked. Then he laughed. "That's true."

"You may be glib, Mr. Foster, but I'm sensible." Violet ladled up some soup for the next recipient. She gave the needy woman a smile, then received a warm thank-you in return. The line of recipients moved up a pace. "As you can see, I'm quite busy here, as well. So if you want to talk charming nonsense to me, I'm afraid you'll just have to do it later."

A shared gasp came from nearby. Evidently, her colleagues were still eavesdropping, and they fully expected her to fall at Cade's feet, lovesick with longing, at the first opportunity.

He gave her another grin. "You think I'm charming, then?"

"And glib. I also said 'glib.' Didn't you hear that part?"

"I heard it. But I don't think you believe it."

Violet smiled. "I wouldn't say it if I didn't."

"Truly?" Mr. Foster seemed intrigued by that notion, commonplace as it was. He moved closer, nearly shoulder to shoulder with her. "Do you always say exactly what you think?"

"Why not?" Violet stirred her soup. "Don't you?"

"I'm a professional sporting man, Miss Benson. I make my living on hope and happenstance. Honesty doesn't enter into it."

"It seemed to do so last night. Between us."

At her words, he seemed taken aback. "Well, I *was* honest with you about *not* being a desperate man," Mr. Foster said, "so if that's what you mean regarding honesty between us—"

"No," Violet interrupted gently. "I mean that, after we danced, you told me I would be swamped with suitors. That's what you said. *Honestly.* I didn't believe you, but you were right!" Gleefully, she confided further, "After you left the Grand Fair, I went through *two* more dance cards!"

Alone in her bedroom afterward—with

care and no small measure of disbelief—she'd pressed those signature-filled dance cards between her Bible pages for safekeeping. She'd thought they might be her only mementos of that extraordinary night. But now that Cade Foster had arrived, all broad shouldered and fascinating, at her charity kitchen, the world felt ripe with possibilities. Given his occupation, he seemed twice as likely to be capable of satisfying her urge for extra zest in her dutiful, workaday life.

"*Two* dance cards? You danced that much?" Relief softened his features, lending sparkle to his vivid eyes. "That must have been fun."

"It was unprecedented," Violet told him candidly. She handed a hunk of bread to the next recipient. "I've never danced so much in all my life! I'm sure it was because of you. By dancing with me last night, you seem to have kindled some sort of curiosity about me, Mr. Foster."

"The men in Morrow Creek aren't alone in being curious about you." Intimately, he lowered his voice. "I am, too. I haven't been able to stop thinking about you."

"I'll only be sorry when it's over." Violet sighed, still reminiscing about last night. "Before long, folks in town will forget this, and I'll be back to cheering up the wallflowers at parties while everyone else…" She paused, belatedly realizing the astonishing admission he'd made. "*You?* Thinking about *me*?"

She nearly had to use her soup ladle to close her gaping jaw. The very notion was dumbfounding. And thrilling too!

"Yes. You're going to be very important to me, Miss Benson. I can feel it." Pausing to study the visitors to the charity kitchen, Cade Foster stepped into place beside Violet. Adeptly, he handed a bowl of soup and some bread to the next person in line. The poor woman who received it nearly fainted with glee at being served by him. He didn't seem to notice her obvious ardor. "I'd like to become equally important to you, if you'll let me."

Violet flashed him a dubious look. She might be hopeful, but she was not an imbecile. Nor was she especially naive.

"You could have the company of any woman in town." As proof, Violet gestured to the other volunteers. To a woman, they were gazing swoonily, chin in hand, at Cade Foster's handsome countenance. All three of them sighed. One waved. "Do you expect me to believe that of all the ladies in town, you are interested in me? I know what I look like, Mr. Foster. As

a minister's daughter, I can't bring you a fine
dowry, either. So—"

"I'm not asking for your hand in marriage."
He seemed disturbed by her rebuttal and
maybe a mite perplexed, too. "Is there someplace we can talk about this privately?"

Violet shook her head. As much as she
wanted to be more venturesome, she did have
obligations to consider. Besides, *thinking* about
adventuring was not the same as *doing* it.

"Not unless I quit work," she said, "and
that's—"

Impossible, Violet meant to say.

But before she could, her fellow volunteers
interrupted.

"Very easily done!" one of them said.

Chattering and smiling, they stripped Violet
of her soup ladle. They untied her apron and
smoothed her upswept hair. They filled in her
place in line, then all but shoved her forcibly
out the door with the gambler. At that, Violet couldn't help forgiving them their unkind
gossip earlier. She wasn't a woman who held a
grudge. No doubt they'd simply been surprised
that she'd been so popular with Mr. Foster last
night…and today.

That made four of them. Because she was
surprised, too.

"Go on!" one of her friends urged cheerfully. "You work all the time! If anyone deserves a break, Violet, it's you."

"Yes. Have fun." Another friend winked. "We'll take care of everything here. Don't you worry about a thing. He's a gambler, isn't he? So why don't *you* take a chance for a change? On *him*!"

So, with no further avenue of protest available to her and with Cade Foster standing patiently nearby, Violet did just that: she took a chance...on a gambler.

Sitting beside Cade on a narrow bench outside the charity kitchen next to a sweeping ponderosa pine tree and a branching rivulet of the nearby creek, Violet Benson shook her head.

Plainly surprised, she asked, "You want me to do *what*?"

Cade didn't answer at first. He simply felt too distracted by what she'd said earlier: *I know what I look like, Mr. Foster.*

That admission was telling. It was, as Cade was rapidly learning, characteristically direct, too. If he'd been a crueler man, he would have used Miss Benson's feelings about her appearance to gain an advantage. As it was, Cade could only examine her through clear eyes, wondering what it must be like to live as Violet Benson did: plain featured and overlooked.

Unexpectedly, a kinship arose inside him. He knew what it felt like to be overlooked— to be left behind. He didn't want that for her or anyone.

Of a certain, Violet's pale red hair was not quite as stylishly arranged as the other ladies' was. Her complexion was a mite too ruddy to be called fashionably pale. Her teeth sported a gap in front, and her nose was too assertive to be considered strictly "pretty." But her hazel eyes were vivacious, her mouth was full and gentle looking, and her hands…

Well, her hands stirred in Cade an unlikely wish to be blessed by her touch—to be granted that salvation she'd alluded to last night when they'd danced. Appalled by the realization, he frowned. He repeated the proposition he'd just made to her.

"I want you to be my good-luck charm. To be available to me at a moment's notice before faro games and hands of poker." He spied her mistrustful expression and added, "I'll pay you for the privilege, of course. I wouldn't consider asking you to do this otherwise. It's only fair that you're compensated."

She made a face. "You really believe in good-luck charms?"

"I can't afford not to. Mine is a precarious business."

"And you believe *I* am yours?" She sounded amused. And intrigued. And unexpectedly compassionate, too. Her very presence exuded kindheartedness and care and a certain special exuberance that intrigued him. "Your good-luck charm, I mean?"

"After I met you," Cade said simply, "my luck changed."

For a moment, Violet Benson gazed across the street that bordered the charity kitchen. Wagons and buggies passed by; the clomping of hooves raised drifts of dust. Those drifts reminded Cade of cigar smoke—and of losing sight of Percy Whittier.

He might be a fool, it occurred to Cade, to ally himself with the same woman who'd disastrously distracted him from his search for Whittier last night. He hoped he didn't regret this.

"If you have enough money to pay me, why do you need luck?" Violet Benson asked astutely. "Why do you need to win at all?"

That was easy. "Because I don't gamble to win money."

"Then you're not doing it properly." She gave a pert smile.

Unable to resist as he should have done, Cade returned that smile. "I entered the gambling circuit to track down a man I'm searching for," he explained. "It's been several years now. I've come close. I've had clues and false leads and near misses. But I've never faced him across a gambling table. I've never caught up with him long enough to get what I want from him. To do that, I need to win. I need to get invited to all the best tables. I need to fit in among the men he runs with."

"If you plan to kill him, I won't help you." Suddenly chilly where she'd once been warm, Violet Benson examined him. "I'll help Sheriff Caffey track you down, in fact. I have a fair sense of what you look like, as does every other woman in town."

This time, Cade smiled more artfully. "I'm flattered by your attention," he said in a teasing tone. Deliberately, he flashed both dimples. "I have every intention of rewarding it, too, in ways I think we'd both enjoy...very, *very* much."

"Right now," Violet clarified drily, "I'm memorizing your features so I can help the deputy draw a wanted poster."

Hmm. Charming female subjects was something Cade had learned to excel at. Perversely, he felt impressed that Violet Benson appeared too levelheaded to fall for his misdirection.

"I want answers from him, that's all." Cade leveled a square look at Violet. "I want to know why he ran out on his family back East. They loved him and needed him, and he—"

Unexpectedly, Cade heard his voice break. A powerful sense of bereavement and anger and solitude welled inside him.

He scarcely knew what to make of it. Irately, he reasoned that Violet Benson and her damnable compassion had caused it. For the second time that day, he wondered if he was making a terrible mistake by coming to her—by trusting her even this far.

"He must have had a good reason for leaving," she said in a thoughtful tone, proving his caution was warranted. Naively, she added, "No man would ever abandon his family unless—"

"*Percy Whittier did.*" Hard-faced, Cade stared at her. He needed to hold on to his fury and hurt. It fueled him when he didn't want to continue searching. He didn't need Violet Benson's natural empathy to awaken something soft inside him—something that was better left to wither and die, as it had been on its way to doing before he'd met her. "Percy Whittier left his family. There's no reason in the world that excuses that."

"I see." Violet inhaled. "You seem very intent on finding this man. Are you a detective, then, hired by his family?"

"No." Cade noticed his hands were shaking. He clenched them, hoping to make the shaking stop.

"A U.S. Marshal? A lawman of some sort?"

"No." Hellfire. Why couldn't he quit shaking? "Neither."

"Hmm. You're going to have to be a bit more forthcoming if you expect me to help you." Through inquisitive eyes, Violet studied him. Lightly, she touched his fisted hand. Like magic, he stopped trembling. Awed, Cade stared as she stroked him, soothingly, the same way a parent might calm a frightened child or a caregiver might help a wounded man. "I might be plain and sensible and occasionally overlooked," she said, "but I'm also—"

"Forbidden to talk about yourself that way," Cade interrupted in his sternest tone. It aggrieved him that she kept on referring to herself as ugly and passed over. Surely the folks in this little creekside town weren't so blind that they couldn't see she had worth beyond bland prettiness. "I won't have it. If we're going to strike a bargain between us, you'll have to quit reminding me of how 'unattractive' you are."

"I know, I know." Self-consciously, Violet Benson ducked her head. She rubbed her thumb over the back of his hand, a bit nervously now. "What God gave me is just fine. The Lord doesn't make mistakes in creating us. My father's told me those things many, many times." She lifted her gaze to his face, her eyes flashing with a glimmer of defiance. "But that doesn't mean, Mr. Foster, that you have license to call me unattractive!"

Stricken, Cade gazed at her. "I hurt you. I'm sorry."

"I've made peace with my looks," Violet went on rather huffily, "but I still expect common decency from people. Even you! That was thoughtless and unkind. You must know that."

He hadn't known that. He'd only been repeating what she'd said herself. Maybe he'd been on this hunt for Whittier for too long. Maybe he was becoming unfit for society. Maybe, with every hand of cards and risky wager, he was losing…everything.

"I'm *very* sorry." He was, too. Very rapidly, she was becoming more than a means to restoring his good luck. She was becoming...*essential*. Carefully, Cade raised his free hand to her slender jaw. He turned her face to his. "I like looking at you. I've never known anyone whose emotions were so evident."

"That doesn't sound like much of a compliment."

"It *is* a compliment. From a man who spends all day being as poker-faced as possible." He smiled. "I find you...fascinating."

"Truly?" Violet's lips quirked. Her wide hazel eyes held a challenge. "Can you guess what emotion I'm feeling right now?"

"Suspicion." Cade stroked her cheek, just once, then made himself let her go. He missed her softness almost immediately. "But you don't have to be suspicious of me, Miss Benson."

"Call me Violet. Then perhaps I won't be."

That brought a smile to his face. "I'd be honored to do so. And you should call me Cade. *Please* call me Cade."

"All right. Cade." She gave a self-deprecating laugh. "Heaven knows, you might be the only man who ever invites such familiarity from me. I guess I might as well enjoy it!"

Again, Cade looked at her sternly. "I can

make sure you enjoy it. I can make sure every man in Morrow Creek wants you."

She arched her brow at his certainty, seeming more than a little bit doubtful. "You're not a detective, a marshal or a lawman." Her smile turned playful. "You're a miracle worker!"

He'd had enough. "The real tragedy in life isn't failing to believe that hope exists, Violet. It's convincing yourself that you don't want any hope, even when it's right in front of you."

"Are you talking about me? Or about you?"

Cade snorted. "I'm talking about the likelihood of your choosing from among a dozen smitten suitors if you help me."

"You mean if I behave as your lucky charm?"

A nod. "Once everyone sees us together, people will look at you with new eyes. They'll wonder why *I* want you—why I'm captivated with you. They'll imagine…all manner of things."

She inhaled again, steadying herself. "Good things?"

The lilt of hopefulness in her voice was heartrending.

"Good things," Cade affirmed, feeling touched by her beyond all reason. He didn't know why he wanted to help her—why he wanted to erase her wrongheaded notion that she was undesirable and unnoticed. He only knew that he did. "Everyone wants what they can't have. Especially men. I know more about human nature than I want to, after all these years of wagering, and I know that's true. Let me show you, Violet. Let's strike a deal."

Hesitating, she bit her lip. "Who will know about this?"

"As far as your friends and neighbors are concerned, I'll be courting you," Cade swore, taking her hand. "That's all."

A glance. "But really *I'll* be bringing *you* good luck."

She was smart, he realized. And much less naive than he'd thought. That made Cade feel better about this whole endeavor.

"Yes," he said. "You'll be bringing me good luck." He offered her a winning smile—one he knew was persuasive. "But hopefully that good luck will be shared by us both."

"You know," she mused, giving him another of her patented, too-observant looks, "I think you're an optimist at heart."

"I think you've only just met me," Cade disagreed, "and it shows."

Her smile touched him, suddenly mysterious. "Well, you'd better find some optimism, then. Because I can only do this if my father agrees. That means you'll have to impress him at dinner tonight and obtain his blessing. Will I see you at six?"

Sunnily and capably, Violet gave him the particulars.

Dumbstruck at the realization that he'd have to impress a straitlaced minister to put his good-luck-charm plan in motion, Cade hesitated. Then he nodded. The minute he did so, Violet Benson jumped up from her bench, briskly said goodbye, then left him alone while she returned to her charitable good works.

That was twice she'd left him stranded, Cade realized as he watched her leave. The first time, on the Grand Fair dance floor, he'd purposely allowed her to do so. The second time...

Well, the second time, just now, he hadn't. Damnation. Was it possible that an innocent small-town girl had outmaneuvered him?

Worse, was it possible that a *reformer* had outfoxed him?

No. He was worldly, intelligent and determined. No one could outwit him. Except maybe Percy Whittier. And even then only a few times.

But the man wasn't a god, and he wasn't infallible. He was only irredeemable. With a little more effort, Cade knew he would find him. Then he would get the answers he needed.

The answers he'd promised Judah.

In the meantime, Cade had a few more hours to spend before dinnertime at the Benson household. That was just enough time, he reckoned, to write to his brother, beat Blackhouse at cards a few more times…and strategize how best to turn Violet Benson into an irresistible temptress, all before Cade left town in the next week or two.

Chapter Four

When Violet heard a decisive knock at the door at precisely fifteen minutes before six o'clock that evening, she felt her heartbeat perk up a notch. Jittery and breathless, she untied her ruffled apron. She hung it on its hook in the kitchen. She smoothed down her skirts, then hastened to the front door.

There, she stopped. Staring at that ordinary white-painted, wooden-framed door, so familiar and yet so unremarkable, Violet couldn't resist feeling that something *momentous* was about to occur. For the first time ever, she'd invited a man to dinner. He'd accepted. And now…who knew what might happen.

Fastening a smile on her face, Violet tugged open the door.

The gambler Cade Foster stood on her front porch, with the setting sun and all of Morrow Creek behind him, attired in yet another of his well-designed suits. His dark hair, brushed from his face in waves, framed his features superbly. His white shirt looked crisp. His necktie looked silky. His coat set off his broad-shouldered physique to perfection. He looked... *wonderful*.

The only thing missing in his appearance was—

A smile. Just as she thought it, Cade gifted her with one. At the sight of it, Violet's poor heart pitter-pattered twice as energetically. He really was *so* handsome. And *so* charming!

Unfortunately, while Violet was savoring the sight of *him*, Cade was enjoying an equal opportunity to scrutinize *her*. He sent his gaze roving over her flowing calico skirts, her dress's high-buttoned bodice, her lace-trimmed shawl... and nodded.

"You look lovely." He took her hand in greeting. His fingers felt warm over hers—warm and deft and masculine. "That dress brings out the green in your eyes. They're sparkling."

"That's because I'm happy to see you. Please, come in!"

Violet stepped back with a flourish, feeling

uncommonly pleased that he'd approved of her ensemble. The oak plank floorboards creaked under her feet; the scent of roast chicken and root vegetables wafted from the kitchen's cast-iron stove. Expectantly, she clasped her hands, waiting for him to enter.

Cade didn't move. Instead he gave her a doubtful frown. "I hope it's all right if there's one more for dinner."

From behind him, Cade reached for something. He dragged it forward. At first it looked like a bundle of cast-off clothing. Then it resolved itself into a scrawny child—a boy with wary eyes, sharp features and an overall air of shameful neglect.

"Tobe Larkin, I'd like you to meet Miss Violet Benson," Cade said. To Violet he added, "Tobe is one of the first people I met in Morrow Creek. I...ran into him on my way here and decided to bring him along."

"Why, that's fine," Violet began. "One more is always—"

"He shanghaied me!" The boy, Tobe, jerked his arm out of Cade's grasp. He glowered at Violet. "I tole him, that lady done *dropped* her reticule! I was only gonna return it to her, is all. Nothin' more'n that. Until *this* here knuck picked me up clean off'n the depot platform and said it was the sheriff or *you*—"

Cade kicked his foot. As though recognizing that signal, Tobe quit talking. Instead he raised his chin. Then he sniffed.

"Is that chicken I smell?" Enthusiastically, the boy strode inside the house. "Chicken and biscuits, maybe? Mmm, mmm, mmm."

With a confidence that belied his few years, Tobe stepped farther into the entryway. He propped both hands on his hips. "This might be all right, I reckon. Only don't you get no ideas about sellin' me into white slavery or nothin', Miss Benson," he warned. "I done heard'a you plenty. I aim to be on my guard the whole time I'm here, and that's for certain. I ain't no fool."

"Well, I—" Mystified by his wrongheaded notions about her, Violet hesitated. "We've only just met. I wouldn't think to—"

She glanced to Cade for guidance. He was watching Tobe with a strange, mingled sense of stoniness and nostalgia on his face.

"—*sell* anyone," she continued, wondering all the while at Cade's unusual expression. "I'm certainly not a white slaver!"

Where in the world had the boy gotten such a nonsensical idea? Violet could scarcely fathom it. Indeed, she helped many different people in town, including children, but the people whom she helped were generally grateful for her assistance.

"He's afraid you'll send him to a foundling home," Cade explained, doubtless recognizing her confusion. "He told me so on the way here. Screamed it, more precisely. Not that I can blame him. Those orphanages are nasty places sometimes."

As he made that curious statement, Cade stepped inside, too. He shut the door behind him. His presence filled the entryway. Instantly her household felt twice as exciting with him in it.

"Tobe insists he's happier on the streets," Cade went on, giving the child another odd look, "among his felonious little friends. He says he has everything he could ever need."

"Oh. I see." That couldn't possibly be true. Could it? Where were the boy's parents? Violet might yet suggest that Tobe go to a temporary home of some kind, she knew. Everyone deserved a home and a family who loved them. Violet was fortunate enough to have both and deeply cherished them. "Well, then there's no need to rush to an orphanage, is there?" At Tobe's still-wary expression, Violet tried another tack. "I mean, I'm *very* pleased to meet you, Tobe! Why don't you tell me about yourself."

Tobe regarded her with evident suspicion. His little face was filthy. His hair might once have been blond; now it was tangled and too dirty to discern its true color. A knit cap, doubtless pilfered, partly shaded his eyes. His britches sported holes in the knees. His shirt needed mending, too. Only his woolen overcoat, which was so large it hid his hands and dragged on the floor behind him, appeared to be in reputable shape.

Concerned, Violet gave him a smile. "Are you new to town?"

"I come in off'n the train. With my mam. Only she's—" Tobe broke off. "Gone," the boy finished flatly. As Violet and Cade exchanged a troubled glance over Tobe's head, he looked with interest at the Benson household. "So… how 'bout that chicken?"

Deciding that further questions could wait, Violet nodded. "It will be ready very soon. I made oyster stew to start, a lovely braise of kale and turnips, and chicken with dumplings."

Tobe shot a triumphant look at Cade. "Tole you so!" He held out his small grubby hand, fingers waggling. "Pay up, chump."

With a resigned grin, Cade plunked a nickel

into the boy's palm. To Violet, he explained, "We had a small wager going."

"On the constituents of my dinner?" Violet shook her head in disbelief. "I wonder what you'll make of my dessert then?"

On her cue, both males—one tall and one small—raised their heads to sniff the air like the most persistent of bloodhounds.

"Something with cinnamon." Tobe perked up. "Pumpkin pie?"

"No." With a mien of concentration, Cade inhaled once more. "It's apples. Apple pie… No. Apple pandowdy. With cream."

Slack-jawed, Violet stared. "It *is* apple pandowdy!"

With a genial chortle, the males traded that very same nickel once again. Glimpsing the surprising camaraderie between them, Violet felt unexpectedly moved. Cade Foster seemed like a hard man. He seemed tough and unwavering and more than a little bullheaded. But when it came to a child in need, apparently, he was entirely mush-hearted.

"You two are almost as incorrigible as Papa," she confided with a shake of her head. "He's at a congregant's, offering them counsel, by the way. That means he'll likely be late to dinner."

Cade gave her a piercing look. "Does that happen a lot?"

She shrugged. "Sometimes. Papa's flock needs him."

"So do you." As though guessing at the loneliness that Violet sometimes felt, alone inside the quiet, tidy and modest house she'd grown up in, Cade squeezed her hand. "I aim to give you everything you might need and want, Violet. *Everything.*"

For a long moment, his gaze met hers, private and enthralling. His promise of giving her *everything* swam in Violet's head, making her feel downright giddy. When Cade had first made his unusual proposition to her this afternoon, she'd been taken aback, it was true. But now that she'd had time to consider matters, Violet was entirely in favor of helping to bring Cade good luck. His proposition provided a handy cover for her own plans to become more adventuresome, without forcing her to risk rejection. It would probably be fun, as well.

Provided Papa approved the idea, of course.

"Don't worry, Cade. You needn't keep wooing me. I've already made up my mind. Besides, there'll be plenty of time to clarify those particulars between us later on. In private." She shifted her attention to Tobe, who'd wandered into the adjacent parlor. Surrounded by its humble but comfortable furnishings, the boy appeared even more down on his luck than he had before. "After I ask little Tobe to unhand the statuette he's about to pinch *and* unburden his pockets of my prize collection of sterling-silver spoons."

Cade only gawked at her. "He's been stealing? *Here?*"

"Well, either that," Violet clarified with a nod, "or his pants are growing elephantine pockets all on their own."

Cade scowled. "I'm sorry. I'll handle this."

With a laugh, Violet put her hand on his shirtfront. Beneath her fingers, Cade's chest felt warm and solid and— *No.* She had to concentrate. "You've done enough by bringing him here," she assured Cade. "It was the right thing to do. But if you confront Tobe now, you'll likely scare him away for good."

"Stealing is not polite." Cade clenched his jaw. "I've been spending most of my time at gambling tables, that's true, but I still possess sufficient manners to recognize that much."

"I have no doubt you're *wonderfully* well mannered." In fact, she was counting on that. His inherent gentlemanliness would allow Violet to behave more daringly without risk of getting in over her head. Comfortingly, she patted his chest. It still felt superb. "But you relax now. I'll take care of this."

Cade gave a reluctant grunt. She accepted that as consent.

"In the meantime," she volunteered sunnily, "you can consider when you would like your next dose of good luck!"

Then she left with a smile to deal with Tobe.

Even after he'd savored a delectable meal of home-cooked dishes, prepared with a love and care he'd *swear* he could detect outright, Cade could not stop thinking about what Violet had said before she'd gone to cope with Tobe's thieving tendencies.

You can consider when you would like your next dose of good luck!

Gazing at Violet now from across the gingham tablecloth–covered table, set with its simple pottery and hand-me-down cutlery, Cade wanted his next dose of good luck soon. *Very* soon.

He didn't know how Violet had done it, but somehow she'd captivated him. Her cooking was magnificent, her caretaking was even better and her skills at affable conversation left him as full of contentment as her meal had left him full of chicken and dumplings. He'd come here expecting to employ his usual methods of strategy and artifice and charm. It had turned out, to his surprise, that he'd needed none of those things to earn Violet Benson's goodwill—especially since her father had yet to appear for dinner—or to discern the most important fact about her.

She was *wonderful*. To be precise, Cade decided as he watched her while spooning up the last sugary, cinnamony bites of his portion of apple pandowdy, she was soft and sweet and quick with a joke. She was capable and smart and loyal. She was not beautiful; that was still true. She was not flirtatious or trivial or full of flattering niceties, the way some women were.

Violet spoke her mind, sometimes even to her own detriment. She blushed at the drop of a hat—a hat not unlike the expensive, flat-brimmed model Cade had respectfully removed while entering her household—and she lacked all sophistication. She would not have fared well in San Francisco or New York or any of the myriad big cities Cade frequented and sometimes called home temporarily.

Simon Blackhouse, he knew, would have found Violet both gauche and probably unlovely, with her easy laughter and broad gestures. But Cade, to his incredulity and satisfaction, found Violet to be…endearing. Being around her was stimulating in a way that keeping company with other people never had been.

Violet never failed to surprise him, the way she'd done with Tobe tonight. She hadn't shirked from welcoming the boy *or* from reprimanding him when necessary. Even though Violet was admittedly ordinary in looks, her high-spiritedness and wit more than made up for her lack of rosebud lips or alabaster skin or any of the other features that prettier women were lauded for.

The plain fact was, Cade realized, Violet's face drew him to truly look at her…and to keep right on looking, helplessly entertained and absorbed by wondering what she'd say or do next.

With genuine warmth, Violet leaned closer to Tobe, urging him to take another spoonful of apple pandowdy. Doubtless she hadn't noticed him stuffing his wee pockets full of the yeasted rolls and nuts she'd served earlier, but Cade had. The boy had fast hands and sprightly thieving fingers——fingers that currently clutched Violet's flatware and likely intended to steal it, too.

At Violet's offer, Tobe gave an eager nod. His cheeks bulged like a chipmunk's. Even as Violet served him his extra dessert, Tobe went on spooning up his pandowdy. He ate as though someone might steal it before he was through. In his rough-and-tumble world, Cade knew, someone might. He didn't know why he'd brought Tobe with him tonight; he only knew it had felt right.

It wasn't like him to interfere in someone else's affairs—even the affairs of one small, larcenous boy. Cade reckoned he'd already started going soft, owing to Violet's pure-hearted ways.

He should have known, by now, to steer clear of a reformer.

"Apple pandowdy is not the loveliest of desserts, I'll grant you that," Violet said, "but it's quick and delicious."

Tobe grunted his assent, still eagerly fisting his spoon.

"It's *beyond* delicious," Cade assured her. His own flatware clinked into his serving dish as he set it aside. "And there are many things more valuable than merely being lovely."

"Like…being lucky?" Her smile looked mischievous.

"And being here, right now, to enjoy all this."

"Ah. I see." Violet's eyes sparkled at him.

She set aside her own plate. "You're a man who lives for the moment, then."

"I'm a man who lives for enjoyment. I just said so."

"But what about planning for tomorrow?"

Cade glanced at Tobe. "Plans go awry. Only a fool counts on tomorrow. All you really have is the hand you're dealt today."

"Or the dice," Tobe put in matter-of-factly. "You might have dice to use." He finally set aside his spoon, then gave an exaggerated groan of contentment. "Thanks for them new cheaters, by the way," he told Cade. "I seen right away that you swapped 'em out for my old rough pair the other night. Soon's I've practiced enough, I oughtta clean up plenty."

"I'll give you a few tips after dinner," Cade volunteered.

Openmouthed, Violet stared at them both. "Are you offering to help Tobe learn to *cheat* more effectively?"

The boy nodded guilelessly. Cade did, too, unable to see what the problem was. "It will keep him safer in the long run."

"What would keep him safer is a secure home to live in," Violet disagreed, rallying handily. "And his mother to care for him!"

Concerned, she turned to Tobe. "Where's your father?"

The child shrugged. "Dunno. He run off a while back."

"Before you got on the train to come here?" Violet pressed. "Or after you and your mother arrived in Morrow Creek?"

Tobe squirmed, plainly uncomfortable at being questioned.

"You can tell me, Tobe," Violet urged. "It's important that you do, so I know how best to help you. Unless I know where your mother and father are, I won't know how to proceed. Please, isn't there anything you can tell me about their whereabouts?"

With panicky eyes and a quarrelsome expression, the boy glanced at Cade. His whole demeanor seemed a plea for help—a plea for rescue from Violet's questioning. Tobe seemed either unwilling or unable to answer her...at least right now.

"Can't we leave now? I done ate everythin' I got given."

"And then some." Mustering a courteous smile, Cade pushed back his chair. It was just as well Tobe had spoken up. Cade suddenly felt less than cozy here himself...especially with Tobe's entreating gaze—so much like Judah's—fastened on him that way.

His brother wasn't as tough as Cade was. He never had been. Their orphan life had been harder for Judah than it had been for Cade. That's why Cade, as the eldest brother, had taken it upon himself to settle the discontent he knew Judah must feel.

He'd taken it upon himself to help Judah feel *whole* again.

For himself, Cade figured, it was already too late.

"I guess we'd better get going." Signaling as much, Cade rose. "Thank you for dinner, Violet. Everything was delicious."

"You're welcome." Violet gawked at him, seeming entirely taken aback. "But you're not really *leaving* already, are you?"

"It's time." Cade summoned Tobe with a nod, rescuing them both from further questions. "I'm sorry I didn't have a chance to see Reverend Benson again. I would have liked to say hello—and to get this deal squared between us, of course."

"'Again'?" Violet repeated, seeming stuck on the word. "But when did you and my father ever—" She broke off, her gaze sharpening. "Did you help Papa cheat, too, like you did Tobe? Is that how you knew Papa won at cards the other night?"

Beside her, Tobe rose from his seat. Taking advantage of Violet's distractedness, he swiped a butter knife. He slid the utensil's long silver handle up his shirtsleeve for safekeeping.

Cade raised an eyebrow. The little trouble-maker was on his way to becoming a full-bore criminal, the way he was behaving.

"I may have slipped your father an improv-ing card or two," Cade acknowledged. Rever-end Benson had been on the verge of losing his clerical collar *and* his shirt in the game they'd played together. "But whether he used it or not, I can't say."

"Oh, *I* can say." Violet folded her arms. "You'll be happy to know that those winnings of his went to the church collection basket, though. My father is completely incorruptible."

Cade frowned. "I'm not trying to corrupt anyone."

Her raised eyebrows suggested otherwise. "Even me?"

That was easy. "*Especially* you."

"Oh." Paradoxically, she seemed almost dis-appointed.

That made no sense. At a loss to understand her—and wondering why he wanted to—Cade deepened his frown. Who cared what pious Violet Benson thought or felt? By the time the first snowfall blanketed Morrow Creek, he would be gone from here.

He would be gone from her life, likely for the better.

Tobe wriggled impatiently. "Are we pullin' foot or not?"

"Yes." Cade headed for the entryway. "It's time to go."

Tobe and Violet trailed after him. So did an odd sense of disappointment. He'd been having a nice time…until Violet had kicked off her damn reformer routine and ruined everything.

He should have known that taking up with a do-gooder was an endeavor doomed to failure. The two of them were like oil and water. Trying to put them together was like trying to glue down dice and expecting them to still produce a win. It didn't work.

"You can't leave yet," Violet protested. "What about our…" She cast an aggrieved glance at Tobe, plainly hesitant to speak openly in front of him, then finished, "agreement?"

She meant his reckless offer that she behave as his lucky charm, Cade knew, in exchange for his pretense of a courtship.

"I reckon that's worked about as much as it's likely to."

"For today, you mean?" Violet specified, hurrying in Cade's wake to the front entryway. She handed him his hat along with a perplexed, entirely too-wounded look. "But tomorrow—"

"I don't plan on tomorrow." Cade reminded her. "Besides, your father hasn't given his blessing yet. He might never."

"But you can't just leave!" Violet insisted. Her expression turned insightful. "If you're merely being protective of Tobe—"

Cade scoffed, irked that she'd read his intentions so effortlessly. "Why would I be? I barely know the boy."

"There's no need for that," Violet hastened on. "In fact, I was thinking—Papa and I have plenty of room. Tobe could stay here with us if he wants to. Just until he finds his family."

Now it was Tobe's turn to scoff. "I ain't no charity case."

Reminded of something similar that he'd told Violet himself just yesterday, Cade shifted uneasily. Like Tobe, he didn't want charity from Violet. He wanted…nothing at all.

Except maybe a pinch of good fortune. And another smile.

Hellfire! What was wrong with him? He

was behaving like a besotted fool—and all over a woman whose feminine curves scarcely showed beneath her prim, starched-and-pressed gown.

"I have no claim on the boy. He can do what he likes."

As though freed—unreasoningly—by his statement, Violet crouched in front of little Tobe. Gently, she smiled at him.

"I'd be very pleased if you'd agree to stay here awhile, Tobe. You can have plenty of food and a nice soft bed, and I think we even have some spare clothes in the church's donation box to lend you. You can wear them while I mend yours for you."

"Not my overcoat!" The boy hugged it. "It's new!"

Giving Cade's former outerwear an overly observant glance, Violet agreed. "That's fine. Of course, you'll want a bath—"

Now Tobe looked petrified. "A bath?"

"Careful there," Cade warned, unable to hold back a grin. "If you scrub off the grime, there'll be nothing left of him."

Violet tossed him an amused glance. Unreasonably, Cade felt blessed by her approval... and warmed clean through. too. He *liked* being included in their comfy, bantering conversation this way. It felt curiously as though the three of them were…a family.

That thought hardened Cade's resolve instantly. He had all the family he needed in Judah. Everyone else could go hang. Including spinsterish Violet Benson and her interfering ways.

"Pish posh. There'll be plenty of him left over!" Oblivious to Cade's glowering look, Violet gave Tobe's gaunt shoulders a heartfelt squeeze. She addressed the boy directly next. "I, for one, can't wait to see what color your hair is!"

"It's blond!" Tobe blurted. "Blond like my mama's."

"Truly?" Violet pretended to be flabbergasted. "Blond?"

At that, the boy actually *giggled*. "Yep! You'll see!"

Cade couldn't help staring. He went right on staring as Violet, with no evident persuasion at all, convinced Tobe to stay.

Disbelievingly, Cade stood by as Violet divested Tobe of his overcoat, his various pilfered household goods and even his hoarded-for-later foodstuffs. The latter she wrapped securely in a big plaid napkin and set on top of a cupboard in the kitchen.

"I'll leave this right here for you, in case you get hungry later tonight," she assured the boy. "No one will touch it."

Cade shook his head. "When your father comes home—" Reverend Benson had not yet returned from his counseling mission "—he might mistake that food for his. He might take it himself."

At his blunt statement, Violet blinked. She appeared surprised to find Cade still there. He'd followed her and Tobe into the kitchen from the entryway…just to watch over the boy.

"No one will take it. I wouldn't promise otherwise."

"Tobe, you should put that food with your things," Cade advised gruffly. "Keep it close to you. You might need it later."

Plainly perplexed, Violet turned to Cade. "He'll have it later," she insisted. "It's right there. He doesn't need to hide it." She touched Cade's arm. "Why would you say such a thing?"

Hard-won experience, Cade knew. A long time ago, he'd learned to keep the necessities close and to trust no one.

But he refused to say so. He didn't want to engender any more reformer's pity from Vio-

let…or to reveal any more of his own vulner-
abilities. He'd thought he'd erased those long
ago.

He had. Damnation, *he had*. But Violet
didn't seem to think so. She gazed thoughtfully at him, seeming on the verge of offering Cade a consoling emergency food packet
of his own.

He, foolishly, almost longed for a chance to
take it, if only it would please her. Hell. Would
his gullibility to her never find an end? Cade
had never experienced its like.

Fortunately, Tobe broke the silence between
them.

"All right. That's good enough for me, I
reckon." Happily, the boy took off his hat. He
set to work on his shoes. "Where's that bath?
'Cause I been itchin' somethin' fierce lately."

To her credit, Violet didn't even recoil. "I'll
get it."

Still feeling baffled and discomfited in ways
he didn't understand, Cade stepped into her
path. Determinedly, he took hold of Violet's
arm. He pulled her into an alcove where they
could speak privately, then lowered his head.
"Don't do this."

"Do what?" In the midst of capably rolling

up her sleeves, Violet paused, plainly baffled. "Haul some bathwater? Heat it? I assure you, Cade, that I'm more than up to the challenge."

Her cheerful smile touched him again. Cade resisted it. Frustrated by his inability to make her see the damage she might do to Tobe, he raked his hand through his hair. He fixed her with a warning look, determined nonetheless to have his say.

"Don't give that boy too much hope. It's not fair."

"Oh." In a heartbeat, her face softened. "I see."

He wasn't sure she did. "You don't know what you're doing. If you get Tobe used to a soft bed and regular meals and—" *warm hugs*, he'd been about to say, but he stopped himself just in time "—plenty of silver spoons to line his delinquent pockets with, it will be doubly hard for him when he has to leave."

Violet appeared to consider that. In the hallway they'd found themselves in—lantern-lit, safe and intractably homey—she edged nearer to him. Confidently and somehow sadly, she gave him a long look. "You know, a wise man once told me that the problem isn't giving up on hope. It's convincing yourself you don't want any hope, even when it's standing right in front of you."

Recognizing his own foolhardy words, Cade looked away.

He hoped she didn't mean him. *He* truly *didn't* need hope.

"I agree," Violet continued staunchly. "So I can't see anything wrong with trying to make sure Tobe never gives up on himself. I *can* help him find his parents, Cade. I can! I know almost everyone in town. I volunteer everywhere. I have access to records most people don't. Everyone from Sheriff Caffey to the folks down at the train depot will help me get information. I'm dogged, too. I promise you, I can help Tobe. And I will."

"You shouldn't." Hoping to make exactly that point, however he could, Cade backed them up to the hallway wall. He caged in Violet with his arms, then ladled as much seriousness into his voice as he could. "You heard Tobe before. He doesn't want to talk about his parents, or where they went, or why he's alone."

"He's only just met me," Violet insisted, not daunted in the least by Cade's intimidating posture. "He'll talk later."

Cade couldn't help admiring her spunk. "Now who's the miracle worker?" he asked.

With an amused sound, Cade slipped on his hat. He touched Violet's chin, then smiled. "All right, then. Have it your way." He shook his head, knowing she was much too confident about her plans to find Tobe's parents. "I'd wish you good luck, but I don't seem to have any to spare right now."

She grinned. "Does that mean I'll see you again tomorrow?"

"I can't rightly say."

"You *won't* say, you mean."

Cade shrugged. Determinedly, Violet straightened her spine. Her maneuver put her chest right up against his. It turned out that her shape wasn't quite as washboard flat as he'd imagined it was. Violet Benson was not curvaceous, but she was…affecting.

As though sensing her unexpected advantage, Violet tipped her face to his. She offered a kittenish smile. The mingled fragrances of castile soap, laundry starch and warm, feminine skin reached him next, making Cade go stock-still with longing.

Men at a gambling table didn't smell like that. Neither did roving train cars or impersonal hotel rooms or bathhouses. Cade couldn't remember when he'd enjoyed inhaling quite so much.

"I'd be very happy," Violet said, touching his arm with an utter lack of guile, "if you'd come back to see me tomorrow."

Yes. *Yes.* On the brink of agreeing instantly just to see her smile again, Cade flashed his dimples at her instead. "Mmm. And *I'd* be happy if you'd rub up against me some more, sugar." Deliberately, he gestured at her position. "But this time, move a little slower, please. I want a little more time to enjoy it."

Just as he'd expected, Violet widened her eyes. She blinked, seeming to awaken to their compromising position. Then she smiled up at him. "You're the one who backed us up here. Anyone watching would think *you* wanted to be this close to *me*."

Damnation. She had him there. Cade put down his arms.

"You do, don't you?" Defying his expectations this time, Violet stayed put, arms crossed. "You can't scare me, Cade. As I said, I've done a lot of charity work. I'm not meek or naive."

"But you are inexperienced. And I'm plenty skilled."

She appeared to ponder that. Her expression turned subdued.

"Well," she said. "If you don't turn tail after

this one evening together, I guess we'll find out about that, won't we?"

Her expression now appeared downright challenging.

Cade gaped. "I can't believe you're baiting me. *Me*."

"Then we're even. Because I can't believe you're trying to seduce me into *not* helping one small, innocent boy who's all alone in the world! Even though *you* helped him first. You must have brought Tobe here for a reason." Tilting her head, Violet examined Cade with uncomfortable perceptiveness. "I think I know what it was, too. Cade…how many orphanages did you stay in?"

Shocked, Cade stiffened. Memories rushed at him, black and lonesome and bitter to recall. He'd thought he'd buried them.

It took him a minute to recover. Dimly aware of Violet watching him, Cade sucked in a deep breath. Somehow he made himself toss off a smile. It was not his most dazzling effort.

"I've just decided," he told Violet, "that I won't be back tomorrow. It turns out, if *this* is good luck…I don't much like how it feels."

Then he tipped his hat to her and took himself away.

Violet Benson might have succeeded in

"saving" one male of her acquaintance tonight, Cade told himself darkly as he stepped into the chilly evening air outside on the front porch, but she wasn't getting her angelic hands on both of them. Not if he could help it.

And he damn well could.

Chapter Five

The nice thing about Sunday services, Violet thought as she sat, hands clasped atop her hymnal, clad as usual in her best jade-colored, worsted-wool bustled gown, in her customary place in the front pew of her father's church, was that they afforded folks a much-needed chance to socialize after a busy week.

Of course, church services *also* helped save people's immortal souls. That was of utmost importance, too. But from a secular, practical perspective, everyone liked to mingle. It was as simple as that. Church provided the best possible place to deepen old friendships and forge new ones, which was precisely what Violet had been doing ever since the gambler Cade Foster had left her standing in her own hallway, all flushed and breathless and feeling as hot as a Thursday afternoon in July.

I'd be happy if you'd rub up against me some more, sugar, she remembered him saying in that low, rumbly, undeniably shiver-inducing voice of his. *But this time, move a little slower, please. I want a little more time to enjoy it.*

Heavens! Just thinking about their encounter now—in Sunday service, of all places, while her father droned on with his sermon!—made Violet feel all...*tingly* inside. She hadn't realized exactly how close she'd gotten to Cade in that hallway. She'd been too busy wondering about him, trying to understand him, searching for a reason that explained his odd resistance to her plans to help Tobe. Who was doing just fine now, by the way.

After a hasty glance at the boy—who for today was being watched over by sweet Miss Mellie Reardon, one of her friends, and seemed to be enjoying all the attention—Violet re-clasped her hands, then thought about Cade some more. She believed she was right about his having spent time in an orphanage. He'd been too distrustful of foundling homes to dismiss the idea outright.

But why? Why would Cade be so cynical about a place that only existed to help forlorn and abandoned children? She couldn't think of a single reason. For a man who'd lectured Violet about the need for hopefulness, she decided, Cade seemed in miserably short supply of it himself. In the end, he hadn't even been able to believe in his own gambler's superstition.

If this is good luck...I don't much like how it feels.

Well, that was doubtless because Cade hadn't experienced its full effect yet! He certainly hadn't given *her* a fair chance as a lucky charm, Violet thought in her own defense. At the rate things were going, he might never do so. She hadn't so much as clapped eyes on Cade since he'd left her house the other night.

She knew he was still in town. Morrow Creek's tireless gossipy grapevine—and all her friends, besides—had kept her informed of that much. But Cade hadn't returned to ask for Reverend Benson's blessing of their supposed "courtship" and attendant lucky-charm scheme, and Violet hadn't sought out Cade herself, either.

Why should she? she asked herself as she shifted in her seat. Word had gotten out about the dinner she and Cade had shared. The knowledge that the mysterious new sporting man in town had paid a deliberate social call on plain, unremarkable Violet Benson had already perked up her prospects considerably.

Exactly as their dance at the Grand Fair had done, their convivial dinner had provoked new curiosity about Violet among the menfolk in town. They'd paid her more attention of late than ever before. She was trying not to become *too* foolishly accustomed to their interest. But it was thrilling, all the same.

Not as thrilling as Cade was, she'd admit. But still…

Unable to properly describe *why* Cade's attention was so much more stimulating than the attention of other men, Violet was saved from continuing the effort by the one thing that never failed her: good works. It was time to pass the collection basket, and Violet was responsible for doing so.

Turning her thoughts to that duty, Violet made her way to the back of the church. Her fellow congregants smiled at her; her father's familiar voice comforted her. She wasn't *sure* that his gambling winnings had wound up in the church's charitable offerings, as she'd insisted to Cade, but she felt hopeful they had.

She stood at the backmost pew, then offered the collection basket to the first congregant.

He put in his contribution. The basket passed from hand to hand. Absently, Violet watched it.

A fat wad of rolled-up currency landed in the basket.

Startled, Violet stared at it. That was a great deal of money! Even if all the bills beneath the top one were the lowest possible denomination, there had to be…a *lot* of cash there.

Aching to know who was so generous, Violet nonetheless kept her gaze lowered. She strived to remain neutral to the offerings her friends and neighbors made to the church. Everyone gave what they could; sometimes people took help when they needed to.

But *this* was beyond unusual. Only a lucky gold miner, a railroad magnate or maybe a touring European could afford to give so much to a Sunday collection plate. It was unprecedented.

Interestedly, Violet let her gaze roam down the pew. Near the far edge where the basket was, she glimpsed quality shoes, a pair of strong legs clad in gray trousers, two masculine hands—

The people on either side of the mysterious donor gasped. Loudly. As one, the whole congregation turned to see what the fuss was about. Caught staring, Violet felt herself flush.

The basket moved on. Throughout the small church, the congregants' rumblings rose a little higher. More people spied the wad of cash in the basket. Each row of worshippers swiveled their heads in turn, trying to glimpse the charitable benefactor in their midst. Her father cleared his throat, then preached on.

Steadfastly, Violet collected the basket at the end of its rounds. The unknown donor's contribution appeared to have kicked up some sense of competitive giving among the congregants. There were more coins and bills than ever before—and one small but valuable gold-dust packet, as well. It smelled like whiskey.

Happy for it all the same, Violet carried the collection to her father's modest office. Located in a small room behind the chancel, it contained a rolltop desk for Papa's books, papers and the church register, a well-worn chair, a window, a seldom-used door that led to the churchyard and a reliable safe. In the West, even a man of God couldn't be too careful with money.

Crouching before the safe, Violet made fast work of depositing the collection funds. Ordinarily she would have sorted them. Today she felt much too curious about the identity of the mysterious donor to be too persnickety about organizing the money. Instead, she shoved the whole lot inside, then clanged shut the safe's door. She gave the dial a hasty spin.

"You missed your calling. You should have been a gambler."

At the sound of that familiar voice, Violet started. She rose, her green worsted skirts swirling around her ankles, to see Cade Foster standing there in her father's office. He looked exactly as handsome—and as darkly enigmatic—as she remembered.

"When I dropped my latest bundle of winnings in your basket, everyone around me gasped," Cade said. "But you didn't even bat an eyelash. I'm impressed—you have quite a poker face."

"That's not what you said the other day," she disagreed. "You said my emotions are unusually evident on my face."

"That's true." He came a little closer. "I did say that."

At his nearness, her heartbeat surged. Breathlessly, Violet stood her ground, feeling suddenly impatient and exhilarated and anxious, all at once. She'd thought she might never see Cade again, she realized. She'd thought her turn as belle of the ball might end as quickly as it had begun. Evidently, she'd been wrong.

She'd never felt *so* happy to be wrong about something.

She ought to be more cautious this time, though. It had shaken her when Cade had skedaddled from her house so abruptly.

To that end, Violet lifted her chin, striving to sound as though she bantered on a regular basis with worldly, roguish gamblers like him. "You also said that was a compliment."

"It was." Cade peered at her more carefully. His expression looked unreadable. "But I reserve the right to change my mind."

She couldn't help feeling stung. "About the compliment?"

"About your ability to bluff. Maybe your poker face only applies to other people, not me. Maybe with me, you can't help showing how you feel." Cade nodded. "You're doing it right now."

She was? "No, I'm not."

"You are." Another careful, interested look. "You look as though you feel...excited. Do you, Violet? Do you feel excited?"

More than she ever had. She could scarcely keep her knees from wobbling, she felt so unendurably curious about why he was there. Had Cade only come to assuage his guilty gambler's conscience by dropping off a contribution to the church? Or was there another reason the gambler had come there? To see her?

"I guess it's probably not smart to tip your hand to a renowned gambler." Rallying, Violet smiled. "I'll make more of an effort to be cryptic and unreadable." She did. "See?"

"Nice try." Cade appeared improbably amused by her efforts—and possibly a bit charmed, too…even though that made no sense. "But even when you're trying, you're still you, Violet."

"Meaning what, exactly? Why are you here, anyway?"

"Meaning," Cade clarified as he came a bit nearer, all the way into a patch of October-morning sunlight, "that you're about as mysterious as an open book on a sunny day. At least to me."

She couldn't help feeling vaguely disappointed. Everyone knew that gentlemen liked pretty ladies who kept them guessing.

"And I'm here," Cade added as Violet pondered the devilish impracticality of that, "because I missed looking at your face."

She glanced up. "Oh." That *might* be a good thing. It might be as good as the way he looked just then, with his dark wavy hair all burnished by sunshine and his eyes bluer than blue.

"*You* can't stop being open to me, it seems." Now Cade was close enough to touch her. So he did. He took hold of her elbow, then drew her nearer. "And despite my efforts to stay away—"

"So you *were* avoiding me on purpose!"

"—*I* can't stop wanting to be near you."

Heaven help her, he looked as though he meant it. His gaze roamed over her features, full of enjoyment and remembrance and...surrender? Violet didn't know what to make of that.

"I won that money for your collection plate shortly after we had dinner together," Cade told her. "I even got invited to the next level of play in the qualifying rounds for the private faro tournament. I glimpsed Whittier, too." He dropped his gaze to her bodice. Most likely, he could see her heaving in eager, restive breaths. "But I haven't won a damn thing since then."

"Oh. I'm very sorry to hear that."

"No, you're not." Cade's eyes sparkled at her, full of mischief and something darker... something needful. "Neither am I. Because it's brought me back here to you." He lifted his hand to her cheek. Rousingly, he stroked her. Tellingly, his voice lowered. Huskily, he said, "You see...I need more good luck."

He was going to kiss her. Violet could tell. She'd not been courted much, that was true; but she recognized something primal in Cade's eyes. Possibly because she felt a bit passionate just then herself. Her knees quaked. Her hands trembled. She *needed* to be kissed, it occurred to her. How else to truly know Cade?

How else to know if she could trust him? Rely on him?

"I need more good luck," Cade repeated, "and it seems I can only get that from touching you. Maybe...from kissing you."

From the rest of the church, the sounds of her father's sermon echoed from the pulpit. Its usual emotive vibrancy was muted by the walls that stood, quite properly, between Reverend Benson and Violet. The effect was surreal— and inhibiting, too.

"You can't...get your good luck here. *Now,*" she breathed, thoroughly scandalized by his suggestion. "We're in church! Everyone I know is in there, a few feet away!"

Rakishly, Cade quirked his eyebrow. "So?"

"So..." Vigorously, Violet gestured. "They'll know what we're doing in here! I'll be ruined." She gave him a quelling look. "You might be leaving Morrow Creek soon, but I'm not."

He laughed, then squeezed her hand as

though to reassure her. "I left quite prominently after making my contribution to the church coffers. As far as anyone knows, you're alone here."

Well...that might be true. Cade *had* used the exterior office door very effectively to enter without her noticing. More important... *he was still going to kiss her.* No matter who was nearby to know it or to happen upon them or even to disapprove.

Agog at the realization, Violet backed up. Her bustle bumped into her father's desk, stopping her retreat abruptly.

She guessed this was what she got for toying with a notorious gambler—for pretending to be more sophisticated than she really was. In a last-ditch effort to retain her virtue, Violet tried some distracting chitchat. She pointed to Cade's fine leather brogues. "I thought I recognized those shoes."

Another smile. "Don't be afraid, Violet. I'll be gentle."

"You'll be..." Envisioning the possibilities inherent in that soft promise, Violet sighed. Tellingly. Swallowing hard, she nodded. "You'll be very, *very* gentle? And quick?" She cast a hasty glance at the doorway. "Very, very, *very* quick?"

"You're new at scandalous behavior. I can tell."

"Try not to seem so amused by that. It's rude."

"I'm sorry. I do admire your enthusiasm for the task at hand though. Not every sinner wants to conduct their sins quite so...efficiently as you." Contritely and somehow wickedly, Cade took her other hand. "I never mean to be unkind to you, Violet. Please allow me to make up for my rudeness...with pleasure."

Oh my. "*Gently*," Violet specified shakily. "And *quickly*!"

"Hmm." A low, speculative rumble escaped him. "I can't rightly promise either...seeing as how I've been hungering for this every day since I saw you last." Cade squeezed her hands again, almost longingly. "I want you, Violet. Let me have you."

Let me have you. No one had ever spoken to her that way before. So passionately, so stirringly...so *commandingly*.

At Cade's roughly voiced request, Violet could hardly refuse. Willfully, she nodded. Her entire midsection tightened with eagerness, filled with uncertainty about what came next.

"Yes," she began primly. "Yes, if you like, you may—"

Kiss me, she was about to say, but Cade's mouth came down on hers just as that last puff of breath was about to escape.

Every bit of what she'd been thinking flew from her head. All that remained were Cade's lips, surprisingly warm and firm and soft on hers, and Cade's hands, releasing her hands to pull her whole body tight against his, and Cade's hips, pressing against her skirts, crowding them against the desk behind her.

His kiss was not gentle. It was not quick. It was hard and slow and probing and remarkable, and Violet wasn't quite sure how—given how dizzy she felt with shock and amazement—she remained upright beneath it. Cade's hands cradled her back; his lips slid over hers, making her mouth come alive with new sensations. A wild burst of…it could only be *longing*, she knew, rushed to her toes. Avidly, Violet grabbed his lapels and held on, but even that was not enough to steady her. She needed… *more*.

"Oh, Violet." Moaning with enjoyment, Cade pressed his forehead to hers. Intimacy rushed between them, heady and new. He stroked her cheek, pushing back a few errant tendrils of hair. He curled his knuckles against her jaw. "You're so…"

Helplessly, she froze, waiting for him to say something thoughtless or unkind. Once, a blacksmith's apprentice who'd courted her briefly had kissed her, also. *I never thought I'd find myself kissing you!* he'd tactlessly burst out afterward.

It had taken her days to stop feeling ashamed of that.

"—so perfect," Cade said at last. Seeming truly to mean it, he blessed her with a smile. "So perfect in every way."

"You're joking," she burst out. "You *must* be—"

"Give me more," he urged. "I'll try to be gentler."

Warily, Violet raised her eyebrow.

Sensing her skepticism—and feeling inexpressibly saddened by it—Cade stroked her cheek again. "I promise I won't hurt you," he said.

Markedly unsure of that, all at once, Violet exhaled. She shook her head. "You can't promise me that."

"I just did." A *very* gentle kiss. "Believe me, Violet."

But it was too late. She'd already been reminded of the way her infrequent suitors usually reacted to her. She couldn't help wondering: Exactly what, if anything, made Cade different?

Astutely, the gambler gazed at her. "How many?"

Violet blinked, surprised. "How many what?"

"How many men have hurt you? How many have disappointed you? How many have made you believe in them, then let you down?"

Shakily, Violet scoffed. "None," she lied, subtracting every single man who'd courted her briefly, then revealed that he didn't want to marry her, had found someone else, or had only wanted to meet Adeline. Irked that he could read her feelings and her past so well, she raised her chin. "None at all."

His gaze met hers. "Someday you'll tell me the truth."

"How do you know I haven't already?"

"Because your whole body tells me you haven't." Tenderly, Cade ran his fingers down her arm. He stroked his thumb over her wrist. "I can feel you leaning toward me, wanting more—"

She felt herself flush. Compared with him, she was so inexperienced. So gullible. So defenseless to protect her heart.

"But a part of you always stays behind."

Cade's coaxing hand swept along her arm. He watched its progress, seeming transfixed by the sight of his masculine hand against her lace-trimmed gown. "Give me more. I won't disappoint you, I swear."

Violet tried to laugh. She tried to appear worldly and sure. Maybe if Cade believed she was sophisticated and carefree, he wouldn't recognize the disappointment and worry she tried so hard to keep hidden. But it was too late. He already had.

"Give over, Violet," he urged. "Do it. It's the only way to feel alive."

That was a reckless philosophy. Violet opened her mouth to tell him so, but Cade met her with another kiss. She lifted her chin to muster up a more assertive, more convincing stance, but Cade took advantage of her position to kiss her neck. Shocked to feel his mouth there above the lacy collar of her dress, Violet stiffened. Ardently, Cade kissed her there again. This time, a tiny, barely perceptible squeal of enjoyment escaped her.

"See there?" Cade grinned. "*Now* you feel alive."

She *did*. Her plan to fly to new heights was working, Violet thought in a daze. Never had she felt anything so wondrous as Cade's warm mouth, his faint, raspy beard stubble, his hands and his breath and his body—so much bigger and stronger than hers—holding her close against him. His kisses moved onward, sliding from her neck to her jaw, and all the while he kept on speaking.

"All I want is for you to feel wonderful," Cade said in a low voice. "I want your heart to race…just like it's doing right now." Proving he'd noticed it, he laid her hand, covered with his, atop her heart. The gesture felt almost impossibly intimate. "I want your breath to pant and your knees to weaken."

Obligingly, her body complied. Violet didn't understand. If she didn't yet trust him, how could she be so responsive to him?

"I want you to touch me, too, Violet." Cade delivered another kiss, potent and sweet, just at the junction of her neck and jaw. "I want to feel your hands on me…just like this. Mmm."

At his soft moan, Violet opened her eyes. When had she closed them? Swoonily, she saw that Cade had moved their joined hands from *her* heart to *his*. Specifically, to his chest. Upon finding herself touching him so boldly, she widened her gaze.

But there was more. "*Your* heart is pounding, too!" she said.

His nod exhilarated her. "I like kissing you," Cade said in a matter-of-fact tone. "I *love* kissing you. I knew I would."

Violet disagreed. "You couldn't have known that."

His dimples flashed. "Only you would argue the point."

She smiled. "Only you would dare such an enormous bluff."

Cade merely shook his head. "What will it take for you to believe me? I'm right about us. I'm right about us *together*."

His blue-eyed gaze suggested there was something about them being *together* that Cade knew…and she did not. Trying not to blush any more forcefully than she already had, Violet fluttered her fingers over his shirtfront. What did he look like underneath it? she wondered suddenly. Was he burly? Hairy? Both?

She bet he looked like an Adonis, splendidly come to life.

Shocked by her own prurient curiosity, Violet lowered her hands. Evidently, Cade brought out all kinds of new qualities in her. If this continued, he wouldn't need any persuasive ability to make her do…whatever he wanted. And wasn't that the trouble?

"You can trust me, Violet," Cade said. "You know you can."

He was probably right. Of everyone she knew, Cade was the only one who'd never tried to sugarcoat his opinions of the way she looked or the way she behaved. Cade had never pretended to love her. He'd never even gone out of his way to be particularly solicitous of her. He was characteristically blunt and fully undaunted by the attitudes of other people. He was...*himself.*

On the other hand, Violet remembered, Cade took chances for a living. He wagered on everything from playing cards to dice to her own homemade apple pandowdy. *I make my living on hope and happenstance,* he'd told her once. *Honesty doesn't enter into it.*

Did that mean she could trust him? Or not?

Unhappily, she recalled what her best friend, Adeline, had said upon learning of Cade's interest in Violet. *You'd better be cautious,* Adeline had told her. *You don't want to get hurt.*

What Adeline *hadn't* said was what they both knew: that Cade's newfound devotion might be both short-lived and heartbreaking for Violet to lose...now that she'd sampled it.

"Well, I guess you probably have about a week's worth of luck by now," Violet settled on saying, sidestepping the issue of trust altogether. Brightly, she smiled. "That'll do, right?"

"No." Cade frowned. "Because this isn't about good luck."

"It isn't?"

"Not anymore. You make me want *more* than luck. Much more."

"You're a gambler, Cade." Violet turned away, hoping to divert herself by straightening the papers on her father's cluttered desk. "What more is there for you, besides luck?"

Silence. But only for a moment.

"I was hoping you could tell me that," Cade said.

Violet didn't have the first notion how to do so. Hedging, she said, "Until my father agrees that I may see you on a social basis, I'm afraid I can't comment on our…relationship."

"Then there is one. Good." There was a smile in his voice. "That's a start, at least. That means both of us are anteing up."

"I'm not a poker game," Violet protested, "to be bet upon!"

"I guess we'll see about that." As she turned to him again, Cade tipped his hat to her. "I'll be back. You can bet on that yourself—even without an infamous gambler's credentials to your name."

Then, with an audacious wink, Cade exited to the churchyard, leaving Violet to wonder exactly what he meant—and if she should bet on anything at all where the gambler was concerned.

Outside under a ponderosa pine tree, Simon Blackhouse stood smoking a cheroot. A farmer wandered past, giving the itinerant bachelor an inquisitive look—undoubtedly owing to Blackhouse's fancy suit, air of privilege…and close-at-hand valet, Adams.

Approaching his benefactor, Cade didn't feel as awkward as that farmer undoubtedly did. But he did feel unaccountably grim.

"Will she do it?" Blackhouse asked.

Cade gave a curt nod. Behind him in the church, the people of Morrow Creek went about their Sunday worship—unknowingly, with a freshly kissed Violet Benson beaming in their midst.

She hadn't been kissed much, Cade decided. Or she hadn't been kissed very well. But what Violet lacked in tutoring, she made up for in sheer, stirring responsiveness. With Violet all warm and pliant and soft in his arms, Cade had felt luckier than a riverboat gambler with a handful of aces and no table limit.

"Good. You'll need her." Expansively, Blackhouse offered Cade a cheroot—or rather, at his signal, Adams proffered the box of elegant, square-tipped cigars. Cade accepted one. "I was beginning to think you couldn't catch up with Whittier on your own. I was considering calling in a fallback to make certain."

"I'll catch up with Whittier." Discontentedly, Cade eyed the small, white-painted church. In a minute, congregants would begin streaming out, full of chatter and kindheartedness. Men would stretch and collect their wagons; women would tidy their children's hair; youngsters would let loose the energy they'd kept pent up while stuck in their pews. They'd holler their glee at being free from confinement for the rest of the afternoon.

Dimly, Cade recalled doing all those things with Judah…and his parents. But the memories felt faded and bittersweet, almost too hazy to believe they'd happened to anyone…least of all him.

"Someone else might be even more motivated to find Whittier," Blackhouse was saying. He withdrew his favorite match safe, a shiny gold model engraved with a full house of cards. In a whiff of sulfur and a crackle of fire, he struck a match to light Cade's cheroot. "Your brother, for instance?"

Over the glowing tip of his newly lit cheroot, Cade eyed Blackhouse. "Judah and I agreed. When I won that Jürgensen, I earned the right to track down Whittier. *I* did. No one else."

"Ah, yes. The famed 'luckiest game of your life.'"

"That's right."

Dubiously, Blackhouse perused the gold chain that secured Cade's watch, tucked safely in the pocket of his ornate wool vest. "If only you'd known that it was Whittier across the table from you that night," he said. "That it was *his* watch you were winning. Things might have unfolded very differently."

Cade wished they had. But he refused to say so.

"I've often wondered…" Blackhouse went on in a cryptic fashion. "Do you think Whittier lost on purpose? Maybe he *wanted* you to have that Jürgensen. Just because you didn't know who he was doesn't mean he didn't know who you were…even then."

At that, Cade felt even less talkative. Drawing on his cheroot, he gazed contemplatively at the church. From inside it, the homespun sound of the congregants' singing reached its crescendo. That meant the service was almost over, he reckoned.

"I always liked that hymn," he remarked without thinking.

Blackhouse's raised eyebrow brought him back to himself quickly. Cade didn't want hymns. He wanted answers. Period.

"All this goodness and God talk is giving me a headache." With a jerk of his head, Cade indicated the dusty street nearby. "How about a bolt of mescal and a fast round of Mexican monte?"

"Yes!" Blackhouse appeared immeasurably cheered. "As a matter of fact, I wouldn't feel I'd visited the Arizona Territory properly if I didn't sample more of...*both* those things," he said. "Come along, Adams! We have winning to do."

Just as the worshippers began filing out into the churchyard, Cade escaped in the opposite direction with Blackhouse and Adams hard on his heels. That made twice now that he'd eluded redemption, it occurred to him, and by a narrow margin each time, too. But Cade couldn't help wondering as he headed away

from the church and all its virtuous believers:
Would he ever stop running...if Violet ever
asked him to?

Chapter Six

It was near midnight by the time Cade looked up from the gambling table. Mexican monte with Blackhouse had turned into roulette with Adams, which had led to craps with Sheriff Caffey, which had segued into "bucking the tiger" with a new batch of local gamesters and everyone's favorite sin: faro.

Now, with an almost empty whiskey bottle at his elbow, a pile of cash winnings beside it and a too-friendly saloon girl eyeing both him *and* his latest hand of cards, Cade knew he should have felt on top of his game. Instead he felt morose and brooding and downright solitary. He wasn't alone; not precisely. But he felt as detached from his opulent, risk-engendering, sinfulness-stoking surroundings as he possibly could have.

When had green baize and playing cards become so dull? How had scantily clad women and wagering opponents stopped being stimulating? Where was he supposed to go for satisfaction now?

He hadn't entered into the gambling world for thrills, Cade reminded himself. But somewhere along the way, while searching for Whittier and tracking his movements within the circuit, he'd become used to the distracting pleasures that world offered him.

Glancing around the table now as he idly placed his next bet, Cade couldn't help wondering: When he got the answers he needed from Whittier…what then? What would be left for him then?

As if in answer to that question, a gray-haired man stepped through the crowd of saloon goers. He wore a sober pressed suit, a minister's clerical collar and a starched-looking hat. From beneath its dark brim, his full, silvery whiskers were plainly evident; so was his determined expression. Whatever Reverend Benson had come to the saloon for, it was important to him.

"Foster!" Reverend Benson barked. "I want a word with you."

Aha. The minister had come regarding Violet, then. Cade had been expecting this—for quite a while, in fact.

"Just *one* word?" Cade gave the older man's lowered eyebrows and indomitable features a chary look. He set down his cards, readying himself. "I reckon you want more than that, don't you?"

"Don't be impertinent."

"I'm guessing you've got a whole passel of words saved up, all ready to unleash on me." Cade clinked together his winnings. With deft movements, he pocketed his money. Beside him, the showily painted saloon girl blinked, obviously surprised at his speedy movements. "Let me guess—they start with 'stay away' and end with 'my daughter.' Am I close, Reverend?"

The older man compressed his mouth, seeming displeased.

Knowingly, Cade grinned. "You're not the first father I've run into during my travels. I doubt you'll be the last."

But he was the only one Cade had ever felt disappointed to be having this conversation with. The realization puzzled him.

"That only makes my business with you all the more urgent."

"To you? Maybe." Cade shrugged. "But to

me, this is just the latest town. The latest game. The latest overprotective father, determined to guard his daughter's virtue." Aware of their observers' curious looks, Cade met Reverend Benson's gaze squarely. If the reverend thought they'd forged some sort of friendship just because Cade had slipped the man an improving card...well, he'd better think again. Cade didn't form alliances. "The only thing that makes you different, Reverend, is you're less likely to swear at me. Or to try to swing a punch."

"Keep talking." Frowning, Reverend Benson made a fist. "You might inspire me to show you that you're wrong about that."

Impressed, Cade raised his eyebrows. Maybe he had misjudged this particular soft-spoken father. "Violet wouldn't like that."

"You don't know what my daughter likes."

"Mmm. I think I do." He had when he'd been kissing her. But admitting as much would be beyond indiscreet—and Cade was nothing if not restrained. His lonely life had taught him to be. Carelessly, he dragged on his suit coat. He adjusted his lapels, then made himself smile. "You're here later than I expected," he observed, glancing up at the minister again.

"Most fathers would have voiced their objections to me long before now."

Reverend Benson straightened. "*I* am not most fathers."

"Violet is not most women." Lazily, Cade rose. "So I'm curious to know. Why have you waited this long to protect her?"

Benson's eyes bulged. Growing red faced, he pointed a shaky finger at Cade. "Your intentions *are* dishonorable, then?"

Another smile. "If they were, would I admit it?"

"Talk straight with me!" The reverend raised his voice. "I'm here, man to man, to manage this situation between you and Violet. To offer you a wager! But if you insist on speaking in riddles with me, then it will be impossible for us to—"

"A wager?" His curiosity piqued, Cade went still. No domineering papa or interfering uncle or matchmaking mother had ever suggested a wager. Not to him. Especially not with regard to a woman like Violet. He'd been hoping he could use charm and conviviality to earn Reverend Benson's blessing to call on Violet— eventually—but that tactic no longer seemed available…not given the man's current combativeness. "What sort of wager?"

Reverend Benson glanced around. Across Jack Murphy's boisterous saloon, the piano still pinged out a bawdy tune. Gamblers still placed their bets. But near the table where Cade had done his wagering so far, all was silent in anticipation.

"A private one," Benson said firmly. "Let's talk alone."

That seemed fair. With another shrug, Cade left behind his latest game. "Keep the table warm, gents," he said over his shoulder. "I'll be back directly to clean your pockets."

Amid the genial, profanity-filled objections of his fellow sporting men, Cade followed Reverend Benson to the saloon's back room. Whatever Violet had done to bewitch him into wanting her by his side, Cade realized, it must be nigh irresistible.

Otherwise, how else to explain the fact that he was about to risk angering a man of God— and maybe the Almighty Himself—in a wager that was sure to be foolish at best?

But he didn't have much to lose, Cade reminded himself as he shut the door behind himself and Reverend Benson. His search for Whittier was leaching away whatever hopefulness he'd once had. If a fresh bet could enliven his night, what was the harm?

* * *

Standing in the minuscule, inadequately heated Morrow Creek train station office on a brisk autumn morning, Violet accepted a stack of registers and paperwork from Joseph Abernathy, the clerk. It was an awkward exchange. Joseph had lost partial use of his hand and arm a few years ago during a sawing accident at the Copeland Lumber Mill, so his grasp on the records was a bit precarious. But his smile, which he offered her in conjunction with the leather-bound books, appeared every bit as bright and boyish as it always had.

"Here you go, Miss Benson," he said cheerfully. "All our receipts from last spring all the way up to last week."

"That will be fine. I shouldn't need any more than that." Knowing the records in her grasp ought to provide her with at least a first step in tracking Tobe's arrival with his mother in Morrow Creek, Violet smiled. "Thank you very much, Joseph. I can't tell you how much I appreciate your help. Again. This must be the fourth favor you've done for me in as many months."

"Pshaw. It's no problem at all!" Joseph insisted. "After everything you've done for me, it's the least I could do. If it weren't for you, I don't know what would have happened to me."

He meant after he'd lost his job at the lumber mill, Violet knew. He'd been deeply distraught. But all that was behind him.

"The depot is fortunate to have you." Joseph's position there—wrangled by the combination of Violet and mill owner Marcus Copeland, working together—had been a snap to procure. "You're smart and hardworking, and that uniform suits you, too."

This time Joseph blushed, all the way to his ears. "That's what Miss Hartford told me. That she likes me in my uniform."

"Really?" Intrigued and pleased, Violet hugged the records to her chest. "How are things progressing between you two?"

Somewhat shyly, Joseph confided his plans to propose to his longtime beloved, Miss Letitia Hartford. Violet liked Joseph; she was happy for him. For the first time when hearing such romantic news, she didn't feel even a twinge of jealousy or self-pity. *She* had someone to care for, too, Violet remembered— someone who cared for her, also. Someone who wanted to kiss her!

Cade might be an unusual partner, but he

was a dazzling one. His interest in her now made up for years of disregard.

"Well, good luck with your proposal." Warmly, Violet gave Joseph a parting squeeze to his upper arm. "I have business to conduct at the Lorndorff Hotel—" meaning she had more records to retrieve there "—a few letters to mail and then a sewing bee to get to. My women's group is making quilts for needy families this year, and there's a great deal of work left to be done."

"That's mighty kindhearted of you, Miss Benson."

Violet merely shrugged. "It's as much for me as it is for anyone else. I'm so blessed—how could I *not* share that?"

"Knowing you? You couldn't." Joseph tipped his cap. With a leading look, he added, "I only hope you and your Mr. Foster will be as happy together as me and Miss Hartford are."

"If you're angling for grist for the gossip mill, I'm afraid you're going to be disappointed." Violet grinned. "Despite rumors to the contrary, Mr. Foster and I share a simple friendship." *With kisses. Lots and lots of kisses.* "That's all."

At least until Papa agrees I may see Cade. And then....

"Absolutely," Joseph agreed, eyes wide with sham naïveté. "No one is expecting a wintertime engagement for you at all!"

An engagement. Wouldn't that be extraordinary?

With the notion taking root in her heart for the first time, Violet considered precisely what such a remarkable event would mean: that she was loved...*beloved.* That she could finally give herself to someone on a more personal basis than the broad generosity required for quilted coverlets or charity kitchens.

That would be the fulfillment of her dreams for certain. But did *she*—plain-featured, overlooked Violet Benson—truly dare to hope for such a momentous occurrence? Cade insisted he wanted her. Joseph and several of her friends seemed to agree that they could become a credible couple. So what was stopping her?

"Well, perhaps everyone *should* expect that!" Violet dared to say. At the immenseness of her boast, her heartbeat hammered madly. If she wasn't careful, soon she'd be bluffing as often and as recklessly as Cade. But at the same time, she couldn't help remembering exactly what Cade had told her the other day.

Give over, Violet. Do it. It's the only way to feel alive.

She *wanted* to give over to her wildest impulses. She did. Cade had helped her to recognize that from their very first dance. Already, Violet realized, she was well on her way.

Perhaps now she could go even further.

Joseph blinked, appearing slightly less teasing—and slightly less sure. "We should expect an engagement? For *you*?"

Heedless of the hesitation now edging into her friend's voice, Violet brightened. She *should* do it! she decided. She should do *something*, at least. She should…seize this rare opportunity at courtship and gamble on love herself! Everyone seemed to believe she'd done so already. So why not do it?

After all, Cade believed she could bring him good luck. There was no reason to suspect she couldn't improve her own fortunes at the same time. With Cade still ensconced, so far as she knew, in his luxurious room at the Lorndorff Hotel—her next intended destination—there was no time like the present.

There was no time like now to truly *fly*. With Cade.

Fired up now and full of newfound verve—not to mention a budding hope that what existed between her and Cade might grow into something more—Violet gave Joseph's arm another squeeze.

Then she turned hurriedly to leave.

"By the first snowfall, we could *both* be engaged to be married," Violet told Joseph as she left. "Let's hope so!"

"For your sake," Joseph vowed sincerely, "I *do* hope so!"

Was that more *doubt* suffusing his voice, making him sound uncertain and wary? Violet didn't think so. Assuring herself she was doing the right thing, she offered Joseph a heartfelt goodbye. Then, with her documents hugged to her chest and her heart filled with a heady mix of bravado and sheer until-now-untapped determination, Violet left the train depot and headed for the tall, two-story opulence of the Lorndorff Hotel...and somewhere inside it, Cade Foster's scandalously enjoyable embrace.

To be a good gambler, a man had to be both observant and detached, interested and wary. He had to be willing to risk everything on the turn of a card or the roll of a dice. He had to possess sufficient grit to stay the course even when fortune didn't spin his way. Most of all, he had to keep his word. Otherwise, he'd rightly be labeled a liar and a cheat, and the gambling world would snap shut to him for the rest of his days.

That's why, last night when Cade had lost his wager with Reverend Benson, he'd had to accept the consequences. He'd had to move forward like a man. For the sake of his reputation, he'd had to smile at Violet's father, nod in acceptance of his fate and move on straightaway.

Last night, Cade had done all those things. Today, in the unforgiving light of a bleak new morning, he almost wished he hadn't. The stakes that Reverend Benson had set—and Cade had foolishly and arrogantly accepted—were just too high.

If you win, the minister had said, *you may court my daughter. You may call on Violet and entertain her in public. Eventually, if she agrees, you may even marry her.*

And because, to a whiskey-soaked and over-confident Cade, that prize had sounded nigh irresistible, he'd agreed readily.

But if you lose, the minister had gone on to caution him, wearing a peculiar smile, *you must agree to find yourself honest work, as an honest laborer, and give up all your gambling ways.*

*Even the "gambling ways" that have bene-
fited your church coffers and your own pock-
etbook?* Cade had asked with a grin. It was just
like a pious man, he'd reckoned then, to try to
reform him...even while he profited from his
supposed debauchery.

But the wager had been all but set at that
point. There'd been no way Cade could foresee
losing a bet to a fumble-fingered, outlandishly
overoptimistic minister—especially one who
let tender emotions overrule common sense.
No self-respecting professional sporting man
could have. So Cade had merely shook hands
with Violet's father, requested a fresh deck of
cards from Harry, Jack Murphy's able barkeep,
and begun a new game.

Two hours later, Cade had stared in patent
disbelief as gray-haired, newly jocular Reverend Benson had scraped all his winnings into
his overturned hat, issued an incomprehensi-
ble bit of scripture as a final condolence, then
bade him farewell.

Don't forget! his parting words had rung
out. *Honest work! In an honest trade, with a
fair exchange of labor for wages.*

Cade scarcely knew what that meant. And
he scarcely knew how to explain this disastrous
misstep to Blackhouse, what's more. His bene-

factor wouldn't be pleased with this wrinkle in their plans. Whatever Blackhouse's reasons for wanting to find Whittier were, they'd kept him in the hunt for a long while. The bachelor ne'er-do-well of the rails was unlikely to quit now.

Considering the thorny issue of explaining himself to Blackhouse, Cade dragged his arm over his eyes. He wanted to shield himself both from the daylight shoving its way through his hotel room draperies *and* from his own recriminations.

How could he have been so brash? So reckless? Not only had he put his search for Whittier in jeopardy, but he'd also cut himself off from seeing Violet. She would never understand this.

Wondering if the reverend would tell his daughter the truth about their situation, Cade groaned. Of course he wouldn't. He'd wanted to force Cade to stay away from Violet, and he had—in a fashion that Cade could neither argue with nor back down from.

I believe you're a man of honor, Reverend Benson had told Cade as he'd made ready to leave the gambling table and Murphy's saloon last night. *For Violet's sake, I'm glad of it.*

That was him, Cade thought now with a new sense of irony. An honor-bound gambler:

the first and last of his kind. Because when it came to Violet and what she deserved from him, honesty was paramount...but honor came hard on its heels. For Violet, Cade would have clung to the merest of honorable intentions. How else to explain why he'd entered into such a foolish wager at all?

Sprawled amid his tangled bed linens, beset with regret and the rough aftereffects of too much Old Orchard whiskey, Cade groaned again. The only thing to do was get on with it. If he went on lying here, turning over the events of last night in his mind, he'd surely lose the will to get up altogether. Judah had found him that way once, Cade recalled unwillingly, half-drunk and entirely naked, stuck in a nameless hotel room from which he'd felt no inclination to leave for almost a week.

He'd lost track of Whittier on that occasion, too. That had been years ago now—years and many disappointments...the latest of which had left Cade completely averse to carry on fighting.

Get up, his brother had urged him. *You're scaring me.*

Judah's blue eyes—so like their father's—had looked especially large and fearful that day, set against the youthful features of his familiar face. He'd been not quite twenty then. Cade had just turned twenty-four. It felt a million years ago now.

Please, Judah had said then. *I need you to keep trying.*

But now Cade's brother was hundreds of miles away. There was no one to rouse him from his bed this time. There was no one to lie to him and tell him there was still hopefulness left.

A sharp rap at the door startled Cade.

Judah? he couldn't help thinking. Had Blackhouse really brought him there, as he'd suggested he'd do so many times now?

Impossible. "Go away."

Another knock. It sounded more determined this time.

"Leave me alone." Maybe it was the maid. Yesterday she'd flirtatiously suggested using her feather duster to tickle his fancy. Cade hadn't been interested. "I don't need anything."

That was a lie. He did need things. He needed answers and resolve and maybe a kind word or two. He needed Violet Benson.

"I don't need anything you can give me," he clarified with a certain belligerence. He swore. "Go bother someone else."

The knocking quit. An instant later, the doorknob turned.

Cade gawked at it. It rattled vigorously. Next came the distinctive click of a key being inserted into the lock.

Hellfire. Probably Blackhouse had bribed a hotel employee into unlocking Cade's room—possibly for the express purpose of gloating over Cade's loss to Reverend Benson last night. Cade didn't think anyone knew about the outcome of their wager. But during their acquaintance, Blackhouse had proven surprisingly adept at collecting information—at least when he could be bothered to bestir himself from his usual pleasurable pursuits.

With an even more raw and heartfelt swearword, Cade heaved himself from his bed. Bleary-eyed and shirtless, he padded across his hotel room's plush Oriental rug. With one eye on the door, Cade dragged on his trousers. He'd just buttoned them when the lock finally gave way. The door burst open with a bang.

Violet Benson stood there, her arms full of books and ledgers and papers, all held higgledy-piggledy in her grasp. Her face was flushed, her breath was hurried and her smile was enchanting. Cade knew he must have imagined her. He must have conjured her from some devilish mixture of despair and regret, specifically to taunt himself over losing the chance to be with her. He could be unforgiving that way, he knew. He could be cruel, especially when it came to himself and what he needed.

"I don't want to bother anyone else," Violet piped up with giddy, adorably girlish certainty. "I only want to bother *you!*"

She *looked* real enough. She sounded real enough. She even reacted realistically enough when she belatedly noticed that Cade was tellingly tousle haired and mostly undressed.

Unlike him, Violet did not appear at ease with his near nudity. Blushing even more furiously, she gave a one-handed wave in his direction. "But I can wait until you're dressed. To bother you, I mean. I don't mind waiting for, um, you to—" She broke off, obviously floundering. "That is, I did come here on purpose, you see, but I was not quite prepared for such a speedy entrée into the world of, well, courtship and…things."

"Courtship? And things?"

"Indeed." A nod. "Although I believe it's customary to be dressed, at least for the initial stages. So you should—"

"You haven't spoken with your father yet, then?"

Violet gave him a puzzled look. That only convinced Cade he was probably losing his mind—or maybe was still a little drunk.

Perhaps, he thought with the sudden insight of the formerly sober, he shouldn't have chased his Old Orchard with mescal.

"My father was ministering to a congregant this morning," Violet informed him. "So no, I haven't spoken with him today. But if you're concerned about earning Papa's permission—"

"I'm not." Not with *this* Violet, Cade wasn't. With *this* Violet, he still had a chance to indulge all his fantasies.

Intrigued by the possibility—even if he *had* fabricated an inconveniently prim version of her—Cade took a step nearer.

Violet's upswept hair was mussed, he noticed. Her skirts were askew, as though she'd run all the way upstairs to his room. Which she couldn't have done, of course. Because a proper young woman like Violet Benson—a minister's straitlaced daughter, no less!—certainly wouldn't risk her reputation by taking herself alone to visit a scurrilous gambler like him.

That all but proved he'd conjured her somehow. Whether through some consequence of the liquor he'd drunk or simply his own overwhelming desire to see her, he'd imagined her there in his room. Still watching her, Cade realized that if *this* Violet wasn't real—if this wasn't really happening at all between them— then he didn't need to be gentlemanly or restrained. He didn't even need to watch what he said for fear of scaring her away.

"You're lucky I'm wearing even this much," he said as a test of his theory, gesturing at his low-slung trousers. "Until I heard the knock at the door, I was lying in bed entirely naked."

Her gaze skittered to the unmade bed. Her eyes widened. She was picturing the sight, Cade reckoned…exactly as he'd meant for her to do. If this was the real Violet, she'd scurry away now.

Instead, she lifted her chin. "I bet that was… comfortable."

Cade raised his brow. His imaginary Violet was sassy. He liked that about her. "It was. You should try it sometime."

She nodded, biting her lip in apparent deliberation. At that, Cade's imagination truly galloped away with him. Wholly unbidden, it offered up a tantalizing vision of Violet lying there in his bed, with her skin bare and her luscious curves ready for him to touch. Swallowing hard, Cade shook his head to clear it... even as Violet nodded in thought once more.

"Yes. That's a marvelous idea. Perhaps I will try lying in bed naked." She eyed the bed and its rumpled covers as though considering the notion more carefully. "Perhaps very soon."

As if that outrageous statement were simply a long-expected promise, she met his gaze squarely. Cade scarcely dared to wonder what his make-believe Violet would say or do next.

"I'm here to ruin my reputation, Cade," she announced firmly. "With you."

Stunned by that scandalous notion, Cade couldn't speak.

But Violet didn't seem to mind. "I'm here to make some thrilling memories," she went on, "and maybe change my future while I'm at it. And we've already wasted a great deal of time, so—" perkily, she smiled "—shall we get started?"

Chapter Seven

"Get started?" Cade repeated. Did she really mean what he thought she meant? That they should be together…intimately?

"Yes." With an air of plucky certainty, Violet set down her books and papers and leather-bound ledgers. "We should have all the time we need, so don't worry about that. I told the hotel clerk that I was here on a charitable mission for the church."

"The church?" Cade repeated dumbly, still stuck on the possibility that Violet might willingly lie naked in his bed.

"Yes. I embark on altruistic works all the time, you know," Violet assured him. "Everyone in Morrow Creek is aware of that. So they won't find it the least bit questionable that I'm here visiting you like this. After all, you're new in town, and you're most certainly in need of ministering to. It's undeniable. I mean, just *look* at you!" She beamed at him as if delighted by his debauchery. "I felt immensely clever when I realized that on my way here. Isn't it utterly convenient?"

"Yes." It *was* convenient, Cade realized. Ingenious, too.

Contrary to all expectation, Violet's logic suggested that a virtuous woman could misbehave far more readily than a scandalous one could...and not be suspected of being anything less than upright in the process. No wonder Violet seemed so all-fired pleased with herself. She had a veritable license to sin.

And she wanted to use it with Cade.

"No! No, it isn't convenient," he blurted, realizing too late that he had to backtrack. For honor's sake. "Everyone will find it *very* questionable that you're here. Alone. With me."

I'm here to ruin my reputation, Cade. With you!

"You can't ruin your reputation," he insisted. "You made me promise that *I* wouldn't ruin your reputation. This is madness."

"It's not. It's actually quite sensible. Besides, my feelings have changed on the matter of my reputation. Given our newfound...closeness, I think this will be fine." Her satisfied smile seemed to settle the matter. "The desk clerk remembered you coming in intoxicated last night. He remembered you swearing about losing your latest wager. Because of that, he was fully prepared to believe I'm here to reform you." Violet paused to deliver him a suggestive look. "However long it takes to do so."

For a moment, Cade couldn't breathe. His entire existence was taken up with imagining the authentic Violet Benson seducing him this way...with wondering if she would have wanted him like this. He thought she would have. After all, he *hadn't* concocted the attraction between them. It had seemed unlikely to him at first. But very quickly it had felt real and true—and tempting.

"I think you're mistaken about what 'reform' means, Miss Benson." Cade couldn't help cracking a grin. Damnation, he wished she was real. He wished Violet's idea of "reforming" him really did include alluring looks and promises to lie abed naked with him. "But I confess to liking your take on the notion."

"Yes. I thought you might." Surprisingly, Violet grinned too, leaving him feeling overcome by the impish beauty of her smile. "The truth is, I wasn't intending to go this far when I set out for the Lorndorff a little while ago. But partway here I realized this might be my only chance to experience lovemaking, Cade. *You* might be my only chance. I don't want to miss it."

"Miss...lovemaking?" Cade repeated, scarcely able to form the words. Her frank way of talking left him electrified. He'd never expected to hear such things coming from Violet's mouth.

Then, too, he *wanted* to be her only chance, just as she'd said. God help him, he *wanted* to be the one to introduce her to lovemaking and all the pleasures it had to offer. He wanted *her*.

But this...wasn't real. It couldn't be.

Trying to recover his wits, Cade shook his head. Somehow his harmless fantasy had grown fangs. Now it was torturing him.

Violet was off-limits. Violet was proper and good. Violet didn't want a man like him—a man without a future to offer her.

"Yes. Lovemaking," Violet said firmly. "I might never be married—not the way things are going, anyway—and I can't see why I should be penalized for that. So I have to make this good. I have to do whatever I can to *feel alive* before it's too late!"

Recognizing his own words on her lips,

Cade groaned. He aimed his gaze heaven-ward, desperate now to end this reverie—if that's what it was. He was beginning to have serious doubts.

"I'll never touch a drop of whiskey again," he swore fervently, hoping to snap out of his fantasy. "I swear it."

"See?" Violet's ever-comforting smile touched him. "That's very well done of you to play along! Anyone passing by would believe I've been partially effective in reforming you already."

As if tardily realizing then that any idle passersby could indeed glimpse them, Violet punctuated her statement by pushing Cade's hotel room door completely closed. Its thud-ding slam alerted him to the fact that per-haps—almost certainly—he wasn't imagining things. He wasn't imagining *her*.

What, exactly, was happening here?

"But even if I've licked your awful problem with drinking, there's still the matter of your *terrible* gambling impulses to deal with, Mr. Foster." Violet's expression turned alarmingly teasing. She seemed almost cocksure...for her. "You need my help. You really do," she insisted earnestly, crossing the room to come nearer to him. When she arrived to stand almost atop his big bare feet, she smiled up at Cade coquettishly. "When Henry—he's the desk clerk...I've known him since we were both in the schoolhouse together—gave me my own key to your hotel room, he wished me good luck in coping with your...uncontrollable urges."

Uncontrollable. Yes, that was exactly the way Cade would have described his desire for her just then. Trying hard not to think about that, Cade glanced at the hotel room key she'd used. Even now it mocked him from atop the ledgers and things Violet had set aside. Feeling suddenly beset by those selfsame urges she'd alluded to—or at least by a few illicit impulses exactly as passionately felt—he clenched his jaw. *Violet was real.*

She was real, she was here, and Cade could not give in to any of the things she was suggesting. No matter what.

"This is a test," he announced, realizing it must be true—diabolically so. "It's a test to see if I'll keep my word, the way I promised to. Well, you can tell your father that I did." Cade raised his hand to swear it. "This is one honor-bound gambler who won't endanger your heart *or* your reputation."

"Oh, I don't intend to tell my father about this." Violet raised herself on tiptoe. She clasped her hand with his upraised hand for leverage, then pressed a kiss to his mouth. "Or that." Another kiss, followed by a tentative smile. "Or that. Or anything that might happen between us from now till midnight."

"Midnight?" Maybe he'd misunderstood. After all, he'd never been "reformed" before. Maybe he'd been dreading the notion unnecessarily all this time. "What will take until midnight?"

"More kissing," Violet specified. "More touching. More looking." Audaciously, she sent her gaze over his bare torso. "I like the way you look, you know. I like it very much." Another, bolder perusal. She nodded. "You look very strong. And capable."

It was still possible he could deter her before it was too late. Hoping to do exactly that, Cade said, "I *am* capable."

Her mouth parted. Her cheeks turned a pretty shade of pink.

"I'm capable," Cade went on, gazing into her eyes, "of giving you the kind of pleasure you couldn't possibly have imagined. I'm capable of making you yell with enjoyment—of making you writhe and pant beneath me, begging for release."

Violet swallowed hard. But her gaze never left his.

"I want that," she said. "I want you. I trust you."

She shouldn't do that. *Hellfire.* Closing his eyes, Cade tried to summon whatever fortitude and integrity he had left.

"Don't, Violet. Just…don't." This time, paradoxically, Cade was the one begging—and they hadn't even reached his bed. "You don't know what you're doing…what could happen. This is—"

"Perfect," she breathed. "It's going to be perfect, just as soon as you give in. Just as soon as you realize that I *want* this. I want *you*!" Eagerly, Violet shucked her long woolen coat. Beneath it, her calico dress swayed with her movements, showing him a glimpse of stocking-clad ankle. "Please, Cade. I'm not going to beg. But we've had an understanding between us for a while now. You must have known this was inevitable. Because I know you see me as I am, and I see you, too, the same way."

"No, you don't," Cade disagreed, needing to disillusion her. "There are things about me that you can't conceive. Dark things. Things I can't explain and don't have answers to."

"Then you can tell me all about them. I want to know."

He hauled in a ragged breath. If he had no choice…

"Because I've realized something about us, Cade." Violet offered him a bashful smile. "Something about us together." With her eyes shining in anticipation of her coming statement, she inhaled. "Somehow, I think, we're each other's last chance."

Cade didn't understand. "Last chance for what?"

"For feeling loved!" Violet took his hand. "I know I want that. You must want it, too. Wouldn't it be downright foolhardy to throw away that chance just for the sake of propriety?"

He grinned. "You make a compelling argument."

"And you make a surprisingly reluctant participant," she teased. "For a renowned scoundrel and known chance taker."

"I'm not reluctant. These stakes are higher than most."

If he wanted to behave honorably, Cade knew, he'd tell Violet that propriety trumped all. If he wanted to avoid hurting her, he'd tell her that he *had* felt loved, many times over, and had no need of her paltry caring now. But that would be a lie—an especially egregious one—and Cade could not deliver it. Because all at once, he saw Violet in a new and vulnerable light, and he knew that *not* being with her might hurt her more than being with her ever could. And Cade decidedly didn't want that.

"But I reckon it *would* be a sin to throw away a chance at love," he finally agreed with a reckless grin. "A terrible sin."

Her eyes brightened. "I'm happy you see things my way."

"Me, too," Cade agreed after broadening his smile, and with that, he quit resisting altogether. After all, he'd duly warned Violet. He'd described exactly what would happen between them. He'd even alluded to his frightful past. And still she remained there. No one could fault him for giving her what she wanted.

And if this wasn't following precisely the intent of his wager with Reverend Benson... well, that could be forgiven, too. Especially if no one ever found out about it, as he planned.

Because Cade hadn't called on Violet. She'd come to him. She'd come to him and she'd offered herself to him, and he was just a man, with a man's needs and a man's eagerness to pleasure a woman, and no one short of a lunatic would expect him to refuse her. Particularly not while she stood there, seeming so ripe and inventive and intriguingly innocent. He'd never had an innocent woman, it occurred to Cade. From his first paramour—a kindhearted whore who'd lived down the street from Cade's third set of foster parents—to his last, everyone he'd been with had been experienced and jaded. Like him, his partners had been wholly uninterested in any connection beyond lusty pleasure.

But Violet was different. Violet was sweet. She was caring.

All she'd talked about was *feeling* loved, just this once. They'd both be fools to surrender that chance. So with his mind made up, Cade broadened his smile. He gave Violet a lingering, up-and-down perusal...one designed to heighten her innocent awareness of exactly how close they were about to become.

"It *would* be a sin to throw away a chance at love," he repeated. Then, "Do you know what else is a sin?"

Violet swallowed hard. In a shaky voice, she ventured, "Coveting your neighbor's skill with a knitting needle?"

He smiled. Damnation, but he could have fallen for Violet...if he'd been a settling-down kind of man. Which he was not. Giving her a tenderhearted smile nonetheless, Cade said, "Not understanding what your body is capable of feeling. Not experiencing all the sensations that are waiting for you."

"Oh." She bit her lip. "I see. Such as?"

She was so brave, it occurred to him. Even in this. He couldn't help admiring that about her. Moving closer, Cade skimmed his hands along her hips to her waist. With slow, deliberate movements, he traced the curves he found there.

"Such as…this." He lifted his gaze to hers. "Do you feel that? Do you feel the way your body differs from mine?"

She shivered…even while her body radiated warmth to his fingertips. With sham contemplativeness, Violet crinkled her brow. "I'm not sure. Perhaps if you demonstrated some more?"

"Minx." Cade grinned again. "You're deliberately encouraging me to continue."

"Yet you're decidedly *not* continuing. So…"

"So you hadn't reckoned on my self-control, I guess." *He* hadn't either, he realized. He hadn't reckoned on his resolve crumbling so much in the face of Violet's naive allure. "Try to pay attention this time," he said, "and I'll demonstrate again."

Smiling, Violet stood erect. "All right. I'm ready."

So was he. He was ready to lay her down on the waiting bed, strip off those interferingly fussy clothes of hers and make her his. But that wouldn't be nearly as much fun as this…as much fun as carefully sliding his hands from Violet's hips—again—to her waist. To augment his lesson, he kissed her, exceedingly gently.

"Where you're curvy, I'm straight," Cade explained. "Where you're soft and yielding, I'm sturdy…even rigid." *Damnation, he was rigid.* It felt as though his hastily yanked-on trousers had shrunk in the past few minutes. "We fit together, you and me."

"I hope we fit together," Violet quipped. "Otherwise I've been woefully misinformed about what to expect."

He raised his brows. "What do you expect?"

She breathed out, glancing determinedly away from him. "Some good things. Some touching. A bit of…pain." Her gaze skittered back to his. "My married friends do confide in me."

"Your married friends are the ones who are misinformed."

"What do you mean?"

"I mean lovemaking shouldn't hurt." Cade might not have indulged in the sentimental, hearts-and-flowers version of sexual relations, but he knew that much for certain. He knew it should feel good. "If there's any pain, it should be brief and—"

"Oh, it won't hurt *you*! Don't worry about that!" Violet hastened to assure him. She gave a fretful titter, seeming concerned that she might have alarmed him unduly. "*You* will enjoy it, without a doubt! All men do. If my friend Adeline is right, *I* will enjoy some of what goes on between us too, so—"

"*All*," Cade specified fiercely. "You will enjoy all of the things that go on between us. Or I'll know the reason."

Her eyes widened. "You sound so determined."

That was because he cared about her, Cade knew. Because he wanted her to experience the kind of joy she deserved and had been denied until now...and maybe would be denied in the future, too. It wasn't fair that Violet Benson had been overlooked just because she didn't possess apple cheeks or an upturned nose. In that moment, Cade found her beautiful. He wanted her to feel that way, as well. He wanted her to feel...*everything*.

"*You* sound dubious," he replied with another grin. "But that won't last. I promise you that much."

"Oh? And how will you—"

"Like this," Cade interrupted, then pulled her into his arms. He'd dallied too long with chitchat and preliminaries. Now was the time to make Violet see what she'd been missing. So he did. He lowered his head and took her mouth with his, a prelude to everything that would come next and after. She felt good and warm and eager in his arms, and he felt that he could have kissed her for days and not come up for air. But eventually his lungs protested, so Cade stopped. He gave Violet a loving look, then kissed her once more. "With enough kissing," he explained, "I think your inappropriate dubiousness will go away."

"I'm not so sure," she teased anew. "Perhaps you've lost your touch. Perhaps your kisses have lost their potency."

"Minx." Again he kissed her. And again Cade found *himself* caught up in their coming together. Kissing Violet was like jumping off a cliff...straight into heaven. It was like sunshine and blue skies. It was like needing and *needing*…and getting only a taste of something essential and true. "How do you feel now?"

Appearing dazed, Violet shook her head. "A bit more certain, I guess," she judged with her usual vivacity. "More?"

"More?" She was going to kill him. Any thought Cade might have given to stopping now could not have withstood her provocation. Whether Violet knew it or not, she was giving him exactly what he needed to ignore any lingering doubts of his own. *More, more, more*, she urged him…and Cade wanted to give it.

"Yes, more." She blinked. "Or should I undress first?"

At the thought, dizziness swamped him. The notion of seeing Violet in the altogether, bared and willing and eager, was almost more than Cade could stand. He swallowed. "I'll do that."

"But you're already partly undressed."

"I'll undress *you*." To prove it, Cade toyed with her bodice's topmost button. He contemplated the secrets it hid, and felt himself grow twice as rigid as before. He'd considered what she would look like naked, of course. Any man would have, especially given the time they'd spent together…and the unexpected rapport they'd shared. But to be so close to the real-ity of that daydream… "Mmm. But first, another kiss."

This time, their mouths met unerringly, in a newly practiced glide that paired heat and slickness and softness in ways Cade had never quite experienced before. With Violet, kissing felt new. *Everything* felt new. New and better than ever.

He raised his head, unable to quit smiling at her. She smiled back at him. Then her mouth made an O. She clapped her hand over her gaping dress bodice, her brows raised. "Oh! You've already started!" A dreamy chuckle. "I didn't even realize it."

"I did." Wolfishly interested in the bare skin he'd revealed at her dress's neckline, Cade traced his finger down the center of her chest. Her cleavage was modest and perfect. With effort, he lifted his gaze to her face. "You're beautiful."

Her expression changed. "I'm not beautiful, Cade. Don't say that. *You*, of all people, know that I'm not—"

"Enough." Sternly, he pressed his fingertip to her lips. It required a serious effort of will not to linger there…not to delight in the luscious softness of her mouth and the sweet bow he found there at her lower lip. But since there were things between them that were more important than simple carnal pleasures... "No more talk like that. I won't have it."

As punishment—and diversion—he deftly slipped a few more buttons free of their confining buttonholes. Her bodice gaped a bit more. The effect was enchanting. Her breasts swelled pertly above her tightly laced corset, ready and waiting and...

"But it's true!" Violet protested. "I'm not even pretty."

"You're *beyond* pretty," Cade said, and in that moment, it became his mission to prove it to her. "You have something no other woman does, Violet. You have yourself, in all your glory, for me to delight in and laugh with and touch this way—"

"Hmmph. No other woman *wants* my so-called 'glory.'"

"Some people are beautiful when you meet them," Cade said, giving her an unyielding look. "Others become beautiful as you get to know them. You," he specified with a lingering touch, "become prettier to me with every minute. You *are* beautiful."

With that, her eyes filled with tears. "Truly?"

"Truly," Cade said, and gave her a kiss to prove it. "I love your freckled face and your wonderful nose. I love your crooked, skeptical smile and your warm, giving hands. I love your body—" He broke off, too distracted to continue speaking as he dared to fill his palms with her breasts, now almost wholly freed from her wide, lace-trimmed bodice. He kissed her instead. "I love everything about you, Violet. And to demonstrate that, I'm going to love every bit of you, starting right now."

Her smile enchanted him. "Even my ankles?"

"Even your ankles," Cade told her, and he knew then that he had won. "So lie back and get ready," he said as he gestured to the waiting bed, "because we've only just begun."

Chapter Eight

With an exuberance born of discovery and curiosity and almost unbearable hopefulness, Violet leaped toward the bed.

She landed amid the tangled covers in a veritable heap of calico skirts and lacy muslin petticoats. Her scandalously unbuttoned bodice allowed her bosom to feel the fresh air; her invigorated skin tingled at her first contact with Cade's fancy hotel room sheets. Her mouth felt swollen and her legs felt weak and everywhere beneath her skirts felt uniquely warm—almost effervescently so—and she wasn't sure how much more of Cade's sweet words she could stand before she simply swooned with joy.

Because Cade Foster loved her. He *loved* her! He'd just said so, over and over again. *I love everything about you.* And now, just as she had when she'd first heard those words from his lips, Violet felt overcome with gladness.

She'd done the right thing by coming here to be with him. If not for her burst of boldness today, she might never have known that Cade thought she was beautiful. That he thought she was irresistible. That he *loved* her!

"There!" Violet announced. Bravely, she pushed up on her elbows, then regarded Cade from her perch on his bed. Chirpily, she patted the bedclothes beside her. "I'm ready. Now what?"

"Now—" He gave her an adorably devilish eyebrow quirk…one that made her heartbeat race twice as eagerly. "I'll join you."

He did as he'd promised, making the mattress dip beneath his weight. Keeping her in his sights, Cade prowled his way from the edge of the bed to Violet's place in the very center of it.

"You have lovely big muscles," she observed, eyeing the rippled, corded movements of his arms and shoulders and chest as he approached her. Avidly, she let her gaze roam down Cade's chest, following his dark chest hair to his taut belly, then lower to his… Not yet ready, she whipped up her gaze. "I like your muscles. No, I *love* them," Violet said in fond mimicry of him. "I do. Especially when you use them to hold me close."

"That's one of the best uses for them," he agreed.

"I don't suppose it requires much strength to hold cards at a gambling table," she mused aloud, "but still, you're strong."

"And you're talkative." A grin. "But that won't last."

"I can't see why not." Somewhat nervously, Violet watched as Cade stretched out on the bed beside her. "I'm pretty good at keeping a conversation going," she said. "For instance—" She broke off, noticing then that Cade's trousers had gaped a bit near the waistband. His movements made it evident that if he *was* wearing undergarments, they were exceedingly tiny. Which seemed unlikely. Which could mean only that he was naked under there.

Naked. She'd never seen a naked man before. Enthralled by the notion, Violet tried to envision Cade lolling about in the altogether. She only got as far as his hip, which was probably best explained by the fact that she could actually *see* several inches of tawny, fascinating skin just above his trousers. *Hmm.*

Oblivious to her reveries, Cade trailed his fingertips over her arm. His touch incited a riot of goose bumps, but still Violet could not be distracted from her discovery. Naked. *Naked.*

Somewhere beneath his trousers, Cade was naked. Violet had a powerful urge to know what he looked like under there.

"You know, I seem to be at a disadvantage," she ventured in an effort to satisfy her burgeoning inquisitiveness. "Because I am almost completely dressed at the moment, while *you*—" she gestured at his lackadaisically slipped-on trousers "—are...not."

"That's easily fixed." Smiling, Cade kissed her.

She really loved his kisses. Therefore it took a while for her to summon an appropriate response. She had to wait to catch her breath. Then, "You're not going to put on a shirt, are you? You know, to match up with my level of apparel wearing?"

That hadn't been the point of her observation. Besides, she liked that Cade wasn't wearing a shirt. It let her see his brawny chest muscles and his arms and his middle. Every single part of him was different from her. Intriguingly different.

To Violet, Cade looked as though he could shelter and protect her from anything—and would, willingly, if she asked.

A broader smile. "I'm going to undress *you*. Remember?" He eyed her bodice. "It's past time we finished with that."

"Yes," she said brightly. "We should certainly finish!"

His amused look let her know that hers wasn't the response he'd been expecting. But Violet couldn't help that. She was too preoccupied with more vital things—with wondering about the rest of Cade's arresting physique. His shoulders were bunched with muscles. His arms were sinewy with strength. His belly was flat, his hips were slim, his legs were long and undoubtedly flawless.

Even given all that wonderfulness, though, Violet felt *most* intrigued by what lay between all that. Lying next to him this way, together on his bed, she couldn't help wondering…

Was his, well…*manhood* as muscularly proportionate as the rest of him? If so, how would it feel? Precisely?

Breathlessly, Violet regarded him. With an unreadable expression, Cade gazed at her— then at her chest. She remembered feeling his hands on her breasts, just a few minutes ago. Again her nipples budded with eagerness. She forgot to do anything except wish he would touch her there once more, just that way.

Instead, Cade kissed her. *Then* he cupped her breast in his palm, gently gliding his thumb over the pebbled point of her nipple, and Violet couldn't help gasping against his mouth.

"Does that hurt?" Cade murmured, kissing her neck now.

"No." Shocked to feel herself arching against him, Violet nonetheless continued to do it. She had to. "I like it."

He nodded, satisfied. "I told you you would."

"I do!" she confessed in a breathy voice. She flexed her hands against his back, needing to hold on. "I really do!"

"That's good." Sliding lower, Cade nuzzled the curve of her shoulder, then the angle of her collarbone. He nudged aside her dress a bit farther, then kissed the swell of her breast. "Mmm."

Violet couldn't help mimicking him. "Mmm-*hmm*!"

Never had she felt anything more wonderful or more right. With Cade, she *did* feel beautiful. She felt indispensible. She felt as though with him to offer his hand to her, she could fly.

Cade seemed to believe that was true, too. Because for the next several moments, he set about releasing her from everything that held her to her ordinary existence. Moving over her, murmuring sweet words, Cade made sure that Violet felt loved and beloved and needed. He made sure she felt *wanted*...passionately so. And despite the incredible unlikeliness of any of this happening between them, Violet couldn't muster a single protest.

In fact, she couldn't think of anything at all. She couldn't say a word. All she could do was feel: feel Cade's hands slowly stroking her, feel his breath fluttering over her, feel his mouth moving in an increasingly necessary and exciting arc from her breasts to her neck to her mouth and back again.

Caught beneath his incredible attentions, Violet simply gave in. This was real. It was true. It was right. Through half-closed eyes, she watched as Cade loved her...and she knew that she loved him in return, even if she hadn't yet said so.

To celebrate that, even if only to herself, Violet clutched Cade's head and kissed him back. Happily, she surrendered her high-buttoned shoes, her long dark stockings, her dress and her petticoats and even her corset. Or at least she found herself eventually without them—somehow Cade had peeled away all those garments with her scarcely noticing the movements of his clever gambler's fingers.

But she gave herself full credit for slipping beneath the bedclothes afterward wearing only her chemise—and for boldly, even cheekily, summoning Cade to join her there.

"Are you sure you're ready?" he asked.

"Would I do *this* if I weren't?" Saucily, she crooked her finger in invitation. "Don't keep me waiting. I need you."

For a fraction of a second, Cade seemed hesitant.

Then, "I need you, too," he said. "*You're* what's left for me after all this is done. I didn't know that until right now."

Violet didn't understand him. But before she could ask what Cade meant, he quashed her ability to ask questions by undoing his trousers and dropping them to the floor. If she'd thought his sporting man's hands were clever before... She'd never imagined they could reveal a sight as fascinating as the one that stood proudly before her at that very moment.

"You *are* commensurately huge!" she blurted, wide-eyed.

This time, Cade was the one who appeared momentarily confused. Also, unabashedly pleased with his endowments. He couldn't have known she'd been wondering if his entire body aligned with his impressive musculature. Yet somehow he seemed to. Otherwise, how else to explain the twinkle in his eyes?

"I'm glad you're pleased," he said as he lifted the rumpled bedclothes to join her atop the sumptuous mattress, "but the proof is in the feeling, not in the seeing."

Still awed, Violet sneaked another glimpse. "I'm enjoying the seeing!" She bit her lip, then lifted her gaze to his magnificent, handsome, beloved face. "But I'm curious about the feeling, too," she confessed. "May I touch you… there?"

Cade closed his eyes. His groan rent the stillness.

"Oh! If that's not done, then I apologize!" Violet said hastily. "It's just that you've done *so* much touching me that I've enjoyed, and I can't imagine why I wouldn't want to do the same for you. Why I wouldn't want to make *you* feel beautiful—"

His gaze met hers. "Then you *do* feel beautiful?"

"I mean *handsome*, of course," she nattered on, "so I…" Struck by Cade's needful expression, Violet paused. "Do you truly not know? *Yes*, I feel beautiful." Warmly, she squeezed his hand. "When I came here today, I wanted the experience of lovemaking. But what you've given me is the experience of being *loved*. It's so much more than I ever could have hoped for."

"I see." His voice sounded husky—whether with unshared emotion or with passion, she couldn't guess. Cade cleared his throat. "But we've barely gotten started," he reminded her.

"I know! Just think how much better it will get!"

His smile dazzled her. "I don't think it can get better than that look of joy on your face right now. But I'll try."

As though proving his intentions, Cade cradled her face in his hands. Tenderly, he kissed her. A bit less tenderly, he slid his tongue against hers in that special way that made Violet's belly turn somersaults and her breath quicken. Grabbing his shoulders with both hands, she returned his kiss as passionately as she could. She *loved* kissing Cade. She loved touching him and looking at him and being next to him. Now all that remained was…

The rest of him. The wholly male, enormously interesting rest of him. Which, at the moment, was hidden by the coverlet.

"So…" Shyly but determinedly, Violet slid her hand down Cade's bare chest. His dark, springy hair tickled her fingers. Already today, she'd dared to touch him quite intimately. She'd even stroked his belly, delighting in the taut feel of his muscles tightening beneath her palm. But none of that contact could compare with what she had in mind now. "May I touch you?"

He knew exactly what she meant. Gazing into her eyes, Cade swallowed hard. He tightened his hand in her hair, then kissed her again. "If you do, I don't know if I can stand it."

"But won't it be nice for you?" Honestly confused, Violet stared at him. Her hand stopped its descent midway to her intended destination. Cade's skin felt *very* warm and a bit more coarsely textured than her own. He looked quite sun-browned, too, in comparison with her, she'd noticed. "Won't you like it?"

"I know I'll love it," Cade said with utter conviction.

"Then what's the matter?" Wriggling with newfound freedom in her nearly sheer chemise, Violet blinked. "Because *I* feel, honestly, as though I can't get enough of your touching. It's as though my skin somehow *needs* to be next to yours. My breasts feel all full and tingly," she elaborated, trying to explain, "and my—" She stopped, at a loss to account for the sensations of heat and pulsing she'd been experiencing elsewhere. She pressed her thighs together, though, and somehow that made Cade understand. "The rest of me seems to need you, too. So why—"

"*Yes*," he breathed. "Do it. *Please*. It can't be any more torturous than hearing you explain why you want to do it."

"Truly? You're sure?"

"Violet…"

"Perhaps you should kiss me first."

Another groan. But Cade complied, exactly as she'd known he would. Because when it came to her, her honor-bound gambler seemed unable to refuse her anything. Even this new intimacy.

Daringly, Violet slipped her hand lower. She encountered Cade's hip, then his thigh, then… *Oh, my.* Silken hardness, a sense of throbbing liveliness and a surprising velvety fullness met her grasp. Thrilled, she stroked the entire length of him. Then, full of exploration and curiosity, she encircled his hot, hard girth in her fingers. Mmm. She quite liked the feel of him.

Cade stiffened. Another moan burst from him. Much too soon, his hand closed on hers, stopping her movements. On the verge of asking him why he'd done that, Violet felt herself being pressed into the mattress. With new urgency, Cade kissed her…and then he just went on kissing her, rolling them both together across the rumpled sheets until she could scarcely reckon out where she stopped and he began. Their limbs tangled; their breath mingled; even their hearts seemed to beat in unison. The only things lacking were fulsome words. But as Cade went on kissing her, as he went on touching her, additional conversation seemed less and less necessary. Everything they needed to share could be conveyed with a look, a moan…another tender touch.

Writhing beneath him now, Violet panted with eagerness. "I *never* imagined lovemaking could be like this!" she blurted. "I feel so…oh, Cade! I feel as though there must be more—"

"There is *definitely* more." Another, deeper kiss.

"And yet I don't know if I can stand it." She wriggled anew, pressing together her thighs to stop the ache that had been bedeviling her for what felt like hours now. Gasping, she delved her fingers in Cade's hair as he kissed her breast. By now, her chemise had been cast aside, yet she didn't feel at all awkward or exposed. All she felt was needful…especially when Cade's tongue slowly swirled over her newly exposed nipple. That only made the ache intensify. "Isn't there something I can do?"

"You've already driven me mad with wanting." Cade grinned, his sapphire-eyed gaze meeting hers with a new, heady sense of closeness. "I can't imagine what else you'd want to do."

"Me neither," Violet confessed, "but there must be something!"

"There is." Soothingly, Cade kissed her. Gently, he pushed back her hair, then gazed longingly into her face. "Enjoy this. That's all you have to do. I'll take care of the rest."

"Oh, but then I won't be doing my share. Surely there's—"

Mmm. The feel of Cade's mouth between her breasts stopped her words. Caught up in that novel sensation, Violet tensed as he kissed her again—this time on her belly. She squealed, unable to hold back another yelp as he slid lower still. His fingertips brushed across the reddish curls at the juncture of her thighs.

"So wet," he murmured. "So sweet. So perfect."

Tossing her head against the pillows, Violet knew she should have thanked him for that— at the very least, because his statement had sounded wholly approving, especially when

voiced in that throaty, manful tone of his—
but she simply couldn't do so. All she could
do was writhe and pant and *yearn*. For what,
she didn't know. But Cade seemed to. That's
all that mattered.

"Mmm. I love this," he said, but she knew
that he meant he loved *her*. At least that's the
way it felt to Violet. "I never imagined it could
be this way, with you." Lovingly, he caressed
her. "Are you sure you want more? Because if
you don't—"

"Yes. Yes!" Violet clenched her fists in the
bed linens. Why was he torturing her this way?
Already her whole body moved toward him all
on its own, her hips thrusting toward his hand,
her legs opening wantonly… "Please, Cade—"

"Yes, Violet?"

"I want…" Panting, she tried to conjure up
words. "You."

"That's all I needed to know." With a confusing mixture of vulnerability and bravado,
Cade looked at her. He stroked her. Helplessly,
Violet arched higher. "You feel *so* good," he
said.

Good didn't begin to do justice to these sensations. Caught up amid exquisite sensitivity
and urgent need, Violet moaned. She simply
couldn't help it. Cade's hands felt so skillful.

His mouth felt so soft. So good. His mouth felt…as though it was *between her thighs* now. It was! Shocked to feel his lips *there*, of all places, Violet hesitated. Surely this was sinful.

Surely this was…it was… Oh, but it was *bliss*.

These kisses, like Cade's other kisses, were magical. They were gentle and sure and entirely erotic, and as he continued kissing her in places Violet had certainly never expected to be kissed, she discovered very quickly that she needed this new kind of kissing. In fact, if Cade stopped, she would die. That was all there was to it. Eagerly, she raised herself toward him. His tongue swirled and teased in response; his lips pressed and kissed and awakened sensations she'd never even known existed.

By the time he began caressing her with slow, deliberate strokes of his hand, obviously savoring the slick wetness she'd so recently become aware of, Violet knew she could stand no more. Pleading, she cried out to Cade for…something. She didn't know what. But he seemed to. As a new torrent of sensation burst over her, she knew she'd never forget the dexterous, loving, *protective* way Cade held her as the world fell apart…then reassembled itself again. Pulsing, breathless, damp with sweat, Violet looked up. She blinked. Cade smiled.

Then, unbelievably, he said, "There's more."

She exhaled, feeling replete and limp and somehow exhilarated. Her ears were ringing. "I don't believe it."

"I'll show you." Then, sweetly, Cade did. He guided her hand lower, then lower still, all the way to that rigid, heavy part of him. He closed her fingers around him. "Mmm. *Yes*."

Reminded suddenly of everything she still didn't know about, Violet brightened. "*Yes!* I almost forgot about you."

"I'll never forget about you," he vowed. His eyes closed, even as Violet daringly stroked him. "Never, Violet. Never."

"I should hope not!" Feeling bewilderingly energetic now, Violet traced her fingers over him. Delightfully, he leaped in response to her touch. She loved that. So she did it again. "You know," she mused aloud, aiming a speculative gaze beneath the coverlets where all Cade's stimulating nudity lay, "I have all kinds of ideas now that I didn't possess just an hour ago."

"Then you're not regretful? Not bashful or sorry?"

Violet gave a one-shouldered shrug. It was

difficult to continue talking while exploring his anatomy this way. "I feel *wonderful*," she told Cade truthfully. "How do you feel?"

He swallowed hard. His eyes opened, then focused on her face. "I feel that if I don't have you soon, I'll die."

Unexpectedly, Violet felt quite protective then herself. Also, her body had begun that curious *throbbing* she'd noticed earlier, all over again. She reckoned Cade could cure that.

"I'm yours," she said simply. "Now and always."

"Ah, Violet." Passionately, Cade kissed her. "I'm yours."

She couldn't help smiling at that—even as Cade chose that moment to pull her into his arms again, effectively ending her explorations of his intriguing manly endowments. An instant later, though, Violet didn't mind as much. Because an instant later, Cade had covered her with kisses, situated himself masterfully atop her and settled himself between her legs.

"Is this the lovemaking part?" Violet asked, suddenly apprehensive. He'd promised it shouldn't hurt much, but—

"With you, *everything* is the lovemaking part." Cade kissed her, even as his body pressed insistently between her thighs. "From the moment I asked you to dance, I was lost. To you."

She smiled. "And I, to you. You're awfully charming."

"And you're chatty." His grin mirrored hers, with a devilish undercurrent of lustiness. With pretend fierceness, he said, "From here on, all I want are moans and squeals and sighs of delight."

"Yes, Mr. Foster," Violet promised. "I'll do my best."

"You don't have to do anything except be you," Cade told her. "That's the part I can't resist—not even now." Seeming newly aware of his own arousal, Cade wriggled teasingly. He kissed her, then gave her a look full of concern and care and passion. "We're about to become one, Violet. Are you ready?"

"For you?" Assuredly, she nodded. "Beyond a doubt."

At her response, Cade closed his eyes. Seeming inexplicably moved by the emotion of the moment, he went entirely still.

Violet thought then that *he* must have felt the same connection between them that she did. As if in proof that he did, Cade truly did make them one: he entered her in one sure stroke. He paused to be sure she was unhurt, then went on.

Having him inside her was...*remarkable*. Feeling filled and fulfilled in a way she never had before, Violet clutched Cade nearer, wide-eyed and astonished and enlightened. *This* was what she'd needed. This and everything that had passed between them until now. This was what she'd been made for...feeling this way.

With soft kisses and tender touches and more and more and *more* skillful thrusting, Cade made love to her in a way that felt unforgettable. His body fit perfectly to hers; his gaze melded seamlessly with hers; and even as he brought them both closer and closer to a new pinnacle of pleasure, Cade never let Violet forget one thing: she was beloved. She was treasured and needed and beautiful to him, and she was *his*. They were united.

"Oh, Violet." With a mighty groan, Cade thrust harder. Beneath them, the mattress dipped and swayed. The bedclothes grew yet more tangled. The coming together of their bodies turned even more frenzied, and still Cade gazed only at her. "Yes," he panted. "*Yes. You feel *so* good. So right. So...ah.*"

He went still. Then he shouted. With an utter lack of inhibition, Cade lost himself in her body. He moaned anew, wholly lustily. Then, with his hair tousled and his muscles slicked with sweat, he delivered her his most stunning grin yet.

"Does that mean you're pleased?" Violet asked breathlessly.

He laughed. "I'm *beyond* pleased." He cradled her close, hauling her atop his big, sprawled body while they panted for breath. "I'm exhilarated. Buoyant." A hearty swearword. "I've never felt anything like that before." Cade shook his head. He kissed the top of her head, then smoothed her hair. "It must be because of you. You make everything better, Violet. Everything."

Happily, she snuggled against him. "I guess I do!" Wearing a smug—and this time *authentically* sophisticated—smile, Violet stroked her palm over his bare chest. Now she was free to toy with his lovely muscles all she wished. "That's because I love you," she confessed, unable to hold back any longer. Brimful with the knowledge of it, she yearned to fling open the windows and yell it to the world. "I love you, Cade! And now, thanks to everything we've shared, I can tell you so."

Still wearing his bliss-filled, endearingly enamored grin, Cade gazed at her. "Then I'm the luckiest man in the world right now," he said. "I was right about you all along, Violet— you *are* my good-luck charm. And now you're much more besides."

"Much, *much* more," she insisted giddily.

"Yes." Just for an instant, Cade furrowed his brow. Pensively, he gazed at his hotel room's ornate plaster ceiling medallion. He seemed lost in some remembrance—and this time, it appeared *not* to be a happy one. "You are more. Much more." He paused almost ominously. "You're more than I deserve."

"What? Of course I'm not. You're—"

"No one has ever loved me." Cade went on staring at the ceiling, seeing…something she couldn't guess. His bleak-sounding voice scared her. "There's no reason you should be different."

"There's every reason," Violet tried reassuring him. This new melancholic side of Cade confused her. "I love you! I—"

His gaze swerved to meet hers. "Saying it twice as often won't make it doubly true." He grinned. His usual exuberance returned with his smile, bringing with it a full measure of charm. It was as though Cade's brief, brooding descent had never happened. "But making love twice as often *will* make you feel twice as good." He gave her a provocative look. "I'll show you."

"Oh!" Suddenly diverted, Violet smiled, too. She knew she should address Cade's conviction that he was incapable of being loved. The very notion broke her heart. But just at that moment, Cade was smiling at her and stroking her thighs and gazing at her as though she was the most delectable treat he'd ever encountered, and she simply couldn't muster the mental acuity to cope with his erotic stimulation and his potentially devastating past, all at the same time. She felt too overcome.

"You'll show me, hmm?" Touched and thrilled and aroused, Violet cradled Cade's face. His beard stubble tickled her palm. She couldn't help smiling. "I do hope you're not bluffing."

"With you? Never," Cade swore. "Are you ready?"

His eyes glimmered with mischief, furthering the thought that she'd simply imagined his unhappiness earlier...and making Violet wonder at the abrupt change in him, too.

This Cade—the one who currently charmed her with kisses and scandalous, huskily voiced erotic promises—was familiar to her. *This* Cade looked like a man who'd never entertained a sad thought in his life. He looked like a man who'd always been admired and adored and in complete control of himself and everything around him.

But Violet knew she'd glimpsed something important a moment ago. She'd glimpsed the truth in Cade's face. She meant to explore that truth further. After all, wasn't that what true love meant? Knowing the one you loved and helping him?

But first… "Am I ready for you? Always," she promised.

But she wasn't. Not entirely. Because as Cade surprised her by rolling them both over until *she* straddled him, Violet squealed. Her eyes widened. Her thighs quaked. Even as she splayed her hands atop Cade's massive chest for balance, she realized that she would never be able to predict Cade's next move. *He* was the gambler here, not her. All she could do was hold on and hope for the best. So that's what she did.

"I love you, Cade," Violet whispered as he loved her.

"I love you, too," she would have sworn she heard him say in response. But a heartbeat later, they were both lost to the pleasure they'd found together. Words were beyond them both.

At least they were until later. Then, lolling in a tubful of hot bathwater, laughing as Cade helped her wash up, Violet remembered a few words she'd planned to give Cade herself.

"You really are a good man," she began. "I always knew it."

Cade merely lathered her shoulders, silently and adeptly. His soapy fingers dipped and slid divertingly over her wet skin.

"That's why I'm going to help you," Violet went on. "I'm going to help you live up to the terms of my father's wager."

Cade stopped. His fingers went still. "What wager?"

"His wager with *you*, of course. Since you lost, you'll have to take part in honest labor in exchange for honest wages. Isn't that correct?" Knowing full well that it was, she smiled. "I'm on good terms with everyone in town. I can help you find an apprenticeship as a wheelwright or a cooper or a blacksmith—"

"You said you hadn't spoken with your father this morning."

Cade sounded gobsmacked. She'd thought he might be. That's why Violet hadn't brought up any of these issues until now. They would have interfered with her greater mission: flying with Cade. Experiencing pleasure with Cade. *Loving* him, most of all.

"That's right. But I *did* speak with Papa late last night after he got home from Jack Murphy's saloon." Violet sighed, remembering the rather awkward conversation she'd had with her father in the lantern-lit hours past midnight. "He really can be too overprotective of me at times, I'm afraid. As far as Papa is concerned, no one is ever good enough for me. Not that he's had much opportunity to test that theory over the years, given my dearth of genuine suitors. Most of them," she confessed, "were more interested in my friend Adeline than me."

Slowly, Cade continued soaping her back. "Is that so?"

"It is." Relieved to have this discussion out in the open at last, Violet nodded. "But *you* will be more than good enough for my father. I'm certain of it! In fact, I'm counting on it."

"Counting on it?"

"Yes. So we can be together." Wearing her most joyful smile, Violet tipped up her head. Her new viewing angle brought Cade's hard-edged face into her sight. He appeared thoughtful. "So we can be together, just like this," she clarified, "for as long as we want to be. Isn't that why we're here right now?"

"Right now, yes." Cade continued his sensual soaping. "But I don't plan to stay in Morrow Creek," he reminded her.

Violet found it easy to overlook that detail. Surely Cade would change his mind once he became familiar with his new friends and neighbors. Coyly, she said, "Then I guess we'd better make the most of our time together right now, hadn't we?"

"Minx," Cade said a third time. Then he kissed her and smiled at her, and all was right between them—especially once the soapsuds fight broke out, and a new round of loving began.

Chapter Nine

"I feel certain I'm going to regret this." Full of equal measures disbelief and discomfort, Cade eyed the distant blacksmith's shop. The place hunkered on the outskirts of Morrow Creek, a short walk from the schoolhouse and the town's namesake creek. Even from a quarter mile away, Cade heard the clang of the blacksmith's hammer striking an anvil at regular intervals. The sound came coupled with the persistent smell of smoke. "I once won a racehorse at the faro table. Keeping that beast in horseshoes nearly broke me. I lost it on purpose a week later."

"Well, then. I guess blacksmithing must be lucrative." Striding confidently beside him, Violet looped her arm in his. Her face positively beamed with encouragement. Her voice rang with faith in him. "Besides, you have to start somewhere. You might be excellent at blacksmithing, for all you know!" She gave his arm a heartening squeeze, inadvertently cradling him against her bosom. "You seem to be *very* good at everything else you do."

"Mmm. We're good together, I'd say." Reminded of the languorous time they'd spent in his bed earlier that morning—and the several mornings before that—Cade quit walking. He couldn't help feeling pleased that he'd impressed Violet. Because of her, he felt hopeful for the first time in years. "At least if the past few days are anything to go by. And I'd say they are."

"They *definitely* are," Violet agreed, holding him close.

"In fact, I think we may have left my hotel a bit hastily this morning," Cade continued, pulling Violet toward a copse of ponderosa pines. He leaned against the nearest tree's thick-barked trunk, then drew Violet closer to join him in that sheltered spot. He twined a bit of her hair in his fingers. Tenderly, he smiled at her. "We should have stayed in bed."

"That would have been nice. And definitely warmer too!"

Agreeing with that in the best way he knew how, Cade kissed her. He still couldn't believe that Violet—gentle, innocent, helpful Violet Benson—had enchanted him so thoroughly. Less than a week ago, she'd appeared at his hotel room door, full of cheeky talk of "reforming" him. She'd gotten under his skin. She'd shown him that love *might* be possible for him, despite the hard lessons of his past. Since then, almost against his will, Cade had begun hoping they could be together—hoping her scheme to help him forge a new, gambling-free life could really succeed.

Not that he felt entirely ready to take up that life straightaway, by beginning the one-day apprenticeship that Violet had arranged for him at Daniel McCabe's smithy shop.

"Maybe we should dally here awhile," Cade suggested instead, lowering his hands to her bosom. He loved touching her there. He loved touching her everywhere. Never had he known a partner more giving or enthusiastic or compassionate. Just being in Violet's presence moved him deeply—so deeply, in fact, that Cade had already blurted out his most shameful secret to her, followed almost instantly by his most strongly felt fear.

No one has ever loved me, he'd confessed

to Violet while holding her close. *There's no reason you should be different.*

Yet she *was* different. Cade was powerfully glad of it.

"After all," he went on, forcing himself from that painful memory as ruthlessly as he had on that earlier day, "I haven't yet shown you how stimulating it can be to feel the fresh air on your bare skin—to make love outdoors, where there's no one to hear you cry out in pleasure except the earth and the sky—"

"And that truck farmer working his fields over yonder…"

Cade followed her pointing finger. "Aha." Another kiss. "That only means we'll have to delve deeper into the forest."

She laughed. "You're incorrigible—and apparently immune to the chilly autumn weather, too." She shivered as she glanced up at the cloudy territorial skies overhead. "It's cold outside!"

"I'll keep you warm," Cade promised. He felt full to overflowing with fondness for her, overcome with a mixture of unaccustomed optimism and all-too-familiar swagger. He'd told Violet he loved her, after all…but he didn't think she'd heard him. That's the only reason he'd risked saying it at all.

Because some things weren't meant to be wagered on—especially not love or the burgeoning promise of it. As much as Cade excelled at gambling, he wasn't reckless. Not usually. Not like this—not the way he was with Violet…with hoping they could have a future together despite the sadness of his past.

But maybe finding Whittier—and the answers he could give—wasn't the only route to the future he needed, Cade had begun to consider lately. Maybe abandoning his search for those answers was.

Not that he was keen to tell Simon Blackhouse as much. He still hadn't informed his benefactor of the wager he'd lost with Reverend Benson—and its subsequent requirement that Cade forgo gambling altogether. With that restriction in place and the faro tournament's qualifying games drawing to a close soon, his chance to find Percy Whittier might be slipping away, Cade knew.

But those were problems for another day—a day when he didn't have an armful of kind, generous woman to love…even if he might have to do so amid the pine trees and nosy warbling birds.

"Be with me," Cade urged Violet, wanting to forget everything except this moment…

and this woman. Deftly he worked at her coat buttons, then slipped his hands inside. Blissful warmth, wonderful curves and the promise of Violet's sweet love awaited him there. He could no more resist those things than he could forget why he'd come to Morrow Creek in the first place.

"You're just trying to delay arriving at the blacksmith's shop," Violet averred, giving him a frisky swat. "Don't worry. You can do this, Cade. If not this, then something else. I have several apprenticeships lined up for you. I'm good at helping people, remember? I won't give up on you, no matter what."

"Maybe you should. You wouldn't be the first."

"There you go, sounding gloomy again." Frowning, she took his hand. She cradled it in hers, gazing intently into his face. "What happened to you, to make you believe such things?"

Yanked unwillingly from the warmth of their togetherness, Cade thought of orphan trains and cold nights and potential foster parents who tightened their lips and shook their heads at the notion of taking in two fast-growing, rascally foundling boys. He and Judah had tried appearing especially angelic once, hoping to lure in a decent caregiver. That had only landed them with a temporary "mother" who thought a swat was as good as a hug and hard factory labor was all that orphaned boys were good for.

Running away had seemed the only reasonable response.

"If I wanted work, would I make my living at cards?" Cade asked, hauling himself back to Violet by dint of sheer will—and doing his best to divert her from her troubling questions. "If I was meant for an ordinary life, would I be a sporting man?"

"*My* life is ordinary." Violet crossed her arms, appearing wounded. "But I have good friends and satisfying work and—"

"And more good deeds to your credit than an angel can claim. I know." With a grin, Cade held up his hands. He knew better than to push her on this. "I already promised you I'd go through with these apprenticeships." Reminded then of another vow he'd made, Cade added, "I also promised you once that I'd make every man in Morrow Creek want you. I'm well on my way to having accomplished that. Getting my hands dirty at a few local businesses will be a good way to test the waters, even if the apprenticeships don't work out. Because if you think I'm going to let just anyone have you without vetting them first—"

"'Have' me?" She snorted. "*That's* not for you to say, Mr. Foster." In a cavalier tone, Violet pressed onward. "What do you think we've been doing together all this time? I've already found the only man I want. While it's true that he can be a stubborn, contrary cuss from time to time, I happen to be—"

"He doesn't sound like much, this man of yours."

"—awfully fond of him." Showing that she meant she was fond of *him*, Violet smiled more broadly. "In any case, I no longer wish to be irresistible to the menfolk in Morrow Creek."

"It would be good for you if you were," Cade protested, warming further to the notion of using his trial employment as a way to fulfill his original promise to Violet. He could scarcely allow her to count on *him* for the future she deserved. She deserved better...much better than him. "Then when I do leave town, you'll have your pick of suitors to—"

"We'll cross that bridge when we come to it," Violet interrupted crisply—almost as though she'd forgotten his vow to her and didn't want to be reminded of it now, despite the bargain they'd made when she'd provisionally agreed to be his good-luck charm…and he'd offered to squire her around town in a sham courtship. "Right now, there are a few things you should know about Daniel McCabe, the blacksmith. He's very happily married to the schoolmarm, Sarah, so don't try to corrupt him as a means of avoiding work at his shop. You know you could do it."

At her dire tone, Cade gave a sober nod. He probably *could* do that, it occurred to him. He possessed both persuasiveness and a knack for forging new friendships. He hadn't thought of that work-avoidance strategy until right now, but if push came to shove and he was stuck in a corner…a bit of harmless, well-meant corruption might do the trick to liven up his workday.

"I would never do that," he pledged, tamping down a smile.

"Don't entice Mr. McCabe's customers into a game of dice to help pass the time, either! That would make them like you, but it would *not* lead to accomplishing a productive day's work."

"Yes, ma'am." Playfully, Cade tipped his hat to her.

"Don't swear. Don't dawdle. Don't forget to be careful around the blacksmithing fire.

Whatever else you do, *don't* flirt with the customers, no matter how attractive they are."

"But Violet, farmers wanting their plowshares mended are often *so* appealing." Musingly, Cade tipped his face to the sky. "To say nothing of the lumbermen needing their axes repaired."

"Very funny." Violet's eyes sparkled. "But you told me yesterday when we were having breakfast in bed together after our morning's… *reforming* session—" she broke off, blushing at the undoubtedly racy memory of that clandestine encounter "—that you haven't ever held a traditional job before, so—"

"What I said," Cade protested mildly, "is that it had been a while since I'd had steady employment. I'm not a layabout! I simply happen to be better at collecting foolish men's money than earning a regular workingman's wage. That's all."

"That's enough."

He shrugged. "I can't help it if I have a gift for gambling."

"That's not all you have a gift for." With a devotedly take-charge air, Violet straightened his shirt collar. She patted down his freshly ironed vest, then plucked a bit of errant lint from that selfsame garment. Evidently satisfied, she smiled at him. "Also, *don't* play faro or blackjack at work."

"Right. I'd assumed you'd already covered that with your prohibition on craps. Shall we negotiate roulette next?"

"I just wanted to be certain you understood."

"I would have to be softheaded not to." Cade kissed her. "Has anyone ever told you you have spoilsport tendencies?"

"No." Undaunted, Violet fussed over his hair. She sucked in a fortifying breath. "You'll be brilliant today. So get going!"

"Are you sure you wouldn't rather linger here?" Cade offered her his most winning smile. "Or maybe a little farther along in the forest? I hear the creek is scenic. I could take you there, standing up. Or maybe against a tree." He patted the ponderosa pine behind him, then gave Violet a suggestive look. "You wouldn't even have to remove your skirts. I could just lift them up a bit, slide my hand up your stockings to your garter…"

Hungrily, Cade demonstrated. Beneath Violet's full skirts and layers of petticoats, he encountered warm woolen stockings, snugly fastened garters, delicate drawers…then, rewardingly, warm, soft skin. He stroked her thigh, loving the way she felt.

"All I need is a few inches more, and you'll be mine," he encouraged, feeling aflame at the idea of loving her in such an impulsive, almost illicit fashion. He'd envisioned the notion as a distraction from his impending workday, but now that he'd devised it… "We'd have such fun together, Violet. You know we would. I'd make you tremble and moan—I love it when you do that—and you'd make me forget everything… everything except you."

Urgently, he kissed her. Their mouths met in a bruising pressure, familiar and demanding and passionate. The only thing Cade needed then was a nod, a smile, a breathy *yes*, and he'd be unable to stop himself from making love to Violet right where they stood. He cupped her derriere in both palms and dragged her nearer, grinding himself harder against her, mindless now of the blackbirds and the fallen oak leaves and the steely gray sky.

"Please, Violet," he urged. "Don't say no."

"I won't." She panted, clenching her fists against his shirt. "I can't." She shook her head, even as he kissed her neck, her cheek, her jaw…her mouth. "But I can say…later. *Later*, I promise." With an obvious effort, Violet pulled away from him. Regretfully, she straightened her skirts. Her mouth looked full and luscious, her hair beginning to fall from its twisted knot. Heedless of her own disarray, she smoothed Cade's clothes again. "You're too good a charmer, Cade. You can charm even yourself."

He blinked. That sounded like nonsense to him. "So?"

"So you really need to get to the blacksmith's shop." Violet tucked her fingers in his vest pocket. She withdrew his gold Jürgensen timepiece, then squinted at it. "If you don't go now, you'll be late. I built in some dallying time—"

"You accounted for my wanting to seduce you outdoors?"

"—but that's almost gone now." Smartly, Violet tucked his watch in its place, oblivious to his incredulous look. "You don't want to make a poor impression by being late, do you?"

"At the moment? Truthfully, I don't care."

"You'll care later." She shooed him toward the smithy.

Reluctantly, Cade nodded. He *would* care later. He would care if he had to leave town unexpectedly—in pursuit of Percy Whittier, say, since the man was so cagey and unpredictable—and hadn't had time to find out if there were any bachelor men in Morrow Creek who were good enough for Violet.

For that reason alone, Cade prepared to leave. He might *want* to stay with Violet. He might *hope* they could have a future. But he'd been disappointed too many times to count on that—or to believe that Violet could truly mean what she said when she told him she wanted him, needed him...loved him.

What Cade needed now was a contingency plan. He meant to get one, for Violet's sake. He meant to repay his damn bet to Reverend Benson, too, by proving he *could* perform honest work.

"All right. I'll see you tonight." He kissed Violet again. Their coming together was as tongue-sweet and heady as it always was. "I'll hold you to that promise of yours, too, about our being alone together...*later*. You remember that, don't you?"

"You're dawdling with *me* now," Violet said knowingly. "On purpose." She chuckled. "Did you really think that would work?"

Another shrug—and an answering grin. "It usually does."

"Not with me," Violet alleged with a twinkle in her eyes. Warmly, she hugged him. "I know you far too well to be fooled."

For an instant, Cade feared that she did. Unmoving, he held her. Then he realized…being *known* was nothing to be afraid of. Not unless you were Percy Whittier and deliberately on the run.

Men had been shot, it was rumored, trying to confront Whittier. Men had been knifed and duped and outfoxed. Cade had chased the man at his own peril all these years—but he'd also come closer, he reckoned, than anyone else had to finding him.

Now all he needed was to know if Whittier truly was the man Cade thought he was—and if he was, to get some answers from him.

"It's bad manners to read my mind, Miss Benson," Cade told Violet. "You'll have to quit that pretty soon—or else."

"Or else what?"

"Or else I might find you even more irresistible than I already do. Who knows what wicked ideas you'll spark next?"

She blushed. "Get going, you rascal. I have records to comb through and lists to make. I can't dillydally all day."

She meant for her search for Tobe's mother, Cade knew. *That* was a wild-goose chase he didn't want to involve himself in. On the verge of telling Violet—again—that the boy had been through enough already, he managed to stop himself. "Wish me luck."

"Good luck!" Cheerily, Violet waved him away.

When Cade was partway down the path toward the blacksmith's shop, Violet called out to him again. Inquiringly, he turned.

"Yes?" He nudged his shoulder toward the thickly clustered trees. "Did you change your mind about visiting the forest?"

Violet's expression told him she hadn't. But then she cupped her hands around her mouth and delivered him a statement that was almost as effective as that in brightening his day.

"Did you really mean," she asked, "standing up?"

Helplessly enthralled by her, Cade nodded. He couldn't help picturing the scene, both of them surrendering to a need that was more powerful than common sense *and* a desire to stay out of the chilly autumn weather. He *did* love her. "Indeed I did."

"I thought so. I'm intrigued!" Violet chirped. She gave another jovial wave. "Till later, then. Have a nice day!"

As she turned and headed with her usual vivacity down the path toward the center of town, Cade shook his head. He'd never been more enamored of a woman—or more certain that they probably could not be together for long. Why should Violet love him, the damnably melancholy side of him insisted, when no one else ever had? Why should she stay with him, when everyone else had abandoned him? Clearly there was something wrong with him, Cade knew; something he tried to keep hidden. Inevitably, Violet would discover it—and then she would likely abandon him, too.

Even so, she deserved to be happy. She hadn't asked to be drawn into the complications and secrets that made up Cade's life. If she couldn't love him—not truly—that wasn't her fault.

With those dismal thoughts in mind, Cade strode toward the blacksmith's shop. There was no time to waste. He only had a few days to assess the men of Morrow Creek and set up a backup plan for Violet's future happiness—and it all started with meeting Daniel McCabe and learning to swing a hammer.

Violet was nose deep in a cookery book by the renowned author and home-keeping expert Daisy Walsh, searching for dishes that would be both strengthening and delicious to serve little Tobe, when the boy himself wandered into the kitchen. He wore a knit cap, hand-me-down britches and a shirt liberated from the church's donation box. He carried a stack of schoolbooks bound by a leather strap. He spied her, adjusted that strap so his schoolbooks rode higher on his shoulder, then raised his chin.

That tiny gesture was as close as Tobe ever came to saying good-morning. But Violet was undeterred. "Good morning, Tobe!"

"You don't need to walk me to school today," he announced. Pugnaciously, he frowned at her. "I can get there by myself."

"I know you can. That's what you say every morning."

"I prob'ly don't even need to go to school at all, what with me bein' here in Morrow Creek temp'rarily. I'll be pullin' foot for someplace a little less restrictive pretty soon, I reckon."

Patiently, Violet stood waiting. This happened every day.

"But I can walk there myself," Tobe nattered on, squaring his shoulders as if preparing for a fight. "I ain't a baby."

"No, you're not." Kindly, Violet smiled. "But I aim to walk you to the schoolhouse all the same. Just like I do every day."

"You're dogged, you know that? Prob'ly on account of your bein' a spinster and all. You

ain't got nothin' better to do than pester me."
With studied nonchalance, Tobe shrugged. He
made a wry face. "But I reckon if I can't stop
you doing it…"

"Then you might as well quit trying." With
their daily ritual thus complete, Violet hugged
him. His copy of *McGuffey's Sixth Eclectic
Reader* poked her in the ribs. She didn't mind.
It was nice to hug little Tobe—to reassure herself that his scrawny frame *had* filled out while
he was in her care and to know that every day
he came a mite closer to actually hugging her
back.

For now, he stood statuelike in her grasp,
stoically submitting to her affection. Tobe had
been with her for almost two weeks now. He'd
alternated his time among the schoolhouse, the
Benson household and—during those occasions when Violet had charitable works to do—
the homes of her neighbors. He'd even made
a few friends with children his own age—at
least he had once he'd come to terms with the
necessity of playing jacks or marbles with them
instead of poker or vingt-et-un. The boy hadn't
asked about Violet's search for his mother, although he knew she'd been diligently combing
every possible local record for clues to Mrs.
Larkin's arrival in and departure from town.

Violet reasoned that Tobe didn't want to get his hopes up, only to see them cruelly dashed if she failed to locate his mama. In that way, the boy reminded her curiously of Cade. Both males, one younger and one older, seemed to hunger for something more from life…and both seemed to fear that hope was lost to them forever. If she could, Violet meant to help each of them.

Reminded of her imminent daily rendez-vous with Cade, Violet released Tobe. She took away his books, then set them on the kitchen worktable. "Go on and eat your breakfast now. I have a few chores to do before we leave for the schoolhouse."

Eagerly, Tobe raced to his place at the table. "Oatmeal!"

"With dried peaches," Violet elaborated, "and cinnamon."

She watched fondly as the boy grabbed a spoon and started in. Tasty vittles reliably brought a smile to Tobe's face, but Violet wasn't sure why that was. Perhaps his mother was an accomplished cook? Or maybe he was simply a pint-size gourmand?

Either way, Tobe seemed thoroughly pleased by his meal. Making a mental note to delve more deeply into Miss Walsh's cookery book for Tobe's sake, Violet offered him some accompaniments. "More sugar?" she asked. "And some milk?"

"Mmm. Yes, please!" the boy enthused. While she sprinkled on maple sugar and poured on milk, Tobe watched her face. "You know, you ain't so bad, Miss Benson. For a preacher's daughter, I mean. For someone who don't like craps playing and ain't fond of saloon girls and skullduggery and everything that's fun."

Violet hid a smile. "What do you know about saloon girls?"

"Plenty!" He spooned up more oats. "I know they like *me*."

"Who wouldn't like you? I certainly wasn't able to help myself. I liked you from the moment I met you."

"Yep." He nodded sagely, chewing with evident enthusiasm. "I reckon that's 'cause I'm a natural-born charmer, like Cade."

"Mr. Foster is probably not someone to be emulated." *But he's wonderful, all the same.* "And I can't help wondering if the 'skullduggery' you just referred to is harmless mischief or something more." She eyed him. "Would you care to enlighten me?"

"Nope. If I tole you, it wouldn't be fun no

more." Tobe sent her an exasperated look. "That's why I said you don't like fun. 'Cause you're always tryin' to take it away from me."

"Only in your best interest." Fondly, Violet regarded him. She'd never met a more spirited, bright and resilient child.

Most likely, it occurred to her, Cade had been similar to Tobe in his youth. At least that's the impression she'd gained from their increasingly intimate conversations. She knew Cade had lived in an ordinary home, then an orphanage, then a variety of foster homes. She knew he'd struck out on his own at a young age. She knew he'd done all he could to protect his younger brother, Judah, during those difficult years and afterward.

She only wished she knew how to help Cade now. Because even though they'd spent days together—very *closely* together—Violet still couldn't piece together the scrambled bits of Cade's past. She still couldn't quite understand him. To her, orphanages and foster homes were helpful institutions. They were run by good people. They saved many children who otherwise would have been left on the streets the way Tobe had been. So Violet couldn't figure out why Cade would say the things he did.

No one has ever loved me.

There's no reason you should be different.

Violet wanted to prove to him that she *was* different—that she could restore his faith in himself and other people. Because goodness and kindness and generosity were the norm in the world, not the aberrations Cade seemed to believe they must be. He needed to know that. More than that, he needed to *believe* it.

Violet didn't think Cade had meant to reveal so much of himself to her. But now that he had…it was unthinkable that she would turn away from him. She would sooner sacrifice her own happiness than see Cade disappointed again.

I won't give up on you, she'd told him, *no matter what.*

Maybe you should, he'd replied heartrendingly. *You wouldn't be the first.*

At that moment, Violet had vowed that she wouldn't be included among the people who'd given up on Cade. Whatever it took, she would stick by him. In the meantime…

"Where's your coat?" she asked Tobe, suddenly alerted to the fact that the boy's oversize, much-adored warm overcoat wasn't hanging on its hook where it should have been. "Did you leave it someplace again? It's too cold to walk to school without it. You'll catch your death of cold!"

Tobe quit eating. He gazed downheartedly at his bowl of oats, appearing oddly preoccupied. "My mama used to say that."

Violet went still. "She used to say what?"

"She used to say, 'You'll catch your death of cold!'" His voice was pitched high in mimicry of his mother's. He gave a faint, unsteady smile. "She didn't know it wouldn't be a cold that tore us apart in the end." Tobe's gaze met Violet's. His little brow furrowed. "That's kinda funny, ain't it? All that time spent worryin' about somethin', then…*wham*! I wandered away from that train depot at the wrong time, and that's that."

"Tobe…" Violet hurried closer. "I'll find her. I will."

He looked away, his expression stormy. "For all you know, my mama run off on purpose, the minute I was out of sight that day. For all you know, she was glad to be rid of me."

"That *can't* be true," Violet argued. "It can't."

"My daddy run off like that, too," Tobe informed her bluntly, "when I was just a kid. And what do you s'pose my mama and him had in common? *Me*. That's it." Bleakly, Tobe shifted his gaze back to his bowl of oatmeal. "It was *me* they wanted away from. There's no use saying it wasn't." His lower lip quivered. He swallowed mightily. "But you're awful kind to try an' tell me different. That's what makes you a good person, Miss Benson."

Violet's eyes filled with tears. She simply couldn't prevent them. Her heart felt torn apart at the realization of all that Tobe had been through…was still going through, maybe for a very long while yet. She heaved in a shaky breath.

"Hey." The boy regarded her suspiciously. "Are you cryin'?"

She sniffled. "No. Of course not."

"Because I won't have no truck with cryin'. Not over me."

"I know. You told me that on our first day together," Violet managed to say, "after you had your bath, when you hugged me thank-you and said you were full of joy at being clean again."

Tobe glowered. "You *said* you wouldn't re-mind me of that!"

"I'm sorry."

"I *like* bein' dirty sometimes! It makes me look fierce. Same way as I *sound* fierce, and not like some smarty-pants city kid, full up on book learnin' and useless good manners."

Well, that philosophy explained a great deal about Tobe's initial appearance. He'd been trying hard to appear—and sound and *seem*—as aggressive and streetwise as possible...probably with the hope of feeling less vulnerable than he was. At that insight, Violet felt a fresh sob well inside her.

"I...I think I might have seen your coat in my father's office at the church," she blurted, searching her pockets for a handkerchief to staunch her tears. "I'll see if I can find it."

"Okay." Tobe nudged her as she passed by him. He held out his hand, offering her a handkerchief. "You lookin' for this?"

"Oh!" Surprised and grateful, Violet nodded. "Thank you."

"It's nothin'." The boy went back to his breakfast, his childish equanimity apparently restored. "Cade told me once that a good man always helps ladies in need." He grinned. "In your case, I reckon a whole lotta bawlin' counts as bein' in need."

His newfound sassiness startled her. Even after all this, Tobe was teasing her? Then Violet realized the truth: just as Cade had done, Tobe had learned to counter misery with charm…to bury despair beneath a grin and a quip.

Her heart ached for them both. She'd been fortunate in all aspects of her life, save the niggling matter of her appearance—which she'd come to terms with anyway. But Tobe and Cade had been stuck beneath an unlucky star for a while now. She'd been blessed with love and support, both before her mother's passing and afterward, when the whole of Morrow Creek had come forward to help Papa raise her. Tobe and Cade had been forsaken.

No wonder they both seemed so hard edged sometimes. It likely took all their strength just to keep moving forward.

Determinedly, Violet cleared her throat. "I'll just collect that runaway overcoat of yours from next door. I'll be back lickety-split."

Her reward was a brief laugh from Tobe. "'Runaway overcoat.' That's a hoot, Miss Benson." He pointed his spoon at her. "If you keep up with them jokes, I reckon there might be hope for you yet."

Chapter Ten

Bustling with resolve and in a hurry to get to Cade for their usual morning rendezvous— after she'd safely seen Tobe to the schoolhouse for his lessons—Violet opened the church doors.

She hastened inside, scarcely pausing to enjoy the calm and orderly atmosphere that greeted her. In the mornings, the church was always empty. The rows of pews stood polished and ready; the stained-glass windows let in just enough autumnal light to give the whole place a cozy and heartening glow.

Inhaling the tart scent of lemony polish, feeling comforted by the memory of the innumerable sermons she'd heard inside these walls, Violet rushed forward. Her woolen coat rustled, releasing the frosty air it had captured outdoors and reminding her that she'd come here to fetch Tobe's overcoat. She had to find it soon or else they would be tardy to the schoolhouse.

She didn't want that. That would mean that Violet might arrive at the Lorndorff Hotel too late to see Cade. Today was his apprenticeship at Owen Cooper's flourishing livery stable, and although taciturn Mr. Cooper had agreed to train Cade readily enough, he didn't seem the sort of man to tolerate tardiness. Violet didn't want to push his good nature too far.

With swiftness utmost in her mind, she scanned the pews. She expected to find Tobe's overcoat in her father's office behind the chancel, but since she was passing this way anyway....

A man knelt in the front pew, his head bowed in prayer.

Startled by the sight of him, Violet changed direction.

Rather than charge down the center passageway as she otherwise would have, she edged toward the outer aisle instead, hoping to avoid disturbing the man. She wished she'd used the exterior door to Papa's office, but now it was too late. Backtracking might prove even more disruptive, she reasoned, than moving stealthily toward the front of the church.

Headed in that direction, Violet glanced again at the praying man. She was passing quite near to him now. She wondered if she should offer to help him or to bring the reverend out to speak with him. Sometimes congregants needed guidance.

Trying to decide, she gave the stranger a more thorough inspection. She didn't recognize him, so he wasn't a regular churchgoer. All the same, there was something familiar about him. Had she seen him at the Territorial Benevolent Association Grand Fair? For some reason, the notion seemed right to her.

As Violet reached the alcove near the office, the stranger stood. He moved slowly, as though burdened, and she couldn't help wondering why he hadn't sought out the minister. Sometimes a bit of counseling eased even the heaviest of burdens. This man, who appeared approximately her father's age, definitely seemed to be carrying more than the usual allotment of troubles.

She paused. "I'm sorry to interrupt, but... can I help you?"

The man's gaze met hers. He looked desolate, almost haunted, and more alone than anyone she'd met. Violet recalled too late—and possibly to her detriment—that some men could not be saved by prayer or helpful intervention. Some men were...lost.

She wished she'd summoned Papa. Or even Sheriff Caffey.

The stranger shook his head, silently refusing her offer of assistance. Respectfully, he held his dark, expensive-looking hat in his hands—hands that appeared, to Violet's eyes, to be unusual in some way. But she couldn't untangle how.

"No, young lady," he said in a low voice, "I don't think you can help me. But if you don't mind, I might stay awhile."

"Please do! I'll try not to disturb you again. It's just that there's usually no one here at this hour. I didn't think—"

He held up his hand. Again, some unusual quality about it nagged at Violet's memory. She still couldn't identify it.

"I'm the one who should apologize to you." He offered a brief, surprisingly chivalrous bow. "I'm sorry I startled you."

Where had she seen him before? Violet wondered afresh. The angle of his shoulders, broad but hunched, seemed strangely familiar to her. So did his striking appearance. The gray in his hair and the lines at his temples only complemented his natural world-weary charm. He wore it like a fine suit of clothes.

Which wasn't to say she felt at ease with him. She did not.

"Have we...met?" Unable to help herself, Violet scrutinized him more closely. "Perhaps at some event in town or at church?"

He shook his head. "It's been a long time since I've been in a place like this." As though dumbfounded to find himself there even then, he gazed in wonder at the pews. "The moment I stepped inside, I half expected the whole caboodle to go up in flames."

Violet gave a discomfited laugh. A sensible woman would have fled right then. After all, the stranger had practically confessed to being a bad man. But it wasn't kind to bolt in mid-conversation. So Violet settled for doing the next best thing. She offered the man a wave and a conversational dodge.

"All right, then. Well, please stay as long as you need."

"I'm not sure the church will be standing long enough for that. I need a lot of time." The stranger glanced down as though gauging the relative sturdiness of the structure he rested his boots on. "You see, I have a great deal to atone for."

Caught in midretreat, Violet hesitated nonetheless. The man's regretful tone awakened something empathetic in her.

"The church will hold strong," she said softly. "This is a good place to begin making amends. But eventually your time here will run out." She met his gaze. "After all, no apology is complete unless it's given to the people who've been hurt."

He lowered his head. "And if they refuse to accept it?"

"You can still try to set things right."

The man appeared to consider that. "It's too late for that." He tightened his mouth. "Fifteen years too late."

"It's never too late," Violet disagreed.

"It is if you've done the things I've done."

Again, Violet felt a frisson of unease. Remorse wasn't always enough to keep people from repeating their sins. Was the stranger confessing his wrongdoings to make her understand them—or to warn her away from him? Uncertainly, she took a step back.

"You can't know that unless you try," Violet said. "If you don't try...." She hesitated, trying to decide between telling him the unvarnished truth and mollifying him—which would have been the most sensible option. Sensibly or not, she chose to speak the truth. "Well, unless you try to make amends, all the remorse in the world is nothing more than self-pity in nicer clothes." She gestured toward her father's office. "Shall I fetch the minister for you?"

"I'm not sure. Is he as unforgiving as his daughter is?"

Violet frowned, taken aback by his statement. He couldn't know she was Reverend Benson's daughter. They hadn't even been introduced. Who *was* he? "The church is all about faith and hope," she told him assuredly. "No one here is unforgiving."

"I beg to differ." The man lifted his gaze from his hat. "*You're* mighty unforgiving, Miss Minister's Daughter. No wonder I've stayed away from 'right-minded' folks all these years."

She couldn't resist asking the obvious question. "What makes you think I'm the minister's daughter?"

"It's not tricky to figure out." He aimed his chin at her. "You walk like you own this place. You dress like a nun. And you talk like a damnable do-gooder." He shuddered. "I hate most do-gooders. No offense to present company intended, of course."

"Of course." Violet bristled. "How could I take offense when you've tried so hard not to give it?"

At that, the man guffawed. His laughter transformed him, turning him from a down-trodden charmer to an irredeemable rogue.

"You're feisty. I like you, Miss Minister's Daughter. I can see why—" Shaking his head, the stranger broke off. Wearing a regretful expression, he clapped his black hat over his heart, then gazed directly at her. "It's only too bad I embarked on this cockeyed salvation mission on my way out of town. Otherwise, we might have gotten to know one another better."

"We might have," Violet agreed, halfway to being charmed in spite of herself. "You don't have to leave Morrow Creek if you don't want to, you know," she added in an impulsive rush. "Your destiny is in no one's hands but your own, Mr....?"

"Oh, no. There'll be none of that now," he warned, tsk-tsking with a sparkle in his vibrant blue eyes. "I've gone to great pains to keep my name my own business. I won't surrender it to a chatty, gutsy girl with more courage than compassion."

"I'm plenty compassionate!"

"All the same, I'm afraid I'm leaving." With smooth and nimble fingers, the stranger tugged on his hat. He gave another brief bow. "Thank you kindly for the advice."

"You're welcome. Will you be taking any of it?"

"Probably not." Seeming oddly cheered, he shrugged. "But it's been nice saying something besides 'ante up' or 'how much for a night?' for a change. So thank you for that, as well."

Violet considered his first remark, overlooking his obvious allusion to arranging a liaison with a prostitute. She'd lived in the West her whole life. She didn't find soiled doves or their customers particularly shocking. "You're a sporting man, then?" she asked with interest. "Are you in town for the private faro tournament? I know someone who's in the final rounds."

The man's eyes gleamed with wariness. He didn't deny her guesses, though, and Violet was about to ply him with more questions—such as an inquiry about whether he knew Cade, since she was powerfully curious about Cade's life outside their time together—but at the moment she began to, her father bustled in.

"Oh, you're here, Violet! That's good. I was

about to run to the house with Tobe's over-coat—" he lifted the boy's favorite gargantuan garment in demonstration "—when I heard your voice out here and realized you must have come to collect it yourself."

Reverend Benson stopped in midstride, his face alight with genial inquisitiveness. Doubtless he'd glimpsed the stranger in their midst. Knowing that her father could likely extract the man's name where she had failed to, Violet turned to make a helpful introduction. But she was too late. The man was gone.

Even as she looked, the church door swung shut behind him.

"Not a very friendly fellow," her father observed. "But an early riser and a wearer of very spruce suits! Who was he?"

"I don't know." Violet glanced to both sides, unable to believe the man had simply ducked out—entirely unobserved—when her father had arrived. "He seemed in need of guidance, though."

"I trust you did your best to provide some?"

"I did." She hesitated. "Did he look familiar to you?"

Her father squinted in thought. He shook his head. "No."

"He did to me. There was something about him...."

Still trying to reason out what it was, Violet considered the few things she'd learned during their conversation. The stranger was a gambler, a rogue, an admitted sinner...and he possessed smooth palms and uncallused fingers—fingers uniquely suited for reading altered playing cards, detecting loaded dice and excelling at games of chance.

Just like Cade.

What's more, the stranger had been pointedly secretive about his name, his past *and* his business in Morrow Creek.

Again...just like Cade.

All at once, several pieces of the puzzle fell into place. Starting with something Cade had once told her about Percy Whittier, the man he'd been searching for at the tables...

I want answers from him, that's all, Cade had said on the day he'd asked her to be his lucky charm. *I want to know why he ran out on his family back East. They loved him and needed him.*

Shocked, Violet stared at the church door. Could it be...?

"I think I might know who that was!" Determinedly, Violet snatched Tobe's overcoat from her father. Then she hugged him goodbye. "I'll see you tonight, Papa! Right now I have to hurry Tobe to school. I have a new project to see to!"

"Don't you always?" Ever resigned and proud, her father smiled at her. "This time, make it a less dangerous one than trying to reform that gambler, Cade Foster, won't you? When you took up with him, I endured no end of sleepless nights."

Guiltily, Violet shifted. "You worry too much."

"I worry exactly the correct amount," her father disagreed sternly. "You're my only daughter. Before your dear mother passed on, she made me promise I would look after you, and that's all I'm doing."

"I know." Affectionately, Violet hugged him again. "But Mama would not have wanted you to tire yourself out with the effort. I worry about you, too, sometimes. After all, I should already be married by now. I should be taking care of *you*—"

"Pshaw," her father disagreed. "I won't hear of it."

"—in your dotage," she went on with a teasing grin, "not remaining an old maid living dependently in your household forever. I'm a drain on your strength and your income." Suddenly distraught at the notion, Violet frowned. "I'm sorry, Papa! I never quite thought of it that way before, but it's true. If I never marry, you'll be worried about me forever and ever."

"There now. Don't concern yourself over things that won't ever happen." With a reassuring sound, her father enfolded her in his strong embrace. "You'll get married someday. Just as soon as you find a man who's worthy of you. It won't be easy——"

"Nonsense. There are a multitude of men in Morrow Creek."

"Exactly so. But not one of them has proven himself."

"Not many of them have tried," Violet reminded him, filled with fondness for her overprotective father. "But even if a million men courted me, I doubt you'd approve of a single one."

"Well, he'd have to be mighty special. That's true." With a twinkle in his eye—and a mysterious smile on his lips—her father nodded. "But I could be moved to approve of the *right* man. The man who could make you as happy as you deserve to be."

Violet wished he meant Cade. *He* made her happy. But Papa didn't know that. Reminded of her multiple secret meetings with her honor-bound gambler, she felt swamped with guilt.

She ought to confess everything to her father, Violet knew. It wasn't right keeping such a secret from him. But if she could truly help Cade meet the terms of his wager with her father, then maybe that would help soften the news of her deception. If she could truly help Cade, she would have done a good, charitable deed. How in the world could Papa disagree with that?

Meaningfully, her father cleared his throat. "Didn't you say you had to rush off to Tobe's school?"

"Oh! Yes!" Newly reminded of all she meant to do, Violet hastily clutched the boy's overcoat. "Bye, Papa! I love you!"

"I love you, too," he said. "Far more than you know."

But the last of his words came indistinctly... almost too softly for Violet to hear clearly as she raced down the aisle and hurried away, intent on telling Cade what she'd learned.

The most surprising thing about doing an honest day's labor, Cade discovered midway through his apprenticeship at Owen Cooper's livery stable, was that he liked it.

He liked using his mind in new ways. He liked using his muscles. He liked lifting and straining, putting in an effort and earning results that were less transient—and harder to lose—than poker chips or gold nuggets. He liked knowing that the results of his labor meant something to people. Most of all, he liked seeing the look of pride on Violet's face when she met him at the end of the day and listened to him talk about his work.

What was even more amazing to Cade was that *he* was proud of himself, too. By now he'd probably done enough labor to repay his lost wager to Reverend Benson—and then some. But somehow Cade had passed the point of working merely to repay his debt to Violet's father and protect his honest name. Now he was working to catch a glimpse of the life he'd thought he'd never have...and maybe to grab ahold of it, too.

Because these days, with Violet, that charmed life felt almost at the tips of Cade's fingertips... his newly callused, almost-worthless-for-card-sharping, workingman's fingertips.

Ruefully, Cade staked his pitchfork in a nearby pile of hay. Alone in one of the unoccupied stalls at Cooper's stable, he lifted his hands. His palms were roughened with those aforementioned calluses; his fingers ached with the aftereffects of the varied and unfamiliar work he'd done. Muscles in his arms and shoulders twanged with every exertion, letting Cade know that honest labor required more effort than gambling ever had.

Of course, lately he'd done more than his usual share of exerting himself in other more enjoyable ways, too. Recalling all the times he'd spent with Violet in his bed, Cade felt a smile sneak across his face. Feeling gratified, he leaned on his pitchfork's handle and recollected some more.

Violet kissing him. Violet loving him. Violet promising him that no matter what, they'd be together.

Cade prayed she was right. Since his apprenticeships had gone so well, he'd even begun planning for a future where she *was* right and they *could* be together. He'd begun daydreaming, for the first time since he was a boy, about happier days.

It could work, Cade thought with renewed hopefulness. He could speak to Owen Cooper or Daniel McCabe or the lumber mill owner, Marcus Copeland, or any of the other tradesmen who'd taken a chance on him, and convince them to hire him full time. He could work hard, save his money and eventually build a home for him and Violet. He could abandon his search for Percy Whittier—because it had never brought him anything but misery, after all—and just get on with living his life. He could do it.

It would be a gamble. It would take a long time to set up a sufficient nest egg. It would be a while before he made himself worthy of asking for Violet's hand in marriage. He wouldn't be able to rely on his "sinful" gambling skills, either—not given the reverend's stated opposition to such gambits. But Cade was a patient man. He could hold out, no matter how long it took.

The only question was…could Violet do the same?

Could she wait for him to start their future together? Or would some other man—newly aware of her and beguiled by her, thanks to Cade's initial pursuit of Violet at the charity ball—chase Violet and win her for himself? After all, the local men had a head start on honest living—one that Cade couldn't hope to match. Violet insisted she didn't want anyone else. But if she were faced with a choice between marrying a good man who was ready for her today and Cade—who might not be ready to reputably make her his until years from now—who would she choose?

Alarmed by the query, Cade frowned. He hoped Violet would choose him. On the strength of her faith in him, he could do all of it. He could become a new man with a new life. All he'd need was a straight talk with Blackhouse first, a conversation to free himself of their arrangement, and he'd be ready to begin.

"Well, now. Isn't this a sight?" Wearing an amused look, Simon Blackhouse strode confidently into the livery stable. He glanced around, seemed to assess the unlikelihood of there being a roulette wheel stashed among the draft horses and mules, then stopped at the door to Cade's stall. "I heard it was true, but I didn't believe it—Cade Foster, pitching hay when he could be pitching woo to any number of nubile young ladies in town."

Cade frowned at him. "You're unsurprisingly single-minded, Blackhouse. Everything on earth doesn't revolve around women."

"Not once you've already settled on one of them, I guess." Blackhouse gave the stable another speculative look. He wrinkled his nose with distaste—undoubtedly at the place's earthy aroma—then shook his head. "That's so…limiting of you, Cade. It's too bad *your* chosen ladylove wants you to do things like *this*."

Meaningfully, his benefactor frowned at the stable and its dirty environs. He came no nearer, almost as though he worried that Cade's newfound willingness to perform hard labor might be contagious. After all, Blackhouse wouldn't want to risk his reputation as a renowned bachelor and ne'er-do-well by engaging in productive employment. His expression said as much.

"*I* want to do this." Deciding he'd lollygagged long enough, Cade forked up more hay. With a mighty effort, he lobbed it into the waiting hayloft. "This or something else like it."

Blackhouse boggled at him. "You can't be serious."

"I'm as serious as I've ever been about anything."

"Oh. I see. I thought you were working some game or other. That *is* serious." Blackhouse seemed distressed. "Damn."

"I'm afraid you'll have to find someone else to go carousing with," Cade told him, cutting straight to the point. The truth was long overdue. "I'm thinking of staying here."

"In the stable? But it stinks!" Blackhouse aimed an agitated glance at his boots. He stepped back, his frown deepening impressively. "I don't know if you've noticed, but there's manure on the floor. *Manure.*" He shuddered. "There's a reason I hire people to take care of these things for me."

"I'm thinking of staying in Morrow Creek, I mean," Cade elaborated with a grin. "Settling down here for good."

"Aha. I see." Blackhouse frowned. Musingly, he fiddled with his waistcoat. "Adams will have to burn this damn suit, I guess, now that it's been contaminated with the stench of labor."

"*That* is the stench of manure. You're understandably confused, having not encountered either of those things up close before."

As in old times, they shared a grin. Their partnership may have been rocky on occasion, but it had been fun more often than not. In many ways, Cade and Blackhouse were kindred spirits.

At least they were…until Blackhouse sobered.

"I'm afraid I can't have you quit on me, Cade. You promised you'd find Whittier for me. You haven't done that yet."

Cade offered a good-natured shrug. "I won't be the first to fail," he pointed out. "There's that Pinkerton man who quit on you after he got knifed in a fight with Whittier—"

"Damn coward," Blackhouse muttered. "He had a derringer!"

"—and that U.S. Marshal you were paying to monitor the official reports of arrests. He collected your bonus money—"

"When all he'd seen was a drunk, dead-beat miner who resembled Whittier," Black-house complained, "*if* you were drunk too, and squinted just right." He heaved a sigh. "That's why I partnered with *you*, Cade. That's why I risked sponsoring *your* search. Because you were motivated by more than just money."

"I still am." Stopping work again, Cade leaned on his pitchfork. In the stalls nearby, horses shifted and blew. One whinnied, prob-ably calling out to the freer beasts trotting by on the bustling street beyond Cooper's stable. "Truth be told, I'd still like those answers I've been after," he admitted. "But maybe finding Whittier isn't in the cards for me."

At the livery stable's wide, double-door opening, Cade suddenly spied Violet. Just then, all she was doing was chatting with Owen Cooper, grinning and gesticulating with typi-cal warmheartedness, but all the same, Cade's heart leaped in response.

They hadn't been together that morning. Cade wished they had been. Although he knew Violet must have had a good reason for skipping their usual meeting, he'd missed her. Now, merely at the sight of her, everything inside him felt gladdened.

"Maybe I'm meant for something else—for some*one* else," Cade said. With his mind made up, he faced his benefactor. "I have a future now, Blackhouse—one that can't include gallivanting all over multiple states and territories tracking a man who doesn't want to be found. Whittier dodged me. It's done. *I'm* done."

Now Blackhouse appeared even more distressed than he had upon noticing the dirty, hay-strewn stable floor. He put his hand to his brow. He paced from side to side. He wheeled around to confront Cade again. "You can't quit on me. You can't!"

Surprised by his vehemence, Cade frowned, too. "Why not?" He gave his benefactor a measured look, trying to decipher him. "What's your interest in Whittier anyway? You never told me."

"You never asked."

Cade grinned. "If I remember correctly, that was a condition of our arrangement. We agreed not to ask questions."

"Not even of one another," Blackhouse specified. "That was our stated policy, and it's worked out very well until now." Convivially, he spread his arms, plainly hoping to cajole Cade into resuming his search—or at least dropping his questions about his unknown motivations. "Why spoil a good thing?"

Cade looked at Violet. "Because things have changed."

"Oh, really? They have? I—" Blackhouse broke off. Astutely, he followed Cade's glance to the livery stable's doors…and the one-of-a-kind woman silhouetted in that gap. "I see."

"I still want to know why you're after Whittier," Cade pushed. "It's important." It *was* important—partly because he'd never seen Blackhouse this upset before. His reaction could not be due solely to Cade's quitting his search. "Maybe if you'd told me your own reasons for finding Whittier, it would have helped my search."

"'Would have'? Are you saying you won't continue your search if I don't tell you my interest in finding Whittier?" Blackhouse wanted to know. "Is that your price?"

Cade remained silent. There wasn't much more to say.

Obviously unaccustomed to accepting defeat, Blackhouse offered him a stiff smile. "Fine. I'll tell you." With reluctance—and no small measure of gravitas—he announced, "The reason is... Well, it's a matter of honor. My *honor* is at stake."

He delivered that certain bluff in as straight-faced a fashion as Cade had ever experienced. In spite of everything, Cade was impressed. He'd have sworn Blackhouse believed his own lie. But then all the best liars did. Just like all the best gamblers bought into their own bluffs. They had to, to win.

All the same...Blackhouse thought he possessed *honor*? Truly?

Still boggling at that remarkable idea, Cade guffawed.

His benefactor did not so much as crack a smile.

"You're serious," Cade observed with amazement. He examined Blackhouse through new eyes. "You actually believe that finding Whittier will preserve your *honor* somehow."

Blackhouse was silent. With a tight expression, he swiped his hand over the stable wall. He frowned with distaste.

"I'll make you a wager," he offered in an obvious bid to regain control. "If you find Whittier, I'll tell you why my honor is at stake. I'll tell you everything you want to know."

Cade shook his head. "You're overestimating my curiosity about your past."

"Am I?" Blackhouse simply gazed at him. "Am I also overestimating your inability to resist a juicy wager?"

Hell. Blackhouse had him there. Cade had always had a hard time turning down a bet. He'd proven that much already by wagering with Reverend Benson. But still Cade refused to commit.

"I already know who Whittier is to *you*," Blackhouse pushed, undoubtedly sensing he'd struck a nerve. "If you want to know who Whittier is to me, then find him." Blackhouse paused. "I'll pay you triple the amount we agreed upon. For a man in your position, that much money could set you up quite nicely."

With a significant glance toward the livery stable entryway where Violet and Owen Cooper were still conversing, Blackhouse nodded. It wasn't difficult to guess his meaning. He would give Cade everything he needed to begin a new life in Morrow Creek—*if* in return Cade gave him the means to restore his alleged honor.

"You'll need a stake," Blackhouse pressed. "I can give it."

"I'm not gambling. I haven't been for days. So I don't need a stake of any kind. Not anymore. Not from you." Stubbornly, Cade eyed him. "Besides, some things aren't wagering material."

"Some things," Blackhouse agreed. "But not many, in my experience." He held out an engraved card. "Bring this with you to my private train car tonight. I'm having a party to celebrate the first night of the tournament. I want you to come."

Cade gripped his pitchfork. "I already have plans."

"I'm sure you do." Blackhouse offered a wide smile. He tucked his invitation card into Cade's vest pocket anyway, then gave it a pat to secure it. He delivered him a breezy wave. He turned, seeming for all the world to be completely carefree. "Think about my offer. Give me your answer tonight. And bring your paramour with you, why don't you. I'd love to meet her."

"She won't want to meet you."

"Are you sure about that? She looks friendly." Blackhouse winked at a surprised-looking Violet. Flirtatiously, he tipped his hat to her. She blushed. "Maybe I'll invite her myself."

Cade tightened his grasp on his pitchfork, unhappy with the idea of allowing Blackhouse unfettered access to Violet. There were things Blackhouse knew about him that Violet should not.

Grudgingly, Cade nodded. "We'll be there."

"Aha. Good!" His benefactor smiled more broadly. "I thought you might find a bit of leeway in your busy schedule. You'll be glad you did, I promise." Blackhouse offered another, almost mocking tip of his hat to Cade. "It can't be all manure shoveling and horse wrangling and shoe dirtying all the time, now, can it? That's no kind of life for a man like you. Besides, if all goes well, I may have a surprise for you."

With that cryptic statement, Blackhouse walked off toward a patiently waiting Adams, who stood outside the livery stable with a cigar box, an umbrella and a bulging satchel. Blackhouse passed Owen Cooper and Violet, gave Cade's beloved a second audacious tip of his hat, then hied off to prepare for his soirée.

Chapter Eleven

Feeling flustered and eager, Violet hastened from the livery stable doorway to the empty stall where she'd spied Cade.

"Whew!" Energetically, she fanned her face. "I thought I'd never get here to you! First I had to thank Mr. Cooper for providing you with this apprenticeship, of course. Then I had to inquire about his usual helper, Gus, and find out how he's doing. Then I wanted to talk about Mr. Cooper's daughter, Élodie, who goes to school with Tobe." After pausing for a gulp of air, Violet rushed on. "She's the sweetest little girl—she lost her mother when she was just a baby, poor thing, but everyone in town is helping Mr. Cooper raise her. At least as much as they can, of course." Confidingly, Violet leaned nearer to a bemused-looking Cade. "Confidentially speaking, Mr. Cooper can be a bit of a lone wolf, I'm afraid. He's a hard man to help—a bit like *another* rough-and-tumble Western man I know."

"Hmm," Cade rumbled. "I can't imagine who that would be."

"Oh, me neither!" Violet fibbed with joyful exuberance. She loved teasing Cade. She'd *so* missed seeing him this morning. She'd been too late after all, between fetching Tobe's coat, meeting the mysterious stranger at the church and speaking with her father, to arrive at the Lorndorff Hotel in time. "All the same, though, I do appreciate Mr. Cooper's apprenticeship. It looks as though you're doing wonderfully over here!"

Aiming an admiring glance at Cade's physique, Violet nodded. She'd appreciated the way he looked in his fancy gambler's duds, of course—any woman would have—but she thought he looked mighty fine in his work-ingman's clothes, too. With his shirtsleeves rolled up, she could glimpse several tantaliz-ing inches of muscular, sun-browned arms. With his shirt partly unbuttoned, she could savor the sight of his tawny throat and intrigu-ing chest hair. With his vest loose, she could see the braces that held up his trousers...and remember herself slipping off those selfsame braces to brazenly help *remove* his trousers. She'd taught herself that particular maneuver just yesterday.

With hardly any provocation at all, Violet sighed dreamily. She sent her gaze roaming over Cade's personhood all over again.

"I won't be able to think about working at all," Cade told her roughly, "if you keep on looking at me that way."

Another sigh. Daringly, Violet sneaked her fingertip beneath his rightmost brace, testing its strength. If she tugged a bit, it would fall. With another skillful flick of her finger, so would his left brace. After that, with just the merest nudge, so would his trousers. Hmm... "I can't help it."

"You seemed to be able to help it a few minutes ago. Then, you only had eyes for Simon Blackhouse." Cade offered the name as though it were arsenic. "The world's most famous layabout."

Violet blinked. "Blackhouse? You were talking with Blackhouse just now?" She'd wondered about that. "Your mentor?"

"My sometime *benefactor*," Cade clarified,

his jaw tight. "And yes—he's the one you were flirting with a while ago."

"Flirting?" Filled with disbelief, Violet hooted with laughter. "I wasn't flirting! I wouldn't begin to know how. You know me—I've been a veritable dormouse all these years."

Grumbling, Cade said, "You blushed at him."

"Blushed *at* him?" Growing more amused now, Violet gave his arm a good-natured poke. "Exactly how does one blush 'at' someone? Especially me? I don't possess a single feminine wile that I know of." When Cade didn't relent, she sighed. "Honestly, Cade, if I didn't know better, I'd think you were jealous."

With a powerful, obstinate gesture, Cade crossed his arms. He gazed into the middle distance toward a passing wagon, silently refusing to say more. His profile faced her, all hard and determined…and grouchy. Very, very grouchy.

Realizing the truth at last, Violet boggled.

"You *are* jealous!" she crowed.

"You needn't sound so all-fired happy about it."

"Happy? I'm *thrilled*!" Violet admitted unabashedly. "No one has ever been jealous of my affections, Cade. Not ever."

"They should have been. This town is full of fools."

"You're sweet to say so." She beamed at him. She couldn't help it. *How* could he possibly be so smitten with her? She'd done nothing at all to deserve him. "I remember when your Mr. Blackhouse tipped his hat at me, of course. It did excite me a little. But only because I'm not used to the attention. Frankly speaking, he *is* quite a handsome man, of course, so anyone—"

"Handsome?" This time it was Cade's turn to boggle. "You think he's handsome?" He released an annoyed gust of air, then turned his attention with new zeal toward the street. "I guess some people might think so. If they like the slick type."

His gruffness was beyond endearing. He *did* care. What's more, he was obviously unused to caring as much as he did.

"I especially fancy Mr. Blackhouse's lovely hair," Violet teased further. "It's so very blond, with all those gorgeous waves in it." Unable to resist joshing Cade, she gave a teensy squeal, then clapped her hands together in apparent exaltation. "It makes him look like a sun-kissed angel! Don't you think so?"

Cade snorted. He shook his own dark, tousled hair, undoubtedly without realizing he did so. "The only thing *less* angelic than Simon Blackhouse is old Beelzebub himself. Don't be fooled by his stupid hair," he warned ominously, "or his pretty face or his impeccable manners or his crates full of money—"

"Is this meant to put me off him?" Violet interrupted pertly. "Because you're making him sound like quite a catch."

"—or his private luxury train car," Cade went on relentlessly, "or his valet or his damnable mysterious past—"

"Ooh, how intriguing!" Violet gushed, clasping her hands girlishly. "A mystery man! With his own valet, to boot!"

"—or his constant offers of reckless wagers—"

"Oh! That reminds me!" Violet butted in, forgetting to josh Cade for the moment. "I met someone today, and I think—"

I think he might be the man you've been searching for all this time.

"—because Simon Blackhouse is a damn blackguard, through and through," Cade growled in a plainly possessive and resolute tone before Violet could tell him her news, "no matter how harmless he might seem. He's no good for a woman like you."

With her jaw fully dropped now, Violet stared at him.

"He's not nearly *good enough* for a woman like you," Cade continued relentlessly, "and if you can't see that, well…"

"Well?" Breathlessly, Violet waited. "Well, what?"

"Well…" Exasperatedly, Cade cradled her cheek in his hand. He drank in the sight of her. He drew in a deep breath. He shook his head. Despairingly, he said, "Words aren't enough."

"Enough for what?" All of a sudden she was scarcely keeping up with him, Violet realized. Jealousy, it seemed, was a powerfully confusing emotion for all parties concerned. "What are you trying to tell me? What am I supposed to see? Are you—"

Before Violet could finish asking questions, Cade's mouth was on hers. In the earthy stillness of the livery stable, he kissed her…so expertly, in fact, that Violet forgot all about the dimness and hay and soberly painted wooden stalls. All she could think about were Cade's lips, soft and insistent on hers, and Cade's mouth, warm and wet and delectable against hers, and Cade's hands, steady and arousing against her neck and jaw, and even as she tried to formulate her last, almost-forgotten query—

just to assure herself that she could—all Violet could do was grab ahold of Cade's vest and just hang on. There was something about the way Cade kissed her, with slow, lazy strokes and tiny rousing bites and gentle, soothing glides of his lower lip, that made her entire mind simply shut down to all other sensation.

"You're supposed to see that *I'm* all you need," Cade announced when he was through kissing her. "You're supposed to remember that, now and always, whether I have the words to say so or not." His gaze remained rapt on her face, his vivid blue eyes dark with passion. "But if you need another demonstration just to set that lesson for certain—"

"I do!" Violet avowed, feeling all aflame. With her last dredges of wit, she added, "You'd better hurry up, too, before I run after Mr. Blackhouse and launch myself a comparison scheme."

Growling against her hair, Cade gave her neck a tender nip. The combination of his rumbling voice and naughty mouth made shivers race down her spine. Blindly clutching his shoulders, Violet gasped. They were still in the stable, she remembered belatedly, in public, where anyone could see them. This was risky. It was foolhardy. It was—she realized as Cade framed her face in his hands and brought his mouth to hers again—utterly and completely necessary. She'd stop breathing without this.

"*Ahem*," came a voice from nearby.

Unwilling to acknowledge that intrusion, Violet squeezed her eyes shut a little bit tighter. She went on kissing Cade, telling herself that the sound she'd heard had most assuredly been a snuffling horse or a kicking mule or a distant bit of thunder...never mind that autumn storms were rare in Morrow Creek, and she'd yet to meet the beast of burden who could sound like—

"*Ahem*." That intrusion came again, more loudly this time.

Oh, no. Possibly it was Owen Cooper. She would ruin Cade's apprenticeship! Urgently, Violet pulled away. Through her dazed vision, she glimpsed Cade's face, impassioned and wonderful.

He wore the same expression he always did when he kissed her, which was besotted and determined and arresting in equal measure, and before Violet knew precisely what she was doing, she'd put both palms to the beard-stubbled sides of his jaw and was kissing him again, crowding herself closer and closer...

"You're going to have to let the man do his

work sometime," someone said from nearby. Very loudly. "Otherwise he won't be able to repay his gambling debts—especially his debt to *me*."

With effort, Cade wrested himself from Violet's embrace. In obvious shock, he stared. "Reverend Benson!"

"Papa!" Violet gaped, too. For indeed it *was* her father who'd been futilely trying to get her attention for the past few minutes. He stood beside a curt-looking Owen Cooper, both men impatiently waiting for her and Cade to quit spooning in the stable like addle-headed love-birds.

Too late, Violet recalled that the livery stableman had famously shunned all things frivolous and sinful, from gambling to drinking to carousing with women. Although he was still young and vibrant, widowed Owen Cooper had become the most straitlaced man in Morrow Creek…all for the sake of his little daughter, Élodie. He would not approve of Cade and Violet's behavior.

Of course, neither would her poor beleaguered father.

Chin held high, Cade stepped up. "This was not Violet's fault, Reverend Benson." He put out his palms in an appeal to be heard. "I encouraged her to see me. I took advantage of her naïveté. I know it was wrong, and I'm sorry. But I care about—"

"No! It was me! All me." Violet crowded aside Cade in her haste to take the blame. Earnestly, she faced her father. "I knew you didn't want me to see Cade, Papa, but I did it anyway. I did it because he needs me! Because I care about—"

"It was me, sir," Cade insisted, head bowed. "All me."

"I won't have it!" Determinedly, Violet shook her head. "I knew you made that wager with Cade to make him quit seeing me. But I also knew I could help him repay his debt to you, so I set out to help him, and everything just ballooned from there—"

"Only because I allowed it to," Cade contended with new and convincing forcefulness. "I should have known better, but—"

As he continued, Reverend Benson and Owen Cooper exchanged an inscrutable look. Then Mr. Cooper piped up. "Isn't anyone going to apologize to *me*? It's *my* stable you're besmirching."

Was that a glimmer of amusement behind

his equable facade? Violet wondered. No, it couldn't be. Not with Owen Cooper.

Instantly, Cade did as the stableman wished. "I'm sorry, Cooper," he said in a contrite and resolute tone. He frowned. "I never meant for this to happen, especially here. If you want me to leave, I understand. I'll collect my things and—"

"Of course he won't want you to leave!" Instantly loyal, Violet shook her head. "You've been doing a good job here. Anyone can see that. Mr. Cooper is an understanding man. He—"

At that, Cooper put up his hand, signaling her to stop. Then he *did* grin. He *was* amused! "Enough. I have customers to see to and work to do." He tipped his hat to the reverend. "I trust you can manage this all on your own, Reverend?"

Gravely, Violet's father surveyed her and Cade. He gave a solemn nod. "With some prayer and divine guidance...yes, I can."

Even as she watched Owen Cooper amble away, Violet swallowed hard. Whenever her father decided he needed the help of the Almighty to deal with her, it was not a positive sign.

Seeking assurance—or maybe trying to give

away a smidgeon of it—she shuffled closer to Cade. Behind her skirts, she took his hand. She squeezed it. Cade squeezed back, delivering her a world of comfort in that single familiar gesture.

After her father bade goodbye to Mr. Cooper, he turned again to Violet and Cade. His spine was stiff, his face filled with censure, and at the sight of his obvious disappointment, it was all Violet could do not to crumple in dismay herself.

"I never meant to let you down, Papa," she said.

"I know that, Violet." Contemplatively, her father examined her and Cade. He took in their close-together posture, their tightly clasped hands…even their heads, automatically tilted to faintly and supportively touch. "I also know that you're capable of ignoring my wishes if that's what's needed to follow your heart. Otherwise, you never would have taken to delivering meals to the prisoners at Sheriff Caffey's jail, for instance, entirely against my better judgment and my explicitly stated wishes."

Violet squirmed, remembering that incident from last year. Papa had thought she wouldn't be safe at the jailhouse. She'd insisted on doing her charitable work there anyway, arguing that no one needed aid more than those people who'd been forsaken and separated from the people who knew them and cared for them.

She guessed she still maintained that philosophy—after a fashion—with Tobe and Cade. Her feelings for them had grown far beyond the compassion she'd felt toward the inmates, though.

"It wasn't that I wanted to defy you," Violet said in her own defense. "I had to do what I thought was right."

"I understand that," her father told her. "I realized then that that's the sort of person you are—the sort of person you've always been. You're helpful and kind and determined, and I rightly cherish those qualities in you. I'm proud of you."

For a moment, confusingly, all her father did was smile at her. Violet began to nurture a burgeoning hope that her father would neither disown her nor begin praying for her redemption—nor decide to march her and Cade down the aisle by force. Not that that last consequence would have been entirely unwelcome....

Unfortunately, her father dashed her newfound optimism by frowning at her in a troubling fashion. He inhaled deeply.

"But that incident taught me one important fact—you *do* have a contrary streak, my dear. That streak, coupled with the fact that you're about as wily and cynical as a newborn puppy—"

"Papa!" Violet exclaimed, thoroughly taken aback.

"—meant I could hardly ignore what was going on when you became enamored of a hard-bitten, hard-drinking, dangerous-looking professional gambler who was willing to slip me an 'improving card'…and was able to discern that I would use it." Somewhat sheepishly, her father glanced at Cade. "But I could hardly just rush ahead willy-nilly, either," he told Violet. "Approving your friendship would have sent the wrong message. Yet if I forbade you outright from seeing Mr. Foster, you might have rebelled and begun a relationship purely *because* I'd prohibited it. I'm sure you appreciate the fix I was in."

Violet did not. She felt much too baffled for that.

"I didn't want to increase Mr. Foster's rascally allure by putting him off-limits—" astonishingly, here her father *winked* at Cade "—but I felt duty-bound to step in and protect you if I could. Because the truth is, Violet, you've given too many foolish men far too many opportunities to hurt your feelings—and all because you insist on seeing the best in people."

He meant the times, Violet knew, when she'd given someone a chance to become close to her, only to learn that he was solely interested in her as Adeline Wilson's best friend—as someone who could offer an introduction to the most beautiful woman in town.

"Seeing the best in people is what you taught me to do," she said in her own defense. "It's the Christian thing to do."

"It is," her father agreed. "But it can be dangerous, too. Seeing good where there's also plenty of bad can be misleading. People are a fickle mix of both." He slanted a perceptive glance at Cade. "So when you told me about your Mr. Foster and I saw that telltale sparkle in your eyes, I knew I had to...intervene."

"You mean you had to separate us," Cade guessed in a knowing tone, "before we became too involved in one another."

Astonishingly, her father nodded. "Yes. As a result of my wager with you, Foster, I reasoned that either you would realize my gullible daughter was *not* easy pickings for a scoundrel—"

Violet frowned, unhappy to hear herself

and Cade described that way. "I'm not gullible, Papa! And Cade is no scoundrel."

"—or you would rise to the occasion and prove yourself. Either way, I reckoned things would work out in the end—*without* my inciting Violet's more defiant instincts. Judging by the way you two have been mooning over one another since I've been here, I'm guessing everything is coming along just fine."

"I wish you'd trusted me, Papa," Violet protested. "I wish you'd let me make my own decisions about this."

"But I did!" Her father blinked. "You didn't have to know what I'd done to acquit yourself splendidly—from arranging these apprenticeships for Mr. Foster to helping him quit gambling and drinking. You did all that on your own." At Violet's look of bewilderment, her father explained, "The desk clerk at the Lorndorff told me you'd been visiting Mr. Foster to help reform him of his debauched habits. That's admirable work, my dear."

Violet and Cade exchanged a guarded glance. Violet bit the inside of her cheek, suppressing an urge to confess everything. Too late, she recalled that her father knew just as many—if not many *more*—residents of Morrow Creek as she did. It made sense that he would learn of her comings and goings without much effort. How could she have been so blind? So blithe? So foolish?

At least her father apparently thought that *all* she'd done was legitimately reform Cade by helping him quit drinking and gambling and carousing, though. There was a blessing in that.

"But all that generous charitable work would mean nothing," her father continued in a more fired-up tone, warming to his usual oratory vigor now, "if your Mr. Foster hadn't done his share. I put as many obstacles in your path as I could, sir, but you hurdled them all." Briskly, he saluted Cade. "Well done. I approve of you, *and* I approve of your courting my daughter. The two of you officially have my blessing and my well wishes."

Violet felt delighted. Cade appeared gobsmacked.

"You were *testing* me?" he asked, skipping over her father's hard-earned approbation for the moment. "You weren't trying to get rid of me? You were testing me?"

"I had to." Reverend Benson's tone sounded matter-of-fact. "I had to know if you truly cared for Violet or if you were simply using her for your own nefarious and immoral purposes."

Cade scowled. "I would never abuse Violet that way."

"Well." Her father chuckled. "Of course, I know that *now*. But I also had to know if you were worthy of my daughter, too."

I could be moved to approve of the right man, Violet recalled her father saying earlier. *The man who could make you as happy as you deserve to be.*

Cade *had* been that man, just as she'd hoped.

"You *liked* Cade," Violet accused her father. "You liked him!" She shook her head in astonishment. "Why didn't you just tell me so? We could have avoided all this subterfuge."

Her father gave her an unreadable—but quite possibly playful—look. "Where would have been the fun in that?"

"Fun? Papa!" Exasperated, Violet waved her arms. "What is *fun* about sneaking around, meeting in smithies and stables—"

"You *will* have to quit smooching in public," her father cautioned her. "I can't condone that. I'm old-fashioned that way."

"—and not knowing if your love is doomed?" Growing suddenly overwhelmed, Violet inhaled. Beside her, Cade squeezed her hand. "Don't you know? I worried every day that I would have to choose between you and Cade, Papa. That I would want to be with him and you would say no. That a decision would be forced on me that I was in no way prepared to make. It was crushing me!"

Her father sobered. "I finally guessed as much." He touched her shoulder, then gazed into her eyes, his full white whiskers and earnest expression ever comforting. "I had a feeling there was something you weren't telling me. Just this morning, when we were talking about that stranger in church, I knew it. I knew you were keeping something from me. I knew it was bothering you to do so. That's why I followed you here, so we could talk about it. You, my girl, are not someone who keeps secrets easily."

"That's for certain!" Violet laughed, even as grateful tears sprang to her eyes. She felt *so* relieved to finally have things out in the open. "I can't tell you how many times I wanted to tell you about something wonderful Cade had done—"

At her side, Cade grew suddenly alert. She hoped he didn't think she wanted to confide anything *intimate*. Silly man. She might be a freethinking woman, but she wasn't entirely daffy.

"—and had to rein in my thoughts for fear you wouldn't approve. I meant to tell you everything, Papa," Violet assured him, "once Cade had finished his apprenticeships. I thought I could present the whole thing as another of my charitable accomplishments!" Giddy with relief, she waved her arms and enthused, "You know, just another lonesome soul, brought from darkness into light, saved from demon drink and the perils of gambling…" She paused, grinning. "Something like that."

On the heels of her own dramatic oratorical triumph, Violet became aware that Cade had grown quite still beside her. He'd turned verifiably wary when she'd begun discussing his overall wonderfulness and her wish to describe that wonderfulness to her father. But that previous guardedness was nothing compared with the way Cade seemed now. His face looked stony, his eyes impassive, his muscles rigid with what appeared to be…anger?

"I'm not anyone's charity case." With his jaw tight, Cade clenched his fists. "Especially not yours, Miss Benson."

His gaze swerved to Violet's. In his eyes,

she glimpsed deep hurt, abundant confusion…
and no small measure of defiance.

"I don't need some self-proclaimed do-
gooder looking out for me. I had all the 'charity' I'll ever need when I was just a boy." Cade
swept Violet and her father with a damning
look. "As a grown man, I sure as hell don't
need the blessing of a tippling, wagering, de-
ceitful 'man of God' like yourself, *Reverend*.
I can get along just fine without either of you."

Motionless with shock, Violet stared at
Cade. Didn't he know she'd only been chattering on, only half thinking? She hadn't meant
to conjure up painful memories of foundling
homes and abandonment. But that seemed to
be exactly what she'd done.

"Cade, no!" Violet cried. "I didn't mean that.
I don't think of you as a charity case. I don't!
I couldn't—"

Determinedly not listening, utterly closed
off to her, Cade grabbed his pitchfork. He
stabbed it into a nearby pile of hay, his face as
emotionless and fearsome as she'd ever seen it.

From nowhere, Violet recalled Tobe's childish assertion.

*I like bein' dirty sometimes. It makes me
look fierce!*

But likening Cade to Tobe made no sense.

Not in this context. Cade was no child. And
he legitimately *was* fierce, now more than
ever. He was streetwise and aggressive, too.
If the hay he was pitchforking didn't burst into
flames beneath his gaze, Violet thought in a
dither, it would be a miracle.

Which only served to remind her, in a scrambled and nonsensical fashion, of the stranger in
church today. In a flash, his words came rushing back to her. *The moment I stepped inside,
I half expected the whole caboodle to go up
in flames.*

If that man really was Whittier...

"I think you both should leave," Cade said
roughly.

"But I was only joking!" Violet grabbed
Cade's arm. He shook off her grasp, then went
on working. "Cade, you must know I don't
think of you that way—as one of my charity
projects. I—"

Love you, she wanted to say. But his con-
demning expression and frighteningly lethal
gaze left the words stuck in her throat.

Indomitably, Violet tried again. "I was only
relieved! I was happy to have our courtship out
in the open, that's all. I spoke out of turn, without thinking clearly. I'm so sorry."

"I don't want your apologies."

"But I *am* sorry! Please listen to me."

Cade refused. Obdurately, he shook his head. Again, Violet was reminded of the stranger in church—of his grim expression, his tellingly dexterous hands, his unshakable belief that it was too late for him to apologize for the bad things he'd done.

It's too late for that. Fifteen years too late.

All at once, Violet had an inkling of what the stranger had meant—and she didn't like it. If this misunderstanding hardened between her and Cade, she didn't know how she would cope.

"This is silly," she insisted. "You can't really believe—"

"Just go." Cade turned his back to her. He forked up more hay, then tossed it into the nearest stall. "Leave. Now."

"I won't leave!" Violet planted her feet. "I said I won't give up on you, Cade, and I won't. Not now and not ever."

Cade gave her a bleak look. "Spoken like a true do-gooder. Don't you see? I'm a lost cause—a hopeless case. Just get out."

No one has ever loved me, she recalled him saying. *There's no reason you should be different.*

Well, she *was* different. Determinedly, Violet rallied.

If she couldn't reach Cade with caring or mulishness, then perhaps she could influence him with the pull of something she knew he wanted. "I saw Percy Whittier today. I met him. I talked to him."

Cade gripped his pitchfork. Although his back was turned to her, she thought she glimpsed new tension in his shoulders. Before she could be sure, though, her father touched her elbow.

"Come along, Violet. What's done is done. You can't mend a sock that's still coming unraveled, no matter how fast you darn it."

Totally confounded, Violet shot her father a confused look. Her father knew nothing about mending. What was he saying?

"The reverend's right," Cade said roughly. "You don't want to be here when I come undone." He stabbed his pitchfork again. "A soft, sweet, *kind* person like you could get hurt."

Violet couldn't miss his embittered tone. Cade didn't think she was kind. Not now. Not at all. Maybe not ever. Because just then, everything they'd ever shared felt as insubstantial and unreal as this conversation did.

"It's too late," she said. "I already am hurt."

Then Violet picked up her skirts, nodded to her father and hurried away from the stable just as quickly as she could.

Chapter Twelve

For a man with his own personal valet, Simon Blackhouse required far too long to answer his own front door—or at least what passed for a front door: his train car's rear hatch.

Unhappy with that fact, Cade frowned at the gaily painted hatch. He lifted the bottle of mescal he'd brought, waved it in the air, then bellowed, "Blackhouse! Open the damn door!"

Sounds of a hurried conversation drifted toward him from inside the train car. Thumping footfalls could be heard.

The door's twin locks were disengaged. The door opened.

To Cade's surprise, Blackhouse himself—he of the angelic blond curls and hellaciously cocksure demeanor—stood there in the entry-way. His gaze lit on Cade's liquor bottle.

"Foster! You're early. The party's not for hours yet. But you brought libations, so all is forgiven." With outright merriment, Black-house reached for the mescal. "Thank you."

Cade held it out of reach. He took a delib-erate swig.

"Courtesy demands that you surrender whatever gifts you bring." Blackhouse ap-peared puzzled. "That's what's done."

"What do you know about 'what's done'? You can't even manage your own valet." Tip-sily, Cade scowled. "I expected Adams to open the door, not you."

"Adams is busy preparing for the party later," Blackhouse told him. "I'm perfectly ca-pable of opening a door by myself."

"Hmm. And here I thought I'd witnessed a miracle." With sham concern, Cade peered at him. "Opening a door by yourself is almost akin to work, Blackhouse. Does your hand hurt?"

"My hand is fine." Blackhouse stifled a swearword. He narrowed his eyes. "Which is more than I can say for you, by the way. What happened? You look as though you picked a fight with your conscience—" here, Blackhouse gave a typically devilish grin "—and then crushed that bothersome nag to smithereens."

"Very astute of you." Feeling himself waver slightly, Cade pointed his mescal bottle at his friend. Confidingly, he said, "I'm undoing all the reforming Miss Benson has accomplished on me. So far, I've cleaned house in faro, drank a third of this bottle of firewater, flirted with four saloon girls *and* delivered a mighty sockdolager to a mouthy saloon patron who was rude to one of those fine dancing ladies." Upon remembering that last occurrence, Cade flexed his fingers. He winced. "*My* hand *does* hurt. It's been a while since I've been brawling."

"I see." Blackhouse gazed at him with uncharacteristic—and in all likelihood, imaginary—sympathy. His erstwhile benefactor stepped aside. "Well, come inside, then. You won't find any brawls in here, but in a few hours you *will* find all manner of other distractions. We'll have drinks and hors d'oeuvres..."

As Blackhouse nattered on describing the evening's upcoming festivities, Cade listened with half an ear. Clutching his mescal bottle, he entered the train car. It smelled of exotic fragrances, owing to Blackhouse's enthusiasm for Eastern-influenced objects and incenses.

It looked posh, thanks to Blackhouse's affinity for luxurious fabrics, rare polished woods and expensive metals. It felt safe inside, Cade thought in a nonsensical and probably drunken fashion, as a result of Blackhouse's insistence on sturdy locks and close-at-hand weaponry. He'd hung multiple knives, one wicked rifle and two—no, *three*—pistols on the train car walls like fine artwork.

Frowning, Cade considered all the firepower on display. Why did Blackhouse—ostensibly a carefree pleasure-seeker with no ties to anyone—need to have a veritable arsenal at the ready?

"…will have music, too, of course," Blackhouse was saying as he ushered Cade into the train car's parlor area, "at least whatever this innocuous mountain town can provide for us…"

Cade swallowed more mescal. The liquor seared a path to his gut, joining with the bitterness there to make an unholy brew. After Violet and Reverend Benson had left the stable, Cade had toiled awhile in blind confusion, abrading his hands with fresh calluses and trying to work off the memory of Violet's words.

I thought I could present the whole thing as another of my charitable accomplishments!

Cade recollected unwillingly. *Just another lonesome soul, brought from darkness into light, saved from demon drink and the perils of gambling...*

Violet hadn't seemed to realize what was wrong with that boastful statement. But Cade had, and he'd worked tirelessly to forget it soon after. His efforts had been stymied by a surprisingly compassionate-seeming Owen Cooper, though, who'd wrestled the pitchfork from Cade's hands and made him leave.

Cooper couldn't possibly have understood the demons driving Cade. Yet he'd done everything but shove Cade forcibly out the stable doors. For that intervention, Cade had decided—eventually—to be grateful. At least he had once he'd found himself standing outside Jack Murphy's saloon...and realized he could rid himself of unwanted "salvation" once and for all.

Hell. He should have known he was nothing more than an altruistic exercise for Violet, Cade told himself now as he followed Blackhouse farther into the train car's well-appointed depths. No woman as pure as Violet Benson could have loved a man like him—a man full of flaws. What had he been thinking?

He was lucky he'd escaped before he'd fallen even harder.

"...and a high-stakes game, just to whet their appetites," Blackhouse rambled on. Cade hadn't heard more than one-tenth of what his friend had been saying, but that didn't seem to matter to Blackhouse. Even now, he turned with an excited flourish.

"But all those things pale, I'd say, compared with what's up next." Confidently, Blackhouse gestured to the settee. "I'd planned this to be a surprise for later. Remember? I mentioned it to you at that dingy stable?" He grimaced. "But now that you're here, Foster, and in such a sorry state at that..."

Blearily, Cade tried to concentrate. "You can be damnably long-winded, Blackhouse. Come to the point, why don't you?"

"Fine. But first I'd better take this from you." With gentle insistence, his friend prized the bottle of mescal from Cade's grasp. "I wouldn't want you to drop it in surprise."

"Surprise?" Vehemently, Cade swore. He wanted his alcohol back. He wanted this charade of pleasantries done. He wanted...

Damnation. He wanted Violet. He wanted her to think of him as a man, not a down-on-his-luck recipient of her benevolent good deeds…not a lonesome drifter needing her angelic embrace.

Angelic. Blast. She and Blackhouse had that much in common. They'd both become idealized versions of the people they'd started out to be. They'd both lifted themselves. Cade had sunk. For a while, he'd thought Violet was lifting him, too, but now…

"Nothing surprises me," Cade grumbled. "Not anymore."

Blackhouse disagreed. "Are you sure about that?"

Cade fired off another expletive. He shouldn't have come here. Except something Violet had said—something about seeing Whittier today—had pushed him inevitably toward Blackhouse.

Most likely, some pathetic but still-hopeful part of him wanted to take Blackhouse's triple-the-money offer, Cade knew. Some part of him insisted on hoping that he could still find Whittier in Morrow Creek, get the money he needed to start a new life, impress Violet, make her his…

His pesky, newly awakened optimism had more kick than he'd reckoned on. Annoyed by that, Cade frowned. "Give me my mescal."

"I'll give you something even better!" With a flourish born of innate confidence and inborn good manners, Blackhouse waved his arm. His grin widened like a child's on Christmas morning. "Behold! Your surprise!"

Wearily, Cade glanced in the direction he indicated. A young man sat patiently on the settee, all angular arms and long legs and broad shoulders, wearing a grin that looked several degrees more uncertain than Blackhouse's. His hair was dark, his eyes blue, and in their depths, Cade glimpsed a million close-held memories—memories that stretched from boyhood till now.

"Hellfire, but you've developed a thirst for mescal," the young man said in a husky, emotion-choked tone. He rose, his gaze fixed firmly on Cade's face. "I haven't tried any of that Mexican liquor myself, but I guess I'm going to have to sample some now. If my brother says it's drinkable—" he stretched out his arms for an embrace "—then I reckon there'll be no arguing."

He stood there a moment, leaning markedly on one leg. He kept his arms outstretched, his attitude full of buoyant hope and unabashed optimism—full, in fact, of the selfsame optimism that Cade was currently at war with. This could only be one man.

Cade blinked, still disbelieving. *"Judah?"*

*　*　*

Hunched on her bed, wrapped in a quilt that
her mother had stitched long ago, Violet lugged
another leather-bound ledger onto her lap. On
the bureau beside her bed, her oil lamp cast a
golden glow over the pages. Next to it sat an
untouched cup of tea—brought a while ago by
her father—and beside it, a jumble of jacks belonging to Tobe. They'd played a few games
earlier, but Violet had been unable to keep her
mind on the diversion.

All she could think about was Cade—and
the way she'd hurt him. It had been an accident,
of course, but did that really matter? In the end,
he was as wounded as if she'd kicked him on
purpose. She might as well have screamed that
she didn't want him—that, just like those foster families who'd passed over Cade and his
brother, Judah, she'd found him lacking and
unlovable.

*I had all the "charity" I'll ever need when
I was just a boy.* Of course Cade thought that.
He might have experienced poorly given char-
ity, but he'd never encountered real love.

It was Violet's mistake that he'd somehow
confused the two. She'd offered love. He'd experienced charity. Violet had no idea, espe-

cially now that they'd parted, how to bridge that gap.

Feeling more distraught than ever, she wrenched open the train-station ledger that Joseph Abernathy had given her. Rows of penciled-in names and dates met her gaze, adrift in a sea of swirling cursive letters and numbers. The task before her suddenly seemed nigh impossible. It would have even if she hadn't been despairing and upset just then. Who was she to think she could find Tobe's mother, where others had failed?

Except there had been no others, Violet reminded herself staunchly, forcing herself to rally as she always did, especially when someone needed her. Tobe had not gone to the authorities, she remembered. He'd feared Sheriff Caffey would toss him in his jailhouse or send him to do forced work. He'd worried a "reformer" like Violet would march him onto an orphan train or enlist him in church service. So rather than look to responsible adults for help, Tobe had fended for himself. He'd banded together with vagabond youngsters in similar circumstances, and he'd made himself seem as akin to them as possible, and he'd gotten by somehow.

But that wasn't good enough anymore. De-

termined to help him, Violet rubbed her eyes.
She refocused on the ledger. If she concentrated hard enough, she would think about
finding Tobe's mother, Mrs. Larkin, and not
about Cade. She would grant herself some re-
prieve from worrying about Cade and maybe
do some good in the process. That's what she
always did, wasn't it?

Sometime later, a knock at her door dragged
her away from her records. Drained and gritty-
eyed, Violet glanced up. "Yes?"

Her bedroom door creaked open. Adeline
Wilson, her very best friend, stuck her head
around the door frame. She smiled. "It's about
time you heard me. I've been knocking for
ages!"

"You have?" Violet blinked. "I didn't hear a
thing."

"I thought as much. Let me guess—you
were engrossed in one of your helpful projects,
weren't you?" With a familiarity born of long-
time friendship, Adeline bustled in. Her pretty
face was full of empathy as she sat at the edge
of the bed; her hands were clutched in worry.
"How are you doing? Are you all right?"

"I suppose I will be." Violet's tentative
smile, already shaky at best, didn't improve
under the pressure of Adeline's sympathetic

expression. "I tried to find Cade to apologize," she said, having already confided everything to her friend during an earlier talk, "but he wasn't in his room at the Lorndorff."

Wide-eyed, Adeline regarded her. "You went to his hotel?"

Violet nodded. "And to the places he's apprenticed, and even to the saloon. Mrs. Murphy had to escort me, though. My arrival at that last one wasn't too popular, let me tell you."

"I'll bet! Those men can be bullish when they're drinking."

"The only place left to try is his friend's private train car." Violet explained about Simon Blackhouse, his mysterious existence and his relationship to Cade's search for Whittier. "Mr. Blackhouse is hosting a party tonight. He's invited me."

"I heard about that shindig!" Eagerly, Adeline grabbed her arm. "You should go! You can have fun, forget about Cade—"

"I don't want to forget about Cade."

"—and enjoy some of that long-ignored popularity that Mr. Foster's interest bestowed on you." Knowingly, Adeline nodded. "That's what I'd do. Why not? You knew this day was coming, after all. You must have considered what you'd do after—"

"After what?" Violet felt her gaze sharpen. Her heart pounded. "How was I supposed to know this day was coming?"

"Well…" Adeline appeared uncomfortable. "I only meant this isn't the first time you've been disappointed, Violet," she said gently. "You must have known this fling with the gambler couldn't possibly last…and planned what you'd do accordingly."

Now it was Violet's turn to feel uncomfortable. She made a face, unhappy to realize that even Adeline, her very closest friend, hadn't believed she and Cade could make a lasting match.

Had *she* believed it herself? Violet wondered suddenly. Or had she blurted out that thoughtless statement about reforming Cade with her charity work as a means of protecting herself?

After all, Violet mused, if the whole world thought she was simply *helping* Cade—not falling vulnerably in love with him—then she wouldn't be pitied if he didn't return her feelings.

The notion wasn't unthinkable—it was only disillusioning. She'd thought she was stronger than that. She'd thought that, with Cade's help and encouragement, she'd gotten *much* stronger.

Evidently, she'd only gotten strong enough to hurt him.

"Come now! Don't look so sad!" Adeline broke into her downhearted thoughts with a cheerful poke. "You still have a lot to look forward to. It's not every day that an heir to a world-renowned industrial fortune invites you to his soirée."

"Heir?" Baffled, Violet wrinkled her nose. "Who's an heir?"

"Mr. Blackhouse, silly!" Adeline tilted her head. "You honestly don't know? You've never heard of him? He's notorious."

At her friend's tone of scandalized delight, Violet perked up. "Well, Cade *did* mention that his friend was an infamous layabout," she considered. "But that's as far as it went."

"Typical male." Adeline tsk-tsked. "He left out all the most pertinent details. Everyone knows about Simon Blackhouse—he's been in all the newspapers back in the States. He's the black sheep of the Blackhouses. They're famously estranged."

Violet frowned. "He sounds like a bad influence on Cade."

At that, Adeline laughed. "I can't believe you're still worried about your gambler's well-being! You really are too kind, Violet." She smiled fondly at her. "Anyhow, I reckon Mr. Blackhouse is a bad influence on everyone. Men like that usually are. Not that *I* care, now that I have my beloved Clayton by my side." She flashed her new engagement ring in genuine elation, having gotten very practiced at that showy gesture lately. "But when it comes to you—well, you're long overdue for a proper dose of adoration and flirtation! You deserve it."

Her friend's loyalty was touching. Her concern was sweet. And Adeline *did* have a point about Violet being overdue for her turn as the belle of the ball. Over the past weeks, she'd received invitations of carriage rides and picnic lunches and sightseeing excursions to Morrow Creek in the company of local gentlemen. She'd turned down all those offers in the interest of spending time with Cade. But if *he* thought of her only as a starchy, prudish Goody Two-shoes—if he didn't love her, to boot, then why *shouldn't* she enjoy herself at a party for once?

Belatedly, Violet recalled Cade's insistence that Simon Blackhouse had been flirting with her. Well, maybe he had been!

Tentatively, Violet glanced at the nearby rocking chair where she usually stowed her knitting. Today, in place of balls of yarn with knitting needles stuck through sat a gorgeous spray of apple blossoms, wrapped with greenery and organza ribbon, all done up in a festive bow. Beside it perched an engraved card.

"Well…Mr. Blackhouse *did* deliver all those lovely things with his invitation," Violet divulged, nodding toward them. "He genuinely does seem to want me to attend his fancy party."

Adeline looked too. Her mouth formed an O. She rushed to the chair, then returned a heartbeat later cradling everything.

"A corsage? Ribbons?" A gasp. "An *engraved* card?" Holding it clasped to her bosom, Adeline let everything else fall. "Oh, Violet. You simply *must* attend this party. Do it for all of us."

"But what will I wear? What will I do? What will I talk about?" Clutching her most recently examined ledger to her upraised knees, Violet frowned at her threadbare, well-loved quilt—and the very ordinary calico dress she had on beneath it. "Who am I to go to a party like Simon Blackhouse's party?"

"You are Violet Benson, a *wonderful* person," Adeline said. She took away the ledger, then seized the quilt to wrest it away as well.

It billowed across the mattress. "You will wear your best dress—the one that brings out the stunning red in your hair. You will have a nice time. And you will talk about—"

Here, her friend hesitated. Violet feared she'd run out of steam. Heaven knew, *she* was stumped on this issue.

But then Adeline came through, just as she always did.

"You will talk about your search for Mrs. Larkin," her friend suggested brightly, "and maybe even enlist Mr. Blackhouse's help in your quest. How about that?"

"Well…I can scarcely resist an opportunity like that, now, can I?" Violet asked, feeling cautiously cheered. "It would be churlish of me to pass up any chance, however remote, to help Tobe find his mother," she told Adeline. "Besides, Cade did tell me that Mr. Blackhouse has buckets of money. Maybe he *can* help!"

"That's right. It's decided, then." Looking pleased, Adeline shooed Violet to the wardrobe to select her gown. "You'll be doing a good deed, as usual, *and* I'll bet you manage to do a little dancing, too. So let's get going!"

"Judah?" Cade repeated. "You're really here?"
His brother laughed. "You'd better believe it."

Their host, Blackhouse, laughed, too. "You didn't see that one coming, did you, Foster?" Jovially, he returned Cade's mescal. "Have your bottle. No, wait! I can do that one better." Blackhouse hastened to the sideboard, then rattled around inside it. "We'll have a toast to celebrate. Just as soon as I find—"

"Don't strain yourself with looking." Cade shifted his gaze briefly to Blackhouse before feeling his attention drawn inexorably back to his younger brother. He stared in wonder. "You've already wearied yourself with opening the door, Simon," Cade said abstractedly. "You'd better call Adams. Quick."

At that, Blackhouse grumbled. But he didn't mention Cade's lapse—he'd uncharacteristically called Blackhouse by his first name—and for that, Cade was grateful. He was also damn humbled.

How had Blackhouse known that seeing Judah was exactly what he needed? Not as a push to find Whittier, not as a threat of having his search usurped by his younger brother, but simply as a means of remembering... everything that meant anything to him.

He wished then, foolishly, that Violet was there, too.

In the sudden silence that fell next, Judah

shook his head. He hauled Cade close for a hug—a hug that felt far too brief.

His brother felt thinner, taller… Hell. He had to be imagining those changes in him, Cade decided roughly, just the same way he was imagining the dark circles beneath Judah's eyes.

With a final hearty clap on the back, they ended their embrace. Judah gazed at Cade, doubtless in the same dumbfounded fashion that Cade himself gawked just then—as though he couldn't believe they were standing face-to-face again after so much time apart. Unwilling to let go completely, Cade put both hands on his brother's shoulders. He shook his head in wonderment.

"It's in here somewhere!" Blackhouse said jollily. "Hang on another minute, and we'll have a proper reunion toast."

Cade quirked his mouth. "I think I hear Adams laughing in the next train car. You'll never find anything by yourself."

"Aw, ease up, Cade." Judah grinned. "Simon was kind enough to bring me here, after all. I arrived on the train just today."

"But you're not well enough to travel," Cade protested instantly. Protectively, he looked downward. "Your leg is—"

"Almost healed," Judah insisted, "which is more than I can say for my pride. *That's* pretty well trampled, thanks to that rampaging stallion." He shook his head, undoubtedly remembering the horse that had gotten spooked, thrown him, then accidentally stomped his leg to pieces. "So...where's that drink, Simon?"

Judah pulled away abruptly, ending Cade's contact. He maneuvered, only a little awkwardly, to the sideboard just as Blackhouse emerged triumphantly with a whiskey bottle. Cade stood alone, wondering how it had come to pass that Judah was here at last. He hadn't known how much he'd needed him till now.

From nowhere, it occurred to Cade to wonder: Did Tobe have a brother? Or a sister? He couldn't remember if he'd ever asked the boy those questions. Although they'd spent a bit of time together, Cade had always kept himself at arm's length. He'd been afraid to hurt the little sharper by getting too close...then leaving him behind one day.

Maybe, Cade thought for the first time while watching Judah and Blackhouse salute each other with their whiskeys, he'd been wrong about Tobe. Maybe Violet had been right. Maybe the boy *did* need hope. Even if that damnable emotion had kicked Cade in the teeth a time or two, it might be different for a child.

Especially for a child whom Violet was intent on helping.

Decisively, Cade cleared his throat. "Simon—"

Again, his lapse in calling Blackhouse by his Christian name went unremarked upon. It was almost as though Blackhouse had expected Cade to soften eventually, all along.

"If you were going to find a missing woman," Cade pushed on, ignoring his own newfound pliancy, "where would you begin?"

Blackhouse blinked, whiskey in hand. "Have you mislaid one?"

"Not again!" Judah clucked in disapproval. "How many times have I told you? If you're going to juggle women, you have to have a system for keeping them straight in your mind."

Cade leveled his brother an inquiring look. "Oh, really?"

"Yes." Judah drained his whiskey, then held out his glass for more. He watched with relish as Blackhouse poured a refill. "You have to assign them code names or numbers, something like that. Otherwise you'll be—" Catching sight of Cade's frown and Blackhouse's inquisitive expression, his brother regrouped. He cleared his throat. "A missing woman, you said? Who is missing?"

For a moment, silence descended. Blackhouse caught Cade's eye. "It seems your brother isn't the innocent you described."

Cade couldn't believe it. But that was a problem for another day. "The missing woman is Mrs. Larkin," Cade said. "She's the mother of a friend of mine." Briefly, he described Tobe's predicament and his mother's disappearance. "If you were to track her, with all your resources, how would you begin?"

Blackhouse arched his brows, still nursing his first whiskey. "What makes you think I'd succeed? After all, I've been on the hunt for Whittier for years now with little success."

At his mention of that name, Judah went still. He shot Cade an anxious look. "You're not still looking for him, are you? Simon told me you'd quit. He told me you'd fallen for a titian-haired saint and were out of the manhunt business for good."

Titian-haired saint. That was one way to describe Violet.

Wielder of cruel kindnesses was another, more accurate way.

Cade wished he'd never swept her into that first dance they'd shared. Maybe then

he wouldn't have learned to love her at all.
Maybe then he wouldn't have learned to hope
for more.

"I'm not still looking." Cade delivered that
assurance brusquely. He'd always told himself he was on the hunt for Whittier because
Judah wanted it—because Judah needed it. But
the truth was...Cade had wanted and needed it
enough for the two of them combined. There
had been times Judah had tried to make him
quit. Cade had refused to take them seriously.

"Good." Judah nodded. "That search was
killing you."

Shocked by that, Cade stared at his brother.
Belatedly, he remembered that this wasn't the
first time Judah had said something like that.
But it *was* the first time Cade listened.

In that spirit, Cade aimed a supplemental
frown at Blackhouse. "That means I won't be
taking you up on your latest offer, Simon. I've
given up on Whittier." *And, by extension, on
Violet, too.* Without Blackhouse's money, Cade
would not be able to support her the way she
deserved, anyway. "And I think you can find
Mrs. Larkin," he added, returning to the matter at hand with a determined edge to his voice,
"because unlike Percy Whittier, *she* is not trying deliberately *not* to be found."

Seeming content with that, Blackhouse nodded. "All right, then." He set aside his whiskey, then began pacing. He wheeled about to confront them both. "If I were searching for a runaway mother, I would begin by wiring the police, the hospitals and the mental institutions. I would hire a detective. I would—"

"I doubt she ran away, turned loony or got herself stuck in the clink," Judah grumbled. He poured himself more whiskey, evidently growing tired of waiting for Simon to offer another glass. "That's putting a grim spin on the situation, wouldn't you say? Maybe she's just been...misplaced, as Cade suggested."

Helpless not to remember their own mother's untimely passing, Cade frowned. "Mrs. Larkin might have gotten robbed or attacked. Even now she could be trying to get back to Tobe."

"'Robbed or attacked'?" Blackhouse repeated with a frown. "Nice. And you two think *I'm* the grim one?" He shook his head, then delivered Cade a more serious look. "If you're asking me to look into this, I will. All I need are the details."

"For that, I'd have to ask Violet. She knows all the facts about Mrs. Larkin." No one remarked on the fact that Cade had accidentally quit calling his lost love "Miss Benson." "Or I'd have to speak with Tobe. But he's staying with the Bensons right now, so that would mean confronting the reverend. Or Violet."

Caught, Cade hesitated. He never should have embroiled himself in that little sharper's troubles. From the moment he'd agreed to a game of craps, purposely lost his warm over-coat...

"Your lady friend is a *reverend's daughter*?" Judah boggled. "Damnation, Cade. That ought to be as easy as pie! You just pull out the charm and take whatever information you need from her."

Blackhouse saw the situation differently. "Miss Benson isn't your typical reverend's daughter. And if Foster's pie-eyed appear-ance—and the mescal he's murdered—are any indication, he's had a falling-out with her anyway. We need another course."

"No, we don't." Suddenly resolute, Cade straightened.

As a boy, he'd wished someone had stepped in to help him. He'd wished he hadn't had to shoulder the burdens and concerns of raising himself and Judah all alone. If he'd had a lost parent out there somewhere, if they could have been reunited....

Hell. He'd have wanted that more than anything. He still wanted the family he'd never had. How could he stand in the way of seeing Tobe brought together with his long-lost mama now?

He couldn't. Not if all he had to do was set aside his own heartache for a night and ask Violet for some information.

"If I get all the details about Mrs. Larkin," Cade asked Blackhouse, "will you do what you can to find her?"

Equably, his friend raised his whiskey. "I promise I will. If your faith in me and my money is justified, I might even succeed."

Blackhouse's lopsided grin gave Cade hope—one more morsel of that precious stuff than he'd entered the train car with. As a gambler, Cade knew that meant his odds were improving. From here, no self-respecting sporting man would have failed to push the limits. Not while there was still a chance of winning.

"Fine." Cade nodded. "Then I'm off to get more details."

"Wait." Blackhouse raised his hand, a frown marring his privileged, irksomely perfect face. "Am I dreaming? Or are you actually planning on engaging in an act of selfless generosity?"

Judah shuddered. "That sounds suspiciously

like charity work. I hate charity work—and charity workers, too." He made a face, undoubtedly prompted by bad memories. "Bunch of damn good-for-nothing nuisances. They should mind their own business."

"That's what I used to think," Cade told his brother. "Until I met one who wanted to be with me more than she wanted to change me." *It was true,* he realized as he said it. Violet had never honestly tried to reform him. She'd never pitied him, even after he'd shared so much with her. In fact, with her zest for sinful romps in his bed, Violet had mostly engaged in the opposite of reformation and pity. She'd *adored* him. Openly.

In return, Cade had made her leave him after the first mistake she'd made. His own hoary doubts—his fears that he could neither love nor be loved—had forced him to do so.

Those fears had been too strong to resist. After all, Cade realized, he'd spent years polishing them up. He'd worried over them like crooked dice in his pocket, turning them over until their sides were worn smooth and familiar. Then he'd rolled his fixed dice and spoiled his chances in the worst imaginable way.

It was almost as though it had been fated to happen. Cade hadn't even granted Violet the same easy tolerance that a dissolute bachelor and a travel-weary youth had managed to grant *him* tonight, when his need for friendship had overcome his need to be hardened and remote. When he'd needed them, Simon and Judah had been there for him. If he was lucky, Violet might be there for him again, too.

If not for his sake, then at least for Tobe's.

"Have fun at the party. I may be gone awhile." Cade hesitated, then gave Judah another heartfelt hug. "I'll make this up to you later, I promise. In the meantime, don't get too pie-eyed yourself." He nodded at his brother's third—fourth?—dose of whiskey. "If I can convince Violet to forgive me—" which at that moment he realized he'd have to do to enlist her help "—I'll want you sober enough to meet her—and remember it later."

Accepting his brother's careless nod, Cade left behind his mescal bottle, left the train car and left his damnable doubts in the dust. In their stead, he set out to face the only woman who'd ever made him want to become a better man—and to try to convince her that he was well on his way to doing so now.

Paradoxically, Violet had changed him by *not* trying to change him, Cade realized as he reached the road beyond Blackhouse's parked train car. Violet's openhanded acceptance, all on its own, had been enough to free him—to make him want to do more with his life. But now none of that mattered. All that mattered to Cade, as he loped off into the cold autumn night, was that he found Violet, begged her forgiveness and asked for the answers he needed: new answers, to new questions.

He had to do this. For his own sake. For Violet's sake.

Most of all...for Tobe's sake. Because if Cade could save that dirty-faced, fast-talking, craps-playing, itinerant shyster of a boy from a life spent wondering about his own ability to love and be loved...well, that's what he damn well planned to do. And no one had better try to stop him.

Chapter Thirteen

Cade's newfound courage lasted *almost* all the way to the Bensons' snug, cozy home on the other side of Morrow Creek. It lasted him past the train depot and the saloon, past the stable, past the Lorndorff Hotel and the jailhouse and the telegraph station and the homespun idyll of the central town square. It lasted as he strode through drifts of dried fallen scrub-oak leaves. It lasted as he clenched his hands at his sides to warm them—he really had to replace the overcoat he'd lost to Tobe—and it lasted as he pushed past gossiping townspeople with their friendly faces and even friendlier greetings. It lasted...

Hell. It lasted until the moment when the Bensons' modest house came into view down the street, with its lace-curtained windows aglow with lamplight and its chimney puffing wood smoke. Then his damnably fickle courage fled like the fair-weather friend it really was. When the chips were down, Cade's bravado deserted him in two seconds flat. Frankly, he resented that.

Grumbling a swearword, Cade quit walking. His boots thumped on the hard-packed dirt street for a final time. There, shielded by darkness, he squinted at the Benson household and tried to imagine what it would feel like to be welcomed inside it.

His mind turned blank. Hellfire. Panicked and impatient, he tried again. Again he could not conceive of being forgiven.

It's too late, Violet had said. *I already am hurt.*

Feeling regretful and beleaguered, Cade frowned anew. What he needed was an approach, a maneuver, a fail-safe plan of the variety he'd managed to spin for half his lifetime now. But faced with a real problem—with a real need—Cade felt stymied.

Maybe he was no good at selflessness. Maybe among all his other faults, self-interest was seated as king of them all.

Or maybe he simply needed a new dose of

courage. With his mescal forsaken, he'd have to look elsewhere. Casting about for a solution, Cade glanced to the church. That would have to do.

Gussied up, polished up and not entirely comfortable with either process, Violet stepped into her family's front parlor. The skirts of her second-best gown rustled softly. The gems in her borrowed earrings and necklace sparkled. The hammering of her heart was most assuredly, she thought, audible to everyone.

Her father sat reading in his armchair. Tobe squatted on the rug, frowning in concentration as he assembled a painted jigsaw puzzle that the McCabe family had given him. Between them, Papa and Tobe were the very picture of warm conviviality.

Loath to disturb them, Violet turned—and almost ran smack into poor Adeline, who'd been following close behind her. Her best friend, undoubtedly sensing what Violet had been thinking, firmly took Violet's shoulders and spun her to face her family once more. It wasn't for nothing that they'd been chums since girlhood. Adeline Wilson knew exactly what she needed.

"Look, everyone! Doesn't Violet look beautiful?"

Reverend Benson glanced up. He smiled. "Very lovely!"

Behind his assurance lay several unasked questions. Violet could glimpse them in his drawn-together brows and pensive look. But she was grateful, just then, that Papa didn't push her.

"Tobe?" Adeline prompted. "Did you see Violet?"

The boy nodded. He inserted another puzzle piece.

"Doesn't she look nice? She's going to a party tonight."

A shrug. "Git goin', already. I ain't gonna applaud you for leavin', if that's what you're waitin' for. So just go on. Git."

"Tobe." Feeling an enormous tug of affection for him, Violet plunked down on the rug. Heedless of the need to protect her fancy dress, she crawled close to him. "I'm coming back, you know. If that's what you're worried about, you don't have to."

"I ain't worried." His little face screwed up tight. "I done survived bein' deserted once already. I can do it again." Tobe refused to look at her. But he *did* drag something forward from around his neck—something grimy, hung on a tied length of twine. "See? I got me the trophy to prove it an' everythin'."

Violet squinted. "The 'trophy'? What's that?"

Confused, she caught hold of it. It appeared to be a rectangular scrap of paper, printed with dates and destinations, punched with a hole for the twine to fit through. It was almost too discolored to make out its original function. Almost.

"Where did you get this? I've never seen it before."

"Sure you have." Tobe tucked it beneath his shirt again. "It's on me every single day." He shook his head as though she was being silly. Peevishly, he went back to his puzzle. "I don't never take it off. Well, 'cept for sometimes, for them baths you make me have, even though I don't want no part of *them*—"

"Tobe, that's a train ticket," Violet said.

"So?" His one raised eyebrow formed a perfect pint-size imitation of Cade's oft-cynical demeanor. "You want one? Git it yourself, why don't you? Maybe after your blasted party."

Aware of her father's and Adeline's gazes fixed on her, Violet inhaled. Sometimes she had to fight to remember that, despite having survived partly on his own, Tobe was only a little boy. He was neither mature nor capable of true cynicism.

What he was, she remembered, was vulnerable and alone.

"Can I please see that ticket again?" Violet asked.

Tobe raised his skinny shoulders in a shrug. "I reckon."

With his permission, Violet shakily brought her fingers to the loop of twine around his neck. Carefully, she pulled the train ticket forward. She read the issuing date. The price paid. The departure and destination stations. This could only be…

"I don't know why you're so int'rested," Tobe complained. "That ticket didn't help me none, not when I was in the clutch. Not like it was s'pposed to. Not like my mama promised."

"Your *mother* gave this to you?"

Tobe nodded. "In case I got lost or missed the train."

Violet gawked. "But you *did* miss the train!"

"No, I didn't," Tobe insisted with the inimitable indignation of a misunderstood child. "My *mama* did. Not me. I was right there, at the train, and she wasn't. I looked."

Openmouthed, Violet gawked at him. Tobe

must have gotten confused about which train to board, she realized. On a crowded platform during a hasty stop, it was easy to get separated and confused. Especially for a woman and her son traveling alone.

"Did you ask the stationmaster to help you?"

Another boyish shrug. "He tole me the train I needed was gone already. He tole me he'd have to call the sheriff about it." Tobe frowned. "I didn't want him to turn me in to some mean ole' lawman. I'd heard some older boys on the train talkin' about what *that* meant. That meant I wouldn't never see my mama again, if the law got me and sent me away someplace. So I skedaddled away when nobody was lookin'."

In dawning enlightenment, Violet stared down at her hands. She held the key to locating Mrs. Larkin. It had been so close, all this time. All she'd needed were the right questions to ask.

"Why didn't you ever show this to me before, Tobe?"

The boy gave her an impatient look. "Can I do my puzzle?"

"In a minute. Please, Tobe. Why didn't you show me this?"

Now he only seemed perplexed. "T'weren't no big secret or nothin'," Tobe said blithely. "I figured you'd rifled through my stuff when I was havin' that very first bath on chicken-dinner night. That's what people do, you know, if you don't keep watch over your kit—they pilfer things. When you didn't pinch that ole' trophy of mine, I reckoned it didn't mean nothin' to nobody."

Violet could scarcely believe it. "*This*," she said, "is everything we need to reunite you with your mother, Tobe."

He scoffed. "No, it ain't. You're pullin' my leg." He set another puzzle piece in place. "My mama was wrong 'bout what that dumb ole' train ticket could do for us. I know that."

There in the parlor, Violet held her breath. Beside her, Adeline stood stock-still, doubtless sensing the drama of the moment. Her father clutched his copy of the *Pioneer Press* news-paper, gazing from Tobe to Violet with evident solemnity.

"Tobe," the reverend said, "that ticket can take you home."

In the flickering lantern light, the boy glanced up. His gaze swerved to Violet's face, obviously seeking confirmation.

She gave a brief nod. Tobe swallowed hard. His chin wobbled. Wearing an impatient frown, he grimaced peculiarly.

He was trying not to cry, Violet realized. *He was trying to remain strong—to remain fierce, just as he'd done for so long.*

"You ain't fibbin'?" Tobe asked in a choked voice.

Silently, Violet shook her head. So did her father.

"I can really go home?" Tobe asked. "To my mama?"

"Yes," Violet said. "Just as fast as we can get you there."

Suspiciously, Tobe examined her face. He frowned once more.

"I'd like that," he said simply, then he began to sob.

Soon the whole room was ablubber with tears. Violet bawled with happiness and relief, Adeline cried with sentimentality and sympathy, and Reverend Benson...well, he was the worst of all.

"I don't know what I was thinking, reading that awful heartrending story just now," her father complained as he dabbed at his red-rimmed, tear-filled eyes. "It's plainly affected me."

"Papa, that was just the boring newspaper," Violet said.

"Tsk-tsk, daughter. You go on to your party

now. I'm going to help Tobe with this puzzle, then look up train schedules."

Still concerned, Violet glanced at the boy. She'd been hugging him close until quite recently, but Tobe had finally wiggled successfully from her grasp and gone back—contentedly—to his waiting puzzle. He truly was an irrepressible, rascally boy.

"Will you be all right if I go, Tobe?" she asked.

"*Pshaw.* Go on. I'll be right as rain now!" he said in an immodest tone. "Nothin' could get me down now that I done solved the mystery of how to git myself back home to my mama again."

"*You* solved—" On the verge of correcting him, Violet stopped. Instead, she smiled. "Is that what you'll tell your mother? That you solved the problem all by yourself?"

Tobe gave her a mischievous grin. "Nah. My mama ain't half so credulous as you, Miss Benson. She won't never believe me. I'll tell her the truth—that a kindly spinster helped me out."

Flabbergasted, Violet stared at him. Then she laughed.

She would have expected no less from such a unique boy.

"All right, Tobe." After giving him another

hug and a quick tousle to his hair, Violet stood. "I guess I'm off, then!"

Stepping into the humble clapboard church that stood closely adjacent to the Benson household, Cade held his breath.

He didn't make a practice of seeking divine guidance. Undoubtedly, a repeat sinner like him would have been denied it. And although he'd come here not long ago to donate his gambling winnings to the church collection plate as a means of seeing Violet again, Cade did not feel comfortable inside the church.

Ostensibly, it was peaceful. Even he could appreciate that. From the bracketed wall sconces, lamplight filtered over the pews. On the air, the aromas of old hymnals and lemony furniture polish lingered faintly. Underfoot, the floorboards creaked as Cade stepped forward. Belatedly, he snatched off his hat. Holding it in hand, he made his way to the rearmost pew. A short prayer couldn't possibly hurt. If the Almighty took pity on him...

Well, if the Lord took pity on him, Cade would be equipped to help Tobe *and* himself—and maybe Violet, too, by dint of loving her. He would have to try very hard to make things up to her.

Guardedly, Cade stepped into the row of pews. He held his hat over his heart. He bowed his head, preparing to begin.

Tarnation. He didn't remember how to pray.

Surely he'd done this as a boy. Urgently, he tried again.

"Well, if this don't beat all," a man said from nearby.

Cade recognized that voice—that laconic drawl and that elusive tone. Instantly alert, Cade wheeled around.

A tall, well-dressed, partly gray-haired man stood inside the church's entryway, studying him with what appeared to be cynical detachment. It shone from his eyes like the glimmer of fool's gold, obscuring his true emotions in a fashion that Cade recognized well. He'd used that tactic himself a time or two. Like that worthless rock's shine, the man's expression was meant to mislead. Doubtless it usually succeeded—especially when aimed at the gullible. But Cade didn't count himself among them.

"Whittier."

A nod. "That's what they call me."

Muddled by the man's appearance in church, Cade stared. He lifted his weapon a mite higher, realizing just then that he'd automatically drawn it. His hat, which he'd been holding, now lay sideways, abandoned on the pew where he'd dropped it.

"I should have known you'd sneak up on a man," Cade said.

"That's rich, coming from the boy who's been tracking me all this time. I can barely turn around without seeing your face." Whittier strode farther inside. His boot heels clunked against the pristine floorboards. "You sneaked in here just like I did the first time," he observed with a sidelong glance, "as if you expected the whole place to go up in flames."

"With you in it? I still do." To Cade, it felt as though Whittier's presence sullied the church. A man like him didn't belong there. Not after everything he'd done. Not when he was probably packing firepower—never mind the pistol that Cade had drawn. He'd never killed anyone with it. "Show me your hands."

A head shake. "That's not necessary. I'm not armed."

Cade aimed his chin at Whittier's hip. "I can see your gun belt from here." He felt curiously disappointed as he added, "Your bluffs aren't what they used to be, old man."

A frown. "I mean I would never draw on you."

Well, there was that. *Why* hadn't Whittier

drawn on him? Cade wondered suddenly. By all accounts, he was a dangerous, amoral professional gambler—one who backed down from no one.

Certainly he didn't voluntarily get himself cornered. Yet there he was, in the church, making his presence known to Cade. Whittier could just as easily have ambushed Cade where he stood.

Befuddled, Cade kept his pistol aimed at his target.

Evidently unconcerned to find himself at gunpoint, Whittier raised his palms. Amiably, he nodded at Cade's elaborate watch chain. "Still carrying the Jürgensen, I see."

Tensely, Cade nodded. He'd be damned if Whittier didn't seem oddly pleased to glimpse his former timepiece. "If I recall correctly, you didn't seem motivated to keep from losing it."

An easy shrug. "I wanted you to have it."

"You've got things backward," Cade told him. "I took it."

Even as he said it, though, Blackhouse's onetime musings returned to him. *Do you think Whittier lost on purpose? Maybe he wanted you to have that Jürgensen. Just because you didn't know who he was doesn't mean he didn't know who you were even then.*

"You've changed since then." Whittier gave Cade a measured look. He seemed peculiarly... nostalgic? "You look...meaner."

Cade didn't want to discuss his own progression from a green youth to a hardened man. If he was right, Percy Whittier was partly responsible for changes in him.

Trying to cut to the heart of the matter, Cade squinted at Whittier. It felt impossible to match the man before him with the man in his recollections...or with the man in the faded tintype he always carried. It had been years since he'd seen Whittier this close.

It had been many more years since he'd seen....

Cade gestured with his pistol. "Come closer."

Obligingly, Whittier did. Cade still wasn't satisfied.

"Where did you get that Jürgensen?" he asked.

He wished he'd asked that question years ago, when he'd first won it. But it hadn't been until later that Cade had spied the message engraved on the back of the timepiece—the message that had made him connect Percy Whittier with...everything.

Whittier lowered his arms. "It was a gift from my wife."

"The truth." Cade cocked his pistol. "Please."

That courteous touch was Violet's influence, Cade reckoned. He couldn't help feeling a little bit proud of himself for that.

As if sensing her angelic inspiration even now, Whittier glanced around. "Have you seen a little redheaded gal around here anyplace? She and I had a talk the other day. She told me—"

He had to mean Violet. "Answer the question."

Tight-lipped, Whittier glanced to the door. Then he relented. "My wife, May, gave me that watch on our wedding day."

Cade's hand wavered. "My mother's name was May."

It was her name that had been engraved on that watch, along with his father's name and the year of their marriage. For that reason alone, Cade had considered himself lucky to have come across it, even by capricious gambling—even by winning it from a man whom he hadn't recognized when sitting down with him. At that point in his life, Cade had only been trying to find his way in his new world of cardsharps and roulette-wheel spinners.

Then, he hadn't been as good—or as lucky— as he was now.

Then, he hadn't deserved to win that watch. But he still had. Those paradoxical facts had niggled at Cade for years.

Whittier gazed at him, not speaking. But Cade could still hear his last words reverberating in his head, all the same.

My wife, May, gave me that watch on our wedding day.

At the recollection, Cade felt dizzy. His heart hammered. He willed it to slow down, but it didn't work. He wondered…

No. He'd come here looking for courage, not a damn miracle.

"That little redhead." Whittier rambled on. "She seemed to think it was never too late to say you were sorry. I reckon—"

"But my mother, May *Foster*, never married Percy Whittier." Regaining his nerve, Cade clenched his pistol more tightly. His shoulders felt as hard as granite. His feet felt rooted to the floor. "So here's what I think. I think you met my father, and you stole that watch from him, and then when I won it from you—"

"Cade—"

"Don't call me that." His father would have called him that. This could not be his father. Not after all this time. Not like this. The only thing that had gotten Cade through the past years

was believing his father was dead—believing he'd left his family not by choice, but by a cruel quirk of fate. Knowing this could not be happening, not like this, Cade closed his eyes.

Unfortunately, that paltry act was not enough to shut out Whittier. He just kept on talking, talking as if he'd kept the words bottled up for years and couldn't hold them in now.

"You know Whittier isn't my real name," he said in an uneasy, falsely jocular tone. "You've known that all along. *You* of all people—you weren't fooled by my name or my running away—"

At that, Cade snapped open his eyes. "You're wrong about that. Your running was too real to ignore. For all of us."

Whittier swallowed. His gaze looked imploring. "Is Judah—"

"Stop." *This couldn't be happening.* Cade strode sideways. His grasp on his pistol slackened. He glanced at it with sudden dismay, then rammed it into its holster. "You're dead." He shot an angry glance at Whittier. "I mean you're not him. *He's* dead."

"If you mean Ben Foster...then I guess you're right."

At the sound of his father's name, Cade quit moving.

"Ben Foster might as well be dead," Whittier went on, "for all the good he did for his family. His wife. His two boys—"

"You're lying," Cade insisted. He mustered up a mighty scowl, a fearsome expression designed to show the world that *he* should be feared. He balled his fists, refusing to look squarely at Whittier. "You're standing in church and you're lying to an armed man. You really are crazy."

"You put away your weapon," Whittier pointed out. "And this little church happens to be the only reason I didn't skedaddle already, like I usually do—or at least that redheaded girl I met in here is. She talked to me, and she made me see some things, and she convinced me to stay in town awhile."

Violet. Again. At the irony of that, Cade shook his head. He didn't want to believe it had been Violet, not him, who'd stumbled upon Whittier. Violet who'd talked to him. Violet who'd persuaded him to stay in Morrow Creek. But she'd told him so herself. *I saw Percy Whittier today. I met him. I talked to him.*

"If not for her," Whittier went on, "I'd have pulled foot for the next town already. I'd have kept right on running, just like I have been. But I wouldn't have found any peace in it."

"You don't deserve any peace."

"That may be true." Whittier gave him a level look. "But you do. Judah does. Once I realized that, I couldn't leave."

Hell. Whittier talked like his father would have. He looked a little like his father would have—at least like Ben Foster would have looked, years later. But after all this time, Cade couldn't risk believing this *was* his father. Feeling newly shaky, he searched the ceiling, looking for courage. For so long, he'd wanted answers. But now that they were imminent...

Cade wasn't sure about any of them. This wasn't the conversation he'd imagined. This wasn't the man he'd imagined. This wasn't the reunion he'd longed for, alone in the unfamiliar households where he and Judah had been fostered, put to work, ignored in their idle time, then made to leave when the harvesting season was through or the factory work was done.

"There's nothing you can say," Cade told Whittier in a harsh tone, "that will explain away everything that's happened. Maybe, when I was still a boy, if my father had come back then—"

"I couldn't come back. I left for *you*! I left

to protect you and Judah and your mother—"
Whittier broke off, his careworn face full of
regret. "I didn't hear she'd taken ill until it was
too late. By then, you and your brother were
gone, on your own."

"I don't believe you." Mulishly, Cade shook
his head. His feelings veered, wildly, from belief to fear to skepticism. "Maybe, before you
stole that watch from my father, you heard him
talk about us. Maybe *he* missed us." That had
always been Cade's secret hope. "Maybe *he*
wanted to come back and couldn't."

Whittier only gazed at him. "You were stubborn like this as a little boy, too. You didn't
believe the fire was hot till you touched it.
It didn't matter how often we warned you
away—"

Cade wished someone had warned him
away from *this*. "Stop."

"I can't. Not now." Whittier shook his head.
"That's what that little church gal told me, and
I believe her." Raggedly, he inhaled. Loudly,
he blurted, "I'm sorry, Cade. I'm so sorry for
everything I put you through! I didn't mean for
any of it to happen. I made a wager and I lost—
I lost so much more than I knew I would. If you
knew the kind of people I was indebted to—"

"*I know them.*" Seemingly from nowhere,

Simon Blackhouse appeared. Wearing a troubled, deeply determined look, he strode nearer. He glanced at a dumbfounded Cade. "Hell, I'm *related* to them, and I wish I wasn't. He's right, Cade—they're bad people."

"Simon?" He had to be imagining things, Cade realized.

Simon Blackhouse—the Simon Blackhouse he knew—was neither this serious nor this stealthy. The Simon Blackhouse that Cade knew was an irresponsible layabout with nothing on his mind beyond the next willing woman or the next pleasurable game.

But *this* Simon Blackhouse...this Simon Blackhouse proved his transformation by continuing in stark, plain-speaking terms.

"If you hadn't gone on the run, you would have been killed," Blackhouse told Whittier. "They meant their threats."

Thoroughly confounded, Cade stared. Again, "Simon?"

"My uncle meant those threats," Blackhouse continued relentlessly. "He meant to have you—and probably your family—killed if you didn't repay that rigged wager of his. For years, that's what my family has specialized in—extortion, cheating, legalized stealing...all in the name of business or 'pleasure'

or whatever caught their fancy. I'm the first to break the mold," he said, "and believe me, the Blackhouses don't like it much."

So *that* was why Simon was estranged from his family, Cade realized. The situation was much more dire than he'd thought—much more dire than the idle society gossip had implied.

"But me, being me… Well, frankly, I don't care what they think about what I do." Here, Blackhouse offered a vivid grin. "I forgive your debt, Mr. Foster—" upon saying that name, he aimed a decidedly confirming glance at Cade "—which is something I have all rights to do. My uncle's death passed his authority to me. What's more, I have the money you lost in that rigged wager to repay you with, with interest, at my private train car. If you'd like to come with me, I'll give it to you."

Now Whittier *and* Cade both gawked in astonishment.

"I can't trust you!" Whittier said. "This must be a trick."

"You can trust him," Cade said, astonished to hear himself admit it aloud. "*I* trust him. It's not a trick. It's…incredible, but it's not a trick. I'd stake my whole bankroll on it."

"Thank you, friend." Gratefully, Blackhouse

inclined his head toward Cade. "That, all on its own, makes sponsoring your search worthwhile." He turned to Whittier. "It *isn't* a trick," he emphasized, "but I knew you might think so if you heard I was looking for you with the stated purpose of giving you money."

Whittier gave a cynical snort. "Sounds like a trap to me. I haven't survived all these years by keeping up with long odds."

"All I want in return," Blackhouse said, "is for you to accept the money, the settled wager and my humble apologies. No one will bother you again. You won't have to run anymore."

"I see." Still seeming rather dazed, Whittier gave him a chary look. "If I do all that… What do you get out of it?"

Cade knew the answer to that one. "He gets back his honor. Or at least a little piece of it." Still stunned, Cade shook his head at his friend. "Because it really *was* a matter of honor to you, wasn't it? Why didn't you tell me, you bastard?"

Blackhouse shrugged. "I thought your reason for conducting your search was more compelling than mine. Finding your father—"

"He's *not* my father," Cade interrupted willfully. "He—"

"—was more important than correcting another heinous familial wrongdoing, even if I *have* been traveling the country doing exactly that for years now. I have a long way to go, too. Your father's was one of the simplest cases to resolve."

"He's *not* my father!" Cade insisted. "He can't be."

Simon gave him a sorrowful look. Behind them, the church's door slammed shut. Steady, measured footsteps could be heard.

"Are you sure about that, Cade?" Judah asked. Painstakingly, he made his way to their position, his gaze fixed on Whittier all the while. "Are you sure he's not? Haven't you seen what he's been doing with that match safe in his hand?"

Taken aback, Cade looked. Whittier froze in place, his attention fixed, too, on the silver match holder in his hand.

It rested now, its glimmer temporarily dimmed, between his agile fingers. But until seconds ago, Cade realized with a perception he'd lacked until just that moment, Whittier had been tumbling that match safe between his fingers like a magician with a conjuring trick, juggling it with scarcely any effort at all.

"That's what Papa used to do whenever he was worried," Judah said. "Don't you remember, Cade? He taught us how to do that trick, too. You were especially good at it, I recall."

Mutely, Cade shook his head. He was afraid to believe...

Whittier tossed him the match safe. Without thinking, Cade caught it. He juggled it as he did so—in the same showy way—to prevent it from falling to the floorboards.

"Well done," Blackhouse observed. "Like father, like son."

Like father, like son. Dumbstruck, Cade stared at Whittier.

But Judah only smiled. "I *knew* we'd find you!" His injured leg scarcely slowed him as he went to Whittier with a smile on his face. Gruffly, he embraced him. "Simon said he'd almost tracked you down. I wanted to be here when he did."

Near them, Blackhouse nodded. He glanced at Cade. "How much more proof do you need?" he asked. "Just look at your hands."

Cade did. He was, he saw instantly, still nervously juggling that match safe—exactly the same way his father had just done.

A huge wellspring of emotion surged inside him. Buffeted by it, Cade watched silently as Judah and Whittier—*Foster*—parted.

They both looked at Cade. He cleared his throat. "Papa?"

The smile on his father's face erased all doubt. "I'm sorry, Cade. It wasn't right, what I did. I need you to know—"

For once, Cade didn't need answers. "It's *really* you?"

His father nodded—or at least Cade thought he nodded. It was hard to tell, because his vision went blurry, his eyes stung…and he could as soon have flown as he could have spoken past the lump of emotion stuck in his throat. He tried to move—

But his father moved faster. With urgent strides, he crossed the short distance separating them. He gazed at Cade, who was trying desperately not to bawl, then hugged him.

He felt different from the man Cade remembered. He felt leaner and tougher and older, but he still felt…right.

A heartbeat later they separated, curtly and awkwardly. There were more apologies, more promises—and more vexing, perceptive grins from the likes of Blackhouse and Judah.

Feeling overcome, Cade scowled at them. He swiped at his eyes, then demanded, "What are you two doing here anyway?"

Blackhouse shrugged. "You didn't think

we'd let you go on this adventure all alone, did you?" he queried with his usual jauntiness. "We followed you from the train car, of course."

"That's right," Judah agreed with a nod. For the first time, Cade noticed he was tottering— probably on account of the whiskey he'd drunk. "I've just found you again. I wasn't going to let you sneak away so soon after our reunion. I'm a little slow these days, on account of my leg—" he gave that appendage an impressive frown "—but I'm pretty hard to stop, all the same."

"We thought we'd be witnessing your groveling to Miss Benson," Blackhouse admitted, "but as a secondary feature—"

"This is mighty fine, too," Judah alleged. He slung his arm around Whittier's shoulders with genial—and possibly drunken—aplomb. "Although I *was* keen to meet the minister's daughter."

Blackhouse clucked with dismay. "Yes, that's too bad."

Violet. Suddenly reminded of her, Cade went still.

Nothing had gone the way he'd planned this night. But everything had turned out providentially, all the same. Could it be, he wondered, that his good luck was back for good?

He would have been a poor gambler not to think so.

Filled with new resolve, Cade raised his hand. He turned to Whittier—to, remarkably, his *father*. "I have more questions for you. There are so many things I want to know. But first—"

"First he has to settle accounts with a girl," Blackhouse said, a knowing grin on his puckish face. "With a special girl."

"With a damn go-gooder of a reverend's daughter," Judah specified, plainly having learned a few more pertinent details from Simon—and then having editorialized them further, "with lovely red hair, an excess of kindness and—near as I can tell—woefully poor eyesight, if she's smitten with my big lummox of a brother."

Cade let that insult slide. He felt too relieved just then—too amazed and grateful and hopeful—to quarrel with Judah.

"A redhead?" Whittier raised a brow. "Is she skinny? Fearless? Fond of calico and cockeyed pep talks?"

The trio of Cade, Blackhouse and Judah nodded.

"I think I know her," Whittier mused. A nod. "Nice girl."

Cade only shook his head. "I let her get away from me once. I couldn't forgive myself if I didn't try to get her back."

With that, his friend, his brother and his long-lost father all agreed to return to Blackhouse's train car. "After all," Simon eagerly pointed out, "I'm having a party tonight!"

Watching them make plans, Cade knew it would take a while to resolve everything. It wouldn't be easy to come to terms with the Fosters' long separation and decide where to go from there.

For the first time, though, Cade felt the stirrings of belief that they could do it. For now, that was enough.

Determinedly, Cade tossed back his father's silver match safe, then straightened his shoulders. "I'll be next door," he announced with twice the bravado he felt, "winning back Violet, finding the means to locating Tobe's mother, dazzling Reverend Benson with my wholesome good intentions and—now that I won't be carousing through town—possibly saving the whole of Morrow Creek from descending into debauchery."

Blackhouse raised his eyebrows. "That's a mighty tall order you've set for yourself."

"I know," Cade replied with a grin. "But I feel up to it."

At least he *did* feel up to it—until he arrived at the Benson household and learned, too late, that Violet had left for the rest of her life as the belle of the ball...without him.

Chapter Fourteen

I𝐭 was an altogether different experience, Violet realized as she wandered through the crowded, elaborately decorated rooms of Mr. Blackhouse's luxurious private train car, listening to the music provided by a small group of musicians and carrying a fluted glass filled with an assuredly alcoholic beverage, to attend a party as a woman of interest, rather than a person who hung decorations and cheered up all the wallflowers.

Where once she'd spent her energies volunteering, fetching refreshments for elderly friends or chatting with other plain girls on the fringes of events, now Violet found herself smack in the middle of things. Handsome men flirted outrageously with her. Popular ladies pursued her with invitations to their own upcoming soirées. Even the waiters—and the kindly gentleman valet, Adams, who'd admitted her to the private gala—seemed to treat Violet with a mixture of burgeoning respect and interest.

Feeling overwhelmed by the newness of it all, Violet maneuvered to the train car's window. Through it, she saw that the town she knew and loved—and had been born in— might as well have vanished for good. From her vantage point, only the barest hints of Morrow Creek's existence remained. Some lantern light could be seen, faintly, coming from establishments like the Lorndorff Hotel and Jack Murphy's saloon—and the nearby train depot, of course. Otherwise, all the houses looked dark. From inside the warm, festive, brightly lit train car, the entire town could have disappeared with a snap of her fingers.

If it had, Violet never would have known it—and just at that moment, she realized, she'd already lost enough. Her first real love. Her pure-hearted motivation for doing good works. A part of her innocence. She didn't want to lose Morrow Creek, too.

Why had she come here, anyway? She no longer needed Mr. Blackhouse—or his fortune—to help her track down Tobe's mother. She no longer needed the validation of other men's interest to make her feel beautiful. All she needed, truly, was Cade. And he was as lost to her, just then, as the lights of her friends' and neighbors' houses were. They stood nearby, it was true; but it felt in the evening darkness as though they were gone forever.

Then Violet remembered something— something Cade had once said to her: *the real tragedy in life isn't failing to believe that hope exists, Violet. It's convincing yourself that you don't want any hope, even when it's right in front of you.*

Was hope right in front of her? What if Cade was here—what if her second chance was *here*—and she was overlooking it?

She was no gambler, Violet assured herself. But maybe it was time she took one more chance with her life. After all, it was possible that Cade *was* at his benefactor's party. With a little looking—and a little luck—maybe she could find him.

Determinedly, Violet gulped down her drink. She set down her glass. She straightened her shoulders, then faced the animated crowd of partygoers again. They were a mix of visiting strangers, professional gamblers and their associates, and townspeople who either knew Simon Blackhouse or wanted to.

None of those smiling men was Cade.

But if he was here, Violet knew she could find him.

She began in the parlor car, weaving through laughing women and groups of cigar-smoking men. No Cade. She progressed to the library car, where a variety of games of chance were taking place. Cade was not among the sporting men there, either. She sneaked into the rearmost quarters, where the staff was bustling with gala preparations. Cade was not there, unsurprisingly, but the valet, Adams, was. He rebuffed her with cordial firmness.

"I'm sorry, Miss Benson, but you shouldn't be back here."

"I know, Adams. But I'm searching for someone."

"Mr. Foster, perhaps?" His respectful face betrayed no sign of where he'd gained the knowledge that Violet knew Cade. "Have you tried the central car, miss? That's where the musicians are. It's the liveliest by far. If Mr. Foster has returned—"

"He was here and now he's *gone*? Where did he go?"

"—that's undoubtedly where he'll be." A bow. "Good luck."

"But where did he go?" Violet persisted. "I must know."

"I'm afraid I'm not at liberty to disclose that." Adams offered a regretful expression. "I'm terribly sorry."

Frustrated, Violet considered pressing him for more. At the same moment, Adams crossed his arms. He offered a slight frown. He was, it occurred to her, quite formidable when he had to be. Why on earth did Mr. Blackhouse need such an intimidating valet?

"Thank you, Mr. Adams," she said. "I'll try elsewhere."

Feeling increasingly dismayed, Violet hurried back to the central train car. Strains of rollicking music reached her, carried on the same currents of air that held the fragrances of ladies' perfumes, exotic incenses and cigar smoke. The party had grown even more crowded during her short absence. Now she could scarcely see past all the packed-together men and women.

Where in the world was Cade? Had he left town altogether?

Just as she conceived that awful notion, someone touched her shoulder. "There you are!" a man said from behind her, in a firm, self-assured voice. "You're missing our dance!"

She'd heard those words before, from Cade. But he couldn't be here. She'd have seen him. This was an unkind joke. It was...

It was...*wonderful*, Violet realized as she turned. It was wonderful because Cade stood there, close enough to touch, looking handsome and manly and exactly as dapper as he had on the night they'd met—the first time she'd heard those words.

He also appeared, she noticed with a second distressed glance, a little beleaguered... and a little apprehensive. Did he truly believe that she might refuse his invitation to dance?

There you are! You're missing our dance!

Well, if he did believe that, Violet had the perfect solution to offer. Stepping into his outstretched arms, she gave him her sauciest smile. "Oh no I'm not!" she said, just as she had on the very same night. "I'd never miss a dance!"

Like magic, Cade whirled her into the dance. Never mind that the train car was jam-packed with revelers. Never mind that they risked stomped-on toes and jostled shoulders. With the same command that he'd displayed on that oft-remembered night, Cade drew Violet into the crush of the celebration…and then made her feel that they were alone in the midst of all the frivolity.

"I was afraid," Cade said, "that you'd say no."

"To you?" She could scarcely believe he was here. "Never."

"You appeared engrossed in something. I saw you rushing from car to car, but I couldn't catch up. If not for Adams—"

"Adams?" Maybe that rascally valet *did* know much more than he let on.

"—slowing you down and then sending you back here, we might not have crossed paths all night." Cade twirled her. His hand felt warm against hers; his hold on her waist felt perfect. "Do you need help finding something? You seemed to be searching—"

"I *was* searching. I was searching for you."

He didn't seem to know what she meant. "I was trying to find *you*," Violet said. Smiling with relief and hopefulness, she explained, "You've been searching, yourself, for so long now. I thought it was about time that someone came looking for *you*."

At that, Cade appeared humbled. "I won't be searching anymore. Tonight I found what I

was looking for." He gave her a tender smile.
"It turns out it was right here, all along."

"You found Whittier?" Excitedly, she
grabbed his arm. "See? He *was* in Morrow
Creek! I knew it. I told you I'd seen him."

"Yes. I did find Whittier," Cade confirmed.
"I found even more than that, too. I found my
father, and my brother—"

"You *have* been busy! No wonder Mr.
Adams couldn't explain."

"—and I found some of the answers I
needed. But that's not what I meant. What I
meant…" Here, Cade pulled Violet to the side.
Away from the frolicking dancers, he brought
his hand to her face. He gazed at her, exactly
as though she were precious. "What I meant
was that I was looking for *you*. I needed *you*,
all along. But because I was foolish and cruel
and too blind to see the truth—"

"No!" Violet hurried to stop him. "It wasn't
you. It was me. I was so unkind, Cade. When
I suggested that I was helping you as one of
my charity projects… I never meant that! I was
only afraid. I was afraid to love you—afraid to
believe that you could love me! Because who
am I? Only plain Violet Benson—"

Just as she'd hoped, Cade kissed her. Hard
and fast.

"Plain Violet Benson," she tried again, breathlessly.

Another kiss. This time, Cade hauled her against him, too. He'd told her so many times not to refer to herself that way.

With her heart hammering, Violet managed to stammer, "P-plain Violet Benson, who's never known a courtship that lasted and who's never—" She broke off, casting Cade a mischievous glance. "What's wrong? Aren't you going to kiss me this time?"

Cade's answering smile beguiled her. "Vixen. You were hoodwinking me all along. I'm fairly certain that *I*, as the professional sporting man here, should be taking that role."

"Oh, I like the role you're playing just fine." Feeling happy and effervescent, Violet grinned. She *knew* she'd manage to take advantage of Cade's unusual method of "chastising" her with kisses eventually. "Whereas when it comes to *me*, plain Violet Benson—" She stopped. Suggestively, she arched her brows.

"When it comes to you," Cade growled obligingly, *not* kissing her yet, "I can't get enough. Before I met you, I was lost. After I met you, I thought all I wanted was a dose of good luck—a bit of good fortune to see me through my lonesome days and the games of chance that filled them. But now—" Seeming downright overcome, Cade broke off. He kissed her again. "Now I know that what you gave me, Violet, was more than good luck. What you gave me was love. Like a fool, I almost threw it away—"

"Not while I'm here to have a say in it!"

"—but I came to my senses just in time. Or at least I hope it was just in time." With a concerned glance at the revelers surrounding them, Cade frowned. "I know you could have your pick of men here. I know that I'm not nearly good enough. I have a long way to go before I settle down, quit wagering and stop feeling a need to indecently ravish you any chance I get—"

"And the trouble with ravishment is…what exactly?"

"I know you deserve an upright husband," Cade said, "a *good* man to call your own, a protector and a conqueror and a hero—"

"Oh, Cade." Violet sighed. Adoringly, she stroked his jaw. "Don't you know? You already *are* all those things to me."

"But I love you, Violet," he forged on, sounding raspy and determined and fierce. "I think I've loved you from the start, from the moment when I pulled you into that dance. You looked at me with that impish grin of yours, and you took my hand as if we were meant to be one, and you trotted onto the dance floor with me without the least hesitation. I was so grateful for that. I was so grateful for *you*. I couldn't take my eyes off you."

Violet knew she must be blushing. Raptly, she gazed into her beloved gambler's face. While looking at him, it was easy to ignore all the hullabaloo and revelry going on around them.

"That's because I must have loved *you* from the start," she insisted. "You spun me into that dance and straight into another way of being. Without you, I would have contented myself with giving and volunteering and working. Without you, I would have had friends, and my family, and maybe even a husband someday." Here, Violet clutched his hand, needing him to know everything. "But I wouldn't have known how it felt to be carried away—to be made to feel special and lovely and beautiful—"

"You *are* beautiful," Cade swore. "You've never been anything less to me. All I had to do was open my eyes."

"—and I wouldn't have known how it felt to love someone with all my heart and soul.

Because that's the way I love you, Cade. If I could give you contentedness, I would. If I could give you surety, I would. But all I can give you is *me*. I hope it will be enough. If only you would consider staying here, in Morrow Creek, I know that eventually things will work out."

"They already are working out," Cade told her. "Even with your father. I saw him when I came for you—when I went to your house this evening, after leaving Judah and Blackhouse and my father. That's who Whittier was, you know, all this time."

Violet boggled. "I *knew* it! I almost guessed as much when I saw him at the church." The truth of it all was remarkable. "You actually left your long-lost *father* to come find me at home?"

Cade nodded. Assuredly, they would need to have a long catching-up conversation when all this was through.

"He's with Judah. For now. We'll talk again later," Cade continued, surprising her anew with the news of his brother's arrival in town. "Your father told me that you found Tobe's hidden train ticket. I knew you'd persist until you found the lead you needed." Proudly, Cade smiled at her.

Violet nodded. "Now all we have to do is take Tobe to see his mother. If our guesses are right, she's just a skip away."

"Hmm. I think I know someone who'd be willing to undertake that mission." Cade cast a slanting glance at Mr. Blackhouse, who'd arrived at the train car sometime during their reunion. His former benefactor gave a somber nod. Cade regrouped. "But the whole point is," he said, "that I spoke with your father tonight—"

"Well, of course you did. You just said so."

"—and I made my case as best as I could, without resorting to flattery or beguilement or outright professional charm—"

"Well, now. For you, that sounds impossible!"

"—and eventually I made Reverend Benson see the truth."

"Oh." Perplexed, Violet inhaled. "Which was?"

"That he's going to have to come to terms with having a reformed, scoundrelly sporting man in his daughter's life," Cade said. "Because I can't live without you, Violet. I tried, and I can't. Without you, there's no substance to life. There's no laughter. There's no joy—" Cade stopped, quite obviously searching for more. "There's not even any fun to be had with drink or dice or dancehall girls!"

Feeling vexed, Violet arched her brows. "Oh, really?"

"What I mean is…" Soberly, Cade held her hand in both of his. He lifted his gaze to join with hers. "I want you to be mine. Please. I love you, Violet. Having you as my good-luck charm is not enough. It never was." Watching her closely, Cade drew in a fortifying breath. "I want you as something more."

For a single, heart-stopping moment, Violet thought he was asking her to be his mistress. After all, these were sophisticated people in very sophisticated surroundings. And she was *almost* prepared to accept.

But then, astonishingly, Cade dropped to one knee, right there in front of Mr. Black-house and everyone who stood nearby and the dauntingly intimidating but well-mannered valet, Adams, and all the most daring gamblers in the whole territory, and then Cade— her very own honor-bound gambler and the man who'd unrepentantly stolen her heart— took on the very biggest risk of them all.

"Please, Violet. Will you marry me?" he asked. "I know I'm not what you probably hoped for, but I love you. And if you give me half a chance, I swear I'll make you happy. I know I can."

"Yes." Filled to overflowing with love for him, Violet dropped to the floor, too. Her skirts fanned out in a majesty of color. They should have been trodden upon, but party-goers miraculously made way for them. Her knees wobbled. They should have buckled, but Violet amazingly managed to remain steady. Her voice broke as she repeated her answer. Somehow, again, she managed to say, "Yes! Of course I'll marry you."

Smiling almost too broadly to pucker, Violet leaned forward and kissed Cade anyway. At her instigation, he pulled her into his arms, lowered his head, then made her his more thoroughly than he had all night—and through it all, all Violet could do was rejoice. She'd reunited with Cade. She'd made him hers and rightly become his. Now all that remained was one final detail.

"I will be *delighted* to marry you," Violet said when at last they parted amid the cheers of the crowd. Blushing for certain now, she added, "I have just one tiny stipulation."

Cade appeared concerned. "Stipulation?"

"Yes."

In his face, caution warred with an evident

determination to fulfill whatever demand she made. "What stipulation?"

"Earlier tonight," Violet told him, "you said that you weren't a good enough man—that I probably hoped for more."

Cade nodded. "I'm *not* a good enough man for you. I—"

Determinedly, Violet kissed him. Hard and fast.

He appeared perplexed. "I'm not good. I gamble. I drink—"

Again she kissed him. This time, Violet wrapped her arms around his neck and devoted her entire being to the task. But when she'd finished—when she next peeked expectantly at him—Cade merely drew a breath and forged onward. "I'm *not* good enough—"

Wholeheartedly, Violet kissed him once more. Then she reared back to give him a serious look. "You *are* good enough," she insisted vigorously, "for me and anyone else. But you're mighty slow to recognize when someone's giving you a dose of your own medicine." Coquettishly, she smiled. "Shall I demonstrate again, or are you catching on to this game at last?"

Then—only then—Cade seemed to understand her meaning.

With a knowing gleam in his eyes, he adopted a very pensive demeanor. Elaborately, he furrowed his brow. "I'm not—"

Her punishing kiss almost bowled him over. Laughing, Cade caught her in his arms and then raised them both. He'd never looked happier—or more handsome—than he did in that moment.

"I have a feeling," he said as he cradled her close before rejoining the party, "that you're going to keep me on my toes."

"With me," Violet promised, "life will *never* be dull."

With that much settled for certain, they turned delightedly to face their friends and neighbors. As one, the people of Morrow Creek cheered. The shadier visitors to town offered gamblers' odds on the probable wedding date they would set. In the center of the melee, a satisfied-looking Mr. Blackhouse encouraged everyone to raise their glasses in a toast.

"Three cheers for lasting love!" he roared. "However improbable, however difficult, however unlikely it is to occur for *some* of us—" Here, Blackhouse stopped for a properly dramatic pause. He glanced at an older man and a younger, dark-haired man standing nearby. "—we can see tonight that sometimes Lady

Luck delivers more than a bounteous payout. Sometimes she delivers us a second chance at living our lives. And for that—"

"He always was a bit of a show-off," Cade grumbled privately in Violet's ear. "We'll be here for days before he's done."

"For that," Blackhouse finished, "we salute her. To Lady Luck! To Miss Benson! To Mr. Foster!" With a triumphant flourish, he raised his glass. "And most of all, to love!"

Together, the women nearby swooned. The men downed their whiskeys. And Violet tugged Cade's arm. Smiling, she whispered, "Let's dance before Mr. Blackhouse starts in again."

"Ah. A woman after my own heart," Cade pronounced.

Then, with an even broader smile, he danced them both into the party, long into the night, and all the way to tomorrow...with all the wonderful tomorrows that lay beyond it still to come for them both to share.

Chapter Fifteen

There was nothing like a wedding to bring out the good spirits of everyone involved, Violet thought. Women commended the bride and told her how lovely she looked. Men congratulated the groom and joked about the coming wedding night's ribaldry. Even children, who were rightly oblivious to most adult goings-on, seemed to sense the crackle of celebration in the air. They participated by whooping, hollering and teasing each other mercilessly. Now, eyeing those selfsame boisterous youngsters as they raced down the aisle of her father's church, Violet sighed.

Upon hearing that telltale sigh, her long-time friend, Adeline Davis, stopped on her way out of the church. Together in their best dresses, she and Violet watched through the open church entryway as the ring bearer and his cousins chased two of the tiny, squealing flower girls down the steps outside.

Beyond the children, autumn-leafed trees embellished the townscape of Morrow Creek. Above those trees, clear territorial skies stretched forever, promising that the mild weather they'd enjoyed would last. In the distance, a train whistle called.

Upon hearing that sound, Violet started. She sighed again.

Adeline gave an empathetic smile. "Still missing Tobe?"

Swallowing hard, Violet nodded. "I know he's been happily reunited with his mother in California, thanks to Mr. Blackhouse's generosity—" the enigmatic magnate had employed his private train car to see to that mission personally, surprising everyone except Violet "—but I still miss the little scamp." Violet smiled at the memory of him. "I'm not at all certain Tobe will write me as often as he promised he would." She hoped he would. "I'm afraid I grew awfully attached to that boy."

"I did, too," Adeline admitted. "He was very sweet."

With a commiserating nod, Cade stepped

up. Sentimentally, he added to their reminiscences. "That little sharper," he said fondly of Tobe. "He took my best warm overcoat with him."

"That was *your* overcoat all along? I never knew that!"

At that, Cade smiled. If his attention had been on the many townspeople exiting the church around them, it wasn't now. Now his attention was all for Violet. Dotingly, he took her hand.

"With Tobe, I lost a bet on purpose," Cade said. "With you, I won a lifetime of riches by accident. I'll take those odds."

With a chuckle, Clayton Davis approached. As befit his wedding day, he was decked out in his finest suit. He stopped beside Adeline, his blushing bride, then hugged her tightly.

"I still say I got luckiest of all, Foster," he said. "But if you take away anything from your attendance at our wedding…"

Clayton paused, even as Adeline cast him a curious look.

"…it's that you ought to elope when it's your turn." With a beleaguered grin, Clayton shook his head. "The planning, the decorating, the meeting up with all the distant relatives—I swear, we should have just run away to Avalanche to exchange vows. We could have skipped to the 'married' part straightaway."

"However it happened, I'm glad it's done." After a loving smooch, Adeline caressed his cheek. "When it comes to matters of the heart, you know I can be a mite...*impatient* myself."

Clearly that was a private joke between them, because Adeline gave her groom a teasing, enigmatic wink. Clayton winked, too, then grinned right back at her.

The two of them were so full of love and admiration and wonderment that Violet would have found herself hopelessly consumed with envy...had she not had a partner by her side who'd brought her every bit as much happiness. So rather than feel covetous, Violet only smiled. She was glad that Adeline had finally wed her long-beloved Clayton, glad that Tobe was finally with his mother and glad—*so* glad—to have Cade by her side, now and forever.

As though illustrating his willingness to stand by her, help her and love her, Cade extended his arm in a decidedly romantic and chivalrous fashion. "Shall we head to the party?"

"Oh yes, *please*!" Violet said.

As a group, she and Cade and Adeline and

Clayton tromped down the church steps, heading for the back room of Jack Murphy's saloon where the wedding reception was to take place.

Spying her father on his way from the other direction with some congregants, Violet waved and blew him a kiss. He'd been wonderful since her engagement. He'd even gone so far as to invite Cade to live with them—in the room Tobe had vacated—while he and Violet made their own wedding plans and got settled in.

"If we get to the reception early," Violet enthused as they walked onward, "there will still be plenty of cake!"

"Spoken like a woman who knows her mind." With a grin, Judah joined them, not seeming to notice when they all slowed their pace to accommodate his injured leg. "I approve, Cade."

"You approved of Violet from the moment you met her at Simon's party and she allowed you to beat her at billiards," Cade said. "You would approve of anyone who did that."

"There's more to it than that!" Judah insisted earnestly. To Violet, he tossed a flattering smile. It looked *almost* as charming as Cade's smiles did...only a shade darker and more evocative of sin. "I approve of Violet because I approve of your new life, Cade," Judah said as he moved with a determined effort to keep up. "It's been good for you, settling down."

Cade tilted his head as if considering his new position as a purchasing agent—an unusually persuasive and hard-driving one, at that—at Marcus Copeland's lumber mill. He smiled.

"You ought to consider doing the same," he suggested to Judah. "Settling down, I mean—now that you're here in Morrow Creek and intend to stay."

But his brother merely laughed. "If only I could find the angel who'd have me!" he pronounced with an almost Blackhouseworthy sense of drama. Hand over his heart, he surveyed Violet and Cade, then Adeline and Clayton, each in turn. "I'm afraid you four have laid claim to all the available love and locked it away. Poor romantic fools like myself have no recourse at all."

This time, everyone *else* guffawed. "The last thing *you've* faced is a shortage of romantically minded company," Violet pointed out as they arrived on the main street. They all took to the raised boardwalk to traverse farther. "The women in Morrow Creek are all aflutter over you, Judah, and you know it!"

"Hmm. Maybe so." Enigmatically, he

sighed. "But all the spooning in the world doesn't add up to love, Miss Benson."

"If anyone's made a thorough study of that supposition," Cade said as they arrived at the saloon, "it's my brother."

Wearing good-natured smiles, they all trooped inside. In the newly decorated saloon, Grace Murphy welcomed them. So did all the gamblers, drinkers, partygoers…and one very special faro dealer. Wearing a handsome suit and tie, he came forward.

Violet hugged him. "How is your work progressing, Mr. Foster? Is Mr. Murphy treating you fairly? Are the gamblers all tipping you generously? Are the dance-hall girls all flirting with you between sets, the way I told you they would?"

"Very well. Yes. Yes. And not nearly enough, but I think I'll remedy that soon." Cade's father gave her a boyish grin. It was easy to see where the Foster boys had gotten their devilish ways. "Some of the sporting men in town are a little confused about my new— *old*—name." Since Simon Blackhouse had freed him from his unfair debt, Cade's father had reclaimed *Ben Foster* as his name instead of Percy Whittier. "But here in the territory, things have a way of sorting themselves out.

I'm just happy to have my name and my rightful reputation back." He widened his grin to include his two sons. "I'm happy to have *all* of it back. If not for you, Miss Benson—and that cagey Simon Blackhouse, too—things might have progressed very differently."

"Well, I *do* have a powerful knack for helping people," Violet admitted with a dose of pride. She hugged him again. "If you find a break in the wagering, please come join the party."

"Yes, please do!" Adeline and Clayton agreed. Even as they spoke, strains of fiddle music came from the saloon's back room, luring them toward the nuptial festivities. "We'd love to have you there. The more the merrier!"

Seeming grateful to be included, Cade's father nodded. He turned to Cade and Judah. They recognized their cue to nod as well, letting him know they wanted him to be at the party, too.

The Foster men hadn't yet resolved all their concerns. They had many years of separation and misunderstandings to make up for. But between themselves, with Reverend Benson's wise help and Violet's ongoing support, the three were well on their way to forging a new kind of family. Violet could not have been more pleased about that…especially for Cade's sake.

There could be no denying that her now-retired gambler had thrived since he'd decided to make Morrow Creek his home. As though that little town of theirs possessed some sort of magical good luck that even Cade hadn't counted on, it had carried him and Violet forward from their first dance to their latest… from their first meeting to their own upcoming wedding. And despite Clayton's advice that they should simply elope and have done with it, Violet had some very specific notions about that event.

Because of that, as everyone headed into the next room for the party, Violet hung back. To her surprise, Cade did, too.

She raised her brows. "Is everything all right?"

"With you? It couldn't be better." He smiled, then held out his arm to escort her. "I was only thinking about *our* wedding."

Violet laughed. "That's serendipitous. I was, too!"

"And I think," Cade went on, "that we should—"

"Have it sooner," they said in unison.

"Tomorrow?" Violet proposed.

"The next day," Cade amended. "I'd like to

give Marcus Copeland at least that much notice. I wouldn't want to leave him in the lurch at the lumber mill. After that...I'm all yours."

"And I am yours." Violet couldn't help smiling with new anticipation. "If ever I'd wondered whether a charming, wagering, altogether disreputable rascal of a gambler could settle down and become a good husband," she mused aloud, "I don't anymore. You're perfect for me, Cade."

"And you, for me. Why else would I bother giving up all the glories of my previous life of pleasure and debauchery?"

With an undoubted twinkle in her eyes, Violet thought about that. "I'd wager there will still be *some* pleasure and shared debauchery in our lives from now on. Wouldn't you?"

"Absolutely." Cade caught on to her naughty teasing right away. With a roguish grin, he leaned forward to kiss her. Then he kissed her again, even more lingeringly. "That's one bet I'd be happy to break my withdrawal from gambling to make."

"Good. It's settled, then." Taking his proffered arm at last, Violet headed into the wedding reception.

For today, she was not the belle of the ball. Adeline was, and rightly so. But as Violet glanced at Cade and saw him standing proudly beside her while they greeted several of their friends and neighbors, she knew one amazing fact for certain.

When it came to Cade, she *was* the belle of the ball.

Now and forever.

With him in her heart, she could not have asked for more—not even if it made her beautiful in the eyes of everyone in town. Because for the first time in all her life, Violet realized then, she *felt* truly beautiful, both inside and out...and it was loving someone that had made her feel that way.

Love was the magic in Morrow Creek, she understood in that moment. And with the good people of the town to keep that love flowing, there really was no end to the magic that might occur...for every single one of them.

* * * * *

Join the Mills & Boon Book Club

Want to read more **Historical** books?
We're offering you **2 more** absolutely **FREE!**

We'll also treat you to these fabulous extras:

-  **Exclusive offers and much more!**

-  **FREE home delivery**

-  **FREE books and gifts with our special rewards scheme**

Get your free books now!

**visit www.millsandboon.co.uk/bookclub
or call Customer Relations on 020 8288 2888**

BS/ONLINE/H1